A GLIMPSE AT HAPPINESS

1844: When Josie O'Casey returns to London after twelve years in America, she is overjoyed to discover childhood sweetheart Patrick Nolan, alive and well. But happiness is short-lived – Patrick now belongs to another. Heartbroken, Josie attempts to settle back into the East End but there are some who resent that Josie left behind the slums of London to return as a lady. Torn between two worlds, Josie is drawn back to her childhood haunts and Patrick. When the couple are finally offered a glimmer of hope, Josie must decide if she is willing to forsake everything for the man she loves...

A GLIMPSE AT HAPPINESS

A Glimpse At Happiness

by

Jean Fullerton

Magna Large Print Books
Long Preston, North Yorkshire,
BD23 4ND, England.

British Library Cataloguing in Publication Data.

Fullerton, Jean
    A glimpse at happiness.

    A catalogue record of this book is
    available from the British Library

    ISBN   978-0-7505-3276-1

First published in Great Britain in 2009 by Orion Books

Published in Large Print 2010 by arrangement with
Orion Publishing Group

Magna Large Print is an imprint of Library Magna Books Ltd.

Printed and bound in Great Britain by
T.J. (International) Ltd., Cornwall, PL28 8RW

*For my three daughters, Janet, Fiona and Amy,
to thank them for their love and support and for
putting up with a constantly distracted mother.*

Acknowledgements

As with my first book, *No Cure for Love,* I have used numerous sources to get the period setting and feel of *A Glimpse at Happiness* right, but I have to mention a few books and authors to whom I am particularly indebted.

First and foremost, Henry Mayhew, deceased, for his detailed contemporary accounts of the poor in *London Labour and the London Poor* (edited by Neuburg, Penguin, 1985) and *The London Underworld in the Victorian Period* (Dover Publications, 2005). His painstaking reporting of the worries, concerns and language of the people he interviewed and scenes he witnessed allowed me to hear the voices and see the lives of the men and women of London as if I were there myself. My fellow East End author Gilda O'Neill's book *The Good Old Days* (Penguin, 2007) has given me an invaluable insight into various aspects of 19th century life in East London, as did the out of print *The East End of London* by Millicent Rose (The Cresset Press, 1951). This account of East London was written before the slum clearances in the late 50s and early 60s and gives a tantalising glimpse into tight-knit communities clustered around the London docks before they were dispersed to high-rise flats and post-war estates.

Judith Flanders book *The Victorian House* (Harper Perennial, 2003) helped me with the little details of Ellen and Robert Munroe's family life, while Lisa Picard's *Victorian London* (Orion Books, 2005) helped me with the details of Victorian London life, such as public baths. I also want to mention *Love and Toil: Motherhood in Outcast London 1870-1918* by Ellen Ross (Oxford University Press, 1993). This detailed academic study has vivid accounts of the trials and tribulation of mothers struggling to raise their children in squalor and poverty in Victorian London. There are several photographic books of old East London that helped me visualise what the streets of East London looked like when Josie and Patrick walked them. These include *East London Neighbourhoods* by Brian Girling (Tempus, 2005) *Victorian Street Life* by John Thompson (Dover Publications, 1994) and *Dockland Life* by Chris Ellmers & Alex Werner (Mainstream Publishing, 1991). One photo in particular, The Bustle of the Pool of London at Black Eagle Wharf Wapping, which is part of the Museum of London collection, is particularly evocative. Google it and see what I mean. Lastly, and by no means least, I would like to mention author Lee Jackson's brilliant website The Victorian Dictionary (http://www.victorianlondon.org/) which is packed with everything you could ever imagine about Victorian London.

I would also like to take the opportunity to thank a few people. My friend Dee, for being there for me always. My fellow historical author Elizabeth Hawksley, for her help in untying the knots in my plot. My many friends in the Romantic Novelist Association who encourage me, in particular Janet Gover and Fenella Miller. My lovely agent Laura Longrigg, who gets long emails from me detailing everything I'm doing and thinking but still smiles warmly at me whenever we meet. Finally, but importantly, a big thank you to the editorial team at Orion, especially Sara O'Keeffe and Natalie Braine, firstly for loving my stories and secondly, turning my 400+ pages of type print into a beautiful book.

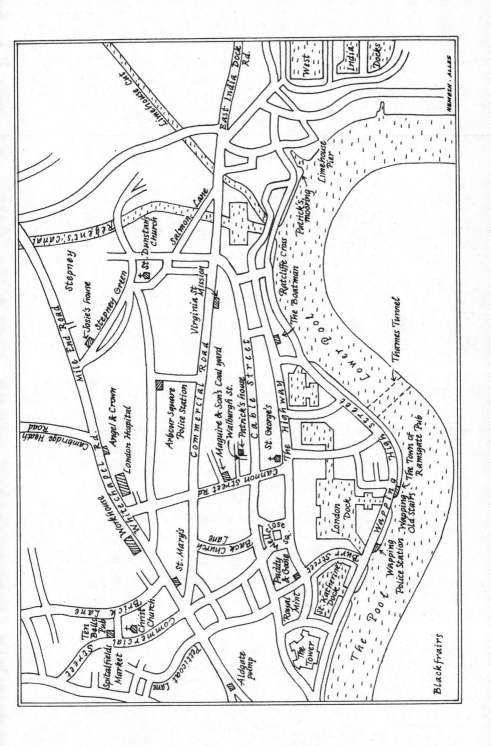

Prologue

Wapping, East London, 1844

Ma Tugman, owner of the Boatman freehouse, wedged herself into her usual chair beside the counter of the main bar. The pub was the only thing of any worth she'd got from her old man. Snapper, her stubbed-nose terrier with a temper as short as his docked tail, shuffled under her chair and lay down with a loud huff. Ma's broad hips spread across the surface of the seat and her feet just skimmed the sawdust-covered floorboards. She could feel the tightness around her ankles so she wriggled her toes inside her scuffed boots. The pain was always worse at the end of the day.

The Boatman was set a few streets back from the river and tucked up the side of Lower Well Alley. It wasn't frequented by watermen with wages burning holes in their pockets, as the Prospect or the Town were, but then it didn't have the peelers from Wapping police office passing through its doors either.

Ma rested her hands on the curved wooden arms of the chair and leant back. It was just after six and they would light the lamps in a while, but for the next half hour or so the light from outside would be enough. Not that it could illuminate much of the interior: most of the windows were

17

covered by packing cases instead of glass, leaving the light from outside to cut through the darkness in haphazard shafts. Daylight never reached the back of the narrow bar, so the full extent of the beer stains and ground-in dirt on the floor remained hidden.

In the dim recesses of the room, men hunched over their drinks while a few of the local trollops jostled for their first customers of the night.

Ma thrust her hand under one pendulous breast and scratched vigorously. She had been a looker years ago but had long since given up wearing stays. She glanced across the bar at the thin young woman cleaning the tankards and yelled across at her to bring a brandy.

The girl dried her hands and brought over a bottle and short glass, just as the door opened to admit Harry, Ma's eldest son. He stumbled in with his brother, Charlie, a step or two behind, then a wild-eyed Tommy Lee, a bargeman from Chapel Street.

Ma's gaze ran over her first-born. He had his father's looks – square and stocky. Unfortunately, he also had his father's hair, which had started to disappear in his early twenties. Rather than try to comb over what was left of it, Harry had shaved his head clean with his razor. Ma shifted her gaze to her other son, Charlie, ten years Harry's junior, and smiled. He had her slighter build and topped his brother by half a hand. He also had her golden hair, which she had spent hours combing and curling when he was a small boy.

Elbowing aside the men clustered near the door, Harry stomped across the floorboards,

18

Charlie and Tommy Lee following close behind.

''Ows me best gal?' Harry asked, kissing his mother on her forehead.

'All the better for seeing my sweet boy,' she answered smiling at his brother.

Harry's lower lip jutted out. He fumbled in his pocket and pulled out a red and green apple. He threw it in the air, bounced it off his bicep and caught it again. 'I got this from Murphy's stall. He said I was to give it to you, to brighten your smile.' He handed it to her.

Ma slid her knife from her skirt pocket. She held it in her palm for a second to feel the smoothness of the ivory handle. It had been her Harry's and his father's before that, and it would no doubt pass to her son Harry in time. It was well crafted, balanced and razor-sharp. She ran her thumb up to the pin at the top of the handle and pressed it. The blade sprung out.

Suddenly, Tommy stumbled and looked for a moment, as if he might fall to the floor. Charlie dragged him upright and, holding him tight by the arm, said, 'Look who we found skulking in the Ten Bells.'

Ma looked Tommy up and down. 'The Ten Bells? What took you so far from home then?'

Sweat glistened on Tommy's narrow forehead.

'Me ma's talking to you,' Charlie growled, 'and I 'ope for your sake you've got an answer.'

Ma waved her knife in the air and it gleamed in the light. 'Now, Charlie, Tommy didn't mean no 'arm.' She began paring the skin from the apple.

'Nah, nah, I didn't mean no 'arm at all, Mrs T,' Tommy replied, his body losing some of its

19

tension. 'I just fancied a stroll and found myself up Shoreditch way.'

Harry snorted. 'Long bloody stroll! Your old lady hasn't seen you for a week.'

'And neither 'ave we,' Ma added, slicing into the apple and popping a wedge in her mouth. 'Bring 'im 'ere.'

Snapper, who'd settled under the table to gnaw at his haunches, heard the change of tone and sprang to his feet. Tommy yelled and lurched away but Harry and Charlie thrust him towards Ma and held his hands down on the table.

Tommy's eye fixed on the blade in Ma's hand as it twinkled in the light. She paused, savouring his terrified expression then, with a twist of her fingers, she gripped the knife and slammed the blade through Tommy's outstretched hand.

An ear-piercing yell tore through the bar. Snapper barked and danced around their feet. Some of the patrons looked up but most, knowing where their best interests lay, continued to stare into their glasses.

Still clutching the ivory handle, Ma leant forward. 'And how is your old lady and those four lovely kids of yours?' she asked in a conversational tone.

A rivulet of blood was rolling off Tommy's hand, staining the tabletop beneath.

Charlie shook him. 'Me ma asked you a question.'

'She ... she's f ... fine, Mrs Tugman.'

'And the children?'

Tommy was all but on his knees now in an effort to minimise the pull on his injured hand.

'Grand. They're grand.'

Ma's free hand shot out, grabbed the tattered scarf around Tommy's neck and hauled him towards her. He lost his footing and would have fallen but for his hand nailed to the table.

'If you want 'em to stay that way, Tommy Lee, when my boys give you something to take up-river, you fecking take it.' Ma wriggled the blade. 'Understand?'

He nodded and, as Ma yanked the knife out of his hand, he collapsed. Snapper barked a couple of times at the crumpled heap then waddled off.

Ma's hand went to her chest.

'Has 'e upset you, Ma?' Harry asked, glaring at the man on the floor.

'Just catching my breath,' she replied.

Harry circled around Tommy, who was now coming to and scrambling to his feet.

'You upset me ma,' he shouted, and booted Tommy in the stomach.

Tommy fell sideways, holding his bleeding hand, and vomited into the beer-soaked sawdust. Charlie went to boot him, too.

'That's enough!' Ma barked. 'Throw him outside. And you' – she jabbed her index finger at the girl behind the bar – 'get a bucket and clear up this mess.'

Harry and Charlie heaved Tommy up once again, dragged him to the door and threw him out to the street.

Ma wiped the blade of her knife on her skirt and resumed eating her apple, but felt a sudden sharp sting under her arm. Letting the knife fall to her lap, she slid her right hand between the

21

buttons of her grubby blouse, over to her left armpit, where she caught her minute tormenter between her thumb and forefinger. She extracted it and idly studied the flea as it struggled. 'You can hide from Ma and give 'er a nip when she ain't looking,' she told the insect as she cracked it between her black-rimmed nails, 'but she'll get yer in the end.'

Chapter One

Stepney Green, 1844

With her hand on the polished banister, Josephine O'Casey, known as Josie ever since she could remember, lifted her skirts and made her way down the uncarpeted stairs from the main part of the house, to the kitchen. The heat from the room burst over her as she opened the door. Tucking a stray lock of her auburn hair back behind her ears, she stepped down to the flagstone floor.

The kitchen of number twenty-four Stepney Green was half below street level. The range, with its two ovens, roasting spit and six hotplates, dominated the space. Daisy, the maid, lit it at five in the morning and it supplied the household not only with food but, thanks to the copper incorporated into its design, a constant stream of hot water.

Standing with her back to Josie was Mrs Woodall, the Munroe family's cook. Her wide hips shook as she furiously stirred the contents of one of the large saucepans.

On a normal day Mrs Woodall accommodated the erratic working hours of Josie's stepfather, Dr Robert Munroe, as well as the vagaries of the tradesmen and the children's fads and fancies; however, today was not a normal day, and the usually unruffled cook looked as if she was about to boil over, just like one of her pots.

'Oh, Miss Josie, it's you. I thought it was your mother again,' Mrs Woodall said, some of the worry leaving her face.

Josie smiled. To her knowledge her mother, Ellen, had already been down to the kitchen three times in the last two hours and by the look on Cook's face she was expected again.

'You'd think the Queen of Sheba was coming, the amount of dishes I've got to prepare,' Mrs Woodall continued.

Queen of Sheba! No, someone much more important: Mrs Munroe, her stepfather's elderly mother.

'Can I do anything to help?' asked Josie, skirting around the stained chopping block which still had the odd chicken feather stuck to its surface. She, too, had escaped from the turmoil upstairs.

Apart from her trips to see Cook, Ellen had visited the guest room twice to check that the bed linen was properly aired, and her temper was shortening by the minute.

'Thank you, Miss Josie, but I've taken the plates up and now I just have to wait for the meat to cook and the fruit to arrive.'

There was a crash from the floor above. Josie and Mrs Woodall looked up.

'Your poor mother,' tutted Mrs Woodall, and, turned her attention to the pile of cabbage sitting ready to prepare. 'She shouldn't be running about in her condition.'

Josie agreed and, pushing her way past the basket of potatoes on the floor, went over to the roasting hook to rewind the clockwork that had begun to slow.

Mrs Woodall gave her a grateful smile. 'I could do with Daisy down here to help,' she said, attacking the wrinkled leaves of the Savoy cabbage with her vegetable knife. 'I don't know why nurse needs help with the children.'

Josie repositioned the dripping tray under the roasting side of beef turning in front of the fire. 'George and Joe have been up since dawn,' she said. 'Their racket woke Jack, who grizzled for an hour, and then the girls got out of bed. Poor Nurse has to help Miss Bobbie and Lottie into their best clothes and take the rags out of their hair, and at the same time try to soothe Jack, who's teething. She needs Daisy to make sure they are all ready on time.'

Mrs Woodall looked unconvinced. Josie noticed the jam tarts on the cooling tray by the open window.

'I can see your eyes, Miss Josie,' Mrs Woodall said, a small smile lightening her face. 'I suppose I had better let you make sure they're all right before I send them up with the afternoon tea.'

Josie grinned, then went over and scooped up a tart. She blew on it for a second and then popped

24

it in her mouth, licking her fingers.

Mrs Woodall's gaze ran over Josie and her eyes grew soft. 'With your sweet tooth, I'm surprised you stay so slim. It must be all that dashing about you do.'

Large windows let light into the kitchen but, since the kitchen was below street level they remained firmly shut to keep out the dirt that would blow down from above. To keep the temperature of the room down, Mrs Woodall worked with the back door ajar.

'And where *is* the grocery boy?' she asked herself now, glaring around the room as if the pots and pans might know.

'I'm sure he'll be here soon. Mr Grey is very reliable,' Josie assured her.

'He is, but that boy of his, Jaco, is a bit flash for my taste. I caught him chatting with Daisy outside the back door last week,' Mrs Woodall replied. 'How am I supposed to make Dish of Orange without oranges, I ask you?'

At that, there was a double-tone whistle and the young man in question stepped through the back door.

'Morning, Mrs W,' he said, swinging his basket up onto the work surface beside the deep sink.

Mrs Woodall pointed at Jaco with her knife. 'I've been expecting you for hours and I'll have something to say to your master when I see him.'

'Now then, hold your horses there, it ain't my fault I'm late.' Jaco repositioned his cap at a preferred jaunty angle. 'The missus' brother been away at sea for nigh on two years and he come back last night. They're all a bit foggy, you might

25

say, this morning after the celebration.'

'Where has he been?' Josie asked, thankful to talk about something other than Mrs Munroe's imminent arrival.

'According to him, everywhere – India, China and other savage lands,' Jaco replied, squaring up the bottom of his colourful waistcoat. 'Brought back all sorts of things, he did. Some strange cups with no handles from Japan, a bolt of silk from Bombay and some carved masks that scared the nippers.'

'It's a pity he didn't bring some oranges with a bit of juice in them,' commented Mrs Woodall, squeezing one of the fruits with a work-worn hand.

Jaco turned to Josie. 'As I said, all around the world and sailed back on the *Jupiter* on the evening tide.'

Josie's mind whirled.

The Jupiter!

Why did that name ring bells in her head?

'Anyhow, Mrs W, Mr Grey says to tell you he'll be by in the morning for the rest of the week's order,' Jaco said. He winked at Mrs Woodall. 'Oh, and tell Daisy I was asking after her,' he said, dashing up the steps two at a time.

'I'll do no such thing,' Mrs Woodall called after him.

Turning back to the table, she seized a large potato and jabbed her knife into it. 'The cheek of him,' she muttered, scraping off the skin in short strokes.

The kitchen door opened and Bobbie, Josie's twelve-year-old-sister, appeared around it. Nurse had worked a miracle on Bobbie's straight hair and her young face was now framed with reddish-blond ringlets.

'Mother's asking for you,' Bobbie said.

Giving Mrs Woodall a brief smile, Josie followed Bobbie up the stairs.

Shoving the niggling issue of the *Jupiter* aside, she reached the ground floor of the house and stepped back onto the hall carpet, the smell of lavender and beeswax tickling her nose. The door to the parlour, the main family room to her right, was open wide and Josie glanced in.

The sofa and chairs sat at right angles to each other with their cushions plumped and the what-nots standing ready to receive books and drinks as required. Josie's embroidery hoop lay across her needlework box on the table by the window. Ma had wanted to tidy it away but Josie had argued that it would show Mrs Munroe that they spent their leisure time in industrious pursuits.

Mounting the stairs to the first floor, her eye caught the print of the steamship her stepfather had bought shares in. A smile lifted the corners of her mouth. That's it! The *Jupiter.*

She peered at the name underneath the picture. It wasn't the *Jupiter,* it was the *Juno.*

For goodness' sake, she thought. The *Jupiter* was threatening to turn into one of those questions that tap at your brain for hours until you remember the answer.

'Josie!' her mother's voice called from above her.

'Just coming, Mam.' Josie hoisted her skirts and made her way up to the next floor.

When Robert Munroe had left New York ahead of them to take up his post as Chief Medical Officer of the nearby London Hospital, and to find his family a suitable house, he had asked Josie what she would like in her bedroom. She had said two words: pink and lace, and now her bedroom incorporated both with pink candy-striped wallpaper, darker toned curtains and lace bed hangings. The room also had a rosewood wardrobe, a chest of drawers and a marble-topped washstand. As Josie had spent the first half of her life in a one up, one down cottage by the Thames she hadn't yet grown tired of the pleasure of her own room. It was a far cry from the creaky wooden bed with the straw-stuffed mattress that she, her mother and her gran used to share all those years ago.

Josie stared around her bedroom as images of her old house, its cracked glass in the windows and its ragged curtains, drifted into her mind. Instead of the Turkey rug on the wooden floorboards she saw the old rag rug covering the beaten earth and shabby furniture.

Ellen's voice cut through her musing.

'For goodness' sake, Josie, where have you been?' she asked, laying the skirt of Josie's best dress on her bed alongside four petticoats. 'You need to get ready. They could be here any moment.'

Josie shut the door. 'There's hours yet. Pa has to get to the Black Swan to collect her and then get a cab back.' She began to unbutton the bodice of her workaday brown dress. 'Mam, stop worrying or you'll get a headache and then Pa'll have something to say.'

Robert Munroe wasn't actually her father.

Michael O'Casey had died before she could walk, let alone remember him, so Robert was the only man she'd ever called Pa. She'd first met him when she was twelve and he had just set up his medical practice around the corner from where they lived in Anthony Street. Her gran had called Dr Munroe to their old ramshackle home one night after Josie had returned home from school with her throat feeling as if she'd swallowed broken glass. From that very moment, he became one of her favourite people, and had remained so ever since.

A soft look crossed Ellen's face and she ran her hands over her swollen stomach.

'Why don't you sit down while I freshen up, then you can help me with my laces,' Josie said soothingly.

Ellen duly sat down and patted the dark auburn bun at the nape of her neck. She glanced out of the window again and her fingers drummed on the armrest.

'Don't worry. I'm sure Mrs Munroe isn't as fierce as all that,' Josie said, as she sponged herself down.

'Maybe so, but I'm sure she still regards me as a godless papist who nearly ruined her son and forced him to live in America for the last twelve years,' her mother replied, fiddling with her hair again.

'I'm sure she thinks no such thing.'

Ellen raised an eyebrow.

Before they married, Josie's mother and stepfather had been at the centre of an infamous trial. Danny Donavan, who had the look of a

29

bulldog chewing gristle, had ruled the dockside area for years with a fist and a blade of iron until Robert Munroe exposed his corrupt practices. Donavan was sent to trial at the Old Bailey, and it was Ellen, who used to earn a few coppers singing in Danny's pubs, who supplied the vital piece of evidence against her boss. The trial was reported widely; so too was Ellen's relationship with the reforming young doctor. They had married, but because of the scandal, Robert had been forced to practise in America for the past twelve years.

Although Robert's father, the Reverend George Munroe, had gone to his grave refusing to acknowledge his son's marriage to an Irish Catholic, his mother was more pragmatic. After Ellen and Robert had been married for eight years and produced five children, Robert's mother had graciously condescended to acknowledge Ellen.

Josie put on a bright smile. 'Besides, I'm sure that once she sets eyes on her grandchildren she won't mind if you're the Pope's sister.'

'It's been hard on your father being apart from his family. He has longed for his mother to meet us all and I am determined that nothing should mar his joy.'

Josie reached for the towel. 'Mam, what was the name of the ship we sailed to America on?'

Ellen shrugged. 'I can't remember.' She stood up slowly and then, going to the bed, picked up the new, finely worked corset she had bought for her daughter in Regent Street.

Ellen shook it at Josie and grinned. 'Now then, Josie Bridget O'Casey, turn around and prepare yourself.'

She slid the corset on Josie, who fastened the hooks at the front. Josie held her breath and her mother pulled the laces at the back. Pulling each side together she worked her way down and tied it off temporarily. Josie let out her breath.

'We're not done yet, my girl,' her mother told her.

'You know Pa said it can be dangerous to lace too tight,' Josie said, hoping her mother gauged her waist to be slender enough.

'Just a pinch more,' Ellen said. She repeated the process.

After five more minutes of being pulled back and forth, Ellen drew the two sides of the corset together at the back and finally tied the laces. She tipped her head to one side and admired her daughter. 'That's not too tight, surely,' she said. 'I read in the paper that there are young women of your age with waists of eighteen inches.'

'What, fainting in the street?' Josie replied, twisting back and forth. 'It's all right for you. You don't have to wear one.'

Ellen laughed 'You look grand, so quit your fussing and get dressed. You can't greet Robert's mother in your underwear.'

Josie stepped into her fine petticoat and then the other three padded ones and Ellen tied them at the back. She held Josie's dress aloft so she could slip into it.

'The turquoise and green in that fabric really suits you,' Ellen told her as she snapped the last metal clip in place.

'I loved the colours when we saw it in the ware-house.'

'It brings out the colour of your hair and eyes,' Ellen said. 'And I'm not the only one to think so. That young doctor, Mr Arnold, your father invited to dinner last week could barely find his food on his plate for looking at you.'

'We were talking about his work, that's all,' Josie replied, lowering her head. She was acutely aware that her cheeks were turning red.

'It doesn't matter what you were talking about,' Ellen said, straightening the pleats around the neckline of the dress. 'He is from a good family and his grandmother left him well provided for.'

Josie had noticed William Arnold's interest but hoped that her mother hadn't. He was pleasant enough but when he shook her hand there was no strength in it. She pulled a face.

'And if not him, what about Mr Vaughan? I could see he was very taken with you and his father owns most of the High Street.'

'Mother! We have only been home a month and already you're wanting to marry me off. Will you just stop throwing young men at me?'

'Only when you decide to catch one. You want to marry, don't you?'

'Of course I do, but you didn't marry Pa to be provided for,' she said, and her mother's eyes flew open. 'You married Pa because you loved him.'

'That is entirely a diff–' she caught Josie's amused expression. 'I just want the best for you, sweetheart,' she said. 'I don't want you to have to wash other people's dirty clothes to put food on the table or–'

'Sing in a public house to keep my daughter from the workhouse,' Josie said.

The iron-rimmed wheels of a coach sounded below. Josie and Ellen dashed to the window. A carriage had slowed and the driver halted the horse. He stowed his whip, then hopped down from the top box. The door opened and Josie's stepfather jumped down. He straightened his coat and held out his hand. The coach lurched and a woman stepped out. She was dressed completely in black and her hat had a modest brim by fashionable standards, with only a Petersham band around the crown by way of adornment. The half-veil of the hat hid all but the tightly drawn lips of the woman. She straightened up stiffly and stared up at the house.

Taking her son's arm with one hand and leaning on her cane with the other, Mrs Munroe mounted the seven whitened steps to the front door.

Ellen rushed from Josie's room. 'Judy! Daisy! Quick, quick! Mrs Munroe has arrived and we should already be downstairs. Bring the children down at once.'

As Josie joined her mother, Bobbie, and ten-year-old Lottie, were already making their way down to the parlour below. Both wore their new clothes, and their tight ringlets bobbed either side of their faces.

Following them was Nurse in her navy uniform and starched white apron, carrying baby Jack while guiding six-year-old Joe down the stairs. Nine-year-old George followed in his new sailor suit, complete with a hat.

Josie just stood, caught in the moment, hardly

33

able to breathe.

Patrick! The *Jupiter* was the first ship he had sailed on.

Her head spun for a second as memories of her first love, Patrick Nolan, danced in her mind. The ache of a loss that had dulled but never disappeared rose up in her.

Josie continued to stand unseeing, as her mind took her back twelve years to when she and her mother had lived in the tiny cottage by the river. She was thirteen then and her head had barely reached Patrick's chin. He had been her 'fella' and she had been his 'gal'. He had signed articles on the *Jupiter* just before she and her mother had sailed for America and he had visited them each time his ship brought him to New York.

It was seven years since she had waved goodbye to him from the quayside in New York. She remembered thinking that, with a strong wind behind him and a swift turn around in London, he would be back to her within the year. As he kissed her goodbye he'd told her that when he came back he would ask Dr Munroe's permission to court her.

He had never returned.

Chapter Two

As the sun dipped behind the wharves that lined the Thames waterfront at Wapping, Patrick Nolan leapt nimbly onto the quayside, looped the rope in his hand around the squat iron mooring then pressed the coil firmly with his studded boot. From Ratcliffe Cross to the Regent Canal Basin the sail barges, like the one Patrick captained, were being tied up and made trim for the next day.

Running his hands through his unruly black curls, Patrick stretched his body to relieve the knot in his back. The soft breeze ruffled his open shirt as he untied his red kingsman – the handkerchief around his neck – and shook the coal dust out before retying it, setting the knot at a jaunty angle. The brightly coloured squares were almost a symbol of the bargemen and were as important to their safety as the tarred keels of their boats, especially when they carried the highly prized and lucrative coal up river. Although the job turned a good profit, coal dust seeped into lungs day after day and rotted them unless the men were careful to keep it out as they worked.

Adjusting his knot again and with a last glance over the boat, Patrick snatched up his jacket and slung it across his shoulder, leaving his shirt sleeves rolled up.

He'd had a good day. He'd loaded a full hold of

coal from a Newcastle collier before the sun was up and, helped by the strong spring tide, had landed it by mid-morning at Pimlico Pier. He'd trimmed the sails and made it back to the Regent Canal Basin just after two, when he'd picked up another half hold of coal that he then ferried to Blackfriars.

Now, turning his back on the jagged black mountains of coal heaped in the yards, Patrick Nolan fell in step with the other men tramping home over the cobbles. He passed many people who greeted him with a cheery wave and a smile, their teeth flashing white in their coal-blackened faces. He had known most of them since they were children, and when he'd arrived back in Wapping five years ago he'd been surprised by the ease with which he had slipped back in to old friendships. He'd even secured a lucrative captaincy on one of Watkins & Sons new barges, but then the fact that he'd worked his way up from deck hand to able seaman had helped to establish his credentials.

Although it was not yet six o'clock, some of the local trollops were already milling around between the warehouses. They eyed Patrick boldly and one blew him a kiss, but though he grinned and winked in response, he didn't pause. He had more sense than to risk his health by accepting an invitation from one of the riverside doxies.

Putting his hand to the polished doorplate of the saloon bar door of the Town of Ramsgate, Patrick shoved it open.

Inside, the narrow bar was packed. The Town did a brisk trade with all those who worked on

36

the river. As it was Saturday, those men who had been paid at the end of the week would stop in at any one of the dozens of public houses in the area for a swift pint before the more reliable of them headed home to give their wives the weekly housekeeping. The first customers in that evening had found themselves seats on the benches against the wall, but most stood elbow to elbow while they sank their foaming pints.

Patrick elbowed his way through the throng. He was a regular customer in the Town of Ramsgate, most of whose patrons were his neighbours, living in two-up, two-down houses like his own in the streets surrounding the London Docks. And, like Patrick, although most of these men had been born in the overcrowded slums of London's East End their names – Docherty, Murphy, Riley, Sheehan – told of their 'Old Country' origins. Many of them greeted him with a slap on the back and a 'Good man yerself, Pat', while others pressed him to have a drink.

By local standards, the Town was a respectable house. When, a few years back, it was still common practice for riverside ale houses to act as recruitment agencies for casual labourers, Arthur Kemp, the landlord, hadn't expected a man to spend half his earnings on drink at the bar before giving him work. For that reason alone Patrick gave the Town his custom. Although the Town looked as if it had been hammered in between the warehouses, it had been there forever, long before the warehouses were built. Arthur was fond of telling people that Nelson had stopped at the bar before Trafalgar, a tale which some wag always greeted by asking if he'd had to wait as long as the rest of them to get served.

The smell of newly laid sawdust drifted up and mingled with the bitter aroma of fresh beer and stale sweat, and men vied for space, shouting and laughing under the grey haze of tobacco smoke. Shouldering his way to the bar, Patrick caught sight of his boyhood friend Brian Maguire, who could almost match Patrick's height but was of slighter build. He was to marry Mattie, Patrick's eldest sister, in three months' time.

Brian grinned at his future brother-in-law. 'I thought you'd be in,' he said, flicking back a wedge of unruly red-gold hair. 'Where have you been today then?'

Patrick smiled. It was common knowledge that he'd sailed around the globe twice, and the men around the port never tired of asking if he'd seen any elephants or sea monsters. It was good-hearted banter and Patrick took it as such, but it was a constant reminder that he now had to be content with the Thames when once he had sailed the oceans.

'Pimlico and Blackfriars,' he replied. 'And no, I didn't see any whales, just a couple of mermaids.'

Brian laughed and Patrick caught Arthur's eye. The landlord wiped his hands on his apron and swaggered over.

'Evening, Pat. Good to see you,' he said, reaching up and taking a battered pewter tankard down from the ironwork above the bar. 'What'll you have?'

'Pint of your brown,' Patrick replied.

Arthur hooked the tankard under the brass

spout, pulled on the pump handle and the ale spurted out. He placed the drink on the wooden counter.

Patrick handed him thruppence and then sipped the frothy head off in a noisy slurp before gulping down a couple of refreshing mouthfuls of the ale beneath.

Arthur Kemp rested his hands on the bar and leant forward. 'I was down by the river earlier and saw your top sail full up and cutting upstream,' he said. 'How'd you get that new boat straight off the blocks?'

A grin spread across Brian's face. 'I'll tell you, Arthur, it's because he's got such a pretty face.'

Arthur laughed, and then glanced down to the other end of the bar. 'My new barmaid seems to think so.'

Patrick followed his gaze to where a young woman at the other end of the bar was studying him. When she caught his eye, a blush spread across her cheeks and she looked away.

'New girl?' Patrick asked. She was curvy enough and her rear swayed pleasingly as she moved.

'Started yesterday. She's a bit slow with the orders but the customers like her.' Arthur winked at him. 'Your brother Gus seemed to think so when he was in here earlier.'

Patrick studied the girl again and a smile creased his face. 'I'm sure he did.'

Brian called for another drink. Patrick put his hand over his tankard. 'I'm heading off after this one. Annie and Mickey will be waiting for me.'

'You know, Pat, those nippers are a credit to you,' said Brian. 'That young Annie is as bright as a button and pretty as a flower in the sun, and Mickey's got the same quick cheek about him as his old man, so he has.' He used the back of his hand to wipe the beer froth from the fair bristles of his top lip. 'After Rosa left not many men would have done what you did. After all, you with only six months from sitting the captain's exams and getting your own ship, yet you gave it up over night to look after your kids and see them right.'

'They are my children,' Patrick replied, remembering coming home three years ago to find Mickey in a filthy bum-cloth, two-year-old Annie trying to feed him a crust of bread, and his wife nowhere in sight.

'Even so, you could have left them with yer mam and gone back to sea. That's what most men would have done,' Brian replied.

'I'm not most men.'

'No ... no you're not,' Brian agreed, picking up his tankard only for someone to shove him from behind. His mouth slipped from the tankard's rim and beer splashed down his front.

'What the fec–' Brian stopped as he saw who had jostled him.

Patrick eyed the newcomer coolly. Harry Tugman was about five years older than Patrick but his baldness made him look even older. The top of his head just reached Patrick's chin, which meant he had to crane his short neck to look into Patrick's face. He wore tight corduroy trousers that sagged at the knees, a grubby grey shirt and a shapeless, oversized checked jacket, but there was no way on God's earth that any of its remaining buttons could ever now be fastened into their corresponding buttonholes.

Harry Tugman was tough, but not as tough as Patrick Nolan, who had learned to handle himself in some of the roughest ports on the globe.

Harry smiled, revealing a set of uneven brown teeth. 'Ma wants to know when you'll be calling.'

'Does she?'

'Aye. She's asked you twice before and is a bit surprised you haven't been by, considering she wants to put a bit of business your way.' Harry leant on the bar between Patrick and Brian. 'For a few easy hours' work you could earn yourself double what you'll earn in a day hauling coal.'

The buzz of voices stopped, and out of the corner of his eye Patrick noticed Arthur grabbing two bottles from the counter, hiding them underneath and locking the money drawer. Brian left his beer and stood at Patrick's right shoulder.

Patrick drained the last of his drink and turned to face Harry. 'I'm sure that Dan Riley thought the same until the police caught him. Now he's in the clink and his wife and kids are on the parish.' He drew himself up and stared down at Harry. 'I know your ma's business and I want no part in it,' he said in a clear voice.

Harry poked a black-nailed finger into Patrick's chest. 'Now, you listen here, you thick Paddy. Ma don't have the likes of you saying no. If you know what's good for you, you'll not get 'er riled.' Spit sprayed from his mouth as he spoke.

'You might still wet yourself when your ma looks at you, Harry, but I don't.'

There was a low rumble of laughter from the back of the room and Harry's face flushed crimson. 'Why you–'

A hard smile spread across Patrick's angular face. 'Now you listen to me, Tugman. Tell that old mother of yours that if she wants to move her pilfered stuff upstream she can look somewhere other than at my barge.' He paused and cast his gaze around the pub. 'Now, I'm just having a quiet drink so I suggest you hurry home like a good boy, and give your ma my message.'

Harry's knuckles cracked. A number of the men around the bar stood up.

For one moment, Patrick thought the man's temper would get the better of him and a part of him hoped it would – but then Harry's toothy smile returned.

'That's right, lads, you have a quiet drink before you head home to your old ladies,' he said with a forced laugh.

The men sat down again but their eyes remained fixed on Patrick, and on Harry, who thrust his face up close to Patrick's. 'You and your bog trotters had better think again, Nolan, or be careful where you walk at night.'

Patrick held his gaze until Harry turned and shoved his way back towards the door.

When he'd gone, Brian whistled through his front teeth. 'Jesus, I thought there'd be blood.'

Patrick downed the last mouthful of his ale. 'I didn't. The Tugmans don't fight you face to face; they slit your throat in the dark. I judged we were safe enough.'

Brian signalled for the barmaid and she hurried over, all blue eyes and eagerness. Patrick guessed she wouldn't be behind the bar for long; some eager fellow was bound to persuade her to marry him. She smiled and a dimple showed itself on her right cheek.

'Same again?' she asked, running her gaze slowly over Patrick.

He held up his hand. 'Not for me. I have to get home.'

'You married then?' she asked, looking disappointed.

Patrick gave her the smile that had served him well in every port he'd ever been in. 'Not necessarily,' he said, sliding his empty tankard towards her and turning to leave.

'Tell Mattie I'll be around later,' Brian said, searching in his pocket for the price of his next drink.

The barmaid pulled hard on the pump. As she leant over the bar her cap caught in the ironwork above her head. Her hair tumbled out and Patrick stopped in his tracks as he watched the rich auburn curls sliding over her shoulders.

Suddenly, he wasn't in the crowded bar of the Town but at the May fair at Bow Bridge by the river Lea, with a laughing girl on his arm. He could almost smell the lavender she had used for rinsing her dark, auburn hair. It transported him back almost thirteen years, to a past before their lives had changed completely.

Although he'd tried not to think about Josie O'Casey, over the years and in different places the memory of her dark green eyes and inviting smile had stolen back to him in dreams. He pushed the thoughts away. There was no point. He could never go back, and remembering the future he'd planned with her on that bright May morning would only add to his other regrets.

Tapping her foot lightly on the carpet in time to the music, Josie watched her two younger sisters at the piano. Lottie was turning the pages for Bobbie, who had been practising for weeks in anticipation of her grandmama's visit. Now her playing was perfect.

Josie's gaze moved on to the person her sisters were so eager to please: Mrs Munroe, in widow's black, sitting straight-backed on the sofa beside her son. Josie hadn't realised how much her stepfather resembled his mother. They had the same broad forehead and strong jaw. He'd also inherited his commanding height from her and his strongly defined nose, although on her it had a beak-like quality, especially when she tilted her head back.

Bobbie came to the end of the piece and everyone applauded. She jumped down from the bench and went over to stand in front of her grandmother. 'I hope you enjoyed that piece, Grandmama.'

The severe lines of Mrs Munroe's face softened as she took Bobbie's hand in her bony one. 'It was beautiful, Robina,' she said. 'I think the pianoforte is an excellent instrument for girls.'

Robert's face registered surprise. 'I don't recall your having a musical ear, Mother.'

Mrs Munroe shook her head. 'I do not commend it for its musical merit but because it forces a girl to sit up straight, and reading music helps her to develop an eye for detail, which is so necessary for checking tradesmen's bills.'

Next, Lottie bounced off the piano stool, hopped across the floor and collided with Bobbie. 'I turned the pages, Grandmama.'

Mrs Munroe regarded Lottie for a long moment and the little girl shifted her weight from one foot to the other.

'So I noticed, Charlotte. Now, I'm sure your governess will be coming to take you upstairs.'

'No, the children stay down until bedtime and then Mam takes them up,' Josie put in. 'I help her, of course, and it's great fun isn't it, Mam?'

'It certainly is,' Ellen agreed.

'How quaint,' Mrs Munroe said coolly, 'but one must always beware of spoiling children. I was most diligent in that regard myself, was I not, Robert?'

Josie had always thought that her stepfather's Scottish childhood sounded bleak. Since meeting Mrs Munroe, she understood why.

'No one could ever accuse you of spoiling your children, Mama, but Sir Robert told me that the Royal family themselves favour a more informal family life,' said Robert.

Mrs Munroe's substantial eyebrows rose up. 'Sir Robert? You mean Sir Robert Peel?'

'I met him last week in the House of Commons to discuss the defeat of Graham's Factory Act. The care of children in general came up.'

Mrs Munroe looked suitably impressed. Josie knew that as part of his work on the Government Health Improvement Board her stepfather met members of the Cabinet regularly but it was a rare day when he mentioned it.

'Now children, play nicely until supper time,' Ellen told them. 'And no, Lottie, you and George can not go out and play in the garden. It's too late and – will you look at the sky? – before the clock strikes the hour the rain will be falling.'

Mrs Munroe's expression chilled as Ellen's Irish lilt, always more pronounced when she was agitated or worried, crept into her speech.

The children did as they were bid. Lottie delved into a large pine chest in the corner of the room and handed Joe his wooden soldiers. George pulled out a stagecoach with a brightly painted horse pivoting between the shafts and trotted it across the rug in front of the fire.

'Do they have toys in the parlour in America, too?' Mrs Munroe asked, as George started making clip-clop sounds.

'Certainly,' Robert replied. 'They spend all day with Miss Byrd, their governess, so when I am home Ellen and I like to enjoy our children together.'

'Well, they *are* utterly delightful, and so clever. You have done well, Ellen. Five children in twelve years and three of them boys.'

'We were blessed with seven but...' Ellen said quietly.

'You must expect to lose an infant or two,' Mrs Munroe replied briskly. 'One must not question God's will.'

'That does not lessen the grief,' Robert replied. His mother made as if to speak but he continued. 'But now we are to be blessed again.'

Jack, who had been sitting contentedly, playing with his rattle on the rug between his parents' feet, started to fret.

Josie jumped up immediately. 'Let me, Mam,' she said, scooping the infant off the floor and placing him on her lap.

Mrs Munroe turned to Josie. 'And what do you intend to do now you have returned to London, Josie?'

'I am going to visit the British Museum and, of course, I can't wait to visit the Tower of London and see the Queen's jewels. Mrs Martin, who lives two doors down, told us how she visited the Tower of London when she was a young girl. The animals have gone to the Zoological Gardens now but Pa said he will try to get us a visitors' pass.'

Mrs Munroe's expressive eyebrows travelled upwards. 'I am disappointed that you do not have plans to spend some of your time in charitable works.' She placed her hand theatrically on her bosom. 'Our Lord himself went amongst the poor and sick. Can we, Josie, do less?'

Josie smiled sweetly. 'I have renewed my acquaintance with Miss Cooper, whose father runs a mission in Wellclose Square. She has a number of young ladies who visit the poor and I plan to join them.' She omitted to add that she and Sophie also planned a trip to Regent Street.

The lines around Mrs Munroe's lips slackened a fraction and she inclined her head at Ellen. 'I have always said that the most effective way of protecting a young woman's reputation is for her to have acquaintances with a serious turn of mind. I have insisted on such with my own daughters and I am glad to hear you do the same, my dear Ellen.'

Lottie left her toys and came over to where the

adults were sitting. 'Grandmama,' she said standing in front of Mrs Munroe with her hands behind her back. 'If you are staying with us for eight weeks that is fifty-six days.'

Mrs Munroe smiled. 'That's very clever, Charlotte, but a young lady shouldn't do multiplication too often as it can upset the female humours.'

Fifty-six days! thought Josie, *I'm sure I'll be crossing them off in my journal.*

Chapter Three

'Honestly, Sam,' Josie said to the young man beside her. 'You will only be gone for a few moments and I will be perfectly safe here until you return.'

Sam, the young lad who helped around the house, didn't seem convinced. 'I don't know, Miss Josie. This is a very rough area,' he said, looking anxiously along the cobbled street. 'And your father insisted that I stay close by you at all times.'

Josie gave him the warm smile that always made him blush. Sam was only a few years older than Bobbie and Josie wouldn't normally have taken advantage of his crush on her. However, after walking the two miles to Miss Cooper's house, her new shoes had raised painful blisters at almost every point they touched.

'The London dock offices are just there,' she said pointing down Wapping High Street to where the tall warehouses surrounding the docks blocked out the late afternoon sunlight. 'There is always a hansom cab or two waiting there for business. It's no more than a two-minute walk.'

Sam eyed a couple of dark-skinned Lascars, slouching against the wall in their loose-fitting tunics, with clay pipes hanging from the sides of their mouths.

'Dr Munroe wouldn't like it if–'

'Sam! I think you forget that I was raised in these streets and I will be perfectly safe for the five minutes or so it takes you to fetch a hansom,' Josie said firmly.

He gave her a dubious look but then turned and sped off, dodging the wagons passing in both directions.

As Josie looked down the bustling thoroughfare that followed the bend of the Thames from St Katherine's Dock through to New Crane Stairs, childhood memories flooded back into her mind. As a child she had thought the main road busy when she'd passed along it on her way to school but she couldn't remember seeing the volume of traffic that now rolled by. Matching carthorses, wearing blinkers and nosebags, hauled laden drays from the wharves towards the city and a driver, his cart piled high with hay just unloaded from a barge from Essex or beyond, called out a warning and Josie stepped back against the wall. She bumped into an old woman with a shovel in one hand and a bucket in the other – the 'pure' collector, harvesting the dog shit to sell in the Southwark tanneries – who gave her a grumbling look, but shuffled off to search for newly laid whorls to harvest.

Josie, using her rolled umbrella for support, picked up one foot and then the other in an attempt to alleviate the pain in her heels and toes, then glanced towards where she had seen Sam going on his way. *Where is he?* she thought, moving along to the end of the wall.

The corners of her mouth turned up in a little smile as she spotted a group of children throwing stones into squares scored in the dirt, then bobbing and hopping up and back in turn. How many times had she done the same? She couldn't remember being as ragged as the barefooted children on the other side of the road, but she must have been just as grimy; even now, the hem of her skirt was covered in dirt after walking only two miles. And the smell! She had completely forgotten the cloying stench at low tide that made you breathe through your mouth, and she hadn't remembered the two-ups, two-downs in the narrow side streets being quite so dilapidated. And although, as Josie knew, there were now street cleaners with carts and stiff brushes, the roads were still filled with all manner of filth.

The rattle of iron wheels over cobbles jarred her from her reminiscence. She stepped back to let the carriage pass, but it stopped in front of her, and a gloved hand lowered the carriage window. A man in a black silk hat looked out, ran his index finger along his moustache and smiled at Josie.

'Looking for a little company, my dear?' He looked her up and down appraisingly.

'I *beg* your pardon?' Josie said, glaring at him,

not quite believing what she'd heard.

The man gave a low chuckle. 'You look like a sparky little minx,' he said, 'and I can be very generous. Ask any of the other girls.' His eyes drifted past her to where two gaudily dressed women, with rouged lips and cheeks, loitered against the buildings.

Alarm shot through Josie. Where on earth was Sam? It was only five minutes to the dock offices and he must have been gone a full ten by now. Ignoring the man, she turned sharply away and, unseeingly, studied the bobbing top sails of the river barges until the carriage moved on. Josie let out her breath, but then heard another carriage approaching. Gathering her wits, she started off towards the police office a few hundred yards away. At least she would be safe there until Sam found his way back.

'Oi! Miss Hoity-Toity,' called one of the whores. 'Sling your hook.'

Josie glanced across at the two young women in their low cut gowns and painted faces.

The other girl stuck two fingers up at Josie. 'You, go find your own pitch.'

Driven by humiliation, and anxiety about Sam, Josie ignored the harsh pain of her blisters and headed towards the police station, hearing the girls sniggering behind her.

As she passed the Prospect of Whitby and New Crane Dock someone shouted from above. 'Watch yer!' Josie looked up and saw a massive wrought-iron crane fixed to the side of the warehouse, its hook dangling from the rope looping around in mid air, and at that moment two

51

empty wagons rolled out from Red Lion Street and blocked her path completely.

Josie tried to squeeze between the wooden side of the cart and the wall but the man steadying the sacks raised his hand. 'Sorry, ducks, you can't go that way.'

'But I need to get to the police station,' Josie protested, increasingly conscious that in her ruby silk gown and tailored jacket she made a strange spectacle beside the other women in their knitted shawls.

She must have taken leave of her senses to send Sam off like that. If she'd been thinking half straight she would have recognised the utter foolishness of wandering alone on the waterfront. She had to get to the station and fast, before anything else happened.

'If you goes down there,' he pointed along Wapping Wall, 'there's a cut through to Coleman Street and that'll take you to the High Street.'

Damping down her annoyance and holding her skirt high to avoid the muck, Josie stepped off the pavement, over the slime congealing in the gutter, and in to the dark alleyway.

Ma Tugman pushed open the front door of the Boatman and stepped out into Coleman Street. Squinting into the bright, late afternoon sunlight, she glanced down the narrow bare earth walkway. Down the centre of the alley a sludgy stream of waste trickled slowly towards the river. It had rained heavily earlier in the day but, even so, the faintly acidic smell of human waste wafted through.

Coleman Street ran between Wapping Wall and New Gravel Lane and was a convenient cut through from the docks to the river. Now, late in the afternoon, those river men who'd sailed up the Thames on the morning tide trudged up the alley on their way home. Ma liked to sit outside at this time to keep an eye on the comings and goings. With Snapper at her heels, she shuffled along a couple of yards and then stopped. Harry, who had followed her with one of the Boatman's wooden chairs, set it down against the wall.

'There you go, Ma.'

Ma pulled a sour face. 'You've put it in the sun.'

'I thought you'd like the warmth,' he said, moving the chair into the shade. 'Loosen up your bones.'

She gave him a sour look. 'You know I have tender skin.' She rubbed her hand over her bare forearm, creasing the flesh. 'Charlie wouldn't have put me in the sun.'

Harry shot her a sullen look.

Ma called to Snapper, who had wandered off down the alley. The dog cocked his leg, then trotted back and settled himself beside her chair. Removing her pipe from behind her ear she tapped out the cinders then thrust it at her son. 'Well, get me a rub of baccy, then.'

Harry pulled out a leather pouch and offered it to her.

'Haven't I told you twice already today that me knuckles are bad,' she said, flexing her hands and grimacing. 'I'm sure you'll be glad when I'm dead and you won't have to bother yourself any more.'

'You know I don't like to hear you talk like that,' he replied.

She thrust the pale clay pipe at him. 'You load it for me ... there's a good boy.'

His pleased expression returned and he pulled out a couple of strings of tobacco.

Ma studied him as he poked it in the smoke blackened cup and thought just how closely he resembled his dad.

She'd fallen under Harry Tugman's spell almost as soon as he turned his lively grey eyes on her. As she'd known men and their bastard ways since her tenth birthday, it was surprising that she'd been so easily taken in by Harry's sweet words.

He'd told her she was his only love, but it wasn't more than a month or two after they moved in together that he had her working the streets alongside his other doxies. When she found she'd been caught with Harry, she considered slipping the baby into the Thames. It wouldn't have been the first unwanted infant washed up on the shore at low tide, and it wouldn't have been the last, but when she'd found out about Harry's other women she decided to stay and make his life as near to a living hell as she could manage. And she'd had seven good years of goading, nagging and robbing him blind before the drinking finally caught him and he curled up his toes.

'Here you go, Ma,' Harry said, handing her the pipe, his face begging for her approval.

Ma clamped the stem of the pipe between her thin lips. 'Give us a light then,' she growled out of the corner of her mouth, 'and tell that slut of Charlie's, Judy–'

'Lucy,' Harry corrected.

'Whatever her fecking name is, to fetch us a drink,' she called after him as he disappeared into the gloom of the pub.

People passing down the alley touched their hats to Ma Tugman as they went by, but despite their friendly greetings she could see the wary look in their eyes – just the way she wanted to keep it. There had been too many of the local bargemen not giving her the respect she was due, especially the Irish scum working with that bastard, Patrick Nolan. The Micks used to know their place before he showed up.

Ma stood up, dragged the chair out of the shade. She settled back down and, closing her eyes, tilted her face to the warmth of the sun.

Harry reappeared with another chair slung over his arm, followed by Charlie's current bit of fancy carrying a bottle and two glasses.

Charlie's a one for the ladies all right, a bit like his father in that way.

She didn't mind that he brought them back to the Boatman as long as they showed proper respect. This one with her downcast eyes seemed to know her place.

The last one Charlie used to warm his bed had thought she was something special, swanning around the bar like the queen of England and giving Ma a mouthful of cheek. But Charlie had put her in her place, smacked her black and blue he had, then sent her to China Rose's knocking shop.

A little smile crossed Ma's face. *I'm sure she's special there.*

'You've moved back into the sun,' Harry said, looking confused.

Ma drew on her pipe. 'You didn't think to bring my shawl, so I had to,' she replied.

Lucy nodded and poured out the brandy. The bottle rattled against the glass as she did.

'Don't spill it, girl,' Ma said, taking the glass from her.

Charlie had been fighting drunk when he stumbled home two nights ago and the bruise he'd given Lucy still showed mauve around her eye.

Lucy poured Harry a drink and passed it to him. He grabbed her wrist and drew her to him and his other hand grabbed her rear.

'You've got a lovely arse, girl, let me have a piece of it,' he said grinning at her and showing his uneven teeth. 'I'll give you better than Charlie ever gives you.' Holding her firmly with one hand he thrust the other hand under her skirt. 'Very nice,' he said. Lucy's feet scrabbled for the floor as she tried to avoid his groping hands. 'Look at 'er, Ma, can't keep herself off me.'

Ma watched with mild interest for a second more then whistled. Snapper jumped up. 'See 'er off,' she told him.

Lucy bolted for the pub door. Snapper dashed after her but then he shot through Harry's legs and down the alley, barking as he went.

Ma stared after him as he ran, his pads barely touching the dirt, towards a well-dressed young woman at the south end of the walkway. The young woman looked to be in her early twenties and was wearing an outfit that would fetch at least ten shillings. Whoever she was she must have been addled in her brain because as far as Ma could tell, she was alone.

Snapper reached the young woman and with a quick double step he sprang at her, teeth snapping. The young woman didn't scream, as Ma expected her to but thrust her umbrella at the dog. Snapper's jaws closed around it and he ripped it from her hand.

Harry pointed at the dog. 'L … look, Ma, old Snapper's...' he laughed. Others in the alley joined in.

Having found something that he could chew his way through, Snapper took his prize over to the far wall. Growling, he shook the umbrella, bit its cane frame into slivers then ripped through the silk cover.

The young woman watched her umbrella being destroyed and then she turned. Setting her mouth into a straight line, she strode over.

'Is that your dog?' she asked in an odd-sounding Irish accent and pointing her finger at Snapper.

'Aye,' Ma replied, drawing slowly on her pipe.

'Well, then,' the young woman said, glancing briefly to where the dog was shredding the last few solid pieces of the coloured fabric. 'If you don't want the police after you, you had better keep it under control.'

As the words left her lips Josie realised that she just should have walked by and ignored them. Now it was too late.

The man and the wrinkled old woman stopped laughing instantly and the old woman blew smoke out of the corner of her mouth. She was bareheaded and without a shawl and a grimy charcoal gown covered her overfed figure. Although her hair was pulled back, a number of greasy strands fell around her face and, as her grey eyes glided slowly over her, Josie suppressed the urge to shudder.

'You threatening us with the nabbers, are you?' the man asked, revealing a set of brown teeth.

A tingle of disquiet crept up Josie's spine. The crowd gathering around them was enjoying her discomfort and, although they seemed good-natured, if this brute turned nasty she knew that every one of them would turn their back and leave her to her fate. She tugged down the front of her coat.

'I'm just saying that it might not be an umbrella next time but a child's leg, that's all.' She set her lips firmly together. 'But as there is no harm done we'll say no more about it this time. Good day.'

She went to walk past but the man grabbed her arm. 'What's your hurry, sweetie? Come and 'ave a drink.'

His fingers closed around her arm and dug through the fabric of her jacket. Josie glanced down at the plump hand with dirty, broken nails and then she fixed its owner with a furious stare.

'Let go of me.'

'A sweet girly like her is too good for you, Harry,' the old woman said. 'She's probably got some man waiting for her, some toff, who ain't got missing teeth or a beer belly.'

Harry sucked in his stomach as he gave his

mother a hateful look, and then turned his attention back to Josie.

'You can have a brandy with me before you run off to your fancy man,' he said, dragging her towards him.

'She don't seem very keen, son,' the old woman said, as Josie's feet skidded on the earth.

Her bonnet fell to one side but Josie ignored it and glared at the man holding her. 'Get your filthy hands off me, you great lummox, or by the Virgin I'll see you swing for it, so I will,' she yelled.

The old woman chuckled. 'Oh, Gawd luv us, she's a Paddy.'

'Well, that's all right then, they all like a drink or two,' Harry said.

With a monumental effort, Josie ripped her arm free. Harry reached out to catch her again then his gaze flickered past her.

'Can I be of some assistance, Miss?' a deep voice with an Irish lilt asked from behind.

Josie spun around and stared up at the face that she'd thought never to see again this side of heaven.

'Patrick?'

There was the mass of black hair that she remembered so well, curled around his ears and forehead, softening the toughness of his face. There was the same strong nose, well-shaped mouth and square jaw, now covered with the dark hue of end-of-day stubble. There was also a spray of dark chest hair poking up through his open shirt that hadn't spread past his breastbone the last time she had seen him.

'Josie?'

She nodded. She had to, because she couldn't speak.

'What are you doing here? What are you do–' Patrick stopped and glanced over her shoulder. 'Is this fellow bothering you, Miss O'Casey?' he asked, stepping between her and her tormenters.

A laugh bubbled up inside and dizziness circled around her head for a moment. Patrick was alive and not at the bottom of the ocean or rotting in his grave. He was here, really here. This oaf with his scruffy mother couldn't drag her into the pub because Patrick wouldn't let him.

'He,' she pointed at Harry, 'was trying to drag me into that that ... cesspit.'

The old woman's face formed itself into an innocent expression. 'The poor lamb was lost and Harry was showing her the road.'

'Feck off, Nolan,' Harry growled.

Patrick squared his shoulders and Josie's gaze ran over them. 'Miss O'Casey is an old friend of mine but I wouldn't want to see you showing *any woman* the road.'

Harry glared at Patrick while the old woman's eyes darted back and forth between the two men.

'I'm fine,' Josie said, wanting only to get away from the alley and put the whole frightening episode behind her. She placed her hand on Patrick's arm. 'Would you walk me to Wapping High Street? I'm sure my young Sam will have found a cab by now.'

Patrick smiled at her and Josie's heart, that had only just returned to a steady beat, set off at a gallop again.

60

Josie! For a moment Patrick thought his eyes and mind were playing tricks on him but, as his gaze ran over her, his brain accepted the irrefutable fact that Josie O'Casey was standing, up to her ankles in slurry, not an arm's reach from him.

She was different, of course. This sophisticated young woman in her straw bonnet, hooped skirt and tailored jacket was not the leggy eighteen-year-old he'd waved goodbye to as she stood on the New York dockside seven years before. But the prominent cheekbones, sparkly green eyes and full red lips were the same.

When he first saw her tussling with Harry Tugman he'd thought she was one of the churchy women who came to 'do good works' among the poor, but when Josie O'Casey turned and smiled at him his mind almost stopped working.

But what on earth was she doing here?

Ma's mongrel started growling. Patrick fixed it with a hard stare and the mutt flattened its ears, wagged what was left of its tail, and then shuffled back under the old woman's chair.

Without a second glance, Patrick led Josie back towards the High Street. She said nothing, just gripped his arm tighter as she walked close to him. Her skirt brushed against his leg and he was suddenly aware of his work-stained clothes. His gaze rested on her small hand. The glove covering it was made of cream kid-leather and expertly stitched. It, and its twin on her other hand, probably cost more than his week's rent.

'I can't believe it's you,' she said, turning to face him as they stepped in to Wapping High Street.

61

The late afternoon sunlight caressing her face illuminated her clear complexion and the red tones of her hair. He noticed her faint Irish accent had a different twist to it now. She put her hand on her chest as if to steady her breathing. 'Oh, Patrick, I thought you were dead.'

'Didn't you get my last letter, the one from Gibraltar?'

Josie's finely arched eyebrows pulled together. 'The last one I got was when you were setting sail for Tenerife.'

His heart sank. Despite slipping out of school and down the river as a boy, Patrick prided himself that he wrote pretty fluently, but the agonising letter he'd scratched out doubled up on the crews' deck of the *Dependable* was the hardest he'd ever penned.

It was difficult enough find a reliable sailor to take a letter across the Atlantic and there was always a chance they would take your sixpence, toss your letter over the side and drink the money. Wouldn't it be just the Devil's own work if the only one of his letters to Josie that had gone astray was the most important one.

'I paid a ship's cook on the *Northern Star* double to make sure you got it when the ship docked in New York,' Patrick said.

Although every word he wrote cut through his heartstrings, he had written her a long letter wishing her well in her new married life and telling her about Rosa. And after all that she had never received it.

'Patrick, I though you were dead,' she said again, her eyes searching his face.

'I thought you were in America still,' he said.

'My stepfather was offered the post of Chief Medical Officer for the London Hospital, so we returned a month ago,' she told him as they stepped around a stack of barrels waiting to be stored in a nearby warehouse. 'We are living in Stepney Green. I have another sister apart from Bobbie and three brothers now, and Ma is expecting another in a few months,' she told him as a tendril of her vibrant hair escaped her bonnet.

'But why are you walking alone down Lower Well Alley? Surely you haven't forgotten what a Godforsaken place some of the backstreets are?' he said.

A faint flush spread across Josie's cheeks. 'I know, but I thought to walk home from my friend in Wellclose Square,' she said. 'But enough of my foolishness, why are you not in India or Africa or Japan or some other far-off land?'

'I had enough of roaming the world and wanted to come home to settle down.' It was his stock answer to the question.

'And how are your family, your ma and pa and Mattie? Hannah, too, and Kate and Fergus. Ma told me that they pulled down the houses in Cinnamon Lane so where are you living now? And I bet Peter and Paul are a handful now – what are they? Twelve?' She gave a joyous laugh and the dimple on her cheek that he'd almost forgotten about appeared.

'A chest ague took Peter when he was two, Paul cut his foot in the mud and died of lock-jaw just after his tenth birthday,' Patrick said. 'We lost Pa, too, three winters back.'

Josie's brows pulled together. 'I'm sorry for your loss,' she said in a soft voice. 'Your pa always had a cheery word for any and I know how hard it was when my ma and pa lost my little brother and sister. I'm sorry to hear your ma's suffered in the same way.'

Patrick gave a tight smile. 'Hannah's a housemaid in Leyton and we only see her a couple of times a year. Kate works in Hoffman's bakery at the corner of Bird Street and Gus is sixteen now and is nearly as tall as me. He's a dock tallyman and earning good money, too. He's lodging up in Jane Street. Mattie's grand though, she's at the Sugar refinery and set to marry in three months. We all live in Walburgh Street and I'm captain of one of Wimlow and Sons barges, working out of Limehouse reach.'

Josie's cheery expression returned. 'I would love to see them all, especially Mattie. She's to be a bride, how wonderful,' she said with a wistful sigh.

Patrick cleared his throat. 'Is your husband with you or is he still in America?'

Josie's brow pulled tightly together this time. 'Husband?' Then she laughed. 'What husband would that be, now?'

A steady thumping started in Patrick's temple. 'The last time I docked in New York I found your house boarded up. One of your neighbours told me you'd got married and moved to Boston with the rest of your family.'

Josie shook her head. 'That wasn't me who got married, it was my cousin Jenny. Uncle Joe's eldest.' She laughed again and somehow a weight

64

Patrick hadn't realised he carried evaporated. 'We had her wedding breakfast at our house just before Pa took his post in Boston.'

'So you're not married, then?' he said, in an idiot-like tone.

Josie shook her head. 'Not yet,' she replied.

Over the years and in numerous places Patrick had pictured Josie being swept off her feet by some tall, handsome, rich young man who'd married her and given her three or four children. And although it had given him no comfort to think of her in the arms of another, it had eased his conscience mightily.

He gave a hollow laugh. 'I'm sure it's not for the want of young men asking you,' he said.

She cast a sideward glance at him. 'There's been the odd one or two who've been interested.' A twinge of jealousy jabbed Patrick.

Don't be a fool, why wouldn't a pretty girl like Josie have young men queuing up to wed her. And none of them barge captains, that's for sure.

'I must visit Mattie. In fact I must come and see everyone, and very soon,' Josie told him, her eyes sparkling with excitement. 'Would your mother mind, if I called one afternoon?'

'I'm sure she'd be right happy to see you,' he replied, wondering what she would think of their home now. Even though she and her mother had lived two streets down from them, in one of the poorest cottages in the area when he and Josie were young, that was a long time ago.

Josie's gaze ran over him slowly as her bright smile returned. 'I can't believe you're here, and praise the saints you're not dead, but Patrick,

65

where *have* you been all these years?'

In that instant, he saw Josie – his Josie whom he had walked home from school and kissed inexpertly behind the gravestone in St George's churchyard – and for a second the urge to kiss her, as he had done so many times before, surged up in Patrick. She was the same Josie he'd wanted for his wife.

Wife! Rosa!

'It's a long story,' he replied flatly.

A hansom cab rolled around the corner, its iron-rimmed wheels grinding over the cobbles after its blinkered horse trotting down the street. The children by the kerb, searching for discarded vegetables for their supper, jumped out of the way as the conveyance screeched to a stop. While the driver quietened the horse, a lad, with a look of utter relief on his beardless face, jumped down.

'Thank goodness you've come to no harm, Miss O'Casey,' he said.

'I'm fine, Sam,' Josie said, glancing up at Patrick again.

The young man opened the cab door. Patrick helped her into the carriage. Despite her glove, his shirt and the jacket fabric, he felt her hand as if it were on his bare forearm.

Josie turned. 'Oh, Patrick, I am so pleased you are alive.'

Patrick swallowed but didn't answer. Josie stepped in; Sam closed the door and jumped up next to the driver.

Josie pulled down the window. 'Tell your ma and Mattie I'll call soon.'

66

Annie and Mickey! Alarm shot through Patrick and he grabbed hold of the cab's brass door handle. 'Will you send word when you're going to visit? I don't want to come home and find that I've missed you.'

How was he going to tell her about Rosa?

Josie's eyes flashed, sending a bolt of the old excitement through him. The cab lurched forward. 'I'll send Sam to let you know when to expect me,' she answered, and then she gave him a sideward glance from under her lashes. 'And when I do, I want to hear that long story.'

Chapter Four

Josie repositioned the flannel over her eyes as the large clock in the hall downstairs chimed seven. She could hardly remember the journey home in the hansom because, the moment the carriage jolted forward, a hundred jumbled thoughts had sprung to mind. By the time they'd reached the front door she had a blinding headache and, after murmuring apologies to her mother, she had dashed upstairs. Since then, she'd lain on her bed with her head swimming and a red zig-zag line dancing at the edge of her vision. She must have slept, for when she opened her eyes the pain had gone, though her troubled thoughts remained.

Well, two troubled thoughts, really. Where *had* Patrick been for seven years and *why* hadn't he come back to her? During the drive home her euphoria at finding him alive had given way to bewilderment. Of course, she told herself, there had to be some perfectly reasonable explanation. It could be any number of things. After all, sailors were often stranded on the other side of the world for months before securing a berth home ... but seven years!

She was truly thankful that he was alive, and quite willing to accept that circumstance had kept him from returning to her, but she felt that the least she was entitled to expect would be a proper explanation of where he had been for all this time.

There was a faint knock on the door and, before she could answer, it creaked open to allow Ellen in.

'Are you any better, my love?' she asked.

'A little,' Josie replied. Ellen sat on the side of the bed and placed her cool hand on Josie's forehead. 'You don't seem feverish,' she said, brushing a stray lock out of her daughter's eyes. 'I am supposed to be the one with headaches, not you. What's wrong?'

'I saw Patrick,' Josie said, the words catching in her throat.

Ellen patted her hand. 'I know how difficult it is for you coming back after all this time. Only you and I know the painful old memories this place conjures up. I can't help thinking of your gran, and how we used to scrub our knuckles raw in the washtub just to pay the rent, never mind putting food on the table. I understand how it must be affecting you because only yesterday, I thought I saw–'

'No, Mam. I don't *think* I saw Patrick, I *did* see him. I met him in the street and spoke to him.' She spoke with a sob in her voice, which made her angry at herself.

Startled, Ellen put her hand to her chest. 'Patrick's alive?'

Josie nodded as a lump formed in her throat.

'Oh, my poor darling ... what did you say to him?'

Josie recounted the conversation.

'But if he's been alive all this time, why didn't he come back, I wonder,' Ellen said. 'And for the love of Mary, where has he been?'

'Apparently, he sent a letter to New York to explain everything, but we had already moved to Boston.'

'What did it say?' Ellen asked.

'I don't know,' Josie replied, taking a deep breath to stop the wavy lines in her vision from returning.

Ellen pressed her lips together. 'I would have thought "where have you been for seven years, Patrick Nolan", would have been the first words out of your mouth.'

Josie's head started to throb again. 'They were, but he said it was a long story. Frankly, Mam, we were standing in the middle of Wapping High Street and all that was going through my head was that Patrick wasn't rotting at the bottom of the sea.' An image of Patrick swam into Josie's mind as she remembered the sensation of his eyes on her. 'I only just managed to ask about his family and what he was doing.' She sat herself up

69

on one elbow. 'When he turned around and looked at me I was so shocked I couldn't think straight ... I just babbled on.'

A faint smile crossed Ellen's face. 'I can understand why. What did he tell you about his family?'

Josie recounted the Nolan family news, and then a smile lifted the corners of her mouth. 'He looked just the same, you know. Tall as a tree and just as solid, but broader than I recall. That old scar on his chin has faded but he has a new one on his right cheek and he still has grand curly hair. He's still Patrick.' She caught her mother's sharp look. 'As I said, I was shocked, so it was only on the way home I started to think clearly about everything.'

Ellen sighed. 'I don't suppose it matters very much, after all this time. It was so long ago and you were both so young.' She patted Josie's hand. 'Now: you know I'll always have a soft spot for Patrick for the way he saved our lives. If it wasn't for his quick actions on the night Danny Donavan tried to murder me, both of us would have long been in our graves. But perhaps him not coming back was for the best. You're in a different position now, Josie, what with Robert's new post at the hospital and everything.'

Josie nodded. 'I may be, but I'm still the Josie who was best friends with Mattie. I'm going to visit her and her mother next week. Patrick said he would be there and I'm determined to get his "long story" out of him then.' The pounding in her temples started again so she lay back. 'I'm sure that, whatever the reason for his disappearance, it will be an interesting one.'

As he turned into Walburgh Street, Patrick's weary eyes rested on his front door at the end of the road. There were already new gas lamps along Commercial Road but he guessed it would be many years before such an innovation reached his street and, until it did, he would only have the candlelight flickering in his front window to guide him home.

Like the rest of the street, number twenty was a two-up, two-down with a small back yard which led out to a narrow alley at the back. Although it was larger than their previous house in Cinnamon Street, the Nolan family packed it to the brim, which is why he was thankful when Gus decided to seek his own lodgings a year ago.

His daughter Annie shared a large bed in the downstairs front room with her aunts, Mattie and Kate, while Mickey bedded down alongside his gran in a truckle bed. As the man of the house Patrick had the small back room above the kitchen to himself. If he stretched his arms wide he could almost touch the walls, but the room did have a small fire and a rag rug and he'd managed to squeeze a compact easy chair next to his bed. Cramped though it was, the room allowed him the privacy that no one else in the house enjoyed.

As he opened the front door, warmth and the mouth-watering smell of oxtail stew wafted over him. On entering the kitchen he greeted his mother and his sister Mattie. Sarah Nolan acknowledged her son with a nod but stayed seated by the fire. Patrick strode over and kissed her on

71

the head then slipped half a dozen coins in her hand.

'That should keep the rent collector happy for another week,' he said.

Mattie looked up from stirring the pot over the fire and smiled at him. She was still dressed in her drab workaday gown but she had taken off the tight-fitting cap that kept her hair clear of the machinery in the sugar refinery where she worked. She shared her brother's colouring, his green eyes and his coal-black hair, but whereas his hair just curled around his ears hers cascaded down her back when it was allowed.

'No Kate?' he asked.

As if she had heard her name, Kate appeared at the back door. She too had an abundance of curly hair but, whereas Mattie's was black like Patrick's and their pa's, Kate's was fair, like her mother's. She looked particularly pale as she entered the kitchen and there was a fine sheen of flour dusted over her.

'You're late,' Mattie said.

'We had a batch of pies ruined so we had to make up another two dozen ready for the morning,' Kate replied, taking off her cap and sending a puff of flour into the air. 'I found this on my way home, too.'

She cocked her head behind her to where Gus was standing. He drew in an exaggerated breath through his nose.

'Am I in time for supper?'

Sarah laughed. 'When are you not?'

Gus grinned. He had yet to fill out and still had three or four inches to go before he would match

72

Patrick's height, but he promised to match Patrick in stature. Like Kate he had their mother's fairer looks, but like the rest of the Nolan menfolk he was always hungry.

'It'll be ready soon, won't it Mattie?' he asked, pulling out a chair from the corner and sitting down.

Mattie rolled her eyes at her younger brother then turned back to Patrick. 'Annie's taken Mickey to bed and is probably reading him a story by now,' she told him. 'Have you been for a drink?'

'Me and Brian had a pint at the Town. He said he'd be around later.'

'Never mind about Brian,' Sarah said, folding her arms across her bosom. 'A birdie told me you were arguing with Harry Tugman outside the Boatman the other day.'

'The news is a bit slow around here if you only heard that today,' Patrick said, shrugging off his jacket.

'If you know what's good for you, you'll give them a wide berth. They'd slit a man's throat without breaking their stride, so they would,' Sarah said.

Mattie waved a spoon at him. 'I don't know why you come home past that gin shop every day instead of just carrying on along Wapping Wall,' she said, sending little specks of gravy flying.

'I go that way because that fecking old bag sits there every day and I want to make sure she sees me.' Patrick jabbed himself in the chest with his thumb. 'I smile at her and wish her a good day with such a grin on my face just to see the frustration in her beady old eyes.' He gave them both an exaggerated smile. 'I'm a free man. I'll walk anywhere I have a mind to and Ma Tugman will not make me do otherwise.'

'Good man yourself, Pat,' Gus said. 'Show that old bag she's no say over you.'

Sarah gave her youngest son a sharp look which he ignored.

'You heard about Peggy Grady's son?' Mattie said, wiping her hands on her apron.

'Of course I did,' he replied. 'And sorry I was for him, too.'

Sarah leant forward. 'By the time Charlie Tugman had finished slicing him he looked more like a butchered pig than a man.'

'Bled all the way to hospital,' Gus cut in.

Katie nodded. 'Those who saw it said they didn't know a man could shed so much blood without the spirit departing his body. Right across his face it was,' she drew her finger across her cheek. 'It's a pure mercy that he still has two eyes. He'll carry the scar to his grave, so he will.'

'I don't need reminding what the Tugmans are like, Mam,' Patrick said, 'but I'll not kowtow to scum.' He stared at his womenfolk. 'And after a day of shovelling coal I would be obliged if you would quit your nagging, at least until me belly's fed.'

'If you were just *passing* how come you and Harry were seen squaring up to each other?' Sarah asked.

'If you must know, I was saving a young lady from Harry's attention,' he replied, remembering Josie in her expensive gown and smart jacket being jostled by the thug. He took the kettle off the stove and poured the water into the enamel ewer, to take to his room for his evening wash.

His mother tutted. 'The trollops in the Boatman are used to Harry's mucky hands so I don't see why you had to int–'

'It was Josie O'Casey,' he said, in what he hoped was a level voice.

Mattie's, Kate's and Sarah's mouths dropped open, and even Gus was lost for words. They all looked at each other in astonishment before Mattie recovered her wits.

'Josie O'Casey? Your Josie?'

He gave a hard laugh. 'She's not mine any-more.'

'Of course not,' Sarah said. 'Is her husband here? Has she any children?'

A lump formed itself across Patrick's windpipe. 'She isn't married.'

His mother's mouth dropped open. 'But–'

'It was her cousin who wed at her house. I heard it wrong,' Patrick said as the constriction around his Adam's Apple tightened.

Sarah gave him a sympathetic smile. 'Oh, well, perhaps it's for the best. You and her are worlds apart now.' A soft look crept into her eye. 'I did have hopes that you and Josie would marry one day, and now she's back, who knows? Although I expect she's a proper lady now.'

'Her money and my lack of it is neither here nor there, nor is the fact that she isn't wed, Mam,' Patrick said in an exasperated tone. 'My being married – to someone else – is why she isn't *my* Josie any more.'

'Why was she outside the Boatman?' Mattie asked.

Patrick told them.

'I bet she was right pleased to see you,' Gus said. 'Especially with that fat Harry mauling her.'

That was true enough. Josie's relief was palpable when she turned and looked at him but, remembering the way her gaze danced over his face, Patrick suddenly hoped the pleasure she showed at seeing him was for more than just deliverance from Harry.

'She asked after you.'

'What does she look like after all this time?' Mattie asked.

What does she look like? Patrick's mind conjured up the picture of her that had barely been absent from his memory – her rich auburn curls escaping from under her bonnet and her slim waist emphasised by the tailored cut of her jacket, her upturned face and large eyes – these images embedded themselves in his mind. Josie had always been a pretty girl, but now she had matured into a real beauty, so stunning it hit right to a man's core.

'Grand. She was grand,' he replied, knowing it was well short of the mark. 'She even said she might visit.'

His mother rocked back in her chair. 'I hope she does. I'd like to hear how Ellen and her doctor are after all this time.'

Mattie stepped forward and placed a hand on his arm. 'Did you tell her about Rosa and the children?'

Patrick raked his hands through his hair. 'I

didn't have time ... we were in the middle of the High Street.' He wished he didn't sound quite so defensive.

Kate gave a flat laugh. 'So when *are* you going to tell her, Patrick?'

'The next time I see her,' Patrick answered firmly. He glanced at the door and lowered his voice. 'She said she'll send word when she's to be expected and I'll make sure I'm here when she arrives.' He grasped the jug of water and opened the door to the passage. 'And *then* I'll tell her everything.'

As Harry opened the small door into the main cellar under Number Six Burr Street, a shaft of light cut into the narrow passage. He stooped so as to avoid braining himself on the low lintel and cursed Ma for not making the secret entrance to their underground warehouse higher.

As he stepped into the main part of the store-room, he shifted his burden into a more comfortable position. The main room was usually kept empty in case the local police wanted to have a nose around, but today it was crammed with crates and barrels, tobacco and tea.

The Maid of Plymouth had arrived from the Indies on the evening tide and weighed anchor mid-stream. Harry had gathered his henchmen and they had swifted away a decent haul from right under the nose of the ship's captain and the police patrols.

Ma sat in a colourless old armchair just to the right of the stairs, her eyes darting back and forth over the goods as they were fetched in. She always came down to supervise the division of a big shipment. The main storage and distribution centre of stolen goods in the area lay under a row of old tenements.

They were owned by some lord or earl but his rent was collected by Messrs Glasson, Glasson and Oakes, a small but respectable law firm with offices in Aldgate. They might be respectable but their chief clerk was not. It was he who had pointed Ma towards the crumbling three-storied houses by the railway arch of the Blackwall to City line. Although Ma could tally in her head as quick as any bank teller, she could only just write her own name, so the lease on the four dilapidated houses was agreed with a spit on the palm and a shake of the hand.

When she'd taken them over, most of the rooms were already used by the local prostitutes so Ma just formalised the arrangement and added some muscle to ensure that the police looked the other way, but the real value of the terrace was in the cellars of the houses. Seeing their possibilities from the first, Ma had left the cellar under the end house open and filled the front of the other three with rubble, then she had bricked up false walls, concealing the cavern that held all their stolen goods awaiting a buyer. Anyone looking down into the area to the old servants' quarters would just think the cellars had been abandoned.

Harry rolled the barrel off his shoulder to join the other four by the stairs. Ma watched, but her gaze ran over him without any obvious pleasure and he wondered again what more he could do to please the old cow.

'What took you so long?' she barked, but before Harry could decide on a suitable reply, the door at the top of the stairs opened. Charlie Tugman sauntered in, wearing a dress suit complete with a threadbare top hat. As it couldn't have been more than seven in the morning, he looked quite ridiculous.

Ma's eyes darted upward to where her youngest son stood and a look of pure adoration spread across her face, giving it an oddly innocent appearance.

Harry's shoulders sagged with despondency. He knew the only thing he could do to please the old harpy: be Charlie.

His brother stomped heavily down the stairs, the treads creaking and cracking beneath his weight. He yawned when he reached the bottom, and took off his tall hat. He scratched his head, setting his oiled hair askew.

The men carrying the crates of sugar and stacks of tobacco back into the inner recess of the cavern acknowledged him and continued with their task.

'Nice of you to join us,' Harry said, glaring at his brother.

Charlie threw himself on the chair beside Ma. She reached out to stroke his hair out of his eyes but he flicked his head away and she let her hand fall.

'You eat and drink the food off the table same as I do, it wouldn't hurt you to work to put it there,' Harry snarled, kicking one of the crates of tea.

'Watch your boot, Harry!' Ma snapped. 'Those chests are like glass. You bust them and there'll be leaves all over the floor and no profit to take.'

Charlie grinned at Harry. 'I *have* been working,' he said, stooping down and picking up the bottle of brandy beside his mother.

Harry gave a hard laugh. 'Work! You don't know the fecking meaning of the word,' he said, stomping across the floor to where they sat.

'And you don't know the meaning of most words,' Charlie replied, taking a large swig from the bottle.

Harry grabbed his brother by the lapels and dragged him to his feet. 'Why, you little bastard, you–'

Charlie shoved back and Harry crashed into the tea chest. The side split and a stream of brown tea leaves poured out.

Ma heaved herself up from the chair and lumbered between them. 'That's enough.' She smacked the back of her hand across Harry's arm. 'I told you to mind the crate.'

Harry pointed over her head at his brother. 'You heard 'im insult me. And where has he been all night while I've been busting my balls?'

Charlie snorted. 'I've been working all right, it's just that I can do it with me head.'

Harry lunged at him again but Ma stood in his way. 'Charlie!' she snapped. He grinned at her. 'Stop riling your brother.'

She turned to the bench and her eyes fell on the spilled tea.

'Oi! Scotch.' The man heading into the tunnel with a barrel on his back stopped. 'Go up to

80

China Rose and tell her to send any of her doxies without a man down here and set them to packing that tea.'

Scotch lowered the barrel to the floor and stomped up the stairs. The treads squeaked and groaned again. He returned a few minutes later with four young women, dressed in gaudy evening gowns, trailing behind him.

Harry knew them all by sight but could never remember their names. They all looked much alike to him, with their scraped-up hair and bright patches of rouge on their cheeks. The clothes didn't help either – they rented their gowns by the day so whoever stumbled out of bed first had the pick.

Charlie tossed the empty bottle away and it skidded across the floor and hit one of the girls on the ankle. She winced.

'Did you find out who she is?' Ma asked.

'Who?' Harry asked.

A smirk spread across Charlie's face. 'Your little lady love. Miss O'Casey. The little darling who Nolan walked away with.' He pulled out a cigar, jammed it in his mouth and then struck a Lucifer on the sole of his boot. 'It seems Miss O'Casey wasn't always dressed in feathers and lace. In fact, her mother sang in old Danny Donovan's pubs before she married one of the doctors at the hospital.'

'Did you find out the doctor's name?' Ma asked.

'Munroe. Robert Munroe. It was his investigation into Danny Donovan's dealings what sent him to the gallows, and Ellen O'Casey, who is now Mrs Munroe, helped put the noose around old Danny's neck.' Charlie drew deeply on the cigar again and blew some smoke rings. 'The little sweetie who gave you the brush-off is her daughter, Josie. They went to America after the trial and only came back a month ago.'

'Danny Donovan was a hard man but fair,' Ma said in a tone of deep respect. 'Your father was one of his top men.'

Charlie let out a long whistle between his teeth. 'I remember I smashed into Danny Donovan in the street one day. I nearly shite meself.'

Harry studied his brother lounging in the chair. He would like to see his lazy, sniggering brother shite himself. In fact he'd give his eye teeth to see Ma look at Charlie, just once, with the contempt she always reserved for him.

It didn't matter to Ma that he'd spent all night on the river lowering barrels and boxes over the side of a ship. Or that, without even seeing his bed, he'd had to hump the same fifty or so crates and sacks down into the storeroom while Charlie snored in drunken oblivion. No. Because anything Charlie did was just dandy in Ma's eyes.

'Hey, Harry,' Charlie said chewing on his cigar. 'What did she look like?' he asked, leaning back.

'She was all right,' he said, trying to sound uninterested to avoid them finding something else to ridicule him for.

Charlie raised his hands and cupped them in front of his chest. 'Did she have a good handful?' he asked flexing his fingers.

Harry grinned. 'Enough.' Thinking about her trim figure and bobbing curls...

Charlie shifted forward and rested his forearms on his thighs. 'What else did she have?'

'Nice eyes,' Harry blurted out.

Charlie snorted. 'Nice frigging eyes! Do you hear that, Ma?'

Ma chuckled. Harry glared at his brother. He hated himself for not being quick enough with a stinging retort but he hated Charlie more.

A faint titter came from across the room and he glared at the sallow-looking redhead at the end of the bench. She lowered her gaze back to the dusty tea leaves but not before her lip curled up.

'Charlie's only having a laugh, aren't you, Charlie?' Ma said, glancing towards the bench. There was a rustle of paper as the four girls returned to their task.

The urge to smash his fist into his brother's smug face swept over Harry but he held it back. One day, he would get his own back when Ma wasn't there to protect her favourite.

She reached into her pocket and pulled out her snuff box. She tapped out two small piles on her hand.

'Well,' she said, closing one nostril with her finger and sniffing the grey powder up the other. 'From what I could see, she'd already caught Patrick Nolan's eye.' The rest of the snuff disappeared up the other nostril and she held her breath.

Yes, Harry had noticed the way that bastard Nolan's eyes glinted when they looked at Josie O'Casey. He had a roguish way about him that women liked and by the way her eyes changed as

83

they rested on Nolan, Josie O'Casey was no exception.

A crafty expression crept over Charlie's face. 'Don't worry, Ma. Our Harry won't let no poxy Mick get the better of him. Will you?'

Get the better of him? Damn, that's just what he *had* done, hadn't he? Outside the Boatman, and in every other fecking encounter he had ever had with Patrick Nolan. That bloody flash Paddy always seemed to out-talk, out-think and out-tough him. He remembered Josie's pleased expression.

'No, I fecking well won't!' he bellowed. Warmth briefly flickered in Ma's eyes and he grinned. 'Too right, Charlie! No poxy Mick's going to get the better of me.'

Chapter Five

Josie pulled her purse from her handbag and snapped it open. She fished around inside it, extracted a sixpence and handed it to Sam. 'It's three o'clock now and I want you to come back for me in an hour.'

Sam touched his cap and pocketed the coin. 'Very good, Miss.'

Josie stood for a moment, watching as he headed off towards the London Docks to buy himself a pie and coffee.

Across the muddy street a front door opened and then another. Two women in the usual garb of dark gowns and head shawls eyed her curiously. A few children in rags edged out of doors and stood clinging to their mothers' skirts.

Josie had put on her cream dress that had just a single ruffle around the neck and sleeves, and had chosen a simple bonnet with nothing more than a ribbon around its crown yet – in this street of modest, tightly packed cottages – she stood out like a duchess in ermine.

She studied the door of number twenty, reflecting how, when Patrick hadn't returned to New York she'd presumed him dead. It had taken several years before she could think of him without tears but now, knowing he was alive, had seemed to unlock her memories.

They had spoken for no longer than fifteen minutes but she could remember every detail of their meeting: the way his hair had moved as the river breeze ruffled it, the dark hue of his jaw with its day's worth of bristle, and the shape of his strong hands, the balance of his shoulders...

Her body had recalled past pleasures as his eyes had travelled over her, their expression changing as they always used to.

Josie studied the panelled door for a second longer, then rapped firmly with her knuckles. Her heart thumped in her chest as she waited. After what seemed like an hour the door flew open and Sarah Nolan stared at her.

Although a little heavier and greyer, Patrick's mother was much as Josie remembered her. The black dress she wore gave her pale skin a waxy look, but her eyes were still soft and kind, as they always had been.

Her gaze flickered down the street and then she smiled warmly. 'Josie O'Casey, as I live and breathe!'

Josie gave Sarah an apologetic smile. 'I hope I'm not early, Mrs Nolan, but I was so eager to see you all.'

It was true. She had been on tenterhooks all day. She woke from a fitful sleep at first light – ravenously hungry but found she'd lost her appetite after the first couple of mouthfuls of porridge. After breakfast she'd tried to read but found herself turning over pages without the faintest idea as to what was written on them. She abandoned the book and took up her needle, but her concentration wandered again and she stitched a red petal on a daffodil without even noticing. All the while the clock tick-tocked out the hours more slowly than ever until finally it was time to put on her coat and bonnet, summon Sam and head off towards the river.

'No, you're not early.' Sarah glanced up the street again. 'Although I was hoping Patrick might be back before you arrived.' She ushered Josie through the door. 'Well, for the love of Mary, what *am* I about? Come in! Come in!'

Josie stepped in to the narrow hallway and Sarah closed the door. 'When Patrick told me that he'd met you in the street I could hardly believe it.'

'Neither could I,' Josie replied. 'I just turned around and there he was, as large as life.'

'Large as life is the truth of it. He fair blocks the sun if he stands in front of you.' Sarah showed her down the passageway. 'Go through – there is someone in the back eager to see you.'

Josie's heart jumped over in her chest. With her mouth dry as tinder she opened the door to the Nolans' kitchen, and cast her eyes around the low-ceilinged scullery. In their old house the whole family had lived downstairs, with another family in the upstairs room but, for all that, Josie realised just how small these old terraced cottages really were.

Mattie turned. She had Patrick's well-defined cheekbones but a small chin rather than a square one. Her dark curls were gathered under the cotton handkerchief tied at the back of her head.

'Josie!' Mattie dashed at her and enveloped her in a tight embrace.

Keeping her eyes from straying to the black mould around the window frames and the mousetrap in the corner, Josie returned her old school friend's hug.

'What am I about, grabbing you like that!' Mattie said, giving Josie a shy smile and wiping her hands down her apron a couple of times. 'You dressed in silks and me in this old thing covered with burnt sugar from the factory.'

Josie embraced her again. 'Oh Mattie,' she said, her voice muffled by her friend's shoulder. 'It's so good to see you.'

'There, didn't I say that our Josie would never be too full of airs and graces to take a dish of tea with her old friends,' Sarah told her daughter, and Mattie's shoulders relaxed.

Josie struggled out of Mattie's embrace. 'Why wouldn't I?' she asked.

Mattie took her hands and drew her into the room. 'Patrick said you were grand.'

The smile froze on Josie's face. Grand! Is that what he thought? A little stab of hurt jabbed at her breastbone.

'Come and sit by the fire,' Sarah urged.

She sat down opposite the fire and noticed that the horsehair stuffing was bursting out from the fabric on the arm of the old chair. She thought of the new furniture she and her mother had bought at Heals, the huge department store in Tottenham Court Road... Josie banished the thought as she untied her bonnet and peeled off her gloves before settling herself back. Sarah sat opposite her and Mattie pulled up a stool. The faint scent of vinegar told Josie that Sarah hadn't give up her daily scrubbing of the floors.

A square table, with an odd assortment of upright chairs ranged around it, dominated the centre of the room. The yellowing linen cloth covering it served as the backdrop for a colourful assortment of cups and saucers. There was a full bucket of coal by the fireside.

'I'm very sorry to hear that Mr Nolan passed on,' Josie said.

'Ah, thank you, my dear. He was a darlin' man.' Sarah fixed a bright smile on her face. 'Now, tell me how your own dear mother is.'

Sarah handed Josie a cup of tea. Josie took a sip. It was weak, and she was just about to say as much when she realised that, of course, Sarah must have used second-hand tea leaves.

She smiled at Sarah. 'Lovely,' she said, and then told them all about her family and their time in New York and Boston.

Mattie and Sarah's eyes grew wide as she

described their house in Brooklyn Heights just across the river from the city and her Uncle Jo's chaotic family, which they had left behind.

'It must be strange being back here,' Mattie said.

Josie nodded. 'It is, although there has been so much to do since we returned I've only just noticed it now and again.'

She glanced at the bare windows and thought of the lace panels hanging in the windows of the drawing room in the house at Stepney Green.

'Patrick tells me you're to be married,' Josie said, abandoning thoughts of West End shopping and her own life. 'Has he got a name, this young man of yours?'

'He's Brian Maguire.' Mattie beamed. 'You must remember him. He and Pat were always together.'

'And getting up to mischief, if I recall,' Josie replied, thinking of the lad universally known as 'Ginger' who had been Patrick's shadow.

Mattie grinned. 'You have that right, although he's filled out a bit and he's a–'

'Lovely Irish fella, that he is,' Sarah butted in. She glanced up at an old clay pipe on the mantelshelf. 'There's no man on earth who can make a woman smile like a lad with green eyes.'

The image of Patrick flashed into Josie's mind. She pushed it aside, for if that lad thought she was too grand to visit an old friend then she certainly wouldn't be smiling at *his* green eyes.

Mattie's face was alight. 'Brian owns a coal yard up at the end of Cable Street and after we're wed I'll be moving in to the house attached.'

'I'd love to meet him,' Josie said, caught up in

her friend's excitement.

'We are going to the Thames Tunnel next Sunday. Why don't you come with us?'

'I will, as long as you don't mind me being a gooseberry,' Josie replied, thinking it would be an exciting excursion as well as a way of getting herself out of Mrs Munroe's sights for an afternoon.

'And Josie, will you come and help me make my dress? You were always good with a needle.' Mattie was brimming over with excitement. 'I paid fourpence a yard for the fabric. It's pink with a thin brown stripe. I thought at a distance it would look like one of those new fashionable, pale wedding dresses.'

Josie stared into her friend's eager face and remembered that she'd just paid Mr Turner, the merchant from Gracechurch Street, sixpence a yard for fabric for Daisy's new dress.

'Of course I will. I'm sure you'll be the loveliest of brides,' Josie said.

She sat back and cradled her teacup. It was comforting being in the Nolans' kitchen. The simple warmth of it took her back to her childhood when she had lived in such a house, but somehow the memories of her old home didn't feature the cracked windowpanes letting light into such a small room or the bare earth floor under her feet. She did remember, though, that her mother had to fetch the water from the pump at the end of the street, as the Nolans must do, and realised that Mattie and her family would have to boil kettles to fill the tin bath she could just about see hanging on the wall outside.

Who knows? If her mother hadn't married Dr

Munroe then maybe she would have married Patrick and been living in a house just like this.

Her mind conjured up an image of Patrick with his sleeves rolled up and his shirt open at the neck and a little bubble of excitement rolled through her. Well, even if she had set up home with him in a cottage like this, cracked windows and all, there would have been some compensation.

'Look, she's away with the fairies,' Mattie's voice said, cutting through her distracting thoughts.

The door from the passageway opened and a little girl of about five or six came in. She wore the same dark serge dress and wraparound apron that Josie and Mattie used to wear for school. Her lace up brown boots looked almost too heavy for her slender ankles.

An expression of alarm shot across Sarah and Mattie's faces as the child skipped over to Sarah, and jumped on her lap.

Josie gave her a friendly smile and the child smiled back. Although her skin was darker than the rest of the Nolans and her black hair straight rather that curly, Josie could see the family resemblance.

'And who's this?' she asked, leaning forward and extending the smile

'This is my darling Annie,' Sarah replied in an odd voice. 'I thought you were playing with Meg Bonney,' she said to the child.

Annie shrugged. 'I was, but we got in Aunt Colly's way so I thought I'd come home.'

Josie was momentarily surprised to find that Sarah had had another child so late in life, but then her own mother was only a few years younger and about to have her seventh.

'My mother used to tie up my hair just like yours, Annie,' she said, indicating the two long, tightly braided plaits hanging over the child's shoulder.

Annie picked up a small square of linen. Josie recognised it as a sampler of the sort her gran had set her to stitching at about the same age. The child pulled out a needle and the thread snagged. She was really a pretty child with a quiet dignity about her. Her eyes were darker than the rest of the family but set over strong cheekbones. With Mrs Munroe monopolising her brothers and sisters, Josie missed the afternoons in the parlour when she helped Bobbie and Lottie with their samplers.

'Let me have a look,' Josie said, reaching out to the young girl.

Annie climbed off Sarah's knee and came over to Josie.

'It's very kind of you, Miss,' Annie said, handing Josie the mangled square of linen.

Josie began unpicking the knotted cotton and, after a couple of jabs of the needle, the thread was free again. Looking over Annie's head, Josie smiled across at Mattie and her mother, both stared back at her with an expression that could only be described as alarm.

What on earth is wrong with them? she thought.

Maybe it had been a mistake to visit. Although she had been overjoyed to see Patrick alive, maybe their lives were too different now and she should go.

It was clear that Patrick hadn't come back to her because he'd written off their youthful dalliance. Now she was forcing herself on his family when he probably didn't want the awkwardness of having to see her again. He said he would be here when she called and, although she'd been here almost an hour, he'd still not arrived.

She returned Annie's untangled sampler. 'There you are. You had just double-stitched it, that's all.'

'Thank you, Miss,' she said taking her work back.

'I really have to go,' Josie said.

A look of relief swept over Mattie and Sarah's faces, and sadness rose up again inside Josie. The front door opened and Mattie and Sarah's eyes shot to the closed passageway door.

The sound of the blood rushing through Josie's ears and the thumping of her heart all but drowned out the heavy boots marching down the hall towards them.

The door opened and Patrick stepped in to the room with a young boy of about four just behind him. His gaze flickered down to the child standing at Josie's side then back to her. An emotion that she couldn't interpret crossed his face as he stood gazing at her for a timeless moment.

'Josie?'

Annie dashed at Patrick. 'Pa, Pa!' she shouted.

Josie felt breathless and light-headed. Without his gaze leaving her face, he lifted the child into his arms and kissed her on the head.

'Pa, Miss Josie's helped me with my sewing.'

Josie rose to her feet. 'You're married!'

'I meant to be here when you arrived to explain. I didn't want you to find out like this,' Patrick said, cursing himself inwardly for the wounded look in her eyes.

'Then why didn't you tell me when we met?'

'We were in the middle of Wapping High Street,' he replied. 'I cut my day short to be here when you arrived so I could explain everything but I was delayed.'

Josie gave him a brittle smile. 'Don't fret yourself, Patrick. I understand completely. You certainly don't have to explain anything to me.' She fiddled with her skirt and then peered over his shoulder. 'I can't wait to meet your dear wife.'

'Me mam's dead,' Annie told Josie in a matter of fact tone. 'She died after Mickey was born.'

Josie's tight expression instantly softened and she made amends by reaching and repositioning a stray lock of Annie's hair.

'I'm so sorry, sweetheart,' she said, then turned to Mickey. 'How old are you?'

'Almost four, Miss,' Mickey answered, gazing up at Josie as if she were a queen.

She tousled his hair lightly. 'You have grand, curly hair just like your father, Mickey.' She glanced up at Patrick. 'You have lovely children. I am truly sorry for your loss.'

'Thank you,' he said, noticing that the cream stripes of her gown not only drew attention to the auburn tones of her hair but also to the slender circumference of her waist.

'What was your wife's name?' Josie asked. The tightness around her eyes had returned but her smile was warmer.

'Rosa,' he said, her name falling like a stone between them. 'She was Spanish.'

They stared at each other and then there was a knock on the door. Josie turned and her skirts swished over his leg as she picked up her bonnet and gloves. 'That will be Sam. I told him to collect me in an hour.'

She flipped her bonnet over her head and started to tie the sateen ribbon. The gloves slipped from her hand.

Patrick scooped them up in one movement and offered them to her. As she took them, his work-roughened fingers briefly glided over her soft ones. A shock of electricity seemed to dart through him.

Since Rosa had left, he'd hardly lived the life of a monk so he was surprised to find himself reacting like a callow youth.

Josie shoved her fingers in her gloves. 'It's been grand seeing you all again and I'll give me mam your regards as I promised.'

'I'm glad you came, Josie,' Sarah said, her eyes fixing on to Patrick. 'And I hope now you've found your way here you'll come back when you have a mind.'

Josie hugged Sarah and Mattie then adjusted her bonnet. Patrick held out his hand. After the briefest hesitation, Josie took it.

'I hope you *will* come again,' he said, taking her hand firmly.

She snatched her hand away. 'I'll be here to help sew Mattie's wedding gown so you'll see me again, I'm sure.'

Mattie stepped forward. 'Josie's coming with

95

me and Brian to the fair in the Thames Tunnel. Why don't you come, Pat? Make up the numbers.'

His sensible mind told him that a social trip in the Tunnel would provide him with the ideal opportunity to tell her the truth about Rosa, but it was his body concentrating on the inviting fullness of Josie's lips that made him answer.

'I'd love to.'

Chapter Six

Josie finished the chapter she had been reading aloud and closed the book. Ellen's eyes remained closed and her breathing steady. Carefully, so as not to wake her mother, Josie leant back in the nursing chair. It squeaked as she sank into its candy-striped upholstery but Ellen still didn't stir.

They had left most of their furniture in America, but her mother had insisted on bringing a few special bits like the cherry-wood nursing chair, and Robert hadn't argued. It now sat where it always had, beside her mother and stepfather's bed.

Mrs Munroe had practically fainted when she found out that her son and daughter-in-law shared a bedroom. She told them in chilly tones that she and her dear departed husband had only shared a bedroom when they visited people. Josie had suppressed the urge to ask if that was the reason why, by Mrs Munroe's own admission, Robert's father had always preferred to stay at home.

Her mother's eyes blinked open. 'I must have dropped right off to sleep,' she said pushing herself up on the bed.

Josie helped her mother to sit up. 'You must be fair worn out; listening to today's suggestions from Mrs Munroe of things "you probably wouldn't know about, Ellen dear."'

'Josie—'

'And I swear by the saints above, if I hear that story about how her brother died at Waterloo one more time, I'll run screaming from the house.'

'And I'll be just behind you,' Ellen said, looking up at the ceiling. She leant over and squeezed Josie's forearm. 'But, praise the saints, she'll be gone in six weeks.'

'And I for one will be waving her off from the steps,' Josie replied.

A wistful smile spread across Ellen's face. 'You look just like Gran sitting there,' she said, a faint tinge of sadness in her tone. 'Now – tell me how the Nolans are.'

Josie told her.

'I'm glad Sarah is well,' Ellen said, biting her lip. 'When Mrs Munroe leaves I'll invite her here one afternoon.'

A crooked smile curled Josie's lips. 'I quite understand. Although Mrs Munroe's heart "bleeds" for the suffering of the poor, we'd have to find the smelling salts quick if we were to suggest that she might like to sit down to tea with any of them.'

Ellen didn't argue the point.

'I remember that Sarah was hell bent on you and Patrick marrying.'

Josie's cheeks felt warm. 'Do you remember I said Patrick still had grand curly hair?' Ellen nodded. 'Well, so does his son.'

Ellen's mouth dropped open. 'What?'

'He's married.' A lump settled in her throat. 'That's to say, he was married but his wife died and left him with two children – Annie, who's just short of six, and Mickey, who's four. They both look very like him although with darker skin. His wife was Spanish,' she said, wondering, not for the first time, what Rosa must have looked like.

Ellen folded her arms tightly over the top of her stomach. 'Well, of all the...' She pressed her lips firmly together for a moment then continued. 'At least we know why *your* Patrick didn't come back.'

The words cut through Josie like a sharp stab of pain. Even after she accepted that he had probably died at sea and was never coming back, Josie always thought of him as *her* Patrick. It was disconcerting and unsettling to think that he had been someone else's Patrick. It was stupid of course, but when she thought about Patrick's lively eyes running over some other woman envy gnawed at her.

'Are you very upset?' her mother asked.

'A little upset, but more put out by the shock of Annie calling him Pa. But, really,' she forced a light laugh, 'we were little more than children when we started walking out together. I mean–'

she laughed again – 'I was only a bit older than Bobbie is now and Patrick was just a lad of seventeen, barely a man.'

He might not have been a man then but he certainly was now. An image of Patrick standing with his children floated back into Josie's mind. She remembered how tenderly he had lifted Annie and kissed her, and the affectionate way his hand had rested on Mickey's head. A pall of sadness settled over her but she pushed it aside, and said, 'In truth, our worlds moved apart and I'm very happy Patrick met someone else. After all, I wasn't short of offers, either.'

'You could have married several times over if you'd just put your mind to it.'

'Yes, I could have. And I *will* marry – as soon as I meet the right man,' Josie replied, trying not to think about how strikingly handsome Patrick looked, even in his rough working clothes.

'I'm surprised he hasn't married again,' Ellen said, cutting through Josie's thoughts. 'Most men would have, if only for the children's sakes.'

'Maybe he still loves his wife,' Josie replied, as envy dug into her.

'Maybe so,' Ellen sat up and Josie patted her pillows back in place. 'Oh, by the way, Mr Arnold is taking tea with us on Sunday.'

'Is he?' Josie replied in a cool voice as she sat back down. 'That's a pity because I'm visiting the Thames Tunnel with Mattie and her intended.'

Ellen raised an eyebrow. 'And now, would I be right in thinking that Patrick is going as well?'

Josie forced herself to seem uninterested. 'He is, just to make up the numbers.'

'I'm sure Mrs Munroe will have a word or two to say on the matter.'

'I'm sure she will,' Josie replied, 'but I'm not going to be dictated to by Mrs Munroe. And it's perfectly respectable for me to take a stroll in a public place, in the middle of the day with Mattie and her fiancé, and an old friend who happens to be a widower.'

'Maybe so,' Ellen replied slowly, 'but I hope you're not trying to fan an old flame, Josephine Bridget.'

Josie gave a hollow laugh. 'For the love of the saints, Mother, *don't* be ridiculous.'

'Well then, tell Mattie you'll go another day and stay for Mr Arnold's visit.'

'It is not polite to put off a *friend* for an *acquaintance,*'Josie replied, not quite managing to hold her mother's gaze. 'I'll take tea with Mr Arnold another time. He visits often enough.'

The door opened and Robert came in. Ellen's face lit up. 'Darling, I wasn't expecting you until late afternoon,' she said, reaching out her hand.

He took it and sat on the bed.

'Braithwaite cancelled so I came home early,' he said. 'How is my patient this afternoon?' he asked, looking across the bed at Josie.

'Mam has done as the doctor ordered and has been resting for two hours,' Josie replied, noting how her stepfather's eyes rarely strayed from her mother's face.

From the moment she'd turned around in the alley to find Patrick standing behind her, the subject of love and what people actually meant by it kept running through Josie's mind. She knew it was absurd to compare her mother and stepfather's enduring affection to her and Patrick's youthful love, but she couldn't help remembering that in order to marry Ellen, a woman whom his family, colleagues and society considered too far beneath him, Robert had turned his back on them all to cross an ocean and find her. He hadn't sworn eternal love and then fallen in love with someone else.

A smile twisted Patrick's lips as he watched Brian turn one way and then the other as he studied his reflection in the mottled glass propped against the wall. He had already tried at least half a dozen such suits on but hadn't been happy with any of them. It wasn't surprising. Although the top floor of Moses Brothers' warehouse was packed from floor to ceiling with jackets, trousers, overcoats and work wear, Brian was after a suit for his wedding and he was looking for something a little more stylish.

Patrick glanced up at the mahogany clock at the end of the room. It was five to ten in the evening. They had arrived just after the store opened at seven and had been there nearly three hours. The two brothers who owned the vast emporium, and whose father had started the business from a hand-cart in Rosemary Street clothes market, were Jewish. In observance of their religion they were obliged to close their business from Friday sunset to Saturday sunset so, to make up for the loss of revenue, the warehouse stayed open until midnight on Saturday. Judging by the way Brian was trying on and discarding jackets, they would still be there when it closed.

Although Moses Brothers was only one of the many clothing warehouses dotted along Whitechapel High Street, it was the most visited, and not just by working men like Patrick and Brian. The well-to-do from all over London caught omnibuses to shop there, while others from as far away as Stratford and Leyton caught trains to Shoreditch Station in search of a bargain in the three-storey building.

The entire upper floor was crammed with all manner of male attire. Rough canvas trousers ticketed at three shillings, cord jackets costing four shillings and buff overalls reasonably priced at two and sixpence, hung from the two-tier rails, alongside expensive worsted day suits and tailored overcoats. There was even a reasonable selection of dinner suits marked up at four pounds, ten shillings in the far corner with silk scarves and white gloves artfully arranged next to them but in a locked cabinet to prevent pilfering. In contrast, and discreetly tucked behind the far pillars, was a selection of quality second-hand items, while against the far wall narrow shelves displayed row upon row of shoes and boots.

Brian and Patrick weren't alone in searching for the right apparel. Under the yellow glare from the dozens of lamps hanging from the ceiling, city types rummaged through the rails of dark suits while, at their elbows, tradesmen searched for serviceable jackets and trousers. As they slid the metal hangers back and forth, dust particles and loose fibres rose up and danced in the artificial light above.

'What do you think?' Brian asked, pulling down the front of a jacket only to have the lapels curl up.

'It's too tight,' Patrick replied. 'I still think the dark green one you tried on two hours ago suited you best. It fits like it was made for you.'

Brian's face lit up. 'Does it? Really?'

'Aye. It hides your beer gut for a start and when you miss your mouth with your fork the gravy stains won't show,' Patrick replied with mock innocence.

Brian laughed and stuck two fingers up at him then shrugged the jacket off. He reached into the tightly packed rail and pulled out another.

'What about this then?' he asked flourishing it at Patrick. 'Is this what a toff like you would wear when the queen invites you to tea at the palace then?'

Patrick grinned as he eyed the garish mustard, green and black checked jacket with a broad, velveteen collar. 'I don't know about that, but it's the sort of dog's dinner Harry Tugman would wear in the Monkey parade.'

They laughed, and the slender floor-walker who supervised the shop assistants and who had had his eyes on them since they arrived, stared at the pair. Patrick stared back and the man lowered his gaze.

Brian shoved the checked jacket back and retrieved the green suit that Patrick had referred to. 'I think I'll have this one. I'm sure Mattie will like it.'

'I'm convinced she will,' Patrick replied, thinking of the ear bashing his sister had given him about making sure Brian got something dignified rather than flash for their nuptials.

Brian threw his suit over his arm. 'We had better kit you out now. What do you fancy?'

'I thought I might treat myself to something a little classy,' Patrick said, moving towards the top end of the rail.

He could have made do with one of the ten bob suits but it was his sister's wedding after all, and he'd had a good few weeks on the river so he thought he might splash out a bit. Besides, it would make a change for him to stand next to Josie dressed in something that for once didn't look as if it had been fashioned out of old potato sacks.

The floor-walker left his position by the till and edged over to them. 'The suits in this section start at two guineas,' he said.

'I can read,' Patrick replied, nodding at the bold lettering in the sign above the rack.

'That's all right, my good man,' Brian said, giving the sallow-faced attendant an idiot-like grin. 'He's the Duke of Dublin, don't you know.'

The supervisor turned his back on Brian and gave Patrick a smile almost as oily as his hair. 'Perhaps sir would consider this?'

He pulled out a brown suit with a broad black stripe. Patrick gave him a frosty stare and the shop assistant slid it back on the rack and reached for a blue checked one. 'Well then, how about–'

'This is more what I had in mind,' Patrick said, lifting a charcoal jacket off the rail.

'A very good choice, if I might say so,' the

assistant warbled. 'Note the fashionable three buttons and the styling on the back. It's the only one we have in that style and skilfully made by one of our local suppliers.'

'It's cabbage then,' Patrick said. The assistant gave a noncommittal smile.

Because the old weavers' houses in the area had large upstairs windows, Aldgate had more than its fair share of tailors eking out a living in them. The large establishments up West sent fabric for a set number of jackets or suits ordered in bulk to the tailors, who often managed to squeeze an extra garment out of the cloth, giving them something to sell on. Such items were commonly known as cabbage.

Patrick shrugged off his jacket, handed it to Brian then slipped on the new one. It sat squarely on his shoulders and hung well. He ran his hand over the fabric, feeling the fine weave with his fingertips. It was so dark it was almost black, and even with his old work shirt underneath it gave him a look of understated elegance. He twisted this way and that, feeling the lining move with the jacket over his body.

Brian let out a rolling laugh. 'Look at yourself, then,' he said. 'You just see how the girlies' eyes light up when they catch a glimpse of you, Pat me boy.'

'Very nice,' the shop assistant cooed. 'It complements your athletic figure. The trousers are ready to fit.' He indicated the unhemmed bottoms and unfinished waistband.

Patrick studied himself in the mirror. Although it might be a sin to say so, he didn't look half bad.

But would Josie think so? Would her eyes light up?

He glanced down at the cuff and caught sight of the paper ticket.

Two pounds, fifteen shillings and six pence!

'Worth every penny,' the supervisor said swiftly, seeing that he had spotted the price.

Perhaps ... but this was nearly two weeks wages.

Patrick looked at his reflection again, and this time imagined Josie on his arm. In his mind's eye he saw her laughing and smiling as she walked beside him. Her eyes would flash and sparkle as they always did, and if they danced, as they very well might, then the silk of her skirt would glide over, not snag on, the fabric of his clothes.

But two pounds, fifteen and six...

'I don't know,' he said, studying the sharp line of the shoulders.

The supervisor's encouraging expression faded a little.

A smile spread across Brian's freckled face. 'I'll tell you what, Pat, it won't only be the local girls who'll be giving you the glad eye.' He winked. 'I bet when a certain young lady catches sight of you looking like the dog's naggers, she'll wish she'd come back from America sooner.'

Patrick slipped the jacket off and handed it to the assistant. 'I'll take it.'

Patrick and Iggy Bonny stood on the stone quayside and surveyed Roy MacManus's barge, the *Mary Ann,* lying half submerged in the ebbing tide. Inside its hull, Roy stood up to his knees in slurry, desperately packing cork into the damaged timber.

Patrick had strolled down to the *Mermaid's* mooring before sunrise and had arrived just before Iggy about half an hour ago.

Ignatius Cassius Bonny, to give him his full name, had joined Patrick on the *Sea Horse* in Kingston ten years before. Sailing around the Cape in the teeth of icy winds and mountainous waves had soon cemented a friendship between this unlikely pair. Although Iggy was as dark as any other native African, his light green eyes and aquiline nose betrayed the other races that were part of his ancestry. When Patrick returned to London, Iggy declared himself finished with the roving life and had crewed the *Mermaid* with him ever since.

He'd met and married Colly, a fair-skinned, red-haired Irish lass, and settled down in Tait Street, around the corner from the Nolans. Colly sold sweets in twists of newspaper to the local children from her front parlour window and presented Iggy annually with an infant – brown-skinned and red-haired, or with a buttermilk complexion and curly black hair, or some other exotic combination. Usually it was Iggy who was early, waiting on the dockside, but since Josie's visit a few days ago, Patrick found himself awake well before dawn with a vision of her imprinted in his mind's eye.

Although the sun was barely up, the waterfront was already alive with dock labourers working under the direction of their masters, the men who oversaw the loading and unloading of the ships. Red-eyed night watchmen slowly made their way home, hunched with fatigue after a night on duty on ships and in warehouses. The slippery jetties were stacked high with crates and barrels awaiting the army of porters to take them into the warehouses standing tall along the docks.

'Don't you worry, chum, we'll soon have her bobbing along good as new,' one of the lightermen shouted down as he started unbuttoning his jacket.

'This can't go on,' Patrick said, to rumbles of agreement on either side of him. 'We all know that Roy told Ma Tugman to sling her hook and this is the result.'

Bert Bunton, who was so ancient he could have sailed with Drake, slipped his cap off and wiped his forehead. 'And much good it did him,' he said, the leathery skin of his face creasing as he spoke. 'All 'e's got to show for it is a hull clogged with mud.'

Patrick nodded. 'That's a fact, but a man can mend a boat. He can't feed his family if he's in prison, can he now?'

Ezra Lennon, a regular in the Town of Ramsgate and one of the dock masters who gave out the daily work tickets, stepped forward. 'Roy's barge isn't the first to be stoved in,' he said. 'Seth Morton's *Dolphin* had its rigging cut and Conner's had his sails ditched in the river. They'd told Ma to look elsewhere, too.'

Bert's rheumy eyes flickered into life. 'That wot I's saying – Ma and her boys will get you. I've been on this 'ere river over forty years, since I was a nipper. In me old dad's time Popeye Wells and the Shadwell boys ruled, then it was Mad Corky and a dozen years ago Danny Donovan held sway. So if it weren't the Tugmans, it would be some other fast crew. As I say, it is the way of the river.'

'Only if we let it be,' Patrick replied, in a voice that carried over the crowd. 'You all know where I stand on the Tugmans, but I'm only one man. If we join together they won't be able to pick us off one by one and they'll have to move their pilfered goods some other way.'

'What's you saying?' Ezra asked.

'I'm saying that all of us who are interested should meet in the Town next Saturday and form an association,' Patrick replied.

Bert pointed a tobacco-stained finger at him. 'You're not one of those Chartists are you, Nolan?' he asked. 'Cos I ain't marchin' on Westminster. Not with my legs.'

Patrick's manner lightened a little. 'No. I'm just after getting us to stand together against those who're trying to take the bread out of our children's mouths.'

There were murmurs of agreement then, from the back of the crowd, a police officer in a navy, high-collared tailcoat and top hat, pushed his way through.

The officer was shorter than Patrick and looked to be ten or so years older, with a girth that spoke of a man who did justice to his plate. He sported a fine pair of sideburns and a broad moustache. Stopping a foot or so in front of Patrick, he looked him up and down slowly.

'Morning gentlemen. You planning a revolution like those frogs across the Channel then?' he asked.

'Someone's taken an axe to Roy's barge,' Patrick replied, flicking his head sideways.

The officer tucked his thumbs into his shiny belt and peered over the side of the quay. He tutted loudly then cast his eyes around the crowd of men. 'Anyone know who did it?'

No one spoke.

The police were a fact of life and as such they were tolerated. They stopped runaway horses and pulled bodies from the river but they weren't to be trusted. No one ever told them anything.

A low-life who sneaked information to the constabulary wasn't regarded favourably by the local population. The crowd shuffled away, and a few climbed down to help Roy bail out the *Mary Ann*. Within a couple of moments only Patrick and the officer remained.

'It's Pat Nolan, isn't it?' he asked, taking a pipe out from the front of his jacket. He stuck it in the side of his mouth and struck a Lucifer.

'Aye,' Patrick replied, not too sure he liked his name being known to the local peelers.

'I'm Plant, Sergeant Plant.' He drew on his pipe. 'I heard you're the one niggling at the Tugmans.'

Ignoring the prickle of uneasiness creeping up his spine, Patrick gave the man an ingenuous smile. 'Our paths have crossed.'

'Harry and Charlie are a pair of wrong 'uns and no mistake. Especially Charlie; I reckon he's got something missing up here.' Sergeant Plant tapped his temple and Patrick was inclined to agree. 'They're almost as bad as that old mother of theirs but then they'd have to go some way to

110

match her wicked streak.'

Patrick wouldn't have argued that one either but his expression remained impassive.

Plant drew on the pipe and let a puff of smoke escape from the other side of his mouth. 'I heard it was Harry who lifted the cargo from the *Maid of Plymouth* last week,' he said.

Patrick tried to look surprised. Plant studied him for a few more minutes then knocked the ash from his pipe before stuffing it back between his brass buttons. 'Ah, well. If you do hear a whisper just come and find me. I've got an interest in the Tugmans' business.'

Hitching her basket on her hips, Josie followed her friend Sophie Cooper along Shorter Alley. True to her word, Josie had volunteered to help Sophie with her round of pastoral visits to the poor of the area, and they were making their way to one of the rundown areas just north of Cable Street. It was the last refuge of the destitute before they were forced onto the parish.

Sophie's father, the Quaker minister, believed that charity didn't begin at home – as Mrs Munroe would have it – but at his ever open front door. Because of Mr Cooper's tireless work in the dark alleyways and stews of the area, Sophie was also well known and respected and therefore never needed an escort.

The shops and businesses that made their living from their proximity to the river were already halfway through their morning by the time the two girls walked past, their baskets of provisions held tightly in their hands. It was hard enough to

111

cross the road with the constant flow of heavy wagons rolling by in each direction, but it was also difficult to navigate their way along the pavement, which was equally busy. The shop frontages were piled high with open barrels and crates displaying the goods for sale, while young lads in long aprons that almost covered their toes stood on sentry duty against opportunistic pilfering.

Between the shops, small businesses that supplied the ships in port with provisions were flourishing. Every other yard had miles of rope, some as thin as your little finger and some as thick as your wrist, coiled around overhead beams. Unwary passers-by lost hats or bonnets if they weren't mindful of the hazards above them. The pungent smell of tar wafted out as ships' pitch was boiled and barrelled, ready for loading. Behind bevelled window panes, watchmakers tinkered with sextons, nautical clocks, barometers and compasses.

As they made their way past quartermasters ordering provisions and shopkeepers replenishing their displays, Josie told Sophie about her visit to Patrick's house.

'I can hardly believe it,' Sophie said, her oval face a picture of concern.

'Of course it was a bit awkward,' Josie replied, as the little niggle of hurt settling around her breastbone jabbed at her again. 'But, as I *keep* telling everyone, it was a long time ago.'

'Well, at least you know why he didn't return.'

Yes, because he fell in love with someone else! Not that I give a jot.

'Where are we going?' Josie asked, turning the

conversation away from Patrick. She stepped over a gutter full of a reeking, slushy brown mixture of something better not investigated too closely.

'Seven Street,' Sophie replied. 'There's a young widow there with two children under five. Her husband fell in the East India dock and was crushed between the dock and the ship's hull.'

'When Mr Arnold, my stepfather's apprentice, came to dinner last week he told us about men killed and injured in the dock,' Josie said. 'He said that drink was one of the contributing factors, which gave Mrs Munroe the perfect opportunity to launch into one of her tirades about the evils of inebriation.' Josie, who had already unburdened herself to Sophie about Mrs Munroe's visit, added, 'I am surprised that she's chosen to "give her life", as she puts it, to the poor, as it seems that almost everything they do or say disgusts her.'

Two women in faded gowns and knitted shawls stepped back as they passed and, out of the corner of her eye, Josie saw them nudge each other and point at her bonnet and gown. They turned left onto Elizabeth Street, where a dog with patches of mange on his hind quarters barked half-heartedly, lifted its leg and squirted urine up the wall, leaving a dark patch on the brickwork. On one side of the alley a couple of muddy pigs scratched about behind an improvised barricade. Sophie stopped in front of an old door that had once been cornflower blue but now only had a few flecks of the paint left on the panels.

'Try not to be too shocked,' Sophie urged, as

113

she pushed the door open with her gloved hand.

Josie nodded, thinking that her old home in Anthony Street was surely not much different from the one she was about to enter.

Sophie stepped inside and Josie followed her down the narrow passage to the back of the house. Something scurried by her foot and she jumped. *Don't be silly, it's only a mouse,* she thought; *a rat would have stood its ground.*

Upstairs, heavy boots stomped across bare floorboards. A man's voice grumbled while a child grizzled. Sophie pushed open the scullery door.

'Mrs Purdy, it's only m–'

Josie collided with her friend who was frozen to the spot. Looking over Sophie's shoulder, she saw that the room was sparsely furnished, if furnished could describe a three-legged table, a milking stool and an upright chair. A pile of rags that had once been blankets were folded in one corner but there was no bed. Beside the empty fire grate an upturned fruit box lined with a knitted shawl served as an improvised cot. On the table was a plate and a broken-handled cup, half a loaf of dry bread and a jug with bluebottles hovering above it.

In the centre of the earth floor stood a pale and thin young woman of about twenty with a baby in her arms and a little girl clinging to her skirt. She stared at the two newcomers with a mixture of relief and dread on her emaciated face. Something caught Josie's eye to her right and she turned to see a familiar figure.

'Good afternoon, Mrs Tugman,' Sophie said,

with a slight tremble in her voice.

The misshapen figure, dressed in what looked like old rags, turned around. Josie found herself facing the same horrid woman whose slovenly son had manhandled her on the day when she'd met Patrick. The fury surged up in Josie as she remembered their first encounter. She gave the old woman a withering look.

A flicker of recognition passed over Ma Tugman's grimy face as she glanced up at Josie.

'Call me Ma, Miss Cooper, everyone else around here does,' she drawled, scratching a finger through her tangled, oily hair. 'And you have the pretty Miss O'Casey with you.'

'You've *met* Ma Tugman?' Sophie exclaimed, a look of alarm on her rosy face.

'I have,' Josie replied.

Amusement flickered across Ma's face and then she thumped her chest and coughed noisily. 'Well, Meg, you have better company than me calling on you, so I'll not intrude.'

A too-bright smile spread over Sophie's face. 'Oh, don't leave on our account; we can always come back another time,' she said in tight voice. 'Can't we, Miss O'Casey?'

Josie looked across at Meg, whose whole demeanour screamed terror, and then to the child staring at the basket on her arm. She couldn't have been more than four, with dirty, worn clothes, no more than rags, covering her thin body. Her bare feet were almost as black as the floor she stood on. There were scabs at the corners of her mouth and her legs were already bowing with rickets.

Josie thought of her brother Joe, only a little

older. She swept past her friend and swung her basket onto the table.

'The children look too hungry to wait,' Josie said, turning her back on the old woman.

She unpacked the fresh bread and milk before her friend could argue. Ignoring the traces of grease on the plate, she set out the bread and poured some milk into the cup.

She held her hand out to the small girl at her mother's skirts who, after the briefest hesitation, ran to the table and snatched up a hunk of bread. She crammed it in her mouth, slurping milk at the same time. Ignoring Sophie, who was glaring at her, Josie turned to Ma Tugman.

Fury passed briefly across the old woman's face before it cracked into an artificial smile. 'What a good heart you have, Miss O'Casey.'

Ma crossed the room and ran a black-nailed index finger slowly down Meg's cheek. The young woman flinched. 'Charity is all well and good, but it's me who can put food in your brats' mouths, regular like. Your friend Lucy's living like a queen since she took up with my Charlie. You'd be wise to study her and see where your best interests lie.'

She lurched back across the floor and stopped in front of Josie, exuding a smell of unwashed body and gin. 'Oh, and Miss O'Casey, when you see your friend Patrick Nolan tell him I was asking after him.'

She shuffled out of the door, banging it shut behind her.

Sophie put her basket on the table next to Josie's. 'I feel rather faint,' she said, fanning her

116

hand in front of her face.

'What on earth is the matter?'

'*That* was Ma Tugman,' Sophie said.

'So I understand,' Josie replied, leading Meg to the chair and handing her one of the small meat pies Mrs Woodall had sent with her.

'No, you don't,' Sophie said.

'Ma controls everything below Commercial Road and from Limehouse Dock to New Gravel Lane,' Meg explained. 'Including the lighthorse men who rob the ships and the heavyhorse ones who move the stolen goods up river. She also runs most of the brothels up Rosemary Lane. Keeps the girls hungry and charges them rent for their clothes and room.'

Josie stroked a stray lock of fair hair out of the little girl's eyes then looked at Meg. 'That's what she was offering you, Meg, a chance to earn some money in one of her stews?'

Meg nodded.

'Don't you worry,' Josie told her. 'We'll find you some work, won't we, Miss Cooper?'

'Of course we will,' Sophie replied, although she looked less than certain.

'It's not just Ma who shoves her weight around,' Meg said. 'There's those boys of hers, Harry and Charlie and the Boatman gang headed by that weasel, Ollie Mac. Between them they have a penny out of every till and cashbox.'

'I've met Harry,' replied Josie.

'Charlie's the devil himself,' said Sophie with feeling. 'It was he who attacked my father last year on his own doorstep because one of those poor girls sought refuge in our hostel. The police

117

couldn't prove anything because the witnesses were too afraid to come forward.' She spread a generous portion of plum jam onto a slice of bread and gave it to the little girl.

'What do you say, Polly?' Meg asked her daughter.

'Fank you, Miss,' Polly answered, spraying crumbs.

The baby in Meg's arms woke up and started to whimper. Josie poured some of the milk into the spoon and carefully dripped it into its mouth while Meg held her.

'Do you know Patrick Nolan, Miss?' Meg asked, looking shyly up at Josie.

'We are old friends,' Josie replied, hoping her voice sounded neutral

'He's the one who helped my Tommy, God rest him, get a job in the dock. He spoke up for him to the dock manger. He's a good man is Patrick Nolan.' Meg winked. 'And he's right handsome, too.'

To her dismay, Josie felt herself blushing.

'But Ma hates him because he won't take her pilfered stuff in his boat upstream. But it's not just that what's got her riled, it's the fact that now, with Patrick leading them, lots of the men – especially the Irish who live around the Knock-fergus stretch of Cable Street – are saying no to her and she don't like it one little bit, I can tell you.'

Josie's stomach fluttered.

'But, Miss, you want to be careful,' Meg said in a trembling voice. 'She's wild to get him and if you're a friend of his you could be in danger, too.'

Chapter Seven

Patrick and Brian shuffled forward a few paces as the queue for the Tunnel tickets moved. It seemed that the whole of London had decided to follow them under the capital's river that afternoon. Although it had been open a year, the novelty of crossing from one bank to the other beneath the Thames hadn't lost its appeal. The north entrance down from Wapping High Street was packed with a variety of people, from smartly dressed men in heavy overcoats escorting elegant women in silk hats and furs to those, like themselves, who were more modestly attired. Brian ran his finger round the starched collar of his shirt and eased it away from his neck.

'Bloody heat,' he said, mopping his brow.

'If you stood still, you great lummox, you wouldn't look like a boiled swede,' Patrick said, grinning at his flushed friend. 'If you get any redder I won't know where your hair stops and you begin.'

'That's easy for you to say,' Brian replied. 'You're not being strangled by your own shirt.'

Patrick smiled. He, too, was hot in his cheap suit and starched shirt but had learnt in the tropics that remaining still helped to stay cool.

Brian nudged him. 'Anyway, man, I thought we were going to the Garrick tonight not to this dog-and-pony show. I can't think why Mattie wanted

119

to come here to see a hole in the ground.'

'Because Mattie wants to spend time with her friend Josie and I couldn't see Dr Munroe allowing his stepdaughter to visit the playhouse in Leman Street,' Patrick explained.

'Is that a fact?' Brian asked, raising an eyebrow as they took a couple of steps forward. 'So it's just that Mattie wants to spend time with Josie?'

'Of course,' Patrick answered.

A mischievous tone crept into Brian's voice. 'Oh, I see. And there's me thinking that *your* sister might have asked Josie along because she's trying to matchmake.'

Patrick raised an eyebrow. 'Well, if that's what *your* future wife is about then I hope you'll put her right.'

They moved forward again. Despite knowing Mattie had asked Josie to join them for that very reason, he'd agreed to his sister's suggestion because this outing might be his only opportunity to tell Josie the truth about Rosa's disappearance before she found out from someone else.

He should have told her immediately, but he'd been so shocked when he found her in his mother's kitchen with Annie that he couldn't think straight. But there was another compelling reason for him to put her right about Rosa – Josie had begun stealing into his thoughts at odd times of the day and he was spending sleepless hours thinking about the shape of her mouth and the way her eyes flashed.

He was a fool not to put her from his mind because, even if he were entirely free, it would be madness for him to imagine she would even look at him again. Nonetheless, his deeply buried feelings for Josie had resurfaced and he had to tell her the truth otherwise his need to see her might put her good name in jeopardy.

They shuffled forward again and Patrick glanced over to the wrought-iron railings, where Josie and Mattie stood, looking down to the vast space beneath. Josie caught his look and his heart ignored his sensible mind and thundered in his chest. He tried to smile but she turned away.

Brian nudged him in the ribs. 'Miss O'Casey looks sweet, doesn't she?'

'Aye, she does,' Patrick replied, unable to take his eyes from her.

'You and her always did make a fine couple,' Brian continued. 'I remembered you walking her home after school and how her mam kept a sharp eye on you to make sure you behaved yourself.'

Patrick gave a half-hearted smile as he continued to gaze at Josie.

When her cab had arrived at the Tunnel entrance and she'd stepped out to meet them she'd fair taken his breath away. He couldn't remember her ever looking quite so lovely, but then he realised he thought that each time he saw her. The dark green gown with frilly lace bits around the neckline and cuffs highlighted her clear complexion and, as usual, odd tendrils of hair had escaped from under her straw bonnet and curled around her cheekbones, drawing attention to their shape.

Not for the first time Patrick's thoughts started to drift towards what might have been, but he willed them away for such idle speculation was

121

futile and painful.

Finally they purchased four one-penny tickets and rejoined Mattie and Josie.

'I thought you'd gone to Timbuktu,' Mattie said, smacking Brian's upper arm playfully.

Josie laughed. 'Oh, Mattie, leave the man alone.'

Someone pushed into Patrick from behind and he stepped closer to her only to catch the faint aroma of violets as he did. 'Don't worry,' he said, smiling down at her. 'Although she'd nag the ears off a donkey, Brian'll be fine because he don't listen to one word in ten my sister ever says.'

'It's my recipe for a happy marriage,' Brian told them, catching Mattie around the waist and kissing her loudly on the cheek. 'Besides, I'm a man of action, ain't I, sweetheart.'

Mattie's cheeks flamed red. 'Brian Maguire, will you stop that!'

He kissed her noisily again. 'You didn't say that last night, now.'

'Brian!' She shot Josie an embarrassed look.

Josie gave a throaty laugh.

A loud chord sounded from below them and Mattie glanced over the railing again. 'I can hear the band.'

It was hard not to as the dome of the Tunnel acted like a megaphone sending the strains of the melody out and upwards, adding its own echoey quality.

Brian held out his arm with an exaggerated flourish. 'Miss Nolan, will you do me the h'utmost h'onour and allow me to h'escort you through the river mud.'

Mattie's face remained stern for a second, and

then she giggled and took his arm. Turning their backs on Patrick and Josie, Brian led Mattie towards the top of the staircase.

Patrick gazed down at Josie, noting as he did so the sweep of her neck and the delicate blush on her cheek. He was so close they were almost touching and the urge to catch her to him and kiss her swept over him. He held out his arm.

'Will you do me the utmost honour too?' he asked.

She gave a restrained smile and rested her hand stiffly on his forearm. 'Thank you.'

He guided her down the spiral staircase. He placed her near to the inside handrail so that she wasn't jostled. Twice he stepped behind her while bracing himself against people pushing past. Finally, they reached the bottom of the stairs where Mattie and Brian were waiting, and there was more room.

Josie immediately let go of Patrick's arm and moved away from him. 'My word,' she said, tipping her head back to see the two high arches that formed the entrance of the Tunnel.

'They'll be building a tunnel to France next,' Mattie said as she joined her.

Brian laughed. 'I shouldn't wonder at it. Now let's be on our way before they run out of beer on the south side.'

Mattie took his arm again and they set off south into the left-hand bore.

'Shall we?' Patrick asked, offering Josie his arm again.

This time her fingers curled around his arm.

The strains of the band were clearer now and

certainly added to the festive atmosphere. Inside the Tunnel, temporary booths had been set up to sell coffee and hot potatoes. Bunting fluttered in the cool draught. There were other stalls offering white pottery tubs of eels and whelks, manned by nautical-looking types in canvas trousers and flat caps who shouted enticements such as 'Swimming this morning!' and 'Fresh from the briny!' The salty sea smell rose up and mingled with the nutty fragrance of coffee and the earthy aroma of the roasting potatoes.

Along the walkway, vendors flourished song sheets for sale as they sang the latest popular tunes in opposition to the tune being played by the band. Patrick slowed his pace and stopped a few times so that Josie could look at some trinket or another.

As they made their way towards the other end of the Tunnel, two children with balloons in their hands dashed towards them with a fraught-looking young woman in a navy dress, hard on their heels. Laughing and jumping as they went, the youngsters were set to collide with Josie so Patrick took hold of her elbow and moved her out of the way.

They stopped by the side to let another party pass. Although he didn't relish explaining to her about Rosa in the crowded thoroughfare of the Thames Tunnel, at least it was a public place and he wouldn't sully her reputation if someone saw them, yet he hesitated. He had to tell her of course, but afterwards there would be no more moments alone with her as she would never consider keeping company with a married man.

Josie stood on tiptoes. 'I can't see Mattie and Brian, maybe we should catch them up.'

He caught her elbow and guided her into the shelter of a column. 'Not just yet. I have something I have to tell you.'

'If it's about not telling me that you were married when we met on the High Street, then don't give it another thought.' Her eyes darted over his face. 'Naturally, I was a bit shocked to ... to realise that you'd gone and married someone, but it's ... it's quite ... understandable that after the passage of time and with all the exotic places you must have been to that you would find someone special.' She attempted a light laugh. 'I mean, we were only children after all when we said we would marry, weren't we? And I *am* sorry for your loss, truly I am.'

'Rosa isn't dead. She left.'

Josie's mouth dropped opened. 'But Annie–'

'We told the children that she'd died to save them from knowing that their mother had deserted them,' he said. He looked away so that Josie couldn't see the anger he still felt towards his wife.

She stared at him for a long time and a faint rosy glow coloured her cheeks. Did she hate him? Was she going to turn and walk away? He didn't know, but he did know that with her dark eyes on him, he couldn't have moved from the spot even if he risked eternal damnation.

'When I realised that my last letter hadn't reached you and you didn't know, I should have told you straight away. I am sorry,' he said, regretting more than just his omission.

She put her hand on his arm. 'You must have been devastated.'

'I really can't talk about it,' he replied. He could live with her accepting his disastrous marriage to Rosa but not with her pitying him for it.

'I understand.'

Patrick ran his gaze slowly over her face again, taking in each detail as if he'd never seen her before.

What a complete fool he had been not to have followed her to Boston and found out for himself if she was married or not. Now all they could ever be was friends.

Without thinking he took a step towards her. 'Josie...'

She looked up at him and for a second he caught a glimpse of something in her expression which was enough to fire his emotions, but he held himself in check as they stood motionless, staring at each other. The words 'I love you' formed on his lips of their own accord but he didn't say them; how could he?

A harsh voice cut in between them. 'Well, fancy seeing you here, Nolan.'

It was only when Josie's confused brain recognised the loutish voice addressing Patrick that she realised someone had joined them. Even then, for the life of her, she couldn't have told you what was said, her mind was still trying to steady itself.

Patrick's wife was still alive but she'd left him!

With his palpable, masculine presence only an arm's reach from her, Josie couldn't imagine why

126

any woman would want to leave him, and to abandon her children. She tore her eyes from Patrick's angular face and then her jaw dropped as she realised that the man addressing them was Harry Tugman.

Although he'd spruced himself up to take in the wonders of the Tunnel, the brown suit with broad white stripes still strained to keep the buttons in their holes. He had no doubt aimed at an air of respectability by carrying an ornate cane tucked under his right arm but it didn't quite work – as hanging on his left arm was a trollop with rouged lips, in a gaudy yellow and black gown.

Patrick offered Josie his arm again and this time she grabbed it, feeling his reassuring strength under her fingers. Drawing her to him he went to guide her past Tugman, but the overdressed, overstuffed ruffian blocked their way.

'It's Miss O'Casey, isn't it?' Harry said, tipping his hat to her. A scraggy lock of hair fell onto his collar. 'We haven't been formally introduced. Harry Tugman's the name and this here is Mrs Curtis, known as Lou to her friends.'

Lou inclined her head and the black feather in her yellow hat dipped over her right eye, giving her the appearance of a theatrical pirate.

'Don't they make a *lovely* couple, Lou?'

The woman beside him giggled. 'Yer, just like us, eh, 'Arry.'

Harry winked at Josie. 'He deserves a bit of 'appiness after the way that slant-eyed, fast-hips wife of his treated him.' He gave Patrick a pitying look.

Josie sucked in her breath. *Surely Patrick wouldn't*

let Harry Tugman insult the woman he loved.

Her eyes darted up to Patrick's face but instead of the fury she expected, his expression was almost indifferent.

Seeing that Patrick wasn't going to rise to his bait, Harry's eyes slid slowly over Josie. The muscles in Patrick's jaw tightened and he stepped in front of her, shielding her from Harry's bold scrutiny.

'Get out of my way, Tugman,' Patrick ordered.

The good humour dropped from Harry's face. 'And what if I don't?'

Patrick right hand shot out and caught Harry around the throat. Harry's piggy eyes opened wide with surprise and he struggled to remove Patrick's hand, thrashing out with his cane, which Patrick caught with his other hand.

'I'm going to make you,' Patrick snarled, as Harry clawed at his hand. 'And if I ever see you casting your filthy eyes over Miss O'Casey again I'll take your cane and ram it down your throat so far you'll roll sideways as you sit.'

People around them were cautiously staring at them as the vaulted arc of the Tunnel amplified their voices.

'Having a bit of a problem, are we?' a mellow voice asked behind Josie.

Josie turned and came face to face with a stout policeman. She let out a sigh of relief. Patrick glanced at the officer then released Harry, who staggered back, pulled his collar away from his neck and gasped for breath. He glared red-faced at Patrick.

'Tugman was having a bit of trouble with his

necktie, Sergeant Plant,' Patrick said, with an innocent expression on his face. 'I was just adjusting it for him.'

The officer tucked his thumbs into his belt and turned to Harry, bent almost double beside him. Lou thumped him on the back to help him clear his lungs but he shoved her aside and started towards Patrick.

'Fecking sod tried to strangle me,' he choked out.

Plant stepped between and his eyes flicked over Josie.

'Watch your mouth, Tugman,' he said. 'You're with decent people.' He gave Josie a paternal smile. 'The young lady here doesn't want to have her ears sullied with your foul language, do you Miss?'

Although the expression on his round, rosy face was kind-hearted there was something in his eyes that didn't quite match his words, but the look vanished as he turned back to Harry.

'I think you had better move on, Tugman, and take Kiss-Kiss Lou with you,' he said.

Harry looked as if he were about to argue but instead he contented himself with shooting Patrick a murderous look.

'Just as you say, officer,' he said, offering Lou his arm. 'And I'll be sure to give your regards to Ma.' As he turned to leave he gave Sergeant Plant a peculiar look, which gave Josie a twinge of unease. Harry tapped his hat back on his head and then he and Lou disappeared into the crowd.

Mattie and Brian came running over.

'Josie, are you all right?' Mattie asked, putting a

solicitous arm around her friend.

'Your friend is fine, Miss, thanks to her beau here stepping in,' Plant told Mattie.

'I'll leave you with your friends now, Miss.' He touched the brim of his top hat. 'Good to see you again, Nolan, and don't forget our last little conversation.'

All four of them watched as the portly officer marched off in the same direction as Harry and Lou towards the north end of the Tunnel.

'What conversation?' Mattie asked, saving Josie the trouble.

'Asked me what I knew about the Tugmans,' Patrick replied.

'What did you tell him?' she asked.

Patrick's mouth pulled into a stubborn line. 'Nothing. A man sorts out his own problems.'

'Meg Purdy told me the Tugmans have you in their sights and you could be in real danger,' Josie said.

Mattie gave a mirthless laugh. 'I'm glad you see that, Josie, because my brother's too stubborn to admit it. Until Pat came back, most people did just as the Tugmans told them – they were too scared to do aught else. But my brother here organised the watermen and river craft captains to say no to Ma's demands. Meg Purdy's right – Ma would give her last few teeth for one of her boys to catch Patrick alone in a dark alley.'

Josie caught hold of Patrick's arm. 'Promise me you'll be careful,' she urged.

The sensible part of her pointed out to her panicky heart that she really shouldn't be clinging onto the arm of a married man, but as she

130

imagined Patrick lying with his throat cut in a stinking gutter, she found she couldn't let him go.

'Of course I will, Josie,' he said in a low, vibrant voice.

They stood lost in each other's eyes until Brian coughed and brought them back to earth.

'Put the worry from your mind,' Patrick said. 'Why, I've fought slippery Chinamen and wild natives dressed in bones and feathers. I think I can take a basin of dripping like Harry.' He shrugged. 'You know how it is. There's always been wrong 'uns snapping at our heels.'

Mattie nodded. 'That's a fact, Pat,' she said, 'but think on this – Harry's seen Josie with you, so now they could be snapping at her heels, too.'

Chapter Eight

Mrs Munroe knocked on Robert's study door, but entered without waiting to be asked. The room had two walls of bookshelves from floor to ceiling, crammed with books of all shapes and sizes, however, rather than being displayed in the conventional way – upright, and arranged by height and binding colour – the medical volumes sat or lay in a disorderly array above labels with subjects scrawled on them in what Mrs Munroe could only call an untidy manner.

A large oak desk at the far end of the room stood under the tall casement window to take advantage of the natural light, and a square red and gold rug with plush fringing covered polished floorboards. There were also two winged arm-chairs on either side of the fireplace, with a small table beside each.

Robert looked up from his desk and smiled at his visitor.

'Mother,' he said, his hand resting on the open book before him. 'This is a pleasant surprise.'

'I told the maid to bring us coffee in here, Robert. I thought we could have a few moments to ourselves,' she said, gliding over to one of the winged chairs.

Robert chewed the end of his quill. 'Very well – just let me finish off this letter.'

'Of course,' she replied, arranging her black bombazine skirt so it wouldn't crease. She could have come out of her widow's weeds two years ago but, as she told any who inquired, she would always be in mourning for dear Mr Munroe.

She noticed with displeasure that two of young George's lead soldiers stood to attention on the side table at her elbow. No one could have faulted her late husband's qualities as a father, but he would never have allowed his children to intrude on his routine the way Robert did. As was only proper, her children had had to wait until the designated hour, when the governess brought them down for the daily visit with their parents.

Mrs Munroe frowned, and wondered again at Robert's curious approach to raising his children. She wasn't surprised to hear that the Royal family followed such a dangerous fashion, the

Queen's husband was foreign after all – but then so was her son's wife. Well, Irish, and that explained a great deal.

Settling back to ease the ache in her back, Mrs Munroe studied her son as his pen scratched rapidly over the paper in front of him.

He had turned forty-three the previous month and there were just the first few signs of grey at his temples but, unlike his father, his hairline was more or less where it had been when he'd left London for New York twelve years ago. He'd filled out a bit, of course, but it suited him. It added gravitas to his new position at the London Hospital.

Her dearest wish had been for Robert to follow her eldest brother into the army and she had been bitterly disappointed when he'd chosen to study medicine instead. Of course, the medical profession was not as respectable twenty years ago as it was now and Robert's brilliant mind and hard work had got him to the top in his field. Well, not quite. His entanglement with Ellen twelve years ago had seen to that. While society might raise its eyebrow at a mistress or two, it would forgive a man if he were discreet. But marrying a woman who sang in a public house and took in washing was quite another matter. Robert's insistence on marrying Ellen rather than setting her up in a little house somewhere meant that instead of rising through the English medical ranks he'd had to waste his talent in America. Who knows, if he hadn't met Ellen he might now be Chief Medical Director.

Mrs Munroe's eyes took in the large portrait on

133

the wall beside the fireplace. The tight line around her mouth disappeared as she looked at the painting of her grandchildren.

Clearly, it had been done some while ago as Jack wasn't included in the group and all the children were much younger. The children's ages aside, she could tell that it had been painted in America as the style was primitive to say the least but, to his credit, the colonial artist had caught the likenesses exactly. Pride swelled up in her and threatened to overflow into tears.

When she'd arrived at Robert's house, every bone in her body was screaming with discomfort from the four hundred-mile journey from Edinburgh by coach. She could have come by boat but felt the coach to be more in keeping with her dignity than being thrown about in the North Sea. As she'd mounted the steps to the four-storey terraced house that was her only son's home, she had intended to make her excuses and seek her bed as soon as possible. But the moment she had set eyes on her grand-children, her energies miraculously returned.

Robert had written to her regularly about his children and when he'd visited Edinburgh four years ago, just after her dear George died, he had brought her a smaller copy of the portrait she now gazed upon. She remembered then thinking his children looked well enough, but seeing them with shining eyes and happy smiles as they welcomed her she realised just how beautiful they really were.

When they came downstairs to greet her for-mally, Mrs Munroe had an almost overwhelming urge to gather the children to her. Thankfully, she suppressed it. Children were naturally emotional and that sentiment, if not forcefully curtailed, could lead to all sorts of unrestrained behaviour and ultimate disgrace, especially in girls.

Casting her eyes over the portrait again, she focused on the young woman seated to one side with baby Joseph on her lap. Irritation replaced grandmotherly pride. Miss O'Casey, as Robert insisted she was addressed, certainly had her mother's striking looks. Her abundance of dark red hair constantly needed repinning while her green eyes flashed as she spoke.

When Robert introduced Ellen's eldest daughter to her, Mrs Munroe had been lost for words. Why on earth hadn't Robert left her in New York with her Irish relatives; surely she would have been more at home there, with her own people...

Her thoughts were interrupted by a knock on the door, and the maid, in her dark grey dress and workaday apron, brought in the morning coffee in a polished silver pot with matching sugar bowl and jug. The milk had a lace cover over it and silver tongs rested on the white cubes of sugar. The delicate bone-china cups and saucers jiggled slightly as the laden silver tray was set down on the table beside Mrs Munroe. Robert folded his letter and set the seal.

Mrs Munroe had mentioned to Ellen only the day before that the maid should change into her better apron before serving the master of the house, but it seemed that her daughter-in-law had yet to tackle the girl on the matter.

'Daisy!' Mrs Munroe said. 'Please change into

your smart apron when you serve my son his morning coffee.'

'Yes, ma'am,' Daisy replied with a brief curtsey.

'Thank you, Daisy,' Robert said, and took the chair opposite his mother when Daisy had left the room. Settling himself with his coffee, he said, 'Ellen runs the house, Mother.'

'Of course she does and I'm not interfering, but she isn't used to running such a large household,' Mrs Munroe said, picking her words carefully.

'She ran a large household in New York, without help,' Robert replied. 'But thank you for your consideration.'

Although she doubted running a house in Brooklyn bore any resemblance to the establishment she now sat in, Mrs Munroe didn't argue the point.

'I must say, I am already *very* fond of Ellen,' Mrs Munroe continued. 'She is quite delightful and without affectation.'

'I think she would appreciate it if you would invite her to call you Mother,' Robert said after a few moments.

Of course, Mrs Munroe knew she should, but she did not want to invite that degree of familiarity. Ellen might be the mother of Robert's children, but she would *never* regard Ellen as a daughter.

'In time, Robert. These things shouldn't be rushed,' she told him.

His brows drew together for a brief second. 'The children are so pleased to meet you at last, Mother.'

Mrs Munroe clasped her hands together on her

substantial bosom. 'Oh, Robert, they are utterly delightful,' she replied. 'And so many – Ellen has certainly done her duty by you.'

The private smile moved across Robert's face. 'She certainly has.'

His mother had observed, during her work with the League for the Moral Improvement of the Poor, that the lower classes seemed able to produce a child a year without the slightest problems whereas her poor daughter, Hermione, after six years of marriage and many miscarriages still struggled to become a mother at all.

'Robina is very like you,' she continued. 'The same broad forehead and dark eyes.'

Robert beamed. 'And she is so clever. I wouldn't be surprised if she *became* the first woman doctor in England.'

Anxiety fluttered through Mrs Munroe. 'You do not want to tax the girl's intellect too much, not as she approaches that difficult age.'

Robert gave a short laugh. 'Don't worry, Mother, I can assure you that education has no detrimental effect on girls, even when they are on the verge of womanhood.'

Mrs Munroe winced. She supposed that Robert's profession caused him to give voice to such matters without regard to delicacy. Although she would be the last to say that women were without natural scholarly ability, she believed their energies and talents should be channelled towards practical feminine pursuits to equip them to be wives and mothers. She failed to see how calculus and science would assist that. She dreaded to think what would become of society if young women started to look outside their God-given domestic sphere for fulfilment.

'Now George is such a fine son, Robert. Upright and strong, confident too.' A burst of joy rose up in her. 'Do you know he marched right up to me yesterday and told me all about his toy soldiers? Have you seen how precisely he arranges them into regiments and battalions? I am convinced he has inherited your uncle's love of the military.' She took out her handkerchief and dabbed the corner of her eye as she had done for the past thirty years. 'Had he survived Waterloo, I know dear Rob would have been a field marshal, maybe even the commander in chief by now.' She fixed Robert with an intense stare. 'You must send George to Oxford. You will have a much better chance of securing him a commission in the cavalry if you do.'

'There is time yet, Mother. He doesn't start at Charterhouse until September.' He drained the last mouthful of coffee and put his cup back on the tray. 'Well, Mother, pleasant though this is, I do have more work to complete so, if you would excuse me...' He began rising from his chair, but Mrs Munroe stayed put and continued talking.

'I was surprised to see that Miss O'Casey came back from America with you,' she said in what she hoped was a noncommittal voice.

Robert sighed and sat down again. 'Why?'

'Well, I thought that you ... that she ... she might be married by now.'

'Ellen and I hoped so, too, but it wasn't to be.'

'I suppose she was pining for this missing Patrick creature who, now it seems, has been

138

alive and well all this time,' she answered with a sniff. 'He sounds like a real scoundrel to me.'

'I would never describe Patrick Nolan as a scoundrel. Josie and Patrick were very young sweethearts and sometimes these things fade with time. I am just thankful he and his family are well.'

Mrs Munroe shifted in her chair. 'In view of their previous entanglement, I am surprised that you allow her to visit his family.'

'I would hardly call a youthful crush an entanglement and I can't see the harm in her visiting her old school friend Mattie and helping with her wedding preparations. Josie has not been without young men eager to speak to me if only she had given them the word.' The frown left his forehead. 'I'm sure she'll find the right young man soon.'

'I pray it is so. She is already losing her bloom and passing the age when most other young women are married,' Mrs Munroe said. 'Couldn't you introduce her to some young man, some shopkeeper or clerk who might take her fancy? She is striking enough, which should make up for her lack of money.'

'Josie is not without money, Mother,' Robert said. 'I will settle four hundred pounds on her and allow her a further two hundred per annum when she marries.'

Mrs Munroe's mouth dropped open. 'Two hundred pounds a year? But she is not even your daughter–'

'I regard Josie as much my daughter as Bobbie and Lottie,' he replied coolly, 'and I would be

139

grateful if *you* would accept her as such.'

Mrs Munroe stifled her annoyance. 'Miss O'Casey is a delightful girl,' she answered carefully. 'A little impetuous and high spirited, but she has many talents. I have complimented her several times on her fine needlework. It's just that her association with this Nolan family – and in particular chasing after this Patrick – might damage your own daughters' reputations. Think of the shame, Robert. Think of the scandal.'

Robert laughed. 'Mother, this is 1844 not 1804. Bobbie is twelve and Lottie just ten; it will be many years before young men start asking me for their hands in marriage.'

Mrs Munroe rose to her feet and faced her son. Although Robert was an inch over six-foot and she was fast approaching her seventy-second birthday, she could almost look him in the eye.

'This might be 1844, Robert, but can I remind you that because of the scandal surrounding your involvement in Danny Donovan's trial and your much publicised liaison with Ellen before you were actually wed, *you* have been forced to practise your profession in America these past twelve years and only now can you return. What if the whole scandal were revived? If Miss O'Casey's feelings for this Nolan man resurface, her impetuous ways might lead her into folly. How many decades do you think you may need to spend in America next time, Robert?'

Annie watched her father take off his coat and hook it on the peg at the back of the door. He smiled at her, then lowered himself into the

140

threadbare armchair. Mickey abandoned the toy ship he was sailing across the rug and climbed up to his father's lap. Patrick snuggled him under his arm and Mickey stuck his thumb in his mouth.

'Had a good day at school?' he asked.

'We studied India today and I told Miss Porritt that you'd been there,' Annie answered. 'Do you want a mug of tea, Pa?'

'I could murder for one,' he replied and Annie giggled.

She couldn't imagine her pa, who had nursed her through scarlet fever and rushed Mickey to the casualty ward at the hospital when he'd slashed his leg on a rusty hinge, hurting anyone. But she knew he could because the boys at school told her their fathers rated hers as a hard man. Even so, Annie still couldn't see it at all. Even the best parents gave their children the odd back-hander when they were out of line but, as far as she could remember, her pa had never laid a finger on either her or Mickey.

'Gran said supper'd be ready soon,' Annie said, picking up the lamp from the mantelshelf and taking it to the table before going over to the fire and making the tea. That done, she took her father's special mug, and hers and Mickey's, together with the brewing tea, to the table. Patrick pulled out a packet from his shirt pocket and gave it to his daughter.

'Spillage,' he said as she took it from him.

Her pa had told her that bargemen were allowed to keep a part of their cargo if it burst or spilled onto their boats. It was a tradition. She didn't quite know what he meant exactly, but she did know it meant a full bucket of coal in the winter and sweet tea from time to time.

Sometimes, if there was a lot, the bargemen would sell it to the local shops. When she went shopping with Gran, things weren't always on display but, if asked for, they would appear from under the counter – unless, of course, one of the local police happened to be walking by.

Annie placed her father's tea in front of him and Mickey jumped off Patrick's lap to sit cross-legged on the floor. Annie handed her brother's tea down to him and he slurped at it noisily and took up his sailing ship again.

'Tell me where you got that cup, Pa,' Annie said, watching her father's large hands cradle the pictures that ran around the bowl.

'I stole if from a maharaja,' he said. 'I crept into his palace one night when he and all his court were asleep and I whipped it out from under his very nose.' He winked. 'Of course, I had to fight off his tigers.'

'Oh, Pa, you do tell 'em,' Annie laughed. She loved it when her father joked, which he seemed to do more often latterly, especially after one of Miss Josie's visits. 'Last time you said you were given it by a chief on a South Sea island.'

'That was the tea pot,' Patrick said, an exaggerated look of outrage on his face.

Annie laughed again. 'Where did you get that?' she asked again.

'Well now, let me see, there was this Chinaman in–'

Mickey abandoned his toy and sat back on his heels. 'Pa! I bet you can't even remember how

142

you got it.'

Her father studied the china mug for a moment and then looked back at his children.

'I'd been at sea for about two years when we shipped out of London. It was a terrible voyage, the worst I'd ever known before or since. There were times when I thought the waves crashing over the deck would take us straight to the bottom. We fought day and night but, finally, with the arms almost torn from our shoulders and the skin nearly gone from our hands, we made it to port. And there on the side of the quay was the prettiest girl I ever saw waiting for me. I'll never forget what she looked like, with her deep brown hair tied up in a green bow and her bright smile. It had been my nineteenth birthday a month before and, as I staggered towards her on my sea legs, she gave me this.' He held up the mug.

Annie turned her face up to him. 'It was Ma, wasn't it? That pretty girl waiting for you.'

Her father gave her a smile that didn't reach his eyes. 'Of course it was.'

Annie knew it wasn't. She could hardly remember her mother. In fact she couldn't remember anything clearly before she arrived at Gran's house; otherwise it was just vague shadows and fears.

Gran and Aunt Mattie occasionally referred to her mother as 'her', when they thought she couldn't hear, and crossed themselves swiftly after. Annie couldn't understand why until one day she overheard Aunt Mattie saying that it was 'wicked how she had treated Patrick'. What had her mother done that had been so wicked? She didn't know, but she knew it made her pa very, very unhappy and she didn't like that.

'Miss Josie's very pretty, isn't she?' she asked, watching her father closely.

'Yes, she is,' he replied, an expression Annie couldn't understand flitting across his face. 'Very pretty.'

'She bought me and Mickey a candy twist today,' Annie told him.

Mickey looked up from his ship. 'It made my tongue go blue,' he said, sticking it out to emphasise his point.

Patrick ruffled his son's hair. 'Don't do that to Gran or she'll fetch you one.'

'When Miss Josie was here yesterday she helped me cut out a shirt for Michael and she says she'll help me sew it properly.'

'That is very kind of her,' her father said.

'Did Ma make your shirts, Pa?' Annie asked.

The relaxed expression on her father's face was replaced by the same taut look he always wore when her mother was mentioned.

'She wasn't too good with a needle,' he replied in a flat tone. Then his face brightened. 'But with Josie's help you'll be like your Aunt Mattie soon and she can sure whip up a shirt in the blink of an eye.'

Annie noticed the change in her father's voice as he said Josie's name. It had a warmth about it that she rarely heard. She got off the chair and took her father's empty cup from him.

'Aunt Mattie told us that you and Miss Josie used to be sweethearts, before she went to live in

144

America,' Annie said in a conversational tone.

'Did she now?' He stretched his legs and settled back in the chair, letting his head rest on the back.

Annie continued to tidy the cups. 'She did, and she said that you used to wait around in Gravel Lane just so you could walk Miss Josie home.'

'I walked her home a couple of times,' he replied, tucking his hands behind his head. 'I hardly call that being sweethearts. I doubt Josie even remembers it.'

'She does, because she told me herself as we were sewing Aunt Mattie's dress. She told us about the time you took her to the fair by Bow Bridge and how she saw a mermaid.'

'What else did she tell you?'

'That you took her to see the jugglers and that there was a dog with a ruff around its neck that jumped through hoops and flipped somersaults,' Mickey chipped in before Annie could answer.

Patrick sat forward and rested his forearms on his thighs. 'Did she say anything else?'

'She said that you bought her a lemonade and knocked three coconuts down on one of the stalls to win her a green ribbon.'

Patrick threw his head back and laughed. 'That lemonade cost me tuppence,' he said. 'A bit of a cheek for a splash of water and a spoonful of sugar. But I remember how that green ribbon shone in her hair.'

Annie smiled. 'Miss Josie said that she still has it and uses it as a marker for her Bible. She said you were at her mother's wedding and danced with her all night.' Annie giggled. 'She told us

145

you could lift your feet to a fiddle second to none, although Aunt Mattie said you had two left feet.'

'She can talk! She might have a right foot and a left, but neither can keep time with a fiddle,' he told her. His grin widened. 'If I say it myself, and I shouldn't, I'm a fair one for the old dancing.'

'Will you dance with Miss Josie at Aunt Mattie's wedding?' Annie asked.

'Perhaps,' he replied, stretching again with his hands back behind his head and crossing his legs at the ankles. 'Goodness, that seems such a long time ago that we danced together in the church hall after Mr and Mrs Munroe got married,' he said, staring at a point on the opposite wall. 'Of course, we were only young then but she was the prettiest girl I'd ever seen.'

Annie giggled. 'Thought you said that was Ma,' she said, hoping her father would laugh at being caught out.

Instead her father sat up. 'So it was.' He stood up. 'That was a lovely cup of tea, Annie.' He smiled at her, but the joy had fled his eyes. 'Pop down and see if your gran's got supper ready yet, there's a good girl.'

He turned away and began to strip off to wash in the bowl on the stand.

With sorrow welling up in her chest, Annie opened the door to the narrow upstairs landing. She didn't know what her mother had done to hurt Pa but, whatever it was, she was still hurting him from beyond the grave.

Chapter Nine

Clutching her package in one hand and holding her skirts tightly around her with the other, Josie side-stepped the wooden privy that served the inhabitants of the twenty or so houses in Walburch and Trench Streets. The alley where the communal toilet sat ran between the backs of the crowded cottages. There was a gully down the centre so that the dirty water and overnight soil from each house could drain into Red Lion Street at the far end.

Although Josie had used the front door on her first visit to the Nolans, close acquaintances always came through the unbolted back door. Not to enter a long-time friend's house this way would have been judged as standoffish. So although it meant navigating her way through the hazards of household rubbish and scavenged scrap metal, Josie respected the custom. She made her way to the yard door and lifted the latch, ducking under the full washing line slung from a hook in the wall to the gatepost, and entered the rectangular space at the back of number twenty.

The length from the back fence to the house was no more than fifteen feet and, unlike some of the yards she'd passed on her way, neat and tidy. There was a small raised vegetable bed at the sides where the first green shoots of the runner

147

beans were already winding their way up the tied canes while, between them, tight fists of cabbage poked out from peaty soil. The tin bath hung on the far wall above the chicken coop in readiness for Friday night. As Josie's skirts brushed against the wire fencing at the front, the brood hens started to trill and cluck.

'Yoohoo! Only me,' she called, as she pushed open the back door.

Mattie got up from the table and hugged Josie, then glanced at the parcel in her hand.

'Just something for Mam,' Josie explained, managing to keep the excitement from her voice. She set the round box tied with a mauve ribbon carefully on the fireside chair.

Mattie took Josie's hands and bobbed up and down. 'I can't believe it's less than a month until Brian and me are wed.'

She stopped her jigging but her eyes still danced. 'Now tell me this, Miss Josephine O'Casey, and tell me no more. Isn't my Brian the most grand handsome man on God's earth?'

Josie thought of another who could fit that description but shoved the notion aside.

'Well, he's certainly filled out,' she replied, remembering how as a lad Brian had always looked as if a strong wind would blow him away.

A mischievous expression crossed Mattie's face. 'It's heaving coal all day that does it. Like with our Pat. Years of heavy work on ships has made him just the same.' Josie gave her a puzzled look and Mattie rolled her eyes. 'You know' – she flexed her biceps – 'pleasing to the eye.'

Josie blushed and snatched up the pile of

148

newspapers. 'I'll lay these out while you get into your dress.'

'All right, and if you move the kettle onto the fire it will be ready to make a cuppa when we're finished.'

Mattie disappeared and Josie dragged the kettle forward, then moved the furniture back to leave them a working space in the middle of the room. She rolled up the rag rug and tucked it under the table then collected the broom from the corner. After sweeping the dirt floor twice she set the newspaper out in a large square to keep the hem of Mattie's dress from gathering dust from the floor. She'd just set the last sheet down when Mattie came back in her gown. She held the skirt up and tiptoed into the centre of the spread papers.

'Fasten me up,' she said, dropping the fabric in her hand and scooping her hair out of the way.

Josie tugged at the back and popped the hooks over the corresponding eyes then stood back. Mattie spun around and they beamed at each other. The two of them had worked hard over the past three weeks and now, with just four weeks until Mattie would walk down the aisle, the wedding gown was almost ready.

Josie clapped her hands. 'Up on the stool,' she said, dragging it from beside the hearth.

Mattie jumped up and turned slowly as Josie checked the fit of the gown.

'Well?' Mattie asked, twisting around and trying to look behind herself. 'Is it fine or do we need to take another tuck?'

'No, I think it's just right,' Josie replied, cocking

her head to the side. 'But there is one thing missing.' She reached across and picked up the parcel she'd brought with her and handed it to her friend.

Mattie pulled at the ribbon holding the lid on and opened the box.

'Oh, Josie,' she said, lifting out the ring of waxed orange blossoms woven together with a green ribbon. 'It's beautiful.' She turned the headdress around in her hand. 'They almost look real.'

'I know. It's very clever how they make the wax so thin without it cracking.' Josie pointed to the join at the back of the wire circlet. 'And look, you can adjust it to fit. As soon as I saw it in Liberty's I knew it was made for you. The shop assistant said it was a copy of the one worn by the duchess of somewhere or other when she got married last year.'

Mattie looked impressed. 'A duchess you say?' Her chin started to wobble and she threw her arms around Josie. 'It is such a darling present and you're a darling girl yourself. I'm so glad you're here to see me wed my Brian.'

The girls clung together then Josie untangled herself. 'Come on then, put it on.'

Mattie nodded and carefully settled the white and green circlet on her ebony hair.

A lump caught in Josie's throat. 'You look so beautiful, Mattie. Brian will fair faint away with pride when he sets eyes on you.'

'Go away with you,' Mattie said, gently touching the headdress with her fingertips, then holding it next to the skirt of her gown. 'It will show off the colour of the dress.' She fingered the lace at her cuffs and then at her throat. 'And the dress fits like a glove.' She smiled at Josie. 'You're so clever. I would never have been able to make my wedding gown so perfect if you hadn't helped me.'

'I learnt it from Gran; she used to make clothes for the girls in the Angel and Crown where Ma sang, until her fingers got too stiff,' Josie replied.

Josie had duly passed on her needlework skills to her two sisters and, though Bobbie approached sampler making in the same thorough manner she did everything else, Charlotte never managed more than a row or two without having to have her thread untangled. The quiet afternoons sewing in the parlour had lost their appeal now Mrs Munroe was there. She sucked all of the pleasure out with her constant demands that Bobbie and Charlotte sit up straight and stop fidgeting.

It was one of the reasons why, when Mattie had asked for help with her wedding gown, Josie had jumped at the chance. And, of course, there was another reason for her eagerness to visit Mattie and her family...

Naturally, she and Patrick were only friends. In view of his confession about Rosa still being alive they could be nothing else, but each time she saw his laughing eyes and flashing smile she remembered just why she'd been eager to marry him all those years ago.

In her sensible moments Josie was almost grateful that Patrick was still married. She couldn't deny his attractiveness but knowing that he was not free stopped her heart from being tempted into folly. Handsome and exciting won't pay the

151

bills she reminded herself when she accompanied Sophie on her pastoral visits, although Josie couldn't help but imagine what her life might have been like if she had married Patrick.

He earned good money compared to many in the area but that wouldn't run to a tenth of the luxury she now had. The two roomed cottage that was her home until she was twelve had a rag rug instead of carpets and bread and dripping instead of cakes and jam, for tea. In those days she only had food in her belly and boots on her feet because Mam and Gran scrubbed their knuckles raw on other people's washing. Her mother had added to their small income by singing in the dockside pubs for an extra copper or two, but even then the three O'Casey women were always just a meal away from the workhouse.

If she'd married Patrick she might still be living as precariously as she had before...

Patrick must have loved Rosa so much to be heartbroken still, she thought. After all, four years had passed since she left.

A twist of jealousy caught Josie in the pit of her stomach. She knew it was completely foolish for her to react so, but every time she thought of Rosa, or heard her name, she couldn't help it.

Now, she told herself, she was just thankful that she and Patrick were friends, just like the old days, but a small voice in her head whispered 'liar'.

An image of Patrick with his sleeves rolled up, revealing the dark hair on his forearms and the rippling muscles beneath, materialised in her mind.

'Do you want to be just friends?' The little voice asked.

Josie stifled her thoughts and knelt down on the newspaper. Tugging down Mattie's hem, she said, 'Now stand still or you'll catch yourself on one of these pins.'

Mattie did as she was told and Josie worked her way around the dress, pinning the hem at the correct length.

'The stitches on this underfrill are very neat,' Josie said, looking at the deep calico frill attached to the hem to anchor it down.

'Annie stitched it,' Mattie said, turning slowly on the stool. 'Since you showed her how to judge the length of the stitches properly she has got so much better.'

Josie made a play of concentrating on setting the hem at an even length. 'I suppose that Annie was too young for her mother to have taught her any of the usual skills,' she said, in a neutral voice.

'*She* wasn't one for domestic pursuits,' Mattie replied, in a measured tone.

'Oh.' Josie picked another pin from her pincushion. 'I mean, Spain must be very different from Wapping, but I'm sure if you love a man you'll follow him wherever he goes. Poor Patrick, he must still love her, despite what she did,' she said. The jealous knot tightened. 'I mean, he can hardly say her name.'

Mattie climbed down from the stool and several emotions passed across her face as she looked at her. 'Now Josie, don't go jumping to assumptions about Pat and Rosa, or anything else for that matter, until you hear the full story.'

Josie's brows pulled together. 'What full story?'

'It's for Pat to tell you, not me,' Mattie replied, folding her arms and looking remarkably like her mother.

'But, Mattie, I–'

The back door handle turned and Patrick walked in.

He was dressed in his corduroy work trousers and rough cotton shirt, with the top few buttons undone. His hair and the bottoms of his trousers were dripping wet and he was without boots.

He smiled at Josie. A warmth spread though her and she smiled back.

Goodness, he was handsome! Even with his unruly damp hair and his workaday clothes, she couldn't think of a man she'd ever met who'd match him for looks.

'Afternoon, Josie.'

'Afternoon yourself, Patrick,' she replied, with more warmth in her voice than she'd greeted him with before.

He threw his coat over the nearest chair and turned towards the fire.

Mattie shrieked. 'Patrick Michael Nolan, don't you take one step more.' She jumped back on the stool. 'You look like you've been swimming in the Thames and if you splash my dress the saints will have to deliver you.'

'Can't a man have a cuppa when he's home, Mat?' he asked.

'It's all right,' Josie said stepping between Patrick and his sister. 'Mattie, you get out of your gown and I'll make Patrick a mug.'

154

Holding her skirt out of the way and with her eyes fixed on her brother, Mattie left the room, closing the door behind her.

Patrick sat down in his father's chair and leant back, while Josie boiled the kettle on the fire then made the tea. All the while, she was acutely aware of his gaze on her.

The Full story... What *was* the full story, she wondered, as Mattie's words turned over in her mind, until the kettle's whistle had cut through her thoughts. When she'd set the tea to brew, she turned to Patrick.

'For the love of all, look at the state of you,' she said, putting her hands on her hips and giving a short laugh. 'Have you fallen in the river?'

'No, I climbed down into it,' he laughed too. 'One of the barges had been damaged and I lent a hand fixing it. I washed most of it off under the pump at the end of the street, but my boots will need scraping.' His eyes twinkled. 'Ma would skin me alive if I traipsed the river bottom into her kitchen so I hope you'll excuse me from appearing improperly dressed.' He wiggled his toes in his socks.

'You're excused,' she replied, reaching up to pull down a towel from the washing line above the fire. When she handed it to him they stared awkwardly at each other for a second before she poured the tea.

She handed him a cup and their fingers touched. They sat in silence. She caught Patrick's eyes on her and gave a tight smile.

Patrick raised the cup. 'Very nice.'

He sat with his long legs stretched out in front

of him and his ankles crossed. The socks covering his large feet were in need of darning.

Josie raised her eyes and studied his shirt. It too was in need of repair. No wife who loved her husband would ever let his work shirt get that frayed.

'I always liked you in green,' he said.

'Thank you,' Josie said. A warm glow spread through her.

He took another sip of tea. 'Annie and Mickey said you told them about the time we went to the Bow fair. I didn't think you would remember.'

The warm feeling intensified. 'Oh yes, I remember,' she replied softly. 'I remember the mermaid in the jar and the rubber man in his bright tights and waxed moustache.'

'I bought you a lemonade.'

'I thought you would faint when you heard the price,' Josie giggled.

'I'd have paid twice that just to see you smile.'

The area between Josie's shoulder blades prickled. 'I remember you were very flash, dressed in your dapper best,' she said lightly.

She must stop this – it was too dangerous.

He slapped his legs and a little puff of dust rose up. 'Like I am now?'

Josie studied Patrick's square jaw with the old scar on it, then moved on to his firm mouth and up to his warm, green eyes. 'And I remember that you kissed me behind the lemonade marquee,' she said in a quiet tone.

As the words left her mouth, she knew she shouldn't have said them. It was too forward, too flirtatious, but the memory of their embrace and

156

the feel of his lips pressed upon hers came back with such force that she couldn't stop herself.

His eyes darkened and the expression on his face changed. She had seen similar looks of admiration from other young men in New York. She'd enjoyed them and accepted them without any obligation. But Patrick's scorching eyes demanded a response. Unable to hold his gaze she stood up and took her empty cup to the table. Patrick rose to his feet and came to stand beside her.

'I haven't forgotten,' he said in a low tone.

They stood so close together that they almost touched. Slowly, she turned to face him and noticed that the front of his shirt had fallen open. With some effort she forced her eyes to remain on his face.

She forgot the years she'd waited. She forgot Rosa and the hurt she'd had in her heart since she found out that Patrick had married. She tilted her head towards him. Slowly, Patrick raised his hand and Josie felt him touch the fabric of her sleeve.

She took a step towards him.

'Josie,' he whispered.

The door opened and Mattie came back into the room.

Sergeant Plant grabbed hold of the frayed rope and hauled himself up the narrow steps from the Boatman's cellar. The other constables had already made it back to the bar but they were all a good ten years younger than he was and hadn't eaten a full oyster supper two hours before. The steps creaked under his weight and he belched noisily, but the burning sensation around his breastbone remained.

Bloody Superintendent Jackson, he thought as his stomach rumbled again. Why couldn't he just send a couple of the young lads around instead of dragging the whole of the nightshift out?

Plant pushed open the door and re-entered the bar of the public house. The four constables who had just searched the low cellar beneath the sawdust-covered floor stood to attention beside Superintendent Jackson.

I'd like to tell him a thing or two about the scum living in these streets, Plant thought resentfully, looking at his superior officer with his well-fitting, navy tailcoat and silk top hat.

Superintendent Jackson's keen eyes rested on Plant and the sergeant's bravado vanished.

There was nothing you could tell Superintendent Jackson about policing the riverside because he already knew it. Known as Long Jackson back in his Wapping court days, and goodness knows what expletive when he was a provost sergeant in the army, the steely-eyed, steely-haired Superintendent was not to be underestimated. It was he who, twelve years before, had put an end to Danny Donovan's murderous reign of terror and who had sent several crooked constables to Botany Bay on the back of it.

Swallowing hard, Plant pulled down the front of his jacket and flicked the dust from his shoulders. He marched over to Jackson and, suppressing another belch, saluted smartly.

'Clean as a whistle, sir,' he told the superintendent.

Jackson ground his teeth under the generous overhang of his moustache then swung around. He glared at the two men leaning back with their elbows on the bar and the old woman sitting on the chair between them.

They all looked back at the H-division senior police officer with expressions of cherubic innocence. Plant ran his eyes over them slowly. The Tugmans were scum of the earth, and no argument about it.

Harry and Charlie were togged out in their usual manner, the eldest in a tight-fitting flash suit with a watch chain draped across his paunch; the younger in a dark frock coat, as if he were quality. Both sported fat cigars. But it was the unkempt, dishevelled woman sitting between them who was the brains of the family.

Before she hooked up with Old Harry Tugman she was known along The Highway as 'up and down' Sally. Looking at her now, it was hard to imagine she was the same woman who sailors fresh off the ship would ask for by name.

Now she just sat around with her swollen legs and broken teeth, taking cuts from all the pilfered cargo and light-skirt along the waterfront. While her two boys barely contained their amusement at Jackson's frustration, Ma sat with her arms folded across her bosom, drawing on her pipe just like any other old woman.

'I'm sorry you didn't find what you were looking for, *Mr Jackson*,' Charlie drawled. 'But do pop by anytime.'

Superintendent Jackson's hand clenched the hilt of his cutlass. But he smiled. 'I'm sure I will.

159

The reward for the *Arcadia* cargo has been raised to fifty pounds.'

Harry whistled though his teeth. 'Did you hear that Ma – fifty pounds?'

Superintendent Jackson glared at them then, with a flick of his head, dismissed the four young constables.

As the door closed behind them, Superintendent Jackson jabbed his finger at the old woman. The dog under her chair growled, then lowered his head submissively as if sensing that a man who'd disarmed murderers and faced loaded pistols wouldn't be intimidated by a mangy old terrier.

'Fifty pounds,' he repeated and left.

With a swift glance at the three by the bar, Plant followed.

Outside in the cool air Superintendent Jackson stood breathing deeply, then started down the alley towards the river. Legend had it that once, to emphasise his point to a felon, Long Jackson had punched his fist through an oak table.

With the superintendent's scarred knuckles showing white in the dim light coming out from the pubs Plant could very well believe it. Reluctantly, he approached him. 'I'd say they'd been warned, sir.'

The superintendent let out a string of expletives that wouldn't have disgraced a sailor.

'Of course they were *fecking warned*, Plant, and if I ever get my hands on the officer who did it, he'll wish his mother had left him in the workhouse.'

The taste of oysters gurgled again and Plant

160

covered his mouth with his hand before asking, 'What makes you think it was one of us?'

Jackson's eyes narrowed. 'Send the officers back to their beats, Plant, and then meet me back at the station,' he barked, and marched off down the street, his footsteps echoing in the narrow alley.

Plant saluted his receding figure and sent the four constables about their business. Pulling out his pipe he lit it and drew on it for a few moments before sidling up the alley towards the back of the pub.

He knocked on the door and heard the lock snap open. With a last glance down the alley he stepped inside. Ma, Harry and Charlie were already waiting for him.

''Ow's you doing, Flower?' Charlie asked.

Plant stifled his irritation. 'You got something for me?'

Ma rummaged inside her stained bodice and pulled out a handful of coins. Plant counted the five sovereigns and slipped them into his pocket.

The young skivvy brought in a brandy bottle and glass and poured him a drink. Plant threw it down his throat hoping the brandy, good French by the taste of it, would settle his stomach.

He turned the glass over in his hand. 'Two hundred pounds reward now,' he mused, and looked up at the Tugmans. 'Lucky Jackson doesn't know about your cellar under number forty-two Burr Street.'

Harry chewed the cigar sticking out of the side of his mouth and glared at him.

'Pour the sergeant another drink,' Ma ordered.

161

The girl did as she was bid. Plant's gaze ran slowly over her. She was a little skinny for his taste but she had a pretty face and nice blonde hair.

As she moved away Charlie caught her and pulled her to him with her back against his chest. With his eyes on Plant he slid one hand down the front of her dress and fondled her. The girl froze with a look of sheer terror on her face.

'Do you want a turn with her, Flower?' he asked.

Plant didn't answer, just watched the other man's hand move under the faded fabric.

'You can have her here, or somewhere more private if you're shy,' Charlie continued.

Plant gulped down the last of his brandy and set the glass on the table.

Charlie released the girl and she darted away. He grinned at Plant and lumbered after her. There was the sound of scurrying and thumping on the stairs, then a sharp scream. Neither Ma nor Harry raised their eyes when the floorboards above started to creak.

Animals, that's what the Tugmans were – disgusting animals, thought Plant. 'I'll drop by if I get wind of anything you might be interested in,' he said, turning to go.

Harry snatched the cigar out of his mouth and strode towards him. 'Make sure you do,' he told him, the spit from his lips spraying Plant's jacket. The oysters rolled around again.

Plant put his hand on the back door. 'As I said, when I hear.'

'Sergeant Plant,' Ma said, as he was just about

162

to step out to the dark night. 'Remember that fifty pounds won't do no one any good if they're face down in the river.' The harsh light above her showed every wrinkle, but her eyes were sharp. A shiver ran up Plant's spine and dried his mouth.

'Of course,' he said, hating the slight tremble in his voice.

He stumbled into the alley. Across the way in the half shadow one of the local sailors was having his sixpence worth against the wall.

Plant turned and walked back up towards The Highway. St George's church bell struck the half hour. He sped up, thankful to leave the Tugmans' dirty back room. The constables would be on their points soon waiting for him to check them. He must hurry if he didn't want to find himself at the wrong end of Jackson's temper.

Within a few moments he reached The Highway with its tightly packed houses and shops on either side. He saw the first of his constables standing on the corner of Ensign Street and waved him on.

Plant pulled out his pipe again and refilled it. He sucked in a lungful of tobacco smoke and watched a couple of hansom cabs trot past on their way to the City. He shifted his weight and felt the five sovereigns in his trouser pocket.

Ah, well! Scum they might be but at least you knew where you were with the Tugmans, he thought, as he turned east and started along to meet the next constable. Maybe it's better the devil you know, and all that.

Chapter Ten

Daisy set the tea tray on the table, bobbed a curtsey and left the room. Through the open window at the back of the house the sound of the children playing drifted through from the garden as Nurse supervised them for the afternoon. Josie heartily wished she was out there with them and not trapped inside with dour-faced Mrs Munroe in her widow's weeds.

She exchanged a glance with her mother and, judging by the irritable look on Ellen's face, Josie guessed she felt much the same. But there was nothing for it. William Arnold had been invited to take afternoon tea and he must be welcomed. Ellen leant forward to pick up the teapot but Mrs Munroe forestalled her.

'Now, Ellen dear, what would my son say if I allowed you to overtire yourself?' she said, grasping the pot.

'I hardly think pouring four cups of tea would send me staggering to my bed,' Ellen replied.

A tremor of annoyance passed over Mrs Munroe's face. 'Even so. Robert's instructions must be obeyed,' she turned to the man beside her. 'Tea, Mr Arnold?'

Josie stifled a yawn.

It wasn't that Mr Arnold was boring; in fact, by any standards he was a very nice young man, pleasant and accommodating, unremarkable to look at but smart in his dress and manner. It was just that Josie often forgot about him, even when she was in his company.

But it wasn't William Arnold who was interfering with her concentration this afternoon, it was Patrick Nolan. She'd put her sewing into the china cabinet yesterday and then poured hot milk in her fruit juice at breakfast this morning.

'Until you hear the full story.' That's what Mattie had said. But what story, and why should she care to hear it anyhow...

But she did care. She cared very much because, although she tried to pretend otherwise, she had noticed the change in Patrick's voice when he spoke to her and she hadn't mistaken the warmth in his eyes.

But where did that leave her? Nowhere. He was married, and that was the end of it. Or it should have been, but images of Patrick kept drifting into her mind and, even though it was wrong to love another woman's husband, she knew she did. She loved Rosa Nolan's man.

Josie glanced across at Mr Arnold, who was sipping his tea and – while Mrs Munroe and Ellen talked across him – gazing at her with a besotted expression on his face. Would he be quite as adoring if he knew the unmaidenly thoughts running around in her head?

Her mind raced on. What would have happened if Mattie had not come back into the kitchen? She had had the distinct impression at that very moment that Patrick was about to kiss her, and the thought that he still cared for her had unleashed feelings that she hadn't realised

165

she still possessed.

'Josie!' Her mother's voice cut into her reverie and Josie jumped. 'Mr Arnold asked you if you enjoyed the church's Sunday tea last week.'

Josie shoved Patrick from her mind and smiled at the young doctor. He smiled back at her, his light blue eyes warm and eager, his pale cheeks still pink from his morning shave.

She'd noticed that, unlike most of the other men in the dock who only shaved on Sundays, Patrick was always clean-shaven. Despite this, the dark shadow of his beard was always visible, and she wondered what it would feel like to run her fingertips over the rough part of his face and onto the smooth...

'I'm sorry, Mr Arnold,' Josie said. 'I enjoyed it very much, especially when the Sunday School children sang.'

Mr Arnold's prominent Adam's apple rose up and then settled back just above his starched winged collar. 'I can see you have a kind heart, Miss O'Casey,' he said.

'I like to see children happy and fed,' she said. 'Some of the children from the poorest families are so thin.'

Mrs Munroe drew herself up. 'Then it would be better if their mothers bought food instead of strong spirits with their housekeeping. Don't you agree, Mr Arnold?'

The doctor opened his mouth but Josie interrupted

'You are mistaken,' she said, noting that Mrs Munroe's lace cap began to shake as it often did when she tried to contain her annoyance. 'Most

166

of the women I have met on my home visits go hungry themselves in order to feed their little ones.' She thought of Meg and her children.

Josie had been as good as her word and, after speaking to her stepfather, had found Meg a job cleaning at the hospital. It was casual work but regular, and a neighbour had agreed to mind the children for a few pence each week.

Mr Arnold's face brimmed with approval. 'Miss O'Casey, your compassion is an example to all.'

Mrs Munroe shot him a hard, sideways glance before her munificent smile returned. 'Are you still thinking of joining the army, Dr Arnold?' she asked.

The memory of Patrick's eyes came back to Josie. She remembered how excited they'd become as he explained to her the shape and form of the animals and birds he'd seen on his travels.

Mr Arnold shifted forward and gazed at Josie as he answered. 'I was, but I have been offered the chance of a practice not too far from here,' he said, with only the faintest trace of eagerness in his voice. 'My father, Sir Henry, went to school with Sir Gerald Morpeth who has a medical practice in the village of West Ham, a rural farming area just on the other side of the river Lea. He is retiring soon and looking for someone to take over. I understand there is a fine house with an orchard at the back of the surgery.'

Ellen smiled at him and Josie felt as if the parlour walls were closing in.

'Cake, Mr Arnold?' Mrs Munroe asked, flourishing the silver slicer at him.

Mr Arnold took the cake offered and sank his

teeth into it, leaving a faint line of white sugar at the edge of his top lip.

'Delicious,' he said. 'One of yours, Miss O'Casey?'

Josie shook her head.

'My daughter is a wonderful cook, though,' Ellen said, 'In fact, she is quite the little home-maker. I don't know what I would have done without her these last weeks. She has practically taken over the running of the house.'

The smitten young doctor looked suitably impressed.

'And I have been adding those little details that are so important in proper society,' Mrs Munroe said, smiling serenely at her daughter-in-law, before adding, 'of course my son looks on Miss O'Casey as his own daughter and he has a regard for her future.'

For goodness' sake, why doesn't the old trout just tell him what Pa has settled on me and be done with it, Josie thought. In fact, why not just tie a big label around my neck with my price on?

She wasn't a commodity; she was a woman who wanted and needed to be loved.

She cast her gaze around the sumptuous furnishings of the parlour, its china fireplace ornaments, the lace at the windows, and the chenille curtains hanging from brass poles, and let out a sigh as she thought of the full larder downstairs and how every bedroom had coals in the grate. But this was the way it was done. For all her mother's assurances of wanting her to marry someone who would care for her, she knew that Ellen would not be easily persuaded to give her consent to any man without a sizable income or future.

Love didn't fill cupboards or buy coal. Josie understood that.

Life had been hard – very hard – before her mother met Robert Munroe, and there had been many nights when Josie had fallen asleep with hunger gnawing at her aching stomach. When there wasn't money for coal, she, Mam and Gran would huddle together for warmth in the creaky bed. Ellen had even crossed over the harsh line of respectability and sung in a public house in order to send Josie to school.

The memories of their earlier poverty haunted Ellen, and Josie understood that. But Ellen hadn't married Robert for security or because he could provide a four-storey house with servants; she had married Robert because she loved him, and Josie vowed that when she married it would be for the same reason. She hadn't actually got around to telling her mother about Rosa. Naturally, she had to pick her moment. Goodness only knew what her mother would say when she found out her unmarried daughter had been on an excursion with a married man. No, that was a lie. Josie knew very well what her mother would say and in undiluted Irish too. She might even forbid her to visit Mattie, which is why Josie hadn't raised the matter. She didn't want to spoil Mattie's wedding.

As Patrick crunched over the cobbles of Wapping High Street in his studded boots, he inhaled the tangy smell of the exotic spices stored in the ware-

169

houses around him. It reminded him of loading the aromatic sacks of cinnamon and cumin and ginger into the *Seahorse's* hold in Calcutta. It also brought an image of Josie into his mind. When he'd waved her goodbye that last time seven years ago in New York, he had been standing on the quarterdeck of that very same ship.

In truth, he didn't need anything to bring Josie to mind because she was with him every moment of his day and every beat of his heart. Why else was he so eager to get home when she was there sewing with Mattie? How was it that he could recall every little detail of what she said and remember how she looked? And how he relished the pleasure he got from hearing that she'd spoken about him to Mattie and Annie...

Turning into Walburgh Street, Patrick's weary eyes rested on his front door at the end of the road. What he wouldn't give to have Josie waiting for him behind it, he thought, as he pushed it open. Although it was early evening, the air was humid and the soot clung to his damp skin. Sarah was stirring the pot on the fire but turned as her son walked in.

'There you are, lad,' she said, her eyes resting gently on him. 'Good day?'

'Fair, though this heat's murder,' he replied, warmed by the tenderness in her voice.

He began to wash his hands and face in the bowl of cool soapy water his mother had left at the end of the table for him. 'Where's the young 'uns?'

'Upstairs. I told them I had a headache.' Sarah reached up to the mantelshelf and picked up a letter, which she handed to him.

Patrick wiped his hands on the towel draped over the back of the chair and took the letter.

Instead of the new-style envelopes that were now generally used, the letter with Patrick's name scrawled boldly across it was a solid sheet of paper, tucked and folded and held together with an old-fashioned wax seal. Above the seal, in smaller letters, was written: Lieutenant Edward Smyth, adjutant to Colonel FitzWallace of The First Anglia Infantry Regiment, Newcastle-upon-Tyne.

Patrick stared at it. It had been over four months since he'd written to enquire after Rosa – just before he'd met Josie again. He hadn't been optimistic about a reply. He knew that the comings and goings of one of the camp followers wouldn't be a high priority for the garrison's commanding officer.

'It arrived at Wardells' store yesterday and I collected it this morning along with a letter from Aunt Bridie,' Sarah said. 'Aren't you going to open it, Pat?'

Patrick's heart pounded in his chest. The squat-sealed letter in his hand might just give him the key to happiness with Josie.

He'd originally written to satisfy his own mind as to his wife's fate, but since Josie had come back into his life, knowing Rosa's fate had become urgent. He unfolded the page and began reading.

The regimental sergeant major informs me that on the last occasion that he saw Mrs Rosa Nolan she was still in the company of Corporal Keble of the Fifth.

She accompanied the regiment when it left for Egypt six months ago.
However, mindful of your difficult situation, I have taken the liberty of forwarding your letter to Mr Watson, chaplain to the garrison in Alexandria, and an old school friend of mine, in the hope that he might have further knowledge of your wife's whereabouts.

My God, Alexandria!

'What does it say?' Sarah sat down opposite him. 'Tell me that she's dead, God forgive me!'

Patrick gave her a disapproving look and Sarah crossed herself hastily.

'She was alive six months ago but now in hell – of sorts,' he replied. 'She went to Alexandria. The colonel has forwarded my letter to the chaplain attached to the fort in Egypt. There is a slim chance we may still hear news of Rosa.'

Sarah folded her arms tightly across her bosom. 'Well, good riddance to her.'

'Maybe, but I don't relish any woman having to suffer Alexandria, not even Rosa,' he said. 'You smell the place on the wind long before you see it, and it's so infested with disease that one in six of the local population is killed by it – and for the English double that. When the *Seahorse* berthed I heaved my gut over the side because of the stench of rotting, bloated animal carcasses – and human ones too – floating in the shallows. Soldiers garrisoned there called it Egypt's arse, and anyone who's been there will know why.'

Sarah regarded him for a few moments, then one eyebrow rose. 'If the place is as bad as you say, Pat, then you might even now be a widower.'

Hope and guilt vied for position in Patrick's mind. He wanted his mother's words to be true so much it was like a physical hurt, but he forced his unworthy thought aside. It was a mortal sin to wish Rosa dead, no matter what she'd done. But as his eyes settled again on the letter Patrick – even if he were doomed to a thousand years in purgatory – silenced his conscience and prayed that his mother's words might come true.

Mattie rolled against Brian as the front wheel of the cart dipped into one of the many potholes along Cable Street. He smiled down at her and snapped the reins lightly on old Flossy's dappled rump. Behind Mattie, carefully packed away in three boxes, was her bottom drawer. Well, bottom three drawers and a chest to be precise, and very soon she would be putting them to use as a new wife.

Brian shortened the right rein to turn Flossy into Cannon Street Road but he didn't need to. The old horse knew her way home and had already plodded around the corner. The iron rimmed wheels squealed as they scraped over the cobbles and through the horse muck and dirt in the gutter.

Sensing her warm stable and her bale of fresh hay waiting for her, Flossy picked up her pace and practically trotted into the yard.

The acrid smell of the coal filled Mattie's nose as she looked around at what would be her new home in less than a week. Brian's father had started the business some twenty years before by filling a hand cart each day at the Limehouse coal depot and then selling it by the bucket around the streets. After two years he'd bought a horse, and after five he'd taken the lease on an old cooperage yard and adjoining house. The oblong plot had the business at one end and the house at the other, with the stable for the four horses in between. At the business end of the yard were four piles of coal divided by wooden fences and ranging from Best Parlour coal to Washed Nuts at half the price.

'Yo there, old girl,' Brian called, applying the brake and winding the reins around the side board.

He jumped down and then held his hands out to Mattie. She slid forward on the seat and his large hand gripped her around the waist. He lifted her effortlessly down but instead of releasing her held her close.

'Give us a kiss,' he said, tickling her.

'Brian Maguire! Not here, in broad daylight. You'll set the neighbours talking,' she said, trying to wriggle out of his grasp. 'Let me go.'

'Plant one on me and I will,' he replied, puckering up.

'What about your men?'

He glanced at the three delivery carts standing in a row in front of the stacked coal. 'The men have gone. It's just you and me, so come on.' He winked. 'A lot of girls would, you know.' He pulled his mouth tight again.

'Well, really,' Mattie said, giving him her severest look but fighting to keep the smile from her face.

Brian made a couple of kissing sounds then

174

Mattie stretched up and did as he asked, feeling the scratch of his end of day bristles on her lips.

Why wouldn't she? Wasn't it what she wanted to do every time she set eyes on him?

'That's better,' he said, letting her go and unhitching Flossy, who trotted into her stall and stuck her head into the trough while Brian took off her harness. He gave the square rump an affectionate slap and hooked the leather straps on the post, then closed the gate. He cast his eyes over the other three horses then strolled back to Mattie.

He had collected her after he'd finished his last delivery and still wore his work jerkin and canvas trousers, both of which were coated with coal dust, although the protective headgear that covered him down to his shoulders lay beside her boxes in the back of the wagon. His face was crisscrossed with black lines where the dust had seeped into the small creases around his eyes, mouth and neck. It contrasted strangely with his bright red hair, sky blue eyes and white teeth. It would take Brian an hour of scrubbing at the kitchen sink to clean the last of it away.

He picked up the largest box from behind the seat and pretended to stagger back. 'What have you got in here, woman, cannon balls?'

'It's the new iron pot that Mam's given me and my bits of china,' Mattie replied, taking up the box with her clothes in.

Brian heaved his load onto one shoulder and then collected her bundle with the cotton sheets and bolster case inside that she had been stitching for the past year.

175

'The chest should be all right there for a moment,' he said.

It had rained earlier in the day so at least the dust that usually blew about the yard had settled, but it now lay as grey sludge under her boots. Mattie lifted her skirts to stop them dragging across the ground and followed Brian towards the house.

The Maguire home was set at the far end of the yard. It was a two-up two-down like the rest of the street but about five years ago, just before he died, Brian's father had built a two-storey extension to the side. The new downstairs room was joined to the house immediately inside the front door and was a large family parlour while the upstairs room became the company office overlooking the yard and reached by an outside wooden staircase. Brian went around the back of the house and through the small garden.

'Mam, we're back,' Brian called as he pushed open the back door with his foot.

Queenie, Brian's mother, stood by the deep kitchen sink but turned from her task as soon as they entered.

Unlike most of the folk in Knockfergus, Queenie Maguire wasn't from the old country. Her family, the Bruntons, had lived along the river long before the Irish arrived, back in the last century. She was finely boned, with a tiny button nose that gave her face a childlike quality. In contrast, a lifetime of housework had developed her thin arms into stringy muscles and given her knotted knuckles perpetual redness. In the light from the kitchen window her fine, almost white hair showed a hint of the gold it used to be.

'Did you get caught in the rain?' she asked, looking anxiously over her son.

'Just for a moment,' Brian replied, sliding the box from his shoulder onto the kitchen table.

The furrows in Queenie's fair brow deepened. She left her chores and went to her son's side. 'Are you wet?' She placed her hand on his sleeve.

Queenie, who barely came up to Mattie's shoulder, was positively dwarfed by her son. Mattie pondered, not for the first time, how a body so diminutive could produce a man the size of Brian.

'No, Mam, I'm not,' he replied, looking down at her with a patient expression on his face.

'Are you sure? Damp will draw a chill to your bones in the wink of an eye. Won't it Mattie?' she asked, looking across to her.

Mattie smiled. Seeing his mother fuss over Brian as if he were eight instead of twenty-eight slightly niggled her but, as Queenie had been brought to bed six unsuccessful times before delivering her son, she couldn't really blame her. Perhaps she would be the same if she were in Queenie's shoes.

Brian took his mother's hands. 'Mam, rest your mind from its fretting. I'm fine. Now is there a brew of tea for me and Mattie?'

Queenie's face crinkled into a smile. 'Of course there is, son.' She shuffled over to the range and moved the kettle to the heat.

Mattie eyed the massive iron oven sitting in what had been the fireplace. Brian had bought it for his mother last year after they got the contract

177

to supply coal to Hoffman the baker's two shops. Having only cooked on her mother's fire Mattie wondered if she would ever master its two ovens and array of hot plates, but she did relish soon having hot water on tap, literally, from the reservoir beside the fire.

'And how is our Mattie?' asked Queenie, turning her attention to her.

'Very well, thank you, Mrs Maguire,' Mattie replied.

'Tush!' she waved a bird-like hand in the air. 'Haven't I told you to call me Queenie? Everyone does. And,' she glanced at Mattie's stomach, 'how are *things?*'

Everyone in the family knew she was with child although her condition couldn't be spoken about openly until after she and Brian were wed, but her Mam and Queenie were forever asking how 'things' were.

Mattie blushed. 'As they should be.'

'Good, good.' Queenie gave a happy shrug.

Brian smiled at Mattie over his mother's head. 'I'll go and fetch your trunk from the wagon.'

'And I'll take my things upstairs, if I may, Mrs ... Queenie,' Mattie said.

'You do that, dear, while I sort you out a splash of tea and maybe a nice bit of fruit cake.' She screwed up her shoulders again. 'Just to keep your strength up.'

Mattie picked up the bundle of linen and left the kitchen. Passing along the newly papered hall she went upstairs and into the front bedroom.

The faint smell of turps still lingered from where Brian had whitewashed the ceiling and walls and put another coat of paint over the window frames. Sadly, it would need doing again in a year or two. The coal dust from the yard meant that Queenie never opened the house windows. Despite this the black flecks of coal still managed to creep into the house somehow.

Mattie rested her bundle on the bed, untied the knot and scooped up the two sets of sheets and matching bolster cases. Folding them carefully, she placed them in the pine chest at the foot of the bed.

Closing the lid, she went and sat on the new cast iron bed with the smart brass knobs at each corner. She ran her hand over the patchwork counterpane, feeling the contrasting fabric under her fingertips. She and Brian had done most of their courting on the sofa in the parlour but in a couple of days they would have the comfort of their new bed and she would have the thrill of waking up beside him in it each morning.

'I thought you might need these, too,' Brian's voice said from the doorway.

She turned and smiled at him. Brian set the box on the chair then sat on the bed beside her. A spring bonged under his weight.

'Don't worry,' he said. 'Mam's a sound sleeper.'

Mattie slapped his upper arm and he caught her and rolled her on the bed.

Mattie looked up into his blue eyes as he gazed down into her brown ones. A fizz of excitement went through her as she felt his weight pressing on her.

'Are *things* well?' he asked, resting his hand lightly on her stomach.

'They are very well and growing each day. I think I felt a movement yesterday.'

Brian gave her such a look that she swore she felt her bones melt. 'Grand,' he said softly.

She reached up and ran her finger through his hair. 'How many do you want?'

'Three boys to work the wagons and two girls to sit on their father's knee and adore him,' he replied, his gaze running slowly over her face.

The image of Josie and Patrick standing together flashed into Mattie's mind and a lump formed in her throat.

What heartbreak, she thought, as tears gathered, to be so very much in love and without any hope. She was so blessed to have found Brian.

'I love you, Brian Maguire,' she said, as a tear escaped and rolled down her cheek.

He pressed his mouth on hers in a long kiss. 'And I love you too, Mattie Nolan.'

Chapter Eleven

Under the benevolent gaze of the Virgin with the Christ child in her sculptured arms, the priest gave Mattie and Brian his final blessing. They had been to the parish church of St George's the day before for legal requirements but the nuptial mass was their real wedding ceremony.

The Virginia Street Mission had been a coffee warehouse not so long ago, but the aroma of roasted beans had now been replaced by the heady scent of incense. With its whitewashed interior, draped high altar and brightly coloured figures of the saints lining its walls, St Mary's and St Michael's was the main place of worship for Knockfergus's Catholic population.

The boy operating the organ bellows jumped from his seat and heaved them up and down. Mattie and Brian turned and faced their family and friends as the organ struck up a long chord.

The choir boys filed out, and the congregation rose and followed the newly married couple down the aisle and out into the bright June sunshine. Squashed between the pews, Josie lost sight of the bride and groom in the crush to get out. Someone caught her arm and she turned to find Kate and Hannah Nolan grinning at her.

Kate's golden locks were swept up into a loose becoming knot at the nape of her neck while Hannah's light brown hair was plaited across the top of her head.

'Wait for us,' Kate said, her bright blue eyes dancing as she held onto the arm of her younger sister.

'Let's head for the side – it's less crowded,' Josie said, pointing over the sea of heads.

'Good idea,' Kate said, heading towards the chapel door.

Gathering her skirt with one hand and holding her bonnet in place with the other, Josie followed the flow of people heading out of the church. Although they were jostled as they went, the three young women laughed and joked and when Josie lost one slim-fitting pump and had to skip back for it, people happily moved aside while she found it.

Hannah smoothed down her new, dark blue gown. Although it fitted her rounded figure well, its lack of adornment or frills marked it out as a servant's outfit. Hannah had done her best by adding a detachable collar but it still looked very like the gown Daisy had made from the fabric Josie had bought her.

'Goodness, so many people,' Hannah said, straightening the collar around her throat.

'Everyone wants to give Mattie and Brian a good send off,' her sister said, 'me included. Now she's gone there'll be a lot more room in the bed.'

'You've still got Pat's Annie,' Hannah replied.

Kate laughed. 'Aye, but she takes no more than a slither of the room and she don't snore all night.'

Josie and Hannah giggled, then Kate took them by their arms, urging them along. 'Come on, or the happy couple will be taking their leave of us all before we've even arrived.'

The procession back to Walburgh Street was a merry affair. People from the surrounding streets came out to wish the young couple well, and women with shawls over their heads stood in open doorways next to working men with pipes stuck in their mouths. Some of them offered advice for a long life to the new bride and groom, while barefooted children darted back and forth, jumping and giggling.

It had rained first thing and the cobbles were still wet, but it had settled the blacks – the small flecks of soot from the local chimneys that fluttered in the air like ebony snow. The downpour had washed the worst of the refuse away too, thereby sweetening the early summer air. The warm June sunlight warmed Josie's cheeks and she turned her face up to feel it.

Kate tugged at her arm. 'Wasn't it a lovely Mass?' she said, picking up their pace.

Josie nodded. 'That it was.' She looked towards the front of the crowd and could just see Mattie in her pink wedding dress, the ring of waxed orange blossoms nestling on her black curls.

'Mattie's dress looked a wonder,' Hannah said, looking Josie up and down. 'You haven't lost your skills with the needle.'

Josie smiled with satisfaction. Hannah wasn't the only one to remark on the bride's pretty gown.

'No doubt you have your own dressmaker now,' Hannah continued, with just a hint of envy in her voice.

Josie flushed with embarrassment. It had been quite difficult to settle on what to wear, for she didn't want to overshadow her less well-off friends. Eventually she'd decided on her apple-green twilled silk day dress, which had a deep frill around the hem and a subtle, but pretty, lace trim around the neckline and cuffs. It also had a nipped-in waist, and for once she hadn't complained about her mother's insistence on a second lacing. She'd thought the dress unremarkable enough but it was clear that it was still grander than everyone else's in the street.

Kate gave her younger sister a sharp look then smiled at Josie. 'The orange blossom headdress is just perfect.'

183

'I saw it and couldn't resist it,' Josie replied.

'You bought it in Bond Street, you say,' Hannah said, still studying the details of Josie's gown.

'No, Regent Street,' Josie replied, giving Hannah a tight smile.

Annie dashed through the crowd. 'There you are, Miss Josie,' she said taking hold of her hand.

Josie felt an instant sense of pride. She had found one of Lottie's old dresses and refashioned it to fit Annie. She'd felt tears start in her eyes when she buttoned the little girl into her gown that morning and saw the utter joy in her face.

'Where's Mickey?' Josie asked.

'He's already at the cake table,' Annie said, rolling her eyes and looking very like her grandmother. 'With Uncle Gus.'

Josie laughed. 'I bet he is. He's spoken of nothing else since I arrived this morning.'

Annie skipped along beside Josie, and her own aunts, and all four soon reached the bottom of the street.

'Your mam looks a picture in her new jacket and bonnet,' Josie said, watching Sarah Nolan as she strolled along behind the bride and groom.

'Aye, and look at Brian's ma in her spruce new outfit,' Kate said.

'Well, Maguire and Son is one of the busiest coal yards in the area. Why wouldn't Brian's mother splash out a shilling or two for her only son's wedding?' Hannah replied, then knitted her fair brow into a frown as she asked 'Who's that with Gus?'

Kate stood on tip-toes and looked across. 'I don't know,' she replied, studying the pretty young woman looking adoringly up at their brother. 'Let's go and find out.'

Josie watched Kate and Hannah weave their way through the crowd, and then her gaze travelled on to the wedding party and fixed on Patrick. She couldn't help it. She didn't seem able to stop herself. Her eyes ran over him again and, with his attention elsewhere, Josie allowed herself the luxury of an unhurried study.

He stood behind his mother, his hand resting lightly on her shoulder. The shoulders of the suit he wore could have done with an inch or so more room to accommodate the breadth of his upper body but, considering it was probably bought at one of the cheap clothing warehouses around Shoreditch, it fitted remarkably well. Even the slight sag at the knees of the snugly fitted trousers didn't detract from his long, well-shaped legs.

As if he knew her eyes were on him, Patrick looked over at her and smiled. Josie's heart turned in her chest.

Why on earth would Rosa have looked elsewhere with Patrick by her side? She wondered, yet again.

Someone spoke to him and he turned, which allowed Josie to study his face. The shape and form of his lips fascinated her as he mouthed words, as did the sweep of his dark brows. She noticed again his square hands and long fingers, with their closely clipped nails. She remembered the strength of his hands too, from the way he had gripped Harry Tugman.

Josie imagined those hands – hands that had once slid around her waist and held her – holding

Rosa instead. Did she, that woman who had played him false, thrill to his touch the way Josie had all those years ago? And did she run her finger lightly over her lips after he'd kissed her in an attempt to keep the memory for as long as possible? How could any woman desire another man if Patrick was beside her?

Now, Patrick himself, smiling, was walking towards her. The breath left her body, and Josie O'Casey knew in that moment what she'd really known all along: she loved Patrick Nolan.

As he came up beside her, a long note from a fiddle cut through the air, the signal to start the dancing. People all around them surged forward and Patrick reached out his hand to Josie.

'May I escort you into the party?'

She curled her hand around his arm and he led her forward.

Walburgh Street buzzed with activity. Sarah's neighbours had dragged tables outside from all their houses. These were now lined up along one side of the street, and the women were bringing out bowls and plates of food. Across from them, the men milled around, talking and pouring beer from jugs.

Patrick led Josie over to greet the newlyweds. Mattie's face lit up as she saw them approaching. She jumped up and hugged Josie.

'I'm so happy for you and you look beautiful in that dress,' Josie said to her friend.

Mattie glanced at her brother. 'And you make a grand couple,' she said in a low voice.

Josie lowered her eyes but her cheeks grew warm.

'I have to stay with me mam for the formalities,' Patrick said, giving her a heart-stopping smile.

'Of course,' Josie replied. She let go of his arm and he stepped behind his mother again.

Someone else came forward to greet the happy couple so Josie walked away to chat with the neighbours. Colly Bonney, whom she'd met before the ceremony, came over with her colourful children and introduced her to some of the other boatmen's wives and, after sharing some good-hearted banter, a comforting sense of belonging stole over her.

She wouldn't wish Bobbie, Lottie or the boys to live the life she'd known as a girl, with barely enough to eat and the terrible spectre of the workhouse if Mam was unemployed, but then again they wouldn't know the comfort of knocking on any door in the street, always sure of a welcome. The people in Knockfergus didn't worry about what next door had, because everyone had the same: nothing.

Patrick's speech was well received and Josie smiled as she listened to him extol Brian's bravery at taking on a Nolan woman as a wife. This brought him a thump on the arm from Mattie and a loud cheer of approval from the men in the audience. A cake of salt and oatmeal was offered to Mattie and Brian and they took three bites each to protect them from evil. They then stood up to lead the dancing. Annie came over and stood next to Josie and the little girl's eyes sparkled as she watched the adult members of her family dance in the middle of the street.

'Why is Aunt Mattie dancing in that funny

way?' she asked Josie, as they both clapped in time with the music.

'Because the fairy people love a bride and if she takes both feet off the floor before she's – err – properly wed,' she said, carefully, 'they can spirit her away.'

The fiddler drew out a long note calling the dancers to order. The men stood up and, with their hands on their hips, started to twist their feet heel to toe. Patrick joined them, stylishly dipping and leaping between the other men. After a few moments, he took off his jacket and cravat and threw them to Sarah.

A couple of his fellow dancers pushed him into the middle. With his thumbs in the armhole of his waistcoat he swaggered around in time with the music then did some high steps, which earned him thunderous applause, before he returned to the circle and another dancer stepped in.

'He's a fair one for the dance is your father,' Josie said to Annie.

'That he is,' Annie agreed. 'He said that he danced with you at your mam's wedding.'

Josie glanced down at Annie. 'He did,' she replied, thinking of how he'd also swirled her onto the front porch and kissed her.

The dance finished and Patrick came over. 'I'll get you a cup of punch.'

Annie saw a friend sitting on one of the doorsteps at the end of the street and so dashed off to join her.

Patrick strolled across the street to the refreshment table, dodging between dancers as he went. A couple of men gathered around the table slapped him on the back and he exchanged a joke with them before making his way back to Josie.

He handed her the glass of punch and their fingers touched briefly. The expression in his dark eyes set her heart racing again. She took a sip of the punch and it scorched her throat.

'My goodness, it's almost pure spirit,' she said, placing her hand on her chest and coughing.

Patrick laughed. 'Jamaican Rum, of course. Just be thankful it's spillage and not brewed from potato scraps in someone's zinc bath.'

Josie took another sip and Patrick swallowed a long draught of his beer. They stood for a while as the dancers swung around.

'It's a wonderful wedding,' Josie said. 'And everyone can see that Mattie and Brian are so much in love.'

'Aye,' Patrick replied. 'And even Mattie's bouquet couldn't hide it.'

'Oh, Patrick,' Josie laughed, and when she glanced up at him she felt the passion in his eyes warm her even more than the fiery punch was doing.

The fiddler struck up another long note to start the next dance. Patrick took her drink from her and put it with his own on a nearby windowsill. He grabbed her hand.

'Come on,' he said. 'It's a mortal sin not to dance when an Irish jig's calling you.'

He shouldn't dance with her of course, it was asking for trouble. When she'd arrived that morning, he had only just managed to hold himself back from gathering her in his arms to kiss her until she was breathless, so holding her hand and waist, even in a dance, was utter madness. But with the sun in her hair and the merriment of the day he couldn't stop himself.

But, even if he were free, what did he have to offer Josie? He was a man with two dependant children, living upstairs in two rooms in a damp cottage with his mother. He worked when there was work, and notched in his belt when there wasn't. He had missed his chance with Josie and he would have to force himself to accept that.

The tune started and Patrick bowed.

'I don't suppose you remember this one,' he said.

She picked up her skirt and swung to one side. 'Of course I do and I haven't got two left feet to dance it with,' she answered, twirling around.

She sidestepped and passed behind him. Patrick stood and clapped as she circled, hopped to one side and then back, his eyes never leaving her laughing face.

God, she was beautiful, he thought, watching as a small tendril of hair escaped from her bonnet.

She doubled-stepped back into place and then it was his turn to circle her. She clapped and beat time with her foot as he strutted past her. Someone knocked her bonnet, tipping it sideways.

She laughed, pulled the ribbon and threw it behind her. Patrick slipped his arm around her waist then they turned around each other. Her hips butted against his and she smiled up at him.

'You told Annie about dancing with me at Mam's wedding,' she said, as they changed arms and stepped back the other way.

'I did,' he replied, enjoying the sensation of his arm around her slender waist.

'That's not all you did! If you remember.'

The tone of her voice caught him in the stomach and stole his thoughts. He only had to dip his head and he could press his lips on hers.

'I've never forgotten it.'

Her eyes opened a fraction and her lips parted. He hadn't lived the life of a monk since Rosa left but the flirtatious glance Josie threw him caught his vitals as no other woman had done.

He *had* to stop this. With her in his arms he was on the brink of doing something he should not. Thankfully, the dance broke them apart. They wove through the other dancers and then back to each other. The music stopped and they stood facing each other. Suddenly for Patrick there were no broken promises and no years of regret, there was only Josie. Josie, who he had walked home from school and whom he'd vowed to marry and who would be his only love until the last breath left his body. Heedless of the press of people around them, he stepped forward and took her hand.

'Josie,' he said, and then suddenly became aware that there was an eerie silence in the street.

She noticed it too and turned.

Ma Tugman, flanked by Charlie to her right and Harry on her left, was standing at the end of the street.

Moving Josie behind him, and fixing the late-comers with an unwavering stare, Patrick strode towards them. Every other man in the street did the same.

Chapter Twelve

Ma stopped at the end of Walburgh Street and six pairs of studded boots ground on the cobble stones behind her. As she recovered her breath Ma glanced up the street.

The wedding party was now in full swing, with children dashing back and forth cramming handfuls of cake in their mouths as they dodged through the adults' legs. The tinny strains of some diddly-diddly tune screeched out while men and women cavorted about in the centre of the road like fleas on a dog's back. Men in their cheap suits, pints of ale in hand, stood chatting while the old women sipped cherry brandy and watched the youngsters dancing.

These men, laughing and joking with each other, were the same men who'd refused to do Ma Tugman's bidding. She watched them enjoying themselves, anger simmering within her, and then she saw Patrick. Her anger flamed into hatred.

She'd have liked to have one of her boys take him out and gut him but he could handle himself, could Patrick Nolan. Even her hardest men were wary of challenging him because there was a fair chance it would be them washed up on the tide with a knife in the ribs, not him.

Even if her lads did get the drop on Nolan, if his corpse was found floating in the Thames she'd have a war on her hands, with every last Paddy down to the Boatman like hounds from hell. Those mealy-mouthed shopkeepers and tradesmen who paid her to keep glass in their windows and their stock from the flames would start whispering to the police and very soon she'd find the filthy nabbers crawling over the cellars in Burr Street.

Ma's eyes narrowed as she watched him enjoying himself in the dance, and then she noticed his partner. A twisted smile spread across her lips.

'I see your little lady love's here,' she said to Harry.

'Oh, is that the famous Miss O'Casey,' Charlie drawled. 'Nice, very nice. She seems very taken with our friend Nolan.'

Ma studied Josie as she dipped and swirled around Patrick.

'Jumped up madam,' she said with a harsh laugh. 'She wouldn't give our Harry a second look and yet she's making eyes at fecking Nolan like one of China Rose's girls after a trick.'

'I wouldn't mind a chance at her myself,' Charlie said, turning to the men behind and grabbing his crotch.

'Now, Charlie, I don't want no trouble,' she said mildly.

Charlie gave her an innocent look. 'I ain't out for trouble, Ma.' The boyish expression changed to a leer. 'But I can't answer for them, can I?'

Ma's eyes settled on Patrick again. He was trouble!

Although she'd long finished with the jiggy-

jiggy she could see that he had that rough appeal women craved. Even with his two half-dago brats, half the women in the neighbourhood were after getting his feet under their table. Her gaze moved to the woman with her arm hooked in his. It would seem that for all her expensive clothes and big house Josie O'Casey had the same need between her legs as any other woman.

A few people at the end of the street noticed the Tugman crew. The music stopped mid-chord and the women called their children back to them and slid back into their houses. The men put down their drinks and picked up bottles. Then Patrick Nolan turned and saw them.

Ma grabbed Harry's arm again. 'Come on then, boys, let's go and give our respects to the 'appy couple.'

She started forward but Patrick stepped in front of her.

'You and your bully boys are not welcome here,' he told her flatly.

'Ah, Patrick, Patrick,' she said in her soft poor-little-old-woman voice, and shook her head. 'Surely you don't mind me wishing your dear sister and her new husband well.'

Patrick's mouth curled into a mirthless smile. 'You? Wishing anyone well?'

Ma put an offended expression on her face as she noticed Miss O'Casey moving alongside Patrick.

'It's only proper. I don't want you Irish to say the Tugmans don't know what's right and what's not.' She stretched her neck and looked past

194

Patrick to where Brian had escaped Mattie's grip and was on his way to join the rest of the men.

'What do they want?' he bellowed as he came abreast of Patrick.

Patrick gave a dry laugh. 'Ma says she's come to wish you well.'

Brian snorted. 'What, with a pack of murderers at her back?' He jumped in front of Patrick and shoved Harry in the chest. 'Feck off, the lot of you!' he yelled. 'I'll not have you scum upset my Mattie.'

Harry pushed him back and Brian raised his fist, but Patrick caught him. The men behind Ma jostled forwards.

Holding hard to Brian, Patrick patted his shoulder. 'Don't give 'em the excuse, pal. They're not worth it.'

Brian stood glaring at Ma for a second then the tension left his broad shoulders. 'Aye, you're right, Pat.'

Patrick let him go and stood alongside the other men.

'See now, Nolan, that's why your Paddy gang here and us are always at odds,' she said, casting her gaze around. 'You're too bloody touchy.'

A smile spread across Patrick's face. 'There's no gang here,' he said, spreading his arms wide. 'We're just honest men enjoying the day.' The pleasant expression disappeared. 'So why don't you and your pack crawl back to that hovel of yours and leave us be.'

Ma assumed a forlorn expression and sighed. 'What is the world coming to?' she asked to no one in particular, then said to Patrick, 'would it

195

hurt you to let an old woman see the smiles of a new bride?'

'You're *not* coming into the street,' Patrick repeated.

The men of the wedding party surged forward and Ma's gang did the same. A couple of Patrick's men smashed the bottles in their hands and raised them while others pulled out knives.

'Get out of my way,' she snarled.

Patrick's mouth took on a hard line. He folded his arms.

Fury and humiliation gnawed at her. Harry had told her to bring more men to even the odds, but she thought that her reputation and the fact that there were women and children in the vicinity would be enough to make Patrick and the Irishmen stand down.

Her hand shot into her pocket and onto her late husband's old knife. She fingered it affectionately, running her thumb over the catch. With one swift movement she could draw it, spring the blade and jab out Nolan's implacable eyes, but as she clipped her nail under the catch, Charlie stepped forward.

He shoved Patrick aside and grabbed Josie's wrist. 'I'm not going anywhere until I've had a dance.'

Josie hadn't seen Charlie's hand reaching for her until it closed around her wrist. She struggled but he held her firm.

'Let me go!' Out of the corner of her eye she saw Patrick step closer.

Charlie grinned. 'Now then, little lady, you were happy enough dancing with Nolan here; I don't see why you can't kick up your heels with me.'

As he held her inches from his face, Josie looked at him. Charlie would probably be regarded as handsome by those who found sharp features attractive but the glint of cruelty in his eyes sent a shiver of fear down her spine. She knew both brothers would slice a man's throat without a second thought, but Charlie would glory in it.

He slipped his arm around her waist. 'Come on, fiddler, strike up a tune,' he called across as he tried to drag her into the centre of what had been the dance area. Patrick stepped in front of them.

'Take your hands off her,' he said, in a controlled tone.

'What's the harm?' Charlie laughed.

The muscles in Patrick's jaw stood out and he forced himself between them. Charlie let go abruptly and Josie stumbled forward. She grabbed hold of Patrick's arm to steady herself and felt the taut muscles through the fabric of his shirt.

Charlie glared at him for a second then in a lightning move he whipped out a blade and slashed it across at Patrick's face.

Josie screamed, but Patrick jerked back and caught Charlie's arm as it completed its arc. The blade hovered frighteningly near to Patrick's eye, then with a grunt he twisted Charlie's arm behind and up his back.

Charlie gasped and Patrick jerked his arm upwards again. The knife clattered onto the cobbles.

Josie's eyes darted around the street and she saw Annie and Mickey over by the fiddler. Before she could tell them to go inside they dashed across the cobbles and clung onto her skirt. She kissed Annie on the head and picked Mickey up. The boy buried his head on her shoulder. Josie stood defiantly by Patrick's side.

Patrick threw Charlie at his mother and he crashed in the dirt at her feet, his shiny top hat rolling haphazardly through a puddle. Then Patrick stepped between them and picked up the glinting blade.

Charlie scrambled to his feet. 'Fecking big man you are with your dirty boatmen behind you,' he yelled, snatching up his ruined hat, 'but you won't be so cocky when I catch you alone.' His eyes flickered over Josie and a brutal smile spread across his face. 'Or your woman.' He gave a hard laugh. 'I bet you're hoping this one stays at home instead of chasing anything in trousers up and down The Highway. I mean, with a wife that fecked and tooted most of the men this side of the river, a man couldn't be sure the brats she birthed were his.'

Patrick didn't move. Charlie gave him a long, mocking look. 'If I remember rightly, I had the old lady meself.'

Annie buried her head in Josie's skirts.

For a long moment there was utter silence, then Patrick smiled.

Slowly he strolled towards Ma and stopped just in front of her.

He threw Charlie's knife in the dirt at her feet. 'Leave the street. I won't be telling you again.'

Charlie and Harry started forward but Ma raised her hand and they stopped.

'I'll not forget this, Nolan,' she managed to force out between clenched teeth. Then, grabbing onto Harry's arm, she turned and shuffled away.

Charlie dusted off his hat, jammed it on his head and blew Josie a kiss before following his mother and the other thugs.

Patrick watched them go then he bellowed. 'Fiddler! The devil's on the run–' a roar went up '–so strike up a merry dance. This is my sister's wedding after all, and I want to see her off in style.'

The fiddler dragged his bow across the strings and the dancing started up again. Josie lowered Mickey to the ground and the boy stuck his thumb in his mouth. Sarah came over and held out her hand.

'Come with Gran and she'll cut you a giant slice of cake,' she said and the lad went with his grandmother across the street. With the music playing, the dancers took to the floor again.

Patrick hunkered down next to his daughter. 'There, Annie, love, it's all over.'

Annie turned her tearful eyes to her father and then, letting go of Josie's skirts she ran into the house. Josie dashed after her, closely followed by Patrick.

Patrick had only just managed to keep himself from plunging the knife deep into Charlie's chest. What he'd said about Rosa was old news and everyone close to him already knew the story –

everyone that is, except Josie, Annie and Mickey and it was his children he was most concerned with just at the moment. At four, Mickey was probably too young to understand what the bastard had actually said, but his Annie was the sharp one and he knew from her stricken face that she understood only too well.

He was just a step behind Josie as they reached the kitchen. Annie sat on his mother's old chair by the fire with her knees drawn up and her face hidden. Josie knelt down on the dusty floor beside her and gathered the little girl to her. A lump lodged in Patrick's throat as his daughter threw herself into Josie's arms and sobbed.

'Aroon, aroon,' Josie crooned.

He placed his hand on Annie's soft hair and then hugged her too, sliding his arm around Josie's shoulder as he did so.

He kissed Annie's hair and smelt Josie's lavender cologne. Annie turned her tear-stained face up to her father.

'Why ... why di ... did he say ... that about Mam?' she asked, a sob catching her voice.

'Because he was trying to make me fight him,' Patrick replied, stroking a damp curl away from his daughter's forehead.

Heedless of the dust from the floor on her silk skirt, Josie sat back on her heels and took hold of Annie's hand. She bent forward and kissed it. 'Charlie Tugman's a bad man, Annie. That's why he said all those hurtful things about you mother. He and his old mother and brother came here to spoil your Aunt Mattie's wedding day and your father wouldn't let them.' She kissed Annie's hands again and then held them firmly. 'I hope you're very proud of your pa because he is a very brave man.'

Annie glanced up at Patrick and gave a nod. Josie smiled at him over Annie's head and he saw something that could have been love in her eyes, but he dared not believe it.

The breath wouldn't leave his lungs as hope flared in him. What if Rosa were dead...

Josie drew her handkerchief out of her sleeve and wiped the tears from Annie's cheeks. 'That's better,' she said cheerfully.

Annie turned. 'Pa, I am your girl, aren't I?'

Patrick felt a pain so deep that for a moment his mind wouldn't form an answer.

Josie took hold of Annie's hands again and squeezed them. 'Listen, Annie. I remember your pa when he was a lad, and your Aunt Mattie too, and you and your brother are the image of them when they were your age. Your pa is your real pa, and no mistake.'

A solemn expression settled on Annie's face. She threw herself in her father's arms and Patrick crushed her to him. He looked at Josie and saw tears in her eyes.

He put Annie from him. 'Now, my girl,' he said. 'If you want to taste any of the sugar-iced cake I think you had better go and see your gran before Mickey eats it all.'

Annie scrambled down from the chair and, giving them a renewed smile, went back down the passageway and back to the party.

'It's hard enough that she and Mickey have had to grow up with no mother, without adding to their grief,' she said, 'but Charlie was speaking the truth about Rosa, wasn't he?'

Patrick opened his mouth to deny it but Josie's unwavering stare stopped him.

'Mattie told me I needed to understand the full story of you and Rosa,' she said. 'And now I want you to tell me.'

A weight lifted off his shoulders. He knew that he'd never stopped loving Josie and that he mustn't lie to her any more.

He sat on the table. 'After I waved you goodbye the last time in New York, my ship sailed down America's eastern seaboard, then onto the Cape. Four days out of Rio we were caught in a murderous storm, and although the old girl managed to stay afloat, when we limped into Montevideo she was so badly damaged that the crew was discharged. Although I was desperate to sail north and back to you, the only berth going was to Freetown in Sierra Leone, so I took it. When I got there I sent you a letter on a French ship bound for New York. Thankfully we headed north, and when I reached Le Havre I found a ship heading for New York and signed on. So almost a year late I sailed up the Hudson. As soon as I was paid off I headed for Brooklyn, only to find your house shut up. I asked around the neighbourhood and heard that the eldest daughter of Doctor Munroe got married and the whole family had moved to Boston.'

'But Patrick, how could you think that I'd married someone else?' Josie asked.

A sad smile spread across Patrick's lips. 'Truly, Josie, with you standing here with me now I must have been clean out of my head to believe such a thing, but each time I returned to New York I noticed how much more your family had prospered. You became the daughter of a wealthy doctor while I was still working my way up to ship's mate. When I heard you'd married, although it tore my heart to shreds, I thought, why wouldn't you choose a son of a well-to-do merchant rather than a bare-footed deck hand.'

Josie gave him a furious look. 'I thought you knew me better than that, Patrick Nolan.'

'I should have, I know,' he said, raking back his hair. 'But every time I waved you goodbye I was afraid that when I came back you would have found a man who could give you a proper home and support you in a way I wasn't able to. So when I heard about the big wedding at your house I thought that was what had happened.'

'Well, as I told you, it was my cousin Jenny who was wed at our house. Uncle Joe had sold his farm and they were living with us until the deeds for the land they bought in New Jersey came through. I wrote and told you that we were moving to Boston but obviously that letter went astray, too. Oh Patrick, if only you'd followed us to Boston, then you would have found me waiting for you.'

'I tell you Josie, not a day passes when I don't curse myself for not doing just that, but I've had punishment enough for being so stupid.'

Josie's expression softened. 'Rosa?'

He nodded. 'After I found your house locked up, I took the first ship signing crew and sailed the next day. It was a hard voyage, in the teeth of the winter storms, but I didn't care. I even went aloft sometimes hoping to be swept away. Having lost you to another man, the cold ocean seemed welcoming.

'We dropped anchor in Gibraltar and I hit the nearest tavern. That's where I met Rosa.' He smiled ruefully. 'She was serving at the bar and was very popular with the men and, as I found out later, they were popular with her, too. I was miserable, and one night when I'd finished one bottle more than was good for me I sought to blot out thoughts of you – in Rosa's arms.' He held Josie's gaze. 'I sailed off the next day to Istanbul, but when I returned eight weeks later she told me she was with child. I couldn't shirk my responsibilities so I married her.'

Josie gave him a warm, understanding smile. 'I would expect nothing less of you.'

'I thought to make her a proper husband and that's when I wrote and wished you well in your new life and told you that I'd also married. I didn't love Rosa, but she was my wife and so I just made the best of it. With a family in Gibraltar I couldn't sign on for the long passages anymore so I took work on the ships passing through the Straits and started to study for my captain exams. I had no idea that while I was away Rosa spent her time at the port drinking and cavorting.' He gave a hard laugh. 'What a fool I was. I thought her a faithful wife, yet all the while she was sleeping with any sailor who'd buy her a drink. I discovered later that she'd taken some of them back to the house, and our own bed, while the children slept in the other room.'

Josie's mouth dropped open. 'How did you find out?'

'One time our ship got blown back to port early and I arrived home to discover Mickey crying in his crib and Annie curled up beside him, filthy and hungry. I found Rosa in the tavern by the quayside. She'd been there for three days.'

'She left her children for three days?!' Josie crossed herself. 'Oh my God, what if the house had caught fire?'

Patrick stood up and paced to the window as blind fury at the memory burst over him again. He stared blankly out for a few moments then turned back.

'I never loved Rosa, though I tried to make it work but, God forgive me, from that day I hated her. We set sail for London the next day.' He raked his fingers though his hair. 'I should have left Rosa in Gib, but I thought if I kept a proper eye on her she'd start to behave as a mother should.'

Patrick ran his gaze over Josie and thought of the ribbon she'd bought for Annie's hair and how she'd darned Mickey's socks. 'I'm ashamed to tell you this, Josie, but Mattie had to cut the children's hair to get the lice and dirt out and it fair broke Mam's heart to see Annie and Mickey's thin bodies. When we got back, I took a house for us all two doors down from Ma's in Cinnamon Street, but inside of a month Rosa had discovered the Tower garrison. I didn't care by then and I let her go her own way. Annie and Mickey ate with Mam, and she did our washing too – Rosa was too busy drinking and fecking to be bothered.'

He was surprised at the bitterness in his voice, but why shouldn't he be bitter? Not at Rosa, but at himself for being such a gullible fool and throwing away any chance of happiness with Josie.

Josie stood up, her skirt brushing against him as she stopped next to him. He only had to reach out his arm to slide it around her waist.

Josie placed her hand lightly on the skin of his forearm.

'I know I should have told you the truth about Rosa before this, but I didn't want your pity. I've never stopped loving you, Josie.'

'I love you, Patrick.' She ran her hand up his arm.

Patrick slid his arm around her waist, pulled her to him and lowered his lips to hers. Sliding one hand up her back, he held her head while the other anchored her body against his.

But he wasn't free to give her either his love or his name. With some effort he dragged his mouth from hers.

'Josie,' he said, as she kissed his cheeks and chin. 'Josie, I love you. I've always loved you but–'

She stopped his words with her lips. 'Nothing matters now.'

She was right. Nothing mattered, not Rosa, not his family, or the years of unhappiness, because Josie was here and they had found each other again.

Lifting her off her feet he moved her back and pressed her between himself and the wall.

'I should never have let you go.'

He pressed another hard kiss on her open mouth as she ran her hands up the front of his shirt under his open waistcoat. Her fingers traced around the inside of his collar, and then stroked the skin of his neck. His hand slid down from her waist and pressed her into him, but after holding her tight and close for a few moments, desire throbbing through him, he untangled himself from her arms. 'We mustn't,' he said, hoarse with emotion. 'It's wrong. I'm a married man.'

Josie let go of him and they stood away from one another. 'I know,' she whispered, lowering her gaze.

'I wish to God that it were not so, but I am,' he said.

Josie nodded and continued to study the dirt floor beneath her feet, then she raised her eyes to his face and tears shimmered on her lower lids. She stepped towards him again.

'No, Josie,' he said, gripping on to the back of the chair until his knuckles cracked.

'But–'

'There are no buts, Josie, only the fact that it's wrong.' His gaze ran slowly over her face again, taking in every detail. 'I want us to be man and wife and, if I could, I would marry you to-morrow, but that's impossible. If I can't marry you, then for the sake of your reputation we can't see each other again.'

'Patrick, my heart won't survive losing you a second time–'

'I love you, too, and I always will, but we have to face the possibility that I may never be free.'

'There must be some way,' she implored.

Patrick tore his fingers through his hair. 'If there was I'd grab it with both hands but there isn't, is there?'

Josie nodded slowly and sadly. 'Without proper sanction of the church we would be condemned. My reputation would be destroyed, my parents would disown me and I would be regarded as little more than a whore,' she said, each word falling like a stone between them.

'And I couldn't live with myself if I had done that to you.'

He gathered her to him and kissed her again, allowing himself to relish the feel of her in his arms. Too soon she broke away.

'I should go,' she said, but she didn't move from his embrace.

He clasped her more closely. 'If God is good, then we *will* be together one day, my love.'

'I pray so,' she replied.

The door to the scullery opened and Josie turned. Sam was standing in the doorway, Sarah and Mattie at his shoulder and a terrified look on his young face.

'Miss Josie,' he said, 'You must come home straight away.'

Chapter Thirteen

Josie sat beside the bed on the candy-striped nursing chair and held her mother's cold hand. Her mind was completely numb.

Ellen lay with her eyes closed and her face as white as the pillowcase beneath her head. Her dark hair curled over her shoulders but her lips were so pale the edges merged with the waxy hue of her face.

Robert left Dr Pym and joined Josie at his wife's bedside. In the light that still shone through the tall windows, his complexion looked grey.

'What did he say?' Josie asked, as Robert sat on the chair at the other side of the bed.

'He's done all he can.' He glanced at the crib in the corner of the room. 'He couldn't save our son but he has staunched your mother's bleeding. She is very weak.'

'She will be all right, won't she?' Josie asked, stroking her mother's hand.

Her father gave her a bleak look. 'She's taken a few sips of water – only time will tell.'

Josie's vision blurred as jumbled images and memories flashed into her head. In her mind's eye she saw her mother laughing while she played with the children and remembered her sharp wit that always brought a smile to Robert's face. But Josie had other memories too, memories she didn't share with her brothers and sisters.

209

Memories of how her mother's hands, raw and bleeding after a day of scrubbing, would always be tender when she tucked Josie in bed at night.

Dr Pym shoved his instruments back into his case and snapped it shut. He held Robert's hand in his for a long moment, before leaving the room. Robert returned to the chair opposite Josie and carefully took his wife's hand. He pressed his lips to her fingers and closed his eyes tightly.

Mrs Munroe rustled in, her widow's weeds adding to the mournful atmosphere of the room.

'How is dear Ellen?' she asked, laying her hand on her son's shoulder.

'Still with us,' he croaked. 'But I don't know for how much longer.'

'Must we prepare ourselves, Robert?' Her hand gripped her son's shoulder. 'God's will shall be done.'

Robert's face took on a tortured expression, and then he pressed his lips to Ellen's fingers again.

Her eyes opened. 'Robert,' she mouthed.

'I'm here, my love.'

'I'm thirsty.'

Robert placed the spout of the invalid cup to her dry lips and she swallowed.

He gave her an encouraging smile. 'That's my girl. Take a little more.' Ellen did. 'We have to feed you up and get you better.'

Ellen lips moved. 'I want to say goodbye to the children–'

'Josie will fetch the children but you're not going anywhere. We're going to get you back on your feet, aren't we, Josie?'

Almost blinded by tears, Josie nodded.

A ghost of Ellen's fiery spirit passed across her face. 'Robert Munroe,' she whispered. 'After living with you for nigh on thirteen years, do you think I don't know when you're lying to me?'

'Ellen,' Robert forced out as he fought for control. 'My only love.'

She raised her hand and ran it down his cheek. 'Shhh. The children, please. While there is still time.'

Robert's lower lip trembled and tears filled his eyes. He nodded and pressed her hand to his cheek.

Ellen gave a ghost of a smile and then closed her eyes. Robert looked at Josie, who stumbled out of the room and made her way upstairs to the nursery.

She stopped outside and wiped her face with the heel of her hand and tidied her hair. It would be difficult enough for the children to see their mother on the brink of death without seeing their older sister buckle, too.

As she opened the door, four pairs of eyes fixed on her. Bobbie and Charlotte were sitting on the window seat together while George sat on the straight-backed chair by the window. Although, at six, Joe couldn't quite understand why everyone was so sad, the fact that his usually lively siblings were all subdued was enough for him to seek comfort in his thumb and ragged blanket. Only baby Jack, sleeping soundly in his painted cot, was unaffected by the mood in the house.

Josie held out her arms to her sisters and they jumped down and dashed over to her. Josie

211

hugged them and kissed the top of their heads in turn.

Bobbie looked up. 'Is Mama–'

'Mama is very ill,' Josie cut in. 'Pa wants you to come.'

Bobbie gave a nod and took hold of Lottie's hand. Josie went over to the boys.

Nurse looked at her with wide eyes and stifled a sob into her handkerchief.

'I'll take George and Joe if you carry Jack,' Josie told her.

The young woman gently scooped up the dozing baby while Josie picked up Joe and took George's hand. 'Now I want you to be very brave when we go in to Ma and Pa's bedroom.'

As they entered the chamber, Josie's eyes went straight to her mother. Robert hadn't moved, but whereas when she'd left the room the bright light of day still streamed in through the tall window, now the heavy curtains were drawn. Only the sputtering of oil lamps and Ellen's laboured breathing broke the silence.

Robert looked up from his vigil and stood. He took Jack from Nurse, who curtsied and left the room. Robert kissed his sleepy son on the forehead.

'Come and kiss your mother,' he said.

Silently the children filed forward and kissed Ellen, then they turned expectantly to their father, who hugged each of them.

Josie took her place on the other side of the bed. Mrs Munroe came and stood beside her. 'You can draw comfort, Miss O'Casey, that your mother is passing peacefully into her eternal reward,' she said, in her best churchy voice.

Josie gave the old woman a withering look. Then, with a determined look on her face she bent and kissed her mother on the forehead. She turned towards the door.

'Surely you're not leaving at such a time,' Mrs Munroe asked. Josie cast her gaze over her mother, hovering between life and death, her stepfather manfully trying to hold himself together while comforting his children.

Her mouth set into a firm line. 'Me mam's not dead yet and, as Pa said, we have to build up her strength. So I'm going to prepare a coddled egg and buttermilk for her supper.'

Mrs Munroe surveyed the parlour as she waited for Robert to bring Ellen down. God in his infinite wisdom had spared Ellen and Mrs Munroe told herself she was pleased he'd done so. While she would never be able to think of her son's wife as a daughter, seeing how heartbroken the dear children were, she was relieved that her darlings had not had to lose their mother at such a tender age.

Ignoring the crick in her back, she let her eyes rest on the children. Charlotte kicked her legs under the sofa but for once Mrs Munroe didn't try to catch her eye to stop her. Bobbie, sitting at the other end, twirled her hair although she'd been told not to. Her gaze moved to dear George, so much the little man. She had heard him running down the stairs but had resisted the urge to scold him. Just for today she would not mark their transgressions. The door opened and Josie entered the room carrying Jack. Mrs Munroe's brows furrowed.

'Mam will be down any moment now,' Josie said, smiling broadly at her brothers and sisters.

Mam! What a way to address your mother, Mrs Monroe thought, not for the first time. Thankfully the other children hadn't picked up the habit, but even so...

Charlotte clapped her hands and Joseph, sitting on Nurse's lap, copied her. Mrs Munroe's forehead smoothed. It was a pity that the stillborn child had been another boy but Robert still had three fine sons and Ellen not yet too old to do her duty again.

Josie dashed across the floor and sat between Charlotte and Bobbie. She turned the baby to face her and held him while he practised standing on wobbly legs.

'There you go girls, isn't Jack a fair one for the jig,' Josie said, putting on the broadest of Irish accents.

The girls either side of her giggled and Mrs Munroe suppressed a shudder.

'He's dancing like the rest of us because Mam's back to her old self again,' Josie said, pulling a funny face at Jack and setting him chuckling.

Mrs Munroe formed her face into an indulgent expression. 'No one is more pleased than I that your mother is recovering, but prayers of thanks might be more appropriate, don't you think, Miss O'Casey?'

Josie's gaze left the child on her lap and she looked across at her. 'Well now, you have more Bible learning than me, so I'm sure you'll be the

214

one to tell us,' she said, still in the unrestrained Irish accent. 'But didn't King David, ancestor of the Lord himself, dance with joy?'

Mrs Munroe's irritation with Josie rose from its usual place and sat just under the surface of her chest.

A small smile crossed Josie's face and she turned her attention back to Jack, bouncing on her knee. 'I should think the saints in heaven will be dancing too with Mam on the road to full recovery,' she said.

Robina and Charlotte nodded.

Mrs Munroe folded her hands carefully over each other and put a sweet smile on her face. 'Well, now that dear Ellen is recovered, perhaps we won't see you each morning at the breakfast table with red-rimmed eyes.'

A look of utter misery shot across Josie's face so swiftly that Mrs Munroe only just caught it. So, she thought, all that weeping she'd heard behind Josie O'Casey's door each night was about more than her mother dying.

Lottie bounced off the sofa and jumped up and down on the spot. 'I think I can hear them!'

The door opened and Ellen appeared with Robert holding her supportively around the waist.

Joe dashed forward but Josie stood up and caught her brother. 'Let Mam get settled,' she said, as Robert guided Ellen to the chaise-longue by the window, where warm sunlight streamed in.

Ellen's skin was still unnaturally pale, but brightness had returned to her eyes. Carefully lifting her

215

feet, Robert settled her and then covered her with a blanket. He kissed Ellen on the forehead, his lips lingering for a moment before he turned to the children.

'Now, I'm sure you all want to give Mama a kiss,' he said, as all the children surged forward, 'but I don't want you to tire her so no jumping on her lap.' He looked pointedly at Lottie.

The girls clambered onto the seat beside Ellen's legs and hugged her in turn while George, after a few moments of manly stiff upper lip, threw his arms around his mother's neck.

The children pressed around Ellen and she held them close, closing her eyes as she hugged them to her.

Josie held back as her sisters and brothers swarmed over their mother. Nurse brought Jack forward and Ellen kissed him before he and Joe were taken back up to the nursery.

Daisy brought in the tea tray and set it on the low table in the middle of the room.

'Now, children, let your Mama have a bit of space. Mrs Woodall has made one of her special cherry cakes and you can all have a slice if you sit still while you have your tea,' Robert said. 'If you would, Mother, please?'

Mrs Munroe inclined her head and started to pour the tea. 'Perhaps, now the children are all here, it would be the right moment to tell them of your planned trip, Robert,' she said, smiling blandly at them all.

Josie's brows pulled together. 'Trip?'

Mrs Munroe smiled serenely across at Josie. 'Yes. My son feels that for your mother to recover

216

properly she'll need the tranquillity and fresh air,' her smile widened, 'of Scotland.'

Josie folded her mother's smalls neatly and placed them in the leather travelling trunk, aware of her mother's gaze on her. Ellen sat by the window, her feet up on a footstool and a large paisley shawl over her legs. Never plump, she was now gaunt, and her clothes hung loosely on her. The waxy look of her skin had gone but it was still so pale it appeared almost translucent. Josie's gaze moved onto Ellen's thin hands with the bones clearly visible under the covering of skin and then back to her mother's eyes, sunken deep in their sockets.

'I don't know what I would have done without you in these past weeks, my love,' Ellen said.

Josie forced a smile. A worried expression crossed Ellen's face and Josie guessed she saw the dark shadows under her own eyes. She picked up a silk chemise and spread it on the bed.

Each day as sleep gave way to conscious thought, Josie enjoyed a brief moment of joy in her dreams of being married to Patrick. For a few moments her heart wasn't torn apart and a picture of a happy life with Patrick at her side and the family they would have enfolded her until the day intruded all too swiftly. Then she would open her eyes and the pain would return, forcing her to put on her happy mask and face another day without him, and without the prospect of a future with him.

After all, people recovered from broken hearts and fell in love again. That's what she told herself every time some small, unexpected thing – a boy in the street whistling a tune, the throaty sound of a man's laughter – reminded her of Patrick Nolan.

'You do understand why Robert has asked his mother to take charge of the household while we are away?' Ellen asked.

'Of course,' Josie replied not looking up.

Her eyes rested on her mother's red gown, neatly folded in the well of the trunk. It called to mind the red necktie Patrick wore at Mattie's wedding and the ache that enclosed her heart tightened. But what could she do? She couldn't marry him and there was no respectable way they could ever be together. Maybe, in their old life, when they'd run through the streets as bare-footed youngsters – but not now. The only way for them was to part and for her to try to live with half her soul missing. Again.

'Dr Pym says I need fresh air and rest and your father has taken a special leave of absence from his post,' Ellen continued. 'It's been very hard on him these last few weeks and although *dear* Mother is more irritating than grit in your eye, for his sake I'm glad she's been here.' Josie looked across at her mother and Ellen gave her a wan smile. 'In truth, I am as weak as a kitten, but I couldn't go unless I knew that you were here with Bobbie, Lottie and the others.'

Suddenly, loneliness swept over Josie and tears started to press at the back of her eyes. She bit her lower lip and just about managed to hold them back. She unhooked Ellen's dark green taffeta gown from the peg and laid it on the bed.

218

'How long will you be gone?' she asked, trying not to let the dreadful prospect of being left in the house with Mrs Munroe betray itself in her voice.

'Just the summer, until September,' Ellen replied.

Three months!

'I know it will be difficult for you, Josie,' Ellen said.

Difficult! Nigh on impossible was more the truth. It was awful enough to have Mrs Munroe around with Mam and Pa in the house. It would be sheer hell with them gone.

'I wouldn't go, Josie, but Robert's been through so much, what with losing the baby and seeing me so ill.'

Josie left the packing to sit on the footstool at Ellen's feet. 'Of course you have to go, Mam. Not just for Pa's sake but for your own.' She took her mother's hands. 'The Highland air will soon put the apples back in your cheeks and you'll be chasing George and Joe around the place again in no time.' A serious expression spread across Josie's face. 'We nearly lost you, Mam, and if you have to stay in Scotland for a whole year before you're back to being my mam again, then so be it.'

Ellen moved a stray tendril of hair away from Josie's brow. 'So it's not that Robert's mother is to run the house that's caused your long face, then?'

Josie gave her a quirky smile. 'I don't relish the prospect but I'm sure I'll survive.'

'What *is* the matter, Josie?' Ellen asked.

Looking at her mother's drawn face, Josie wondered whether she should tell her. She so wanted to. They had shared so much hardship before Robert that they had a bond which would never be broken but, as she took in her mother's pinched face, she knew that she couldn't worry her now.

What could she say, anyway? That she was in love with Patrick but his wife was still alive? Could she also tell her mother, just having risen from her sick bed, that not only was she in love with a married man but in her weakest moment, when her need of Patrick almost overwhelmed her, she'd contemplated becoming his wife without the benefit of the Church?

No. She could not. Not just yet.

Ignoring her aching heart, Josie put on her brightest smile. 'I'll miss you, that's all.'

'Are you sure?' Ellen's sharp eyes examined Josie's face carefully. 'It's not something about Patrick?'

Josie gave a hollow laugh. 'No. I doubt I'll see much of him now that Mattie's married.'

'I'm sure it's for the best,' Ellen continued in a cheerful tone. 'In time you will meet someone else – someone you already know perhaps.' She winked at Josie. 'I thought I might invite Mr Arnold to tea before Robert and I leave.'

Josie ignored the chasm of unhappiness before her and forced a smile. 'That would be nice.'

A satisfied smile spread across her mother's face. She leant forward and patted Josie's hand. 'William Arnold might not have grand curly hair but he has prospects, and his godfather *is* Sir Edgar Wilmore.'

Chapter Fourteen

Josie bit the end of the quill and re-read the first paragraph of her letter.

Dear Mam,
I hope that this letter finds you in improved health and enjoying the sights of Edinburgh. We are all going on fine here although we miss you and Pa greatly. The weather in London is fair although there was a thunder storm last week.

She stopped as sorrow welled up from deep inside. Since her mother and stepfather had departed for Scotland, Josie had found that being in the house with Mrs Munroe wasn't as bad as she'd imagined it might be. It was ten times worse.

The children have had some adjustment to make as Mrs Munroe isn't able to keep up with the younger ones, so she has introduced a few quiet activities to their daily regime.

A half smile formed itself on Josie lips. That was a windy road way of saying that all the fun and laugher and afternoons playing with toys had been replaced by hours of Bible readings and prayers.

She also believes the childrens' diet to be too rich and has asked Mrs Woodall to modify some of her dishes.

Despite her despondency, a quirky smile moved her lips. Unfortunately, she couldn't put Mrs Woodall's lively comments on the matter down in the letter.

The children miss you but I have explained that you will soon be back. Joe has had a couple of nights when he woke shouting but I snuggled him in with me and now he has returned to the nursery without further incidents.

That was true, but she didn't feel that she could add that he had started wetting his bed again or that he clung to her hand when Mrs Munroe undertook her daily nursery inspection.

Mrs Munroe has expressed a desire to have the parlour for her own use in the afternoons so I have moved the nursing chair from your room into mine and now Lottie and Bobbie sew with me in here each afternoon.

And give them a respite from Mrs Munroe's ever critical eye, she thought but didn't write.

George had a fever last week but is now fully recovered.

Josie stopped and chewed the tip of the pen again. Her mother should be resting and recovering and, although Josie didn't want to upset her in any way, she felt she should know the truth about the incident.

I know that Pa doesn't hold with such things, but before I could explain his views on old remedies Mrs Munroe had already secured a blister plaster on George's stomach to draw out the humours. I am sorry to tell you that before nurse informed me of what was happening the vitriol and paraffin had been on George's skin for a half an hour. Thankfully, after applying camomile lotion the redness has completely disappeared. He is quite recovered and back to riding his toy horse around the garden.

Josie's brows pulled together. It looked as if she was telling tales but poor George had practically screamed the house down as the caustic substances scalded his skin. She held the pen aloft as she considered what to write next. It would sound like carping again but there was no other way of putting it.

I am afraid that after I confronted Mrs Munroe on the matter and about her readiness to reach for the rod, our relationship has cooled considerably.

That was to say they barely spoke and if one entered a room the other left; however, Josie felt she'd said enough. Besides, it wasn't to tell tales on Mrs Munroe that she was writing to her mother. She filled the nib with ink again.

I have visited Sophie Cooper twice last week to undertake our regular pastoral visits and Mr Arnold called for tea. He is a very pleasant young man and I know it is your hope that I would look more favourably on him. I have tried but I cannot. It isn't his fault, Mam, but he isn't Patrick.

During the day, with her time fully occupied counterbalancing Mrs Munroe's puritanical rule, Josie had almost convinced herself that she could wait for Patrick to be free, but the nights were a different matter. She jabbed the pen in the inkwell again.

Now, Ma, I know I should have told you this before you went but I hope you will forgive me that I did not and for what I am about to write...

Bobbie and Lottie trod quietly past the half-open door of their grandmother's bedroom and across the first floor landing. Holding her breath, Bobbie nodded at her sister and Lottie nodded back. Bobbie craned her neck forward and peeked in the room. Her grandmama was sitting on the bed with her eyes closed and her Bible open on her lap. Bobbie knew that she should love her grandmother, but since she'd waved her parents goodbye they had all suffered – it was the only word she could use for it – under her grandmother's miserable regime.

Pressing her back to the wall, Bobbie took hold of her sister's hand and they slid along the corridor towards Josie's bedroom. Bobbie knocked quietly and when Josie called 'enter' she and Lottie went through.

Josie was sitting at her small bureau scratching

away at a sheet of her writing paper. She looked up from her task as they entered, and gave them a smile. 'Bobbie, I thought you were with your grandmother. I heard Daisy say she was looking for you a while back.'

'Well, she didn't find us,' Lottie said, kicking off her shoes and jumping on Josie's bed. She propped herself against the wooden headboard and crossed her arms across her white pinafore. 'I know Papa wants us to love her but I don't,' Lottie announced. 'She must be at least a hundred and she had a sort of dark smell about her.'

Bobbie slipped her pumps off, too, and joined her sister on the bed while Josie resumed her letter.

'Josie, you're frowning again,' Bobbie said.

'Am I?'

'Is it because your friend Mattie is married and you're not?' Lottie asked before Bobbie could nudge her.

Josie put a bright smile on her face. 'Good heavens! What ever gave you that idea?'

'Because Grandmama says you should have been married a long time ago,' Lottie said, pulling her face into a creditable resemblance of Mrs Munroe's long features.

'Does she?'

Lottie nodded. 'And she told us that she thinks it would have been better if you'd married someone in America and settled there.'

Bobbie elbowed her sister in the ribs. 'Grandmama thinks all sorts of odd things, Lottie. Like that girls should not eat meat as it inflames their spirits,' Bobbie said, thinking how Mrs Woodall's

225

tasty plates of steak and onions had been replaced by thin broths with grease floating on the surface.

She had overheard Daisy whisper to Nurse that there was more goodness in the washing up water and Bobbie was inclined to agree. It was only after Josie had confronted Mrs Munroe on their behalf that they still had jam on the table in the morning.

Lottie continued undaunted. 'But *I* said if you just wanted to be married you could marry Mr Arnold.'

Josie said nothing and turned back to her letter.

'Are you writing to Mama and Papa?' Bobbie asked, before Lottie could speak again.

'Yes I am. I know you've already sent your letters to them this week, but I'll give them your love again if you like.'

'Yes, please,' said Bobbie. 'Will you be telling them about George and the plaster?' she asked in as neutral a voice as she could.

Josie gave her a little smile. 'I have put in a couple of lines,' she admitted.

Thank goodness, thought Bobbie, wondering how long it would take her sister's letter to reach Edinburgh.

Josie scratched out a few more lines and Lottie picked up Josie's old doll that lived propped up on the headboard.

Waisy was practically colourless now after years of washing and was almost the last reminder of Mama's and her sister Josie's old life.

Bobbie's eyebrows drew together. For some odd reason it was because of the terrible life

Mama and Josie had lived before they met Papa that Grandmama disliked Josie so much. Bobbie couldn't understand it. Surely if Grandmama was a Christian, she should rejoice that Josie was no longer poor.

'Josie,' Lottie said, rocking her sister's old rag doll in her arms. Josie looked up. '*Are* you going to marry Mr Arnold?'

Josie's eyes looked suddenly very bright. 'I don't think so.'

Bobbie drew in a deep breath. 'Are you going to marry Patrick?'

Josie struggled to keep the bright smile in place. 'Of course not, we are just friends, that's all – friends.'

Bobbie felt, rather than heard, the sob in her sister's voice.

Ever since the wedding, Josie had been her lovely sister on the outside – all smiles and kindnesses – but Bobbie knew that inside Josie was sad. She knew that Patrick was the reason Josie appeared at breakfast each morning with red-rimmed eyes. A wave of compassion welled up in her.

'Oh, Josie.'

Josie bit her bottom lip as her eyes filled with tears. Bobbie slid off the bed and Lottie did the same. Both of them dashed over to their sister and hugged her tightly.

'I'm sorry,' Bobbie said as she felt the sting of tears in her own eyes. 'I shouldn't have mentioned Patrick.' That brought another huge sob from her sister. Bobbie patted her shoulders, feeling very grown up.

Josie lifted her tear-stained face and wiped her wet eyes with her fingers. 'I'm just being silly.' She kissed Bobbie and Lottie. 'Now I have to get on with this letter. Mam and Pa are only staying with your aunt Hermione for another week and then they catch the coach north, and who knows how long it will take for the letter to reach them. I must finish soon so that Sam can take it to the post office.'

Lottie skipped back and took Waisy to the window where she started a game with her. Bobbie sat back on the bed and studied her sister. Why did Josie say that Patrick was just her friend when it was obvious that she loved him? And why couldn't she marry him?

Anger rose up in Bobbie. It was Grandmama again, she was sure. Grandmama disliked Patrick because he captained a boat on the river and didn't have any money. But if Josie loved him and he could make her happy then surely God wouldn't be angry, as Grandmama always said he was. Besides, Papa, who knew almost everything, said that a man should be judged by his actions, not his money.

Josie signed her name with a flourish and smiled at Bobbie. 'That's done then,' she said, flipping the envelope over and sealing it.

Lottie propped Waisy back on Josie's pillow and Bobbie jumped off the bed. 'We had better go down to the parlour; Grandmama will be waiting for us.' She held out her hand. 'I'll put your letter on the table by the front door.'

Mrs Munroe closed the Bible and looked at the

three children ranged on the sofa in front of her. Robina, Charlotte and George regarded her respectfully. Tenderness rose up in her as she contemplated her precious angels, and again she thanked God fervently for bringing them back to her.

Although she hadn't realised it when she'd arrived, it was clearly God's will that she should be here to care for her grandchildren while their mother was so ill. Their futures were precarious to say the least. It was true that Robert now had the ear of the Prime Minister no less, but the scandal of his marriage to Ellen could be so easily revived and where would these beloved darlings be then?

Her heart missed a beat and she drew in a deep breath to steady it. *Trust Him,* she commanded her terrified mind, and the pall of dread surrounding her faded.

Her timely visit, the stillborn child, Ellen's illness and Robert's decision to take his wife away to regain her strength were all part of His plan to bring these treasured children under her protection.

Although her joints ached and she couldn't remember small details as she used to, Mrs Munroe wasn't daunted by her years. Moses himself was over eighty when he led his people to the Promised Land, and she still had a few years on him. Although the children could be noisy, they weren't quite as quarrelsome as the tribes of Israel. However, those doing the Lord's work could always expect opposition and Josie O'-Casey was certainly that. She cast her gaze over her pretty granddaughters sitting either side of their brother.

Despite being late, Robina had read the passage faultlessly. George's concentration hadn't wandered and even Charlotte hadn't fidgeted too much.

She clasped her hands together on her lap. 'Now, children, what do we learn from this story?'

'That if you fall out of a window and are killed the dogs will eat everything but your feet hands and skull,' George said, raising his hands like claws and looking at his sisters.

'Before that, if you please, George,' Mrs Munroe said, sharply.

'If the King sends his troops after you you had better run like Elijah did,' George replied, smiling at her.

The corners of Mrs Munroe's lips lifted. George had such a fine instinct for all things military, she thought – just like her dear brother.

She studied each child in turn. 'But it wasn't the King who ordered the death of Elijah, was it? No,' she said answering her own question. 'It was his wicked queen, Jezebel.'

The children's eyes opened wider and Mrs Munroe continued. 'It was her wicked nature that brought about the ruin of her husband and his kingdom,' she said, picturing the godless queen of Israel with long auburn hair and screaming the order to kill the Lord's prophets in a faint Irish accent.

She pointed at the children. 'Because of her unrestrained passions and her sin of worshipping a heathen god, Jezebel was cast down from God's grace and tainted her whole family. It is a lesson for us all,' she concluded in the same solemn tone in which her husband had used to end his sermons.

Robina glanced down at the Bible on her lap. 'The passage doesn't mention her family.'

Mrs Munroe raised her hands and held them, palms together, in front of her. 'Let us pray,' she said, ignoring Bobbie's comment.

George and Charlotte immediately followed her example and squeezed their eyes tight shut, but Robina gave her a perplexed look. Grandmother and granddaughter stared at each other for a moment, then the young girl put her hands together and closed her eyes.

Robert was right. Robina did have a quick mind but she would have to learn that if a young woman appeared too clever she was likely to find herself a spinster long after her less intelligent friends had found husbands.

Mrs Munroe lowered her eyelids, but kept them open a crack to ensure the children remained respectful throughout the intercessions. Then, when all and everyone had been prayed for, she dismissed the children to the nursery for their afternoon refreshments, letting them kiss her cheek dutifully before they departed.

She stood up and stretched, then pulled on the bell to summon tea. Knowing Josie would take her tray in her room meant that Mrs Munroe had an hour or so to herself before overseeing the children's evening meal. She had designated it as her time of quiet reflection but more often than not, after the tea tray was removed, she nodded off to sleep. She glanced at the door and frowned. Where, she wondered as she stifled a yawn, was Daisy.

She stood up and opened the door. She peered down the hall towards the kitchen and then back. Her gaze rested on an envelope lying in the silver salver in the middle of the mahogany hall table. She went over, picked it up and recognised Josie's handwriting. She glared at the rectangular envelope addressed to her daughter's house in George Street, Edinburgh.

Since Robert and Ellen had left, Josie and the other children had written regularly to their parents and received letters back, but the weekly letters had been sent on their way four days ago. Why was the girl bothering them again? Mrs Munroe's heart thundered unevenly in her chest.

The blister plaster!

The fluttering increased as she imagined what her son would say. When she suggested slitting Jack's gums to relieve teething ache he had told her in no uncertain terms what he thought of such remedies. He would be furious if he knew what she'd done to George.

Selfish girl, to worry her mother so, she thought. *George had recovered, so the whole incident was of no consequence.*

Picking up the letter she turned it over and slipped her nail under the edge. It lifted a little. She heard a sound behind her and turned to find Robina at the bottom of the stairs.

'Ro ... Robina, I thought you'd gone up to the nursery,' she said.

'I left my handkerchief on the chair,' Robina told her as her gaze rested on the letter.

The area between Mrs Munroe's shoulder blades prickled under her granddaughter's frank gaze. She raised the letter.

'I thought I would write and tell your Papa just how well you are all getting on,' she said, replacing the letter.

Robina walked into the parlour and then returned with her handkerchief in her hand. She studied her grandmother for a long moment before starting back upstairs.

'Tell Nurse I'll be up at the usual time,' Mrs Munroe called after her granddaughter as she turned at the top of the banisters.

Robina looked down. 'Yes, Grandmama,' she said, and then disappeared.

Mrs Munroe stood with her hands in front of her until she was sure Robina wasn't coming back down, and then she picked up Josie's letter and went back to the parlour.

Sitting on the sofa she turned the envelope over and studied it, then in a swift movement she slid her finger under the seal to snap it open. Ripping out the letter she ran her eyes over the pages and her lips tightened.

Lies, all lies! she thought as she read Josie's words to her mother. Wicked shameless girl. Bleating on about such trivia when poor Ellen was still recovering, even implying that the children weren't happy being cared for by their own grandmother. What nonsense!

Her heart thumped uncomfortably in her chest again. Perhaps she was a little too quick to call for the switch, but she couldn't afford to spare the rod because she loved them so. An undisciplined child grew into an undisciplined adult. In her considered opinion the moral crisis of idleness and dishonesty that was so manifest in society was the direct result of parents who ignored that particular scriptural command.

It was abundantly clear that out of spite and malice Josie O'Casey would do anything and tell any lie to twist the children's affections away from their grandmother.

She continued to the bottom of the page, then her hands clenched the paper, creasing it where her fingers curled as the second part of the letter sprang off the page.

Now, Mam, I know I should have told you this before you went but I hope you will forgive me that I did not and for what I am about to write.

She read on for a moment then she let the letter fall on her lap and clutched her hand to her chest. Under her fingers her heart was beating erratically.

Naturally, it gave her no satisfaction to say so, but hadn't she known from the moment she clapped eyes on her that if ever there was a young girl on the road to destruction it was Josie O'Casey. The way she chased after that rough fellow Patrick Nolan. Pretending she was helping his sister with her dress while it was as clear as the nose on your face that she burned for him. The lust in her eyes when she spoke his name was a disgrace to behold.

Closing her eyes she took a deep breath. She

felt her pulse steady and picked up the letter again. What a viper her son had nurtured in his bosom, she thought as she read Josie's confession of love and desire for Patrick Nolan, a married man. Her heart galloped again.

I fear that although it is wrong and would cause my ruin, I have such tender and enduring feelings for Patrick that I can deny them no longer.

Mrs Munroe could not believe her eyes. How could a young woman think such a thing let alone write it down?

But blood will out, she thought. Ellen had led Robert into indiscretion and she'd been in the family way when she married her first husband. Josie was an appalling example to the two elder girls. Dear Robina and Charlotte were on the brink of the most delicate time of their lives and didn't need their natures aroused.

An image of her grandchildren materialised in Mrs Munroe's mind and her heart started to thump again.

What if Josie threw all discretion aside and actually went to live with this low fellow? Even if they tried to hide the matter it would come out and Robert's name would be sullied again. If the Prime Minister knew that Robert's stepdaughter had thrown aside all moral reason and had attached herself to a married man, her son might be forced to resign his post.

An aching chasm opened up in front of Mrs Munroe as she thought of the long years of Robert's self-imposed exile in America. If he were forced to go again she would be dead before he returned. How would she live without seeing his dear angels grow up?

She stood up, and without any hesitation crossed to the fireplace and tossed Josie's letter into the grate. The vellum paper scorched and the flames caught hold.

She had warned Robert that Josie O'Casey's wild nature would lead to the family's ruin and he hadn't heeded her advice. It was clear that she had been sent by Divine Providence to protect her dear grandchildren and she would do whatever she had to do to save them from destruction.

Chapter Fifteen

Ma Tugman sat in her usual corner in the Boatmen. It was a quiet night with only a couple of locals propping up the bar and staring into the bottom of their tankards. Although she sat with a brandy in her hand and a genial expression on her face, Snapper at least sensed Ma's mood and kept out of range of her boot, his ears low.

The door creaked open and another working man in corduroy trousers entered and skulked down to the far end of the bar. St Paul's church clock chimed ten and Ma, tight-lipped, tapped her toe on the floor impatiently.

Jackson, God rot the man, was squeezing her hard. There had always been the law, of course.

When she was a girl it had been the court's officers whom the other barefooted children of the riverside would pelt with rubbish as their craft skimmed down-river. Back then the only thing they had been interested in was the ships and the warehouses.

The newly founded Peelers, who took over Wapping Office just before her Harry died, had a new interest: the local heavy horsemen who lifted cargos from the ships at anchor and the light horsemen who swifted away dockside cargo. Jackson, an inspector then, had been one of the new nabbers and had sent old Danny Donovan to the gallows.

Of course the old time Johnnies weren't all bad. Men like her husband and Danny Donovan often had a nice little arrangement with the local nabs, and often the two sides of the law worked hand-in-hand, so to speak. A word here and a few coins there made the world go round – at least in Wapping and Shadwell. Now bloody Jackson was squeezing that as well and, although she would have cut her own and anyone else's tongue out for saying it, things weren't looking too rosy. She, however, was going to remedy that.

The door opened again and Harry slipped in. Ma jerked her head in the direction of her back parlour and he nodded. Heaving herself out of her chair, Ma swallowed the last of her drink and waddled towards the parlour door. Snapper struggled to his feet. The poor old bugger was getting old, too, she thought as the dog tottered, trying to get his back legs to support him.

'You stay put,' she told the dog. 'And keep your

eyes on her,' she muttered, indicating Charlie's bird standing behind the bar.

The dog settled back down with a huff as she pushed open the door and stepped through to her parlour. Harry and Charlie were standing by a disgruntled Sergeant Plant while two of their men, dressed in the gang uniform of check trousers, shapeless dark jackets and round-topped billycock hats, held his arms. A broad smile spread crossed Ma's face.

'Sergeant Plant, what a pleasure,' she said, as the police officer glared at her.

She hobbled over to the chair by the fire and flopped down. At her elbow on a chipped plate were the half-eaten remains of a chop. She waved away the bluebottle hovering above it and picked it up.

'Let him go,' she barked, sinking her teeth into the meat.

Harry's men released the officer immediately.

'It a serious offence to assault a police officer, I'll have you know,' Plant said, brushing his sleeves with exaggerated movements.

'And to take backhanders,' she replied, waving the chop bone at him. 'I won't tell if you don't.'

Alarm shot across the sergeant's face for a second before a conciliatory expression replaced it. 'Enough said, but I still don't see why you had to bring me here; a quiet word would have been enough. If anyone had seen me being dragged into the back of the Boatman–'

'They'd know to look away,' Ma cut in, licking the juice from the side of her hand. 'Now see 'ere. We ain't slipping you a couple of guineas each week because we like you, Plant. We're paying you so that we can get our gear through.' She wiped her nose on her sleeve. 'And we ain't, because Jackson is jumping all over us before we can get our feet wet.'

A tick started in Plant's left eye. 'He's found out the boats you use and he's watching for them.'

'We need to find other boats, Ma,' Harry said, his lower lip hanging loose and with his usual eager-to-please expression on his face.

Ma shot him a venomous look. 'Don't you think I knows that?' She threw the bone on the floor. 'I'd have plenty of boats if it wasn't for that bastard Patrick-fecking-Nolan.'

It had been the talk of the dockside streets for weeks after the Maguire wedding, and she'd seen the sly looks sent her way when people thought she didn't notice. By Christ, she was going to make him pay for that, and soon. Her eyes narrowed and the men in the room flinched.

Sergeant Plant cleared his throat. 'I ran into him on the quayside where MacManus's boat was sunk.'

'At least you managed that without any trouble,' Charlie said to his brother.

'He was telling the men to stand together...' Plant shot her a speculative look. 'I hear they meet in the Town every Wednesday.'

Ma slipped her hand in her pocket and closed it around her knife. She drew it out.

'Well, Sergeant, it's a kindness of you to drop by to see an old woman,' she heaved herself off the chair and grabbed hold of the officer's sleeve spreading the grease from her fingers

239

over his uniform.

She released the catch of the knife and the blade sprang out. The tic in Plant's eye sped up as she placed the tip against the brass button of his jacket and tapped it lightly.

She smiled up at him. 'You sort out Jackson and we'll sort out the boats.'

Patrick sat in the corner of the Town bar swilling the last of the beer around in the bottom of his tankard. Roy's barge had been re-floated and was once again carrying cargo back and forth from the Pool to Barking Reach but, since Patrick had called for the river workers to stand together, he had made it his practice to stay a little longer in the pub on Wednesday nights. There was nothing formal about the association. You joined those saying no to Ma Tugman by a handshake and a nod of the head, but nonetheless the cluster of men determined to earn their living by honest means was growing daily.

A wry smile crossed Patrick's face as three dockers raised their tankards to acknowledge him from the other end of the bar.

His sole intention when he refused to carry stolen goods was to keep himself out of prison, but now he found himself the leader of a full scale revolt against the Tugmans' rule. He should have realised that once he'd stepped forward others would follow. It had been the same on the *Seahorse* when he'd challenged the cook over the food served in the galley. All he'd wanted then was a full stomach before a day's work and instead found himself in front of the captain as spokesman for the crew. But victuals was one thing, the Tugmans were quite another. Still, at least with the tension in the street and long hours working on the *Mermaid,* Patrick had little time to think about Josie.

Of course he thought of her when his eyes opened in the morning and he wondered if she, too, had lain awake half the night thinking of him. He thought about her while he sipped a mug of hot, sugary tea and ate a bowl of oats after loading the first hold of coal in the morning, picturing her having breakfast at a table with a starched white cloth on it and the finest silverware. And, if he wasn't careful, as the day went on he would find himself thinking about her warm smile and happy laugh when he stopped for a mug of coffee and a lunch of bread and cheese; or, sometimes when the wash rolled along the side of the boat, he would recall how her hair swirled in the breeze. Thoughts of her caught him unawares most nights when he got home and his children greeted him. He could not help but imagine her there, too, waiting for him. And when he lay in the dark with desire for her coursing through him, he thought of what he would not give to have her in his arms.

The pub door opened again and Brian stepped inside. He scanned the bar and spotted Patrick. He ordered his pint and sauntered over.

'I'm surprised you're still here, Pat,' he said taking the froth off of the top of his tankard.

Patrick smiled. 'I'm just waiting to see a couple of the lads from Richard Street. One of their neighbours had their rigging cut and he lost three days' money re-working it.'

'The Tugmans again?' Brian asked, the light from the lamp making an orange halo around his head.

Patrick nodded. 'Who else? I met Pug Sheppard from Clarke Street. His men have had enough of handing over their wages and running the risk of being captured by the police. They want to stand with us now.'

Brian gave Patrick a smile that had just a shadow of the freckle-faced lad he'd once been. 'We've been mates a long time, haven't we, Pat?'

'Aye, we have,' Patrick agreed, thinking that he couldn't remember a time before knowing Brian.

'Do you remember how we used to come home with bloody noses after fighting with the Leman Street boys?' he said. 'And how your mam used to feed us bread and dripping after school?'

Patrick laughed. 'Aye, and your mam used to think I was too wild for you to play with.'

'Well, you fecking were,' Brian replied. 'I remember the day you faced down that big lad from Cable Street, you know, the one with a face like a monkey.' He shook his head. 'One blow from you and the big bugger crumpled like a paper lantern.'

'You have to know where to hit them,' Patrick said, relaxing back in the chair.

Brian grinned. 'And I remember how we used to sneak up behind the girls walking home from school and pull their hair.'

Pain grabbed at Patrick's chest. Josie, with her hair tightly twisted into two long plaits, had been one of the girls they had teased. But Josie didn't shriek and cry; she'd turned around and swiped at him. If he could pin down the moment he actually fell in love with Josie O'Casey, it was when she belted him around the head with her satchel all those years ago.

Brian's voice cut through his thought. 'Cor, didn't we have some times then?'

'That we did,' Patrick agreed.

'So you won't mind me asking' – he paused for a moment – 'are you all right, man?'

'Same as ever,' Patrick replied, forcing a casual smile.

Brian let out a loud sigh of relief. 'Thanks the Lord, 'cause frankly, Pat, you look like squashed dog's shite.'

'I've just had a couple of long days, that's all.'

Brian gave a nervous laugh. 'Course you have, course you have.' He took another deep draught of beer. 'All right then.' He cast his eyes over Patrick's face. 'I know you're pining for Josie O'Casey, but who knows what's around the corner, eh! It might all come right, even now.' He buried his face in his tankard.

Patrick studied his old friend and now brother-in-law. As Brian had said, they'd always been close, right from the time when they were runny-nosed toddlers sitting on their front steps. They'd had their scraps of course, but they'd taken the other's injuries as their own. When Patrick returned home from his travels to find his friend all set to marry Mattie, he couldn't have been more pleased. Brian had stood beside him through all of Rosa's shenanigans, but even with all that,

243

Patrick knew it had taken a lot for Brian to mention Josie.

He slapped Brian on the shoulder. 'You're a good mate, none better.'

Brian grinned and was about to say something when the door burst open and Harry Tugman stepped in.

It took a moment for Patrick to register that a dozen or so of Harry's hard-bitten bully boys had shoved their way in behind him.

Patrick and Brian stood up and chairs screeched on the wooden floor as other men did the same. Where a few seconds before there had been the low hum of male voices, now there was only the creak of wooden floorboards as men shifted their weight from one foot to the other in readiness for a set-to.

Harry was dressed in his usual visiting outfit: checked jacket and corduroys with a top hat wedged on his head. It was clear from the sneers on his gang's faces and their hands concealed in jacket pockets that they hadn't just popped into the Town for a quiet drink.

Tugman's men stood shoulder-to-shoulder, blocking the exit to the street. Some of the pub's patrons slid along the side towards the door leading to the steps down to the river. The rear door crashed back and half a dozen more of the Tugman gang pressed in.

The pub was probably at least half full, with the regulars outnumbering Harry's men two to one, but they weren't scrappy street fighters and even with favourable odds they'd be hard pushed to hold off Tugman's thugs. Patrick subtly stretched and flexed his hand.

Harry grinned. 'Evening,' he said in a jovial voice. 'I've got a message from me ma.'

There was a flash of light as he snatched a twelve-inch blade from inside his coat. In the same instant Patrick jerked his own knife out, crouched and balanced himself, ready to pounce. The barmaid screamed and the room exploded.

The boatmen pulled out blades or grasped bottles at the same instant that Harry's men dived into them. Glass smashed and shards crunched underfoot as the men lunged at each other. Arthur scrambled to protect his stock behind the bar, but two of Harry's men grabbed him and threw him through the window, taking out the central panes of glass and much of the wooden frame. A couple of the boatmen, seeing a way out, jumped through the gap and ran off down the high street.

Harry's man Ollie Mac, a swarthy bloke with a shaved head dashed at Patrick and criss-crossed his knife at Patrick's face. Patrick arched back but felt the blade breeze by within a hair's breadth of his cheek before Ollie stabbed at his chest. He missed when Patrick sidestepped, catching the man's arm and snapping it over his knee with a satisfying crunch. He screamed out and crumpled to the floor, cradling his injured arm. Mercilessly kicking him aside, Patrick turned to face the next man, a stocky thug with missing front teeth, who threw himself on Patrick and they tumbled across the floor.

He rolled on Patrick, getting him on his back, and fastened his stubby hands on his throat in a vice-like grip. Patrick retaliated, smashing his fist into the face above him, but still the grip around his throat remained. Bracing his foot on the floor, Patrick heaved himself up and over, gasping for air as he pinned his assailant under him. He groped on the floor and felt the cool smoothness of a bottle. He closed his hand around it and smashed it on the side of the brute's face, feeling a sharp sting as the edge of the broken glass sliced though the top of his own thumb. But the man trying to strangle him howled and closed his hand over the bloody gash on his cheek and chin. Patrick sprang to his feet and looked around.

To his right, Brian picked up the chair he'd been sitting on only moments before and smashed it across a pock-marked brute swiping at him with a docker's hook. Other men scuffled and fought with knives, fists and still more bottles. He saw old Bert Bunton lying in a crumpled heap, blood seeping from a wound in his forehead, while another of Arthur's regulars sat with his back to the far wall using his leather belt as a tourniquet to staunch the flow of blood from a thigh wound. Still others lay in the blood-drenched sawdust, either moaning or crawling away from the fight.

Harry Tugman stood by the door, his knife raised in his hand, but watching rather than joining in the carnage. Raging fury rose up in Patrick, as his gaze ran over the fat gang leader. Men who simply wanted to earn an honest living were being slaughtered by Harry's bunch of animals and he, Patrick Michael Nolan, wasn't going to let it happen.

Picking up a chair by its leg with one hand and retrieving his knife from the floor with the other, Patrick smashed the chair on the bar where it shattered to leave a splintered end.

'Come on, lads!' Patrick yelled above the bedlam. Several of the boatmen looked his way. 'We've heard Ma's message, now let's send ours back.'

A howl rose up and the boatmen surged forward. With a look of determination Patrick made his way towards Harry. When someone blocked his way, he jabbed the raw end of the chair leg in his face and the man fell back. Another leapt at him, but Patrick caught him mid-air and flipped him onto a table, which collapsed under his weight.

Now it was Harry's men who were being pressed back. Some of them stumbled towards the door, holding their hands over bloody wounds or shouldering injured members of their gang out into the street.

Harry tried to scrabble back through the front door but his own men were blocking the way. As Patrick reached him he darted away. For a big man Harry was surprising agile and managed to dodge Patrick but, seeing his way to the street blocked, he pushed towards the rear of the pub with three or four of his men. Patrick crashed after him.

'Stop that bastard!' he bellowed, as he saw his quarry disappearing towards the back door.

Brian, who was grappling with a skinny lad, looked up and saw Harry. He smashed his fist into the man beneath him and stood up.

A glint, like a crack of lightning cut across Patrick's vision as Harry's blade slashed through the air. Silently, it travelled down Brian's throat, leaving behind a vivid red line.

The whole scene slowed as Patrick watched his boyhood friend's blue eyes open wide in childlike surprise. His mouth dropped open and a large hand, still black with the coal dust of his trade, went to the gaping wound that ran from his ear to the edge of his collar bone.

Patrick forgot everything as he crashed and stumbled towards his friend. Blood – red, sticky and pumping forcefully out – sprouted through Brian's thick fingers as the large Irishman sank to his knees. Patrick caught him before he hit the floor and cradled his head in his arms. Brian's blue-eyes shone upwards from a rapidly whitening face.

'Pat,' he gurgled.

Patrick couldn't speak. Someone gave him a cloth which he placed over Brian's neck but within seconds it was soaked with blood. Brian started to shiver and Patrick held him closer.

'Pat, take care of Mattie and kiss my boy for me,' his bloodless lips mouthed rather than said.

No. No. No! Please God, no. Not with Mattie and the baby. Oh God, let him see his child at least, Patrick pleaded silently, as Brian grew heavy in his arms.

He stroked his brother-in-law's bright red hair, thinking of them running and laughing together as boys. Always in trouble and always together. This couldn't be happening, Patrick's mind kept saying and then, suddenly, Brian's head flopped forward. Patrick held Brian's face between his hands and gently tipped it back and, with his own tears clouding his vision, he gazed down at his friend's now sightless eyes.

It was so still that outside the rattles of the beat constable could be heard echoing around the streets. The last of Harry's men had sloped away and the remaining boatmen stood silently amidst the debris of the Town of Ramsgate's bar.

As Patrick stared down into the face of his dead friend a tortured howl filled the air. For a second he thought there must have been a dog injured in the fray, but then he realised the piercing scream of pain was coming from him.

Chapter Sixteen

Mid-July, and the weather was so hot and dry that street dust, disturbed by the traffic of horses and heavy wagons, flew into the air, catching at the back of people's throats and stinging their eyes. And, as it hadn't rained for a few days, debris lay undisturbed in the gutters, to reek and ferment unhindered. Josie, wearing her coolest cotton day dress and straw bonnet, and having dispensed with her two heaviest petticoats, gathered her skirts to dodge through the wagons passing in both directions along The Highway. Despite her light clothes, sweat trickled down between her shoulder blades and the backs of her thighs.

She had visited four houses since she and

Sophie had decided to divide their efforts and had parted at the coffee house in Cannon Street Road. Normally, they visited together but as Edith Carp, who was part of their pastoral team, was unwell Josie persuaded Sophie that the most effective course of action would be to split up. This way, all those mothers reliant on their delivery of food baskets would be able to give their little ones a decent supper.

If she were honest Josie welcomed the chance to visit the tenement and houses alone because she couldn't face another conversation with Sophie about how wonderful it would be when William Arnold proposed.

Everything that was sensible in her called her a fool for turning away the prospect of a good income and an amiable husband. Becoming Mrs Arnold would keep her close to her family and, in time, give her children of her own, but how could she encourage him when her heart belonged to Patrick?

If she couldn't be Patrick's wife she would settle for becoming an old maid and draw satisfaction and the joy of motherhood second-hand from her nieces and nephews.

This is what she told her shattered heart at least three or four times a day as it pleaded with her to seek Patrick out.

The postman passed by on the other side of the road with a heavy sack on his shoulder. Josie's brows drew together slightly, and she felt a sense of unease as she realised that she had yet to receive a reply from her mother to the letter she sent three weeks earlier. Surely Ellen couldn't be so angry that she wouldn't have written back...

The grating sound of iron rolling over cobbles cut through Josie's thoughts and she stepped back to let a hay cart pass. The two horses pulling the wagon wore blinkers and had their noses in oat bags as they clopped their way west to the City. Crossing over to the pavement on the other side, Josie smiled at the butcher hooking the newly dressed pigs' carcasses in a neat row outside his shop. The rotund owner stretched himself precariously at the top of a ladder. The tidy, artistic display of jointed meat attracted customers – and, it had to be said, flies.

Josie had one last cloth parcel to deliver and had deliberately saved Meg Purdy's visit until last so she could spend a little more time with her and the children.

Even without the benefit of the sunlight, Tun Alley was stifling as she entered it. Thankfully, the pigs had long gone and the central drainage channel was no more than a trickle. Josie carried on to the end of the alley to Meg's house. She pushed the front door open.

'It's only me,' she called as she entered the one small back room that was Meg's home.

Since Josie's first visit two months ago, Meg's circumstances had greatly improved and the room now contained several more items of furniture. Most noticeable was a second-hand wooden bed in the corner with three or four blankets draped over the end and a bolster at the head, and the baby now slept in a cot rather then a box. There was also a small, worn easy chair by the fire, but what pleased Josie most was seeing a covered loaf of bread in the larder, along with a stoneware pot of jam and a halfpenny's worth of butter on a plate. There was also a jug of milk on the table and a basket on the floor half-full of potatoes and swedes.

'Afternoon, Miss,' Meg said, settling the baby in the centre of the bed. Mary sat on a new rag rug in the corner, where she played with the doll Josie had brought for her the last time.

Meg straightened her hair and came towards Josie. She had improved too, and now wore a brown work dress complete with an apron. She couldn't run to a bonnet but her hair was neatly tied back with a cotton cap pinned over it.

'And good afternoon to you, Meg,' Josie set the bundle she was carrying on the table and took off her bonnet, pleased to have the breeze from the open window to cool her. 'I have two oranges. My father says one of them a day helps to keep children healthy. You can squeeze the juice for the baby and let Mary eat the pulp. You should have the other. There are three eggs and a bit of fatty bacon too. That should make a bit of a special supper for tomorrow but don't leave it until Saturday or it will spoil in this heat.'

Meg gathered up the food. 'Thank you, Miss O'Casey. We'd have been in the poor house long ago if you hadn't helped–'

The door flew open and a young woman with white-blonde hair and rouged lips burst through and fell back against it.

'Oh, upon my soul,' she said, looking panic-stricken as she put her hand above her low neckline.

252

'Nell! Whatever is the matter?' Meg asked.

'Haven't you heard?'

'Heard what?'

Nell's mouth dropped open in astonishment. 'About the battle at the Town?'

Josie felt lightheaded and afraid. The Town! That was where Patrick drank. 'What happened?' she asked.

Nell gave her a suspicious look.

'This is Miss O'Casey,' Meg explained. 'It's her who got me the job at the hospital.'

'Ah, well then, you should hear too Miss. Last night – they say it was about nine o'clock – Harry Tugman and his crew marched down to the Town and smashed up the place good and proper. Old Arthur – that's the landlord, Miss – went through the window and not one stick of furniture was left by the time the police arrived. When I went by this morning there was so much blood and guts you'd think it was a charnel house rather than a pub.' Josie's heart thundered in her chest as Nell continued. 'Word is that Ma Tugman wanted to show the boatmen who's boss.'

'Who was hurt?' Meg asked before Josie could.

'Old Bert, who lodged above the baker's, was killed, but he wasn't the only one.' She paused, and folded her arms across her modest bosom.

Josie, by now imagining Patrick slaughtered on the dirty floor of the pub, struggled to take a deep breath and still her sense of rising panic. 'Who else?' she asked.

If Nell said Patrick's name she knew she would die on the spot – and be glad of it. A world without Patrick in it wasn't one she wanted to live in.

'Two of Harry's mob, and good riddance I say, and Matthew Anders, the loading supervisor at St Katherine's; also, some bloke from Cable Street and that ginger-haired coal merchant, Brian Magu–'

'Brian Maguire's *dead*?'

'Aye, Miss, cut across the throat.'

The earthen floor seemed to sway under Josie's feet for a few seconds then rolled back into place. She took a couple of steps and grasped hold of the chair to steady herself as she pictured Mattie on Brian's arm on their wedding day not six weeks ago.

Meg's voice cut into her tortured thoughts. 'Are you unwell, Miss?'

Josie shook her head. 'I have to go.'

Hurriedly picking up her bonnet, she left the two women staring after her and flew down the alley back to The Highway. The traffic was lighter now as the dock workers' day was coming to an end. She stopped for a moment to secure the ribbon of her bonnet under her chin, then turned east and ran towards Cable Street.

Josie's lungs almost burst as she ran the half mile to Mattie's. She sidestepped dogs and children as jumbled thoughts rolled in her mind. On the one hand, she felt completely ashamed of the joy she'd felt when she heard that Patrick hadn't died in the attack, but now that euphoria had passed and her heart was breaking for her poor friend so recently a bride and now so cruelly a widow.

Turning into Cannon Street Road, Josie caught

a glimpse of the sign, Maguire and Son, Coal Merchants, painted stylishly above the double doors.

Perhaps Nell had got it wrong, Josie hoped and prayed, as she hurried under the arches to the yard. Perhaps he was just injured...

She clung to that hope, imagining the red-haired Irishman, swathed in bandages and laughing his hearty laugh as she told him of the mistake. She'd almost convinced herself that was the truth of the matter, but when she turned the corner, hope was extinguished.

Outside the Maguire house stood a cluster of women with black mourning shawls over their heads and sorrowful expressions on their faces. Josie slowed her pace, conscious that her bright summer dress stood out against the drab greys and blacks the neighbours were wearing as a sign of respect while they waited their turn to offer condolences. Josie stood with them and soon stepped over the threshold and into the narrow passage. A crowd had already gathered in the front parlour. Men, in their Sunday suits, stood by the windows talking in hushed tones while the women sat either side of the dead man's mother and wife.

Josie's gaze immediately fixed on Mattie, sitting ramrod straight in her widow's weeds, her hands resting on the baby bump that had begun to show. Her dark eyes, red-rimmed and shadowed, stared out in a ghastly contrast to her pale skin. As people spoke to her, she politely acknowledged them, but her eyes never wavered from the table in the centre of the room where the open coffin lay.

Mattie saw Josie and stood up. Ignoring the usual practice of filing past the bereaved in an orderly fashion, Josie rushed to her friend and gathered her into her arms. Over Mattie's shoulder, she saw Brian lying in the coffin and the full enormity of what had happened swept over her.

'I've only just heard,' she said, her voice choked with emotion.

'I can't believe that he's gone,' Mattie replied, her lower lip trembling with every word.

Josie glanced at Brian's mother, who looked as near to death as a body could be without actually giving up its soul. Her pain was almost palpable, with her only son before her dressed and ready for his grave.

Letting go of her friend's hand, Josie sat down beside the older woman.

'Mrs Maguire,' she said. Brian's mother turned. 'I'm so sorry for your loss, I truly am. Brian was such a lovely fella, so he was, and there will be many who will weep at his passing.' She spoke the expressions of sympathy traditional amongst the community.

Queenie Maguire's chin trembled. 'When's my Brian coming home?'

Josie, who could hardly bear it herself, patted Mrs Maguire's hand and stood up to let another take her place. She went back to Mattie who stood at the foot of the coffin staring down at her dead husband. Josie slipped her arm into hers and they stood in silent companionship.

'Don't he look peaceful,' Mattie said, a fond smile crossing her lips. 'Me and Mam washed him and laid him out.' She glanced at her mother-in-law. 'His mother's been in a trance since they brought him back.'

'What about you?' Josie asked. Everyone knew that a shock like this could bring a baby early. After seeing her mother's recent brush with death, Josie feared for her friend.

A tear floated on Mattie's lower lashes. 'Me? If it wasn't for the baby moving inside me, I'd think I was dead, too.'

Tears welled up in Josie's eyes.

'Don't worry,' Mattie said, giving Josie a heart-wrenching smile. 'I'll live again when I hold Brian's baby.'

Mattie moved down the side of the coffin to put her hand in and smooth a stray lock of hair out of Brian's closed eyes. She looked at Josie. 'Patrick's fair beside himself,' she said. 'He blames himself. He wasn't as grieved as this even when Pa died and you know how close they were. But it's more than that, Josie ... knowing he can't wed you is tearing him apart.'

Josie thought how it was tearing her apart, too, but she kept silent.

Mattie stroked Brian's cold, lifeless cheek. 'I'm glad him and me became man and wife before our wedding. We'd been having the pleasure for six months before I got caught with this one,' she said, smiling as she looked at Brian, then fixed Josie with a purposeful stare. 'If I'd waited till we'd married proper I'd have nothing of him left.'

Josie's gaze moved back to the pine coffin, but she didn't see Brian lying in his Sunday suit with his arms across his chest, she saw Patrick. She remembered his laugh and the way he flicked his hair back when it fell in his eyes. She thought of the angle of his shoulder and the corded muscles of his forearms, the shape of his fingers and how his thumb knuckle sat at a square angle to his palm. She recalled the fascination she had with the part of his face where his close shaved bristles stopped and the soft skin of his cheek started. How had she lived for the past weeks without seeing all those precious little things?

'Where is Patrick now?'

'On the *Mermaid* – he'll be along in a while,' Mattie replied. 'Where are you going?'

Josie retied her bonnet ribbons. 'I waited for Patrick last time and lost him to Rosa. I'm not making the same mistake twice.'

Chapter Seventeen

As Patrick turned into Maguire and Son's yard, a combination of sorrow and weariness washed over him. He stopped to put on his jacket. When he'd leapt off the *Mermaid* he was encrusted with coal dust as usual and stopped at the Highway pump to rinse it off his hair, hands and face with his neckerchief. Although it was past seven o'clock now the day was still so warm that he was dry by the time he'd reached Sutton Street. He would scrub the rest of the grime off later. They were burying Brian in the morning and tonight the traditional vigil would be kept by the close

258

family and friends.

He yawned. He hadn't slept more than an hour without waking in a sweat, recalling the sight of blood pouring out of his friend's neck.

Even before the fight though, it had been Josie, and his hopeless love for her, that had robbed him of sleep. Over the years, how many nights had he lain awake thinking about her beautiful eyes and innocent, open smile. In the over-crowded house in Cinnamon Street, as Gus snored beside him in the old bed, he would dream of becoming a captain on a tall rigger, sailing the oceans to come back home laden with treasures to give to her.

Even after he'd married Rosa, try as he might to forget Josie, he would find himself remembering the feel of her against him and their innocent, fumbled caresses in dark doorways when her mother wasn't looking.

He thought he had learnt to live without Josie O'Casey in the same way a man accepts a withered hand. He functioned with it but he was never completely whole. But now life in its cruelty, had brought her back to him, opening up the old wound to taunt him with what he had thrown away for ever because of a moment of folly with Rosa...

People moved aside to let him pass into the house. He greeted his mother and Gus who was standing next to her, then he spotted Mattie and made his way towards where she stood at the top of the table.

Mattie looked up with a troubled expression on her face. He glanced out of the window at the fading light and supposed she had been expecting him an hour since.

'Pat?' she said looking past him for a second.

He hugged her to him and kissed her on the forehead before releasing her.

'Sorry, I'm late, Mat,' he said. 'Old Bert was buried this morning. Some of the boys chipped in and paid his rent until the end of the week. I dropped it off on my way here.'

Mattie glanced behind him again. 'Where's Josie?'

'Josie?'

'She was here not half an hour ago. She's gone to the *Mermaid* to find you.'

Blood thundered through his head. 'Alone?'

The docks and wharves weren't exactly the best places for a woman during the day, but after they fell silent at the end of the working afternoon, the whole area became a cesspool of drunks and prostitutes, sleazy, and dangerous.

Several people looked his way and scowled at him for raising his voice but Patrick didn't care. All he could think about was Josie, *his* Josie, in jeopardy.

He turned and pushed his way back through the mourners.

The sun had already set behind the tall warehouses in Butchers' Row as Josie made her way towards Narrow Street in the evening mist from the river. The iron cranes used to lift the goods from the dockside were silent above her and the wide doors that allowed wagons in for loading cargo were bolted closed. A few men finishing late still trudged down the street, but now the small public houses, some no more than cottages with a couple of chairs in the front room and a barrel or two, had opened for custom. The pale yellow glow of their window lights cut weakly through the foggy atmosphere of coal-dust laden twilight.

Out of the dark recesses between the buildings women appeared in gaudy dresses, their cheeks heavy with rouge and their lips brightly painted. They gave her curious glances but Josie didn't care – all she cared about was finding Patrick.

Although she knew she would compromise her good name by chasing through the streets alone at night, she had to see him. She was in hell with no way out. She loved Patrick but they could never be together without the blessing of the church. It was just not done. It would cut Mam and Pa to the quick, not to mention endanger her mam's fragile recovery. If that weren't enough to hold her back, if she were to do the unthinkable and throw all convention aside, it would likely revive the old scandal around her parents' relationship before their marriage. Moreover, someone might discover that Bobbie was born a year before Mam and Pa were actually married and, despite her love for Patrick, Josie loved Bobbie too much to risk exposing her illegitimacy.

But tonight, after looking on Brian's lifeless face and seeing only Patrick in his stead, even those fearful considerations couldn't hold her back from seeking Patrick out.

She hurried on, into the winding thoroughfare that ran alongside the river to Limehouse pier, where Patrick moored his boat. As she neared the river the wisps of mist thickened and, as her feet clattered along the wooden boards, upright moorings and crates seemed to loom out at her.

A couple of drunks waving bottles shouted across to her as they lolled outside one of the drinking dens. Josie turned her head to quickly hurry on, almost colliding with a young woman in a tatty dress trying to lure a German sailor into one of the back alleys. Finally, stepping carefully through the horse manure, Josie crossed over to Limehouse pier. The tide was almost out, so the boats sat low in their moorings and the stench of the river hung rancid on the still air.

Peering at the names painted on the hulls, Josie made her way carefully along the broad wooden jetty where tugs were tied up ready for the next day. She spotted the *Mermaid* at the end.

There didn't seem to be anyone about, but Patrick had to be on board, otherwise she would have met him on his way home.

A damp fog arrived suddenly, swirling around her, and shadows danced over the boat as it bobbed on the shallow water making it difficult for her to see the stern. Then she saw a movement at the back of the boat. Covering the last few paces along the wooden jetty she swung herself onto the ladder. Her skirts billowed as she stepped down to the deck of the boat.

Breathing in the sweet, tarry smell of the coal that the *Mermaid* carried, Josie caught a glimpse of Patrick bending over the side of the boat near the rudder. She steadied herself against the side and made her way towards him. The boats either side knocked into the *Mermaid,* sending up a low boom and causing her to focus on her balance and move more slowly.

'Patrick!' she called, her heart beating in her chest with anticipation.

Patrick turned.

Josie's legs lost their strength and the breath rushed from her body as Charlie Tugman's face loomed out of the fog.

For once, he wasn't dressed in his usual showy manner but wore a nondescript grey jacket and trousers with a cap pulled low over his brow. A neckerchief was tied round his throat.

An amused expression crossed his sharp face and then he grinned as he called out, 'Oi, Harry, look who's come calling.'

Harry Tugman scrambled up over the side of the *Mermaid.* He too was wearing workman's clothes and carried an axe in his right hand.

Oh sweet mother! Where was Patrick? She glanced at the axe, fear clutching at her guts.

With a monumental effort, she forced herself to stay calm. If Patrick was lying unconscious somewhere on the boat, then every moment she delayed put his life in peril. She tried to retrace her steps but her feet stayed rooted to the spot.

Bewilderment flashed over Harry's fleshy face before he dropped the axe and lumbered towards her. Grasping her skirts, Josie compelled her legs to move.

Harry's heavy steps crashed behind her closer every second so, keeping her eyes on the horizon to steady herself, she pushed on. Out of the corner of her eyes she saw Charlie cut around the other side of the boat.

If she could get back onto the jetty she could call for the local policeman on his beat, checking on the warehouses. With black spots in her vision and her heart nearly bursting from her chest, she reached out to take hold of the first rung of the ladder, when Charlie jumped down in front of her.

He grinned at her, revealing his tobacco-stained teeth. 'What's your hurry, missy?' he leered, his eyes lingering on her breasts.

Josie stepped back, straight into Harry. He grabbed her upper arms and held her firm. Charlie ran his index finger lightly over her left cheekbone. She forced herself not to move, knowing that fear would only add to their pleasure.

'You seem surprised to see us, sweetheart,' he said, and traced the outline of her lips with his finger.

With his face close to hers the bitter smell of Charlie's decaying teeth was almost overpowering. Bile stung the back of her throat.

'I suppose you were thinking to find your bit of fancy – Patrick-fecking-Nolan – waiting for you!' he shouted.

His fingernail grazed along her jaw, then down the soft area under her ear and onto the neckline of her dress.

Josie suppressed a shiver. 'What have you done with him?'

'Bastard's not here,' Charlie replied, as his hand slid down and fondled one breast.

Relief flooded over Josie, but where was he? If he'd not arrived at his sister's yet then he wouldn't even know she was here, let alone come and find her.

'Very nice,' he said squeezing hard. 'You want to have a little feel,' he said to Harry over her head. Josie aimed a kick at Charlie's shins but Harry lifted her back so her foot swung in mid-air.

'Get your filthy hands off me, you pig,' she spat at him.

Harry set her on her feet and Josie tried to slip from his grasp but he held her firm. Sliding an arm around her waist he pressed himself against her, rubbing his crotch into her bottom. Josie squirmed away but Harry laughed and held her firmer.

Lust clouded Charlie's eyes. 'It can only mean one thing – a lady like you sneaking out our way to seek out Nolan...' Charlie's fingers curled over the lace trim of her neckline. 'You're after a bit of rough swiving.' He tore at her gown and Josie screamed.

Harry's hand clamped over her mouth, almost blocking off her air. Drawing in a deep breath through her nose, Josie forced her panic down. She kicked back and then scraped the heel of her shoe down Harry's shin bone. He grunted, but his grip remained tight around her and he yanked at her bonnet. The ribbon snapped instantly and he tossed the bonnet across the deck where it disappeared though the opening to the hold. Then he slid his hand around her throat and put his mouth close to her ear and licked down from her ear to her shoulder with a broad sweep of his tongue.

Josie gagged. Charlie then tugged her dress clear of her shoulder and upper arm, leaving only her chemise covering her breasts. His eyes fixed on her undergarment for a moment then he reached out to rip that away too.

Josie lunged forward and smacked her forehead onto his nose. He let out a yelp and put his hand to his face. Venom flashed in his eyes but then his grin returned.

'Oh, Harry, we have a fighter here,' he said, as blood dripped off the end of his nose. 'Get her on her back.'

Josie dug in her heels but she was no match for him. He dragged her to the stern and threw her on an old tarpaulin, knocking the wind out of her. He kept her down while Charlie grabbed at her skirts and thrust his hand underneath them.

Josie summoned all her strength and kicked out wildly. She freed a hand and clawed and raked at Charlie's face with her nails.

He grabbed her hair and shook her until stars started exploding at the corner of her vision. Darkness began to descend on her and she breathed as deep a breath as she could, knowing she had to stay conscious to keep her wits. If she fainted she'd be at their mercy – if you could call it that.

Charlie loomed over her and wedged himself between her legs. His hands went to her skirts again and flipped them up. 'Cussing petticoats,' he said, as he got in a tangle with her white underskirts.

His hands went to the button of his fly and panic took hold of Josie. She screamed and as

Harry tried to cover her mouth she sank her teeth into his hand. He yanked it away and let out a string of unintelligible oaths.

Josie screamed again but Charlie threw himself on her, spreading her legs with his knees.

Harry grasped her hands and held them above her as Charlie kept fumbling with her undergarments. Josie steeled herself for the pain that would surely rip through her at any moment.

Suddenly there was a dull thud and Charlie's weight shifted. Everything went still as he grunted then slumped across her, his weight on her making it difficult for her to breathe.

Josie blinked slowly and shook her head from side to side, then a sob rose in her throat as she saw Patrick. He stood with a length of iron piping in his hand and murder in his eyes.

Although Patrick wanted the pleasure of smashing the pipe against Charlie Tugman's head until it was no more than pulp, he resisted the temptation. The fact that he'd rendered him unconscious was sufficient for now in evening the odds.

He had been almost mad with fear as he ran from Mattie's house to his mooring. He knew that Brian's death didn't bring him and Josie any nearer to a respectable union, but the terrible sight of his friend's sightless eyes staring up at him and Mattie's white-faced grief when they brought her husband home, had caused his resolve to waver. He was sure Josie felt the same way when she got the news.

Knowing Josie, he realised she would ignore the danger of the streets in order to find him, but when he reached Limehouse pier and heard her scream, instinct had taken over. Grabbing the cast-iron pipe from a pile on the dockside, he'd leapt down and run to the *Mermaid,* where he saw Josie pinned down by Harry Tugman and Charlie between her outstretched legs.

Consumed with blinding fury and disgust Patrick, in a lightning movement, had cracked the weapon over Charlie's head so hard the blow had reverberated up his arm while Charlie grunted and pitched forward across Josie. Her eyes flew open and she saw Patrick, but he fixed his eyes on Harry.

'Let her go,' he said in a controlled voice as Josie struggled to get free of Charlie's inert body.

Harry, like the coward he was, dragged Josie out backwards from under Charlie and held her in front of him like a shield. The upper part of her gown had been ripped to the waist and pulled down on one shoulder. Her corset still held but the only fabric covering her breasts was the thin lawn cotton of her under-chemise.

Patrick's hand tightened around the pipe at the realisation of how nearly he'd failed to get to Josie in time.

'Come and get her,' Harry sneered, and caught her tightly around the waist with one arm while reaching for her breast with his other hand.

Patrick fought to keep his control. Harry hadn't reached for his knife yet, and Patrick wanted to keep it that way. 'I said, let her go,' he repeated.

Harry repositioned his grip and grinned at Patrick. 'I'd make myself scarce, Nolan, before Charlie comes round.'

Charlie was lying on his back staring blank-eyed up at the stars, oblivious to all and every thing. The steady rise and fall of his chest showed he was alive, but the right side of his mouth drooped and a damp patch was spreading across his crotch.

Patrick kicked the prone man's foot. 'I don't think your brother's going to wake up any time soon,' he said and, with his eyes fixed on Harry, he heaved Charlie up under the arms and dragged him to the side of the boat with his head lolling back and forth like a rag doll.

Patrick turned and looked at Harry. 'You let Miss O'Casey go or I'll throw him over.'

'You do and I'll kill you both.'

'And by that time your brother Charlie will be lying in the mud at the bottom, and *you'll* have to tell your ma how you let her "sweet boy" drown while you scrapped over a woman.'

Harry's piggy eyes narrowed, and Patrick studied him for a long moment, gauging the distance between them. 'Let her go, or Charlie takes a swim.'

But Harry's hand went back to Josie's breast and Patrick released Charlie.

Before Charlie even hit the water Patrick was across the boat and behind Harry. Gripping the pipe in both hands he looped it over Harry's head, jamming it across his throat. Harry released Josie instantly, gurgling as the iron pressed into his Adam's apple and clawing at the obstruction over his windpipe.

Patrick's fury took hold, but then he caught sight of Josie, slumped on a coil of rope and trying to gather her ruined dress together. He let go and pushed Harry forward, choking and holding his throat.

Harry stumbled clumsily across the deck. 'You'll fecking pay for this, Nolan,' he croaked as he lowered himself over the side after his brother. 'It ain't over yet.'

Patrick raced over and took Josie in his arms. He closed his eyes and kissed her hair, smelling the lavender in it.

'Are you hurt?' he asked, trying to blot from his mind the full horror of what might have happened had he not reached the *Mermaid* in time.

She shook her head. 'I know we agreed not to see each other but I saw Brian lying there and I just had to see you and hold you...' Her body began to shake with sobs and she pressed her tear-damp cheek against his chest. Patrick kissed her hair again, just because he could.

'Shh, it's all right now, I'm here,' he said, feeling her body on every part of him. How had he lived without her? He didn't know.

He glanced around. The dockside was quiet now and, although Harry was probably still trying to haul his brother out of the river near the shore, Patrick couldn't be certain that the brute wouldn't reappear at any moment.

He stood up and held out his hand. 'We should leave and I had better take you home before any one misses you, my love.'

Patrick's words brought an image of Mrs Munroe's disapproving face into Josie's mind. Her urgent need to see Patrick had driven out all other thoughts, but now she realised that it must be well past nine o'clock.

She pulled the front of her gown together with one hand and tried to gather her hair up with the other. 'My bonnet took a tumble into the hold.'

'I'll fetch it tomorrow,' he replied, taking off his jacket and placing it over her shoulders. It was still warm from his body and Josie hugged it around her as he guided her back along the pier.

They hurried up Narrow Street and north towards Stepney Green. The clock of St Dunstan's church chimed the quarter as they turned into Salmon Lane.

Mrs Munroe would almost certainly know she hadn't arrived home, but she wouldn't be unduly alarmed. She knew Josie sometimes stayed out late to have supper with the Coopers, whose manservant would see her safely home. Mrs Munroe tended to retire early and on more than one occasion had already gone to bed before Josie returned.

She hoped that tonight would be one of those occasions as she hurried past the back of the church with Patrick's arm around her. Even so, she couldn't risk anyone seeing her ruined dress and dishevelled appearance.

'We'll have to go in through the kitchen,' she said, as they reached the bottom end of Stepney Green.

'Won't it be locked?' Patrick asked.

'Yes, but Mrs Woodall's room is under the stairs,' she said. 'I can trust her and she'll fetch me another gown.'

They hurried on until they reached number

271

twenty four. Josie glanced up at the house and her shoulders relaxed. It was in darkness.

The wrought-iron gate to the stairs down the side of the house squealed open. Josie prayed that Mrs Munroe had taken a good measure of her Ladies' Night Elixir and was now snoring softly in her room.

Picking their way carefully, Josie and Patrick crept down the stone steps to the kitchen door. The whole house was quiet as once the mistress of the house retired the servants, who were up before dawn, could make for their own beds.

'I think we're safe,' Josie said. She went to knock on the window but Patrick caught her hand.

'I love you,' he said, pressing his lips on her fingers.

'I love you, too,' she said, stepping closer to him in the gathering gloom, 'but will we ever be able to say that out loud for all to hear rather than secretly to each other?'

Patrick placed his hands either side of her face and kissed her gently. 'If I didn't have that hope, Josie, I don't think I could live through another day,' he said in a low voice.

The gas lamp at the front of the house threw a pale light down the steps and as Josie gazed up at the strong angles of his mouth and chin, the urge to throw herself into his arms and beg him to love her was almost too much. She needed to hold him to her, to feel his lips on hers again, and his arms around her. She needed to have him love her in all the ways a man loves a woman.

His arm slid around her waist and he drew her

to him. She stroked her hand up his chest and tilted her head. His lips twisted into a crooked smile.

'I shouldn't do this,' he said. 'But if I have to live without you I must have something to keep my heart beating.'

He covered her mouth with his and Josie gave herself up to the pure pleasure of it. Her hand went to his hair and she grasped it tightly.

A shaft of light cut across her vision. She and Patrick turned. As her eyes adjusted to the glare her mouth dropped open. There in the doorway, with a lamp in her hand, stood Mrs Munroe.

'Good evening, *Miss* O'Casey.'

Chapter Eighteen

As she opened the door and her eyes rested on Josie O'Casey in the arms of Patrick Nolan, Mrs Munroe sent up a small prayer of thanks to the Almighty.

Since she'd read Josie's letter her sole aim had been to find a way to unmask her as the wanton woman she truly was. Now that opportunity had presented itself. Discovering Daisy in the pantry with the delivery boy two weeks ago had been divine intervention as far as she was concerned. She would have dismissed Daisy on the spot but kept her on only on the understanding that the maid report to her everything Josie did. It was Daisy who had told her an hour ago that Josie hadn't arrived home. Mrs Munroe had sat up, waiting in the dark parlour until she'd heard the gate squeak.

With narrowed eyes she studied the guilty lovers.

Look at the strumpet, with her brazen eyes. And him, in his rough clothes, with a wife somewhere and his arm around another.

'Come in,' she ordered. '*I* have a regard for propriety even if *you* have not.'

Josie stepped in and Mrs Munroe went to close the door, but Patrick put his hand to it.

'Not you!' she said fixing him with her most piercing gaze.

Ignoring her, Patrick stepped into the kitchen and stood behind Josie.

Mrs Munroe's gaze slid over Josie, lingering on the torn dress, the unbound hair and missing bonnet. 'A fine way to repay the care my son has lavished on you! It will break his heart when he hears how you have been acting the whore with this ... this *scoundrel!*'

The word adulterer had been on the tip of her tongue but thankfully she remembered in time. If she called him that Josie might realise she'd read her letter to her mother.

Patrick's eyes darkened. 'So you'll not be interested in an explanation then,' he said addressing her with breathtaking impertinence.

'How dare you–'

'I thought you might be concerned by Dr Munroe's stepdaughter returning home in such a ragged state and would want to know what happened to her.'

274

'What has happened is crystal clear. Miss O'Casey has spent the afternoon with you, doing, I shudder to think what, and thought to slip back into this respectable house without being discovered,' Mrs Munroe replied.

Patrick started forward, but Josie caught his arm.

'Mrs Munroe, I was on my rounds with the baskets when I heard that Mattie's husband had been killed,' she said, shamelessly holding his hand. 'I went to comfort her and pay my respects to her family. She is with child. I knew it was getting late but I ... but I also needed to see Patrick. He was very close to Brian and I wanted to ... to comfort him too.'

Mrs Munroe top lip curled.

'On my way I was attacked,' Josie went on, almost sobbing. 'Thankfully, Patrick found me and saved me.' Josie looked up at the man beside her with such tenderness that a rare lump unexpectedly formed itself in Mrs Munroe's throat.

She wavered. Despite what the whole situation looked like, what Josie said had a ring of truth about it. Then the words from Josie's letter burst back into her mind. Words of loving and wanting. Sentiments a decent young lady would balk at but which this girl, standing before her with love in her eyes and her dress ripped to shreds, wrote boldly across a page.

Her mind moved on from Josie's letter to her five grandchildren asleep upstairs, and her heart galloped unevenly in her chest. She studied Josie again.

She may have been attacked, but she had probably had been on her way to a clandestine meeting with this Nolan fellow, rather than to comfort his bereaved sister. Mrs Munroe's eyes flitted to Patrick, standing protectively beside Josie, and her lips drew into two harsh lines as she studied his commanding height and powerful hands. Who knows how many times Josie had pretended to be about on good works but instead had been meeting this Irish oaf to fornicate in secret? And what if there were to be a bastard from their immoral union?

'You expect me to believe that?' she screeched.

'It's the truth,' Josie replied, but Mrs Munroe barely heard her as her mind imagined her dear Robert disgraced and his children tarnished by Josie O'Casey's adulterous liaison.

Oh, dear Lord, no – not again, she vowed.

The door under the stairs opened and Mrs Woodall, in her dressing gown and nightcap, stepped into the kitchen. Mrs Munroe barely saw her as the loneliness of Robert's self-imposed exile swamped her mind, and she jabbed her finger at Josie. 'The truth is you are a wanton light-skirt whose unbridled desires will bring disgrace on your family if I don't restrain them.'

'Restrain? In what way?' Patrick asked, taking a step closer to Josie.

'There are sanatoriums where women with natures such as Miss O'Casey's can be curbed and moulded,' she said, thinking of the one in Leyton she had heard of only the week before.

Mrs Woodall gasped and Mrs Munroe sent her a scalding look. The cook backed away but stood in the doorway.

Patrick strode over to Mrs Munroe. She was used to having people, even men, look up to her, and she was irritated to have to crane back to remain in eye contact with him.

'You're *not* putting Josie in a queer house,' he told her. 'Miss O'Casey has been attacked. Didn't you hear her? She needs care, not locking away.'

Patrick's eyes narrowed and, despite herself, Mrs Munroe's gaze flickered.

Mrs Woodall shot Josie a sympathetic look but slipped back into the doorway of her own room.

'You're taking a lot on yourself, Missus,' Patrick told her. 'Dr Munroe might have left you to oversee the nursery but Miss O'Casey isn't one of your charges, and this is *her* home.'

Mrs Munroe pulled herself up and gave Patrick a caustic look. 'Do not take that tone with me, you scoundrel. And I would like to point out that this is *my* son's home and you' – she jabbed her finger at Josie – 'only live here, in a comfort you were never born to enjoy, because of his generous nature. And might I also remind you that although you have no call on his affection whatsoever, my son has cared for you as if you were his own child and *this*' – her hand swept over Josie's tattered clothes and then onto Patrick – 'is how you repay him. By grinding his good name in the dust.'

Patrick's eyes narrowed and he made to step forward. Josie gave him a pleading look and he stopped, and fixed Mrs Munroe with an impertinent stare instead.

'I was attacked,' Josie repeated, with a tremor in her voice. 'For pity's sake, I–'

277

Mrs Munroe's nostrils flared. 'Pity! You talk of pity! Your dear mother has been gravely ill but do you have pity on her feeble state? No! Do you have pity on my poor son who not only grieves for his stillborn son, but who has ignored his own health and nursed his wife day and night for over a month? No. You have no regard for anyone but yourself. Your mother's health, my son's position, and your brothers' and sisters' reputations are nothing beside your own selfish desires.'

Josie's shoulders started to shake. 'How *dare* you say such things. I love Mam and Pa and would never do anything to cause them harm—'

'I warned my son that he was nursing a viper to his bosom,' Mrs Munroe's voice boomed around the kitchen. 'And that one day your father's base blood would rise up in you and you would bring disgrace on us all.' She fixed Josie with her steeliest stare. 'It seems that day has arrived, you cruel, ungrateful, heartless girl.'

Josie blanched. 'No!'

Patrick put his arm around Josie's shoulder. 'Don't take any notice, Josie.'

Mrs Munroe's lips drew together as she studied their corrupt intimacy, relishing the stricken look on the young girl's face.

Josie raised her head and looked bleakly into Patrick's face then, clutching her ripped clothes around her, she dashed out of the back door.

Patrick looked at Mrs Munroe, his eyes alight with anger. 'May God forgive you.' He turned and disappeared up the scullery steps after Josie.

A smug look stole over Mrs Munroe face. If Josie left of her own free will then Robert could hardly blame her for Miss O'Casey's disgrace, nor could he take her back after she had thrown herself into the arms of a married man. Suppressing a satisfied smile, she glided across the floor and shut the back door, throwing the iron bolt across the top with a crack.

She turned to the cook standing half in and half out of her under-stair room. 'That will be all, Cook,' she said crisply. 'We are locked up for the *night*. Do you understand?'

Mrs Woodall muttered something and went into her room, slamming the door behind her.

Mrs Munroe shot the middle and bottom bolts in place then picked up her lamp and made her way back to her bedroom through the silent house. As she reached the first floor she looked up the stairs and pictured her grandchildren curled up in their beds. A smile crossed her lips as she closed the door to her bedroom behind her. Setting the lamp down, she sank to her knees on the rug beside her bed, clasped her hands together and closed her eyes. Her mouth moved silently as she fervently thanked God for helping her remove the sinful influence of Josie O'Casey from her son's lovely family.

Even though Patrick took the stairs two at a time, when he reached the street Josie was already a hundred yards in front of him, running towards Stepney Green. Grasping the wrought iron railing he swung around and tore after her.

'Josie!' he called, but she didn't stop.

The rain that had threatened all evening suddenly fell from the sky in heavy droplets that splashed onto his face and clothes as he ran. There was a crack of thunder overhead, then a streak of lightning illuminated the street, showing the glistening cobbles in an eerie grey light. The rain plummeting from the sky drenched the trees and pavements and, as Patrick stamped his boots in the newly formed puddles, splashed onto his trousers.

'Josie!' he called again and this time she slowed. The sodden hem of her gown clung to her ankles and impeded her progress. She staggered to a halt and slumped against a wall.

Rolling her head against the rough brickwork, she shut her eyes and tilted her face up towards the storm. The bodice of her torn dress was now soaked and it clung to her shaking shoulders as she sobbed uncontrollably.

As he stopped in front of her she opened her eyes. 'Patrick,' she said.

He gathered her to him and hugged her. 'There, there, my sweet love,' he said kissing her damp forehead.

Her arms slipped around his waist. 'I love my Mam and Pa,' she said, resting her head on his collar bone, her warm breath passing over the dip where his throat joined his chest.

He kissed her again. 'I know you do and so do they.'

She nodded and looked up at him. 'How could she say such hateful things?' Josie asked, her eyes searching his face.

'Because she's a bitter, twisted old woman,' Patrick replied.

He took his jacket off and slipped it around her

shoulders then guided her away from the wall.

'Now let's get you home before you catch a chill.'

She turned to face him and took hold of his arm. 'Oh Patrick, I don't know if I can. Not after she has said all those awful things about me – and about *you.*'

Patrick squeezed her shoulders. 'Come on, Josie, it won't be forever.' He moved a damp lock of hair from her cheek. 'And let her think of me as she will.'

Josie gave him a brave smile. 'I know. But it's at least another month or so before Mam and Pa are back. We were barely speaking before this but now I'll be hard pressed to be civil to her.'

Several large rain drops had settled on her eyelashes. Patrick took advantage of the shelter from the house and drew her closer.

'I know it's difficult but you'll have to, there is no other way,' he said, savouring the feel of her in his arms. 'No matter how dreadful she is to you I'm afraid you'll have to grit your teeth and bear it.'

She nodded. 'You are right. I'll have to try to be polite to her at least. The children have suffered enough with Mam being ill. I don't want them upset further by being caught in the bad feeling between their grandmama and me. And, I promised Mam I'd look after them.' A determined expression spread across her face. 'After all, if I'm not there who will kiss George better and soothe Jack back to sleep after a nightmare? Not Mrs Holier-than-thou Munroe, that's for sure.'

281

'That's my Josie,' Patrick said, looping her hand around his arm and wishing he was walking her home with him instead of back to number twenty-four.

The rain had eased a little and the thunder now rolled eastward towards the River Lea and Essex.

As they reached the top of the scullery stairs Josie turned. 'Will you tell Mattie I'll be around to go to Mass with her on Saturday?'

'Of course I will. I'll see you there myself,' he replied. 'And remember,' he slipped his arm around her and drew her near. 'Above all, remember that I love you.'

'And I love you.'

They kissed briefly then Patrick let her go. She tripped down the steps and smiled up at him as she reached the back door. She turned the metal handle. The knob rattled in its housing but the door didn't move. Patrick hurried down beside her and tried the handle himself. It released the catch but the door didn't budge. He rattled it again knowing that it would do no good.

They both stared at the solid side door for a moment then he kicked the wooden panel, leaving a mark on the paintwork with the studs of his boots. 'Damn, damn!'

Josie gave him a disbelieving look. 'She's locked me out.'

He glared at the unmovable door for a few seconds then turned his gaze to her as the full enormity of the situation swept over him.

Josie was an unmarried woman, her dress torn, her hair unbound, and bolted out of her house at night with a man. Unless he did something immediately, she would be utterly ruined.

Rosalyn Cooper poured the steaming milk from the small saucepan over the coco paste and stirred it vigorously. She had been awoken from a fitful sleep by the thunder. Her husband Henry was away for a few days and as usual she woke at the slightest noise. Although their house was secure enough, with bars at the lower windows and with a high wall around it, Wellclose Square wasn't the nicest of locations to live in.

The elegant four-storied houses that lined the square had been built a century earlier by prosperous merchants. Other than the Coopers' home, and one or two others, the rest of the dwellings in the square were now lodging houses, let by the room to any who had thruppence a week for the rent. Drunken sailors now brawled where liveried carriages had once rolled, while the solid blocked doorsteps once so diligently whitened each day now served as sleeping places for those unable to pay for a bed.

Of course, it was because Shadwell and Wapping were such destitute areas that the Coopers lived there. Mr Cooper was, after all, the superintendent of the Mission that sat across the square from their house, dedicated to rescuing young women from lives of vice and degradation. But, however worthy this vocation, it didn't make living in such an impoverished neighbourhood any easier.

Rosalyn picked up the cup and lamp and was just about to return to bed when the door knocker rapped.

Her heart thumped in her chest. It was almost eleven o'clock and she wondered who on earth could be calling at that hour. It couldn't be one of the trollops looking for shelter because they knew to present themselves to the warden on duty at the Mission and not at the house.

The sound of heavy footsteps on the stairs above told her that Potter, their manservant, was on his way. Knowing that he would have a loaded pistol cocked and ready, Rosalyn put down her drink and left the kitchen.

By the time she'd reached the hallway Potter was already at the door and talking to someone on the step. He turned as he heard her approach.

'It's for you, Ma'am,' he said, standing back to let her pass. Tugging her nightcap over her hair, Rosalyn stepped forward and gasped as her eyes rested on Josie O'Casey standing on her doorstep with a man beside her.

Josie wore no coat or bonnet and her unbound hair cascaded in wild abandon over her shoulders. Her thin summer dress was soaking wet, and clung to her, and was muddy around the hem. Instead of looking like the well-to-do young woman she knew, Josie O'Casey looked as if she'd been rolled in the gutter.

'Miss O'Casey?' Rosalyn was scarcely able to believe that the bedraggled girl standing on her doorstep was the same young woman whom she'd seen walk off arm in arm with her daughter Sophie that very afternoon.

The young man stepped forward. 'Mrs Cooper? Apologising Ma'am, but Miss O'Casey has been attacked.'

'I can see that,' Rosalyn said, handing the lamp to Potter and putting her arms around Josie's shoulder. 'My poor girl. Don't worry, we'll soon have you home.' To the man with Josie she said. 'I am obliged to you for helping Miss O'Casey. Potter will give you something for your trouble, Mr.. ?'

'Nolan,' he replied firmly. 'Patrick Nolan.'

Rosalyn studied him more closely. Nolan? Could that be the man Sophie had talked of, she wondered. Certainly, he had a confident air about him that was at odds with his rough appearance and he held her gaze in too bold a manner for her liking. He was also standing closer to Josie than he ought, and Rosalyn also noticed that Josie's arms were clutched across her chest to hold her ripped clothing together.

'And Josie can't go home,' Patrick added.

Rosalyn looked from one to the other. 'And why is that?'

'Because Mrs Munroe has locked up the house and won't let me in,' Josie replied. She and Patrick exchanged a glance then Josie gave her an ingenuous smile. 'It's a terrible misunderstanding. While I was distributing food packages today I heard that...'

As Josie recounted the events of the day Rosalyn's mind whirled into a confusion of panic. It was as clear as the nose on her face that Josie and this Nolan were more to each other than old friends and, although everything Josie was telling her had the ring of truth about it, it placed Rosalyn in an awful dilemma.

Josie O'Casey's stepfather might be lauded in

285

high places for his contribution to public health and services to the poor, but her mother once took in washing and sang in public houses. Although Josie was a very likable and caring girl, Rosalyn couldn't help but worry about whether her background made her a fitting companion for her daughter Sophie. She had privately chided herself several times for her lack of charity and strove to overcome her doubts, but with her husband in knotty negotiations over their elder daughter Amelia's engagement to a Harcourt, Rosalyn couldn't afford to have the family's name linked with even a breath of scandal. Seeing the tender smile and glances that passed between Josie and Patrick Nolan, and hearing that Josie had been turned out from her home by Dr Munroe's mother, the words disgrace and dishonour screamed in Rosalyn Cooper's head.

Josie's voice cut through her unsettling thoughts. 'I tried to explain to Mrs Munroe that I had been attacked but she wouldn't listen.' An expression of hurt and anger crossed her face. 'She was just horrid, and said some dreadful things about Patrick. I was so hurt I ran out of the house. I was gone for no more than five minutes but when I went back Mrs Munroe had bolted the doors. I thought I might stay with you until she became more reasonable.'

Rosalyn had been introduced to Mrs Munroe at the recent Widows and Orphans' Benevolent Society tea and while she would not describe Robert Munroe's mother as a warm individual, she was clearly a woman of high morals. Although her conscience told her she should take

Josie in, Rosalyn reminded herself that there was a great deal more at stake.

She squared her shoulders and looked Josie straight in the eye. 'I'm afraid that won't be possible,' she said. Josie's jaw dropped and the colour left her cheeks. 'I'm sorry Josie, but if Mrs Munroe felt it necessary to exclude you from your own home then I cannot give you shelter in mine. I have my own daughters' reputations to consider. I hope you understand.'

Patrick placed his hand on the half closed front door. 'Do you understand what you're doing to Josie by turning her from your door?' he asked, his gaze running accusingly over her face.

Of course she did. If she refused to offer Josie refuge the young woman would live without protection and could fall prey to any manner of evil. Rosalyn thought of her two daughters asleep upstairs. If they were to find themselves set upon in such a manner she hoped someone would offer them assistance. She opened the door.

'After a good night's sleep you and Mrs Munroe will be able to iron out this misunderstanding I am sure,' she said smiling at Josie.

Patrick's shoulders relaxed and his face lost its anxious expression. 'I'm right grateful, Mrs Cooper,' he said. He gave Josie a warm smile which she returned. 'Poor Miss O'Casey has been through enough today, what with Brian's death and being attacked by Charlie Tugman, the last thing she–'

'Charlie Tugman!' Rosalyn exclaimed in a horrified tone.

Josie gave her a nervous look. 'I told you. He

287

and Harry caught me on Patrick's boat as I was looking for him. Patrick fought them off and pitched Charlie over the side, after which...'

Rosalyn's mind careered off to the image of her poor Henry lying on his own doorstep beaten and bleeding after being set upon by Charlie Tugman. Terrified thoughts added momentum to her racing heart as her imagination moved from Henry being injured to the nightmare of his being killed. Her vision blurred for a second and her stomach knotted.

If anything happened to Henry, the Trust would require her to quit her home. She would be forced to go to her brother and his penny-pinching wife in Suffolk and live off their largesse. That would be the end of any hope of a well-connected marriage for Amelia, and for Sophie too for that matter.

'I'm sorry, Josie, but you'll have to find somewhere else to stay.' She made to close the door but Patrick wedged his boot in.

'It was no fault of Josie's that Charlie set upon her,' he said, in a low voice. 'If you turn her away you will be as accountable as Mrs Munroe for her ruination.'

Rosalyn's conscience tried to stay her hand but she overruled it. 'I'm sorry,' she whispered as she leant on the door.

Patrick's boot remained. He leant towards her and compassion replaced the anger in his eyes. 'I understand your alarm at the mention of the Tugmans, but I beg you, for the love of Mary, don't let your fear add to Josie's desperate situation.'

Rosalyn stared into Patrick's imploring face for a moment then shook her head. 'I'm sorry,' she said, as a lead weight settled in the pit of her stomach. 'I truly am.' She glanced at his foot.

Fury blazed from Patrick's eyes then he stepped back and put a protective arm around Josie's shoulder.

'Come away, sweetheart,' he said softly, as he drew her to him and guided her down the steps.

'I'm sorry,' Rosalyn said to their retreating figures, and felt a lump in her throat and tears springing to her eyes.

Patrick turned and gave her a look of utter contempt and then he and Josie walked across the square, their reflections elongated on the wet road.

Rosalyn closed the door and quickly went upstairs. She paused outside her daughters' room and then went to her own. She closed the door and leant with her back against it. She stared blindly ahead as her soul accused her of being callous, despicable and loathsome to have turned Josie from her door and she didn't argue. But what else could she have done? She had to protect her family. Tears streamed down her cheeks, then very faintly and far away, echoing somewhere in Rosalyn's head, she could heard Ma Tugman's spiteful laugh.

Chapter Nineteen

Patrick pushed open the door to number twenty Walburgh Street and stood back so Josie could enter. As she passed him their eyes met. In the dim light of the hallway, his face wore a furious expression.

Shaking the water from her hair, Josie continued down towards the scullery. There was a click of a handle and the door to the front room where Kate and Annie slept opened behind them.

'Is that you, Pat?' Kate's voice echoed down the passage.

Patrick's hand rested on Josie's shoulders to keep her in front of him, with her back against his chest, shielding her from his sister's view. She let her head tilt back onto his collarbone as the warmth from his body spread over her.

'Aye,' he called.

Josie closed her eyes, enjoying the reverberation of his deep voice in her own body.

'I'm going around to Mattie's, to sit with her for the night,' she called. 'Mr Hoffman's let me have the morning off for Brian's Mass so I'll see you at the Mission?'

'That you will,' he called back.

'Gus said he'll be down at the Prospect if you're in need of a drink later,' she called out, just before closing the door behind her.

Patrick led Josie to the fire, then took a wick

from the mantelshelf to light the candle on the table. She only had to reach out and she would have been able to trace her fingers along the muscles of his upper arms.

He turned back to her. 'You'll have to stay here and we'll think of something else in the morning. You can have my bed and I'll sleep down here. Annie and Mickey are at Mattie's with Mam, so no one will know you've spent the night.'

Josie shrugged off his jacket and let her hands fall by her side. Patrick's gaze flickered briefly down to the front of her gown.

'It doesn't matter, Patrick,' she replied, her eyes resting on the top two buttons of his shirt, which were unfastened. 'I'm not going anywhere because I am staying with you.'

He raked his hand through his hair. 'What do you think Dr Munroe will say when he hears that? And your mother! They are likely to take the same view of you leaving their home as Mrs Cooper.'

A small ripple of uneasiness ran through her. 'I won't say Mam will dance a jig when she hears,' she said, trying not to dwell on what her mother would say. 'But I wrote to her and told her how I felt. I am hoping that she and Pa will have some sympathy. After all, they were in a similar situation twelve years ago,' Josie pushed the unhappy thought of being cut off from her family aside. 'But if not, then so be it.'

He shook his head. 'No. I can't allow you to throw everything away just because of that bitter old woman. I'll sleep here and we'll go back in the morning.'

Josie gave him a sad smile. 'It will do no good. I will have slept under your roof and that will cast me as a woman of low morals in everyone's eyes.'

'But surely ... if you told them why–'

'I could try, but no one would accept the explanation.' She went over to him and placed her hands on his chest. 'It seems the choice about if and when we would ever be together has been made for us.'

A tortured look crossed Patrick's face. 'But Josie, there must be some way. Something we can do to put this right.'

She shook her head. They gazed at each other for a moment then Patrick's hand slid around her waist and he kissed her.

'I love you,' he whispered, pressing his forehead onto hers. 'I want to come home to you at the end of the day, I want to hold you as I sleep and find you beside me when I open my eyes.' He kissed her slowly. 'I want you to be my wife, Josie, and for you to have my children – but not like this.'

'I know, my love. I know, but life doesn't always play out the way we plan,' she replied, her voice low. She kissed him lightly on the lips. 'Now, Patrick, let us begin our life together even if it is not how we would have chosen to start it.'

The fight was over. Picking up the lamp and taking her hand, he led her silently through the house and up the stairs. He opened the door and she brushed past him and in to his room.

She gazed around at the small items he'd collected over the years, the large pink shell he'd found on a Tahitian beach, a carved mask he'd bought for a rub of tobacco in Bombay. Then her eyes rested on the cast iron bed with the patchwork counterpane, wedged against the wall.

Shutting the door quietly behind him, Patrick slipped his arm around her and turned her towards him. He studied her for a moment then pressed his lips on hers. Her mouth opened under his instantly but he held back, conscious of her innocence. Her hands ran over his shoulders and chest and he pulled his shirt open so he could feel her fingertips on his bare skin, thankful the summer heat had made him leave off his three-buttoned vest. Her hands explored tentatively and sent his senses reeling.

'God, Josie,' he whispered in her ear as he pressed his lips to her neck.

She tilted her head back as he inched the fabric away from her shoulder then slid her hands onto his chest and pushed him away. He stood back and watched in the soft glow of the lamplight as her hands went to the remaining buttons at the front of her bodice.

'I'll turn around?' he said.

'You don't have to,' she replied, pulling at the ribbon.

He stood mesmerised, watching as she revealed her chemise and corset. Then, with her eyes still averted she slipped the torn bodice from her shoulder and let it fall to the rag rug she stood on. Finally, she untied the laces of her skirt.

Patrick's heart crashed in his chest but he forced himself to remain where he was, reminding himself that this was her first time.

293

Don't rush at her, he told himself, as her skirt and petticoats followed the upper part of her gown to the floor.

She stepped out of the billowing fabric, kicked off her shoes and stood before him. His eyes ran slowly over her, taking in every curve and dip of her figure and then his gaze locked on hers.

He reached for her then, feeling the softness of her breasts against his chest. She trembled in his arms, and he kissed her forehead gently.

'There, there, my pretty girl,' he said, stroking her shoulder. 'You don't have to if you're afraid.'

Josie turned her face up to his. A sensual smile spread across her lips as her hands delved inside his shirt and her fingers twirled the hair on his chest.

'Patrick,' she said in a low voice that caught him in the pit of his stomach. 'I am *not* afraid.'

Patrick had listened to birdsong heralding the dawn in the four corners of the globe but none sounded as bitter-sweet as the chirping of sparrows outside his window that morning. As the first streaks of light peeked in through the curtain, he lay propped up on the headrest with his arms behind his head studying Josie's sleeping face.

With the dawn breaking, Patrick couldn't help but think of Brian, who would never hear birdsong, or anything else, ever again. In a few hours he would shoulder his dearest friend's coffin and stand alongside Mattie and the rest of Brian's family as they lay him to his eternal rest. Patrick couldn't imagine never seeing Brian's cheery face again.

Chapter Twenty

Ma wiped the spit from Charlie's chin with the tatty rag she used as a handkerchief and a rare tear stung her left eye. When Harry had brought him home just before midnight, covered in stinking mud, she thought he was dead, but after pouring half a bottle of brandy down his throat he opened his eyes. To her utter relief she saw a spark of recognition. Well, in his right eye at least, as the left one hadn't moved and its pupil remained unnervingly large.

Her eyes ran over his narrow face. What a beautiful baby he'd been! Such a sweet natured child, lying in his cot gurgling at her. Not red-faced and colicky like Harry. She never had to force gin in his mouth to settle him to sleep. No, Charlie had always been a good boy. And so clever, with his sharp wit and quick tongue and sense of style. Although Harry, her husband, had accepted Charlie as his son, it was clear as the nose on your face that he was the by-blow of that nob she'd pleasured a time or two. The one who'd liked a bit of dirt. And now this had happened to her dearest boy!

Her head pounded as a vision of Patrick dancing with Josie sprang into her mind and the small muscle around her right eye started to quiver. The men in the room shrunk back. Charlie gurgled and she turned her attention back to him.

'What is it, my love?' she asked, moving a strand of greasy hair out of his eyes. His good eye glanced down to where damp seeped through his trousers.

'Get that slut of his back in here to change Charlie again,' she called over her shoulder. The girl appeared and Ma struggled out of the chair beside the improvised cot to allow the girl to work. Harry shuffled forward and cocked his head to one side.

'He looks better,' he said, giving her an uneasy smile. The men behind him nodded rapidly and murmured their agreement.

'Well, he couldn't look fecking worse, could he?' she spat back. Harry's bully boys studied the floorboards. 'I sent you down there to sink Nolan's boat and you bring your brother home all but dead.' She lumbered over to her eldest son. 'You should have been looking after him, not trying to get your end away.' She smacked him across the mouth with the back of her hand. 'You're as thick as your old man. I always said I should have strangled you at birth.'

A wounded expression flashed across Harry's face and it appeased her temper a little.

'But, Ma, Charlie was on top of–'

Ma smacked him again. 'Don't blame your poor brother. It was you who let that bastard Nolan get the drop on you. If you'd been about your business instead of waiting your turn, your brother wouldn't have had his brains rattled.'

Harry clenched his fists. Ollie shuffled up alongside his boss. 'He'll be all right,' he said, giving her a too cheery smile. 'Remember, the

Atkins boy kicked in the head by that dray horse? He didn't open his eyes for a week and he's dandy now.'

Harry nodded eagerly. 'Ollie ... Ollie's right, Ma.'

He glanced for confirmation at the knot of men trying to blend into the wood panelling, but they kept their eyes on the floor. Ma chewed her lips for a moment and glanced back at Charlie by the fire.

The left side of his mouth drooped and his left arm hadn't moved since Harry had set him down, but his good eye was alert and she could see by the way it flickered between them that he understood the conversation. As the Atkins brat *was* now the same snotty-nose oick he'd always been, maybe in a day or two Charlie would recover, too.

She gave Harry a more considerate look. ''Appen he will. But Nolan's still going to pay for it.'

'I'll go and fix him now, Ma,' Harry said, dragging his knife out of his belt.

For a second Ma enjoyed imagining Patrick bleeding on the cobbles with his throat cut, and then she shook her head.

'Patience, patience.' She raised her hand towards Harry's face and he flinched. She patted his cheek lightly. 'You have to learn not to rush things,' she said in a kind-hearted tone. 'I don't want Patrick Nolan to feel the sting of a blade just for a second, I want him to feel it every day of his life inching its way to his heart.'

'How?'

Her thin lips drew back in an amiable smile and

the men in the room recoiled. 'Trust your ma. She'll think of a way.'

Bobbie opened the door to the dining room and found Lottie already at the table. Grandmama, sitting at the head, her hands neatly folded, acknowledged her as she walked in. Although Grandmama looked a little tired, her lips weren't drawn tight as usual, even though Bobbie was late.

Behind her, waiting to serve the breakfast was Daisy, her eyes swollen and her chin uncontrollably wobbly.

'Sit down, Robina,' her grandmother instructed in a light voice.

Bobbie gave her sister a quizzical look. Lottie gave as much of a shrug as she could with her grandmother's beady eyes upon her. Bobbie was a little surprised to see Josie's seat empty. Grandmama loathed tardiness, and it put her in a foul temper all morning if any of them was a minute after eight-thirty, so her sister made a point of being early.

'You may serve,' Grandmama said over her shoulder.

'Josie's not down yet,' said Bobbie.

Daisy let out a long sniff and her chin wobble became more pronounced. Strangely, Grandmama didn't reprimand her, just dismissed her with a flick of her fingers. Daisy fled with her hands over her face.

The door slammed and Bobbie and Lottie stared at each other in puzzlement. Grandmama placed her hand on her bosom.

'Miss O'Casey won't be down today – or ever

298

again,' she said in a doleful tone. 'She is gone!'

'Gone where?' asked Bobbie, not quite sure she was hearing her grandmother's words correctly.

'To be with her paramour.'

Although Grandmama's expression was mournful there was a sort of happiness in her voice.

'What's that?' asked Lottie.

'She has turned her back on her family to live in a wicked, sinful liaison with that scoundrel, Patrick Nolan.'

Lottie's shoulders dropped. 'Oh, Grandmama, of course we'll see her again. Mr Nolan's house is only a walk away and Josie'll be back lots of times.'

'I am afraid that is not possible. You may be a little young to understand but Miss O'Casey is lost to her family forever.' Grandmama put her hand to her forehead. 'She has thrown all the care your father has lavished on her over the years back in his face. Ungrateful, dissolute girl that she is.'

Lottie's lower lip jutted out and she glanced across at her sister.

Anger rose up in Bobbie. 'You must be mistaken, Grandmama. Josie loves Papa and would never do anything to upset him.'

Her grandmama gave her a frosty look. 'Your loyalty to Miss O'Casey is commendable but I have ruled on the matter.'

'I want to see Josie,' Lottie cried. She buried her head in her arms for a second then looked up with a tear-stained face. 'I'm going to see Josie and I don't care what you say.'

Mrs Munroe wove her fingers together and

rested her hand on the table in front of her. 'Do not make me lock you in your room until you repent of your wilfulness, Charlotte.'

An image of her grandmother holding Josie's letter flashed into Bobbie's mind. She caught her sister's eye.

'*Charlotte.*' Lottie sat still. 'I am sure that Grandmama knows best.'

'If you think so, *Robina,*' Lottie replied. Bobbie nodded and Lottie formed her face into an innocent expression. 'Please forgive me, Grandmama. You are right in everything.'

Bobbie wondered if that was just a little too much, her grandmother hadn't noticed they were addressing each other by their full names, so probably not.

Mrs Munroe beamed at the two children and rung the bell by her hand. 'Shall we eat?'

Bobbie threw her oats and toast down her throat as quickly as she could then mumbled an excuse, dashed upstairs and slipped into Josie's room. Tearing open her sister's clothes cupboard she sifted though the billowing skirts. She ignored the fine silk evening dresses and pulled out three of Josie's best day dresses and her old housework one, along with her quilted jacket and her strongest boots. She carefully folded them and tied them in her sister's fringed shawl.

Then, just as she opened the door she spotted Waisy on the bed. Bobbie leapt over, scooped it up and closed Josie's door. With her grandmother's voice echoing up from the front hall as she gave Daisy the tasks to complete before the family returned from church, Bobbie sped up to her own room.

She put Waisy out of sight under her pillow, and then pulled out the top drawer of her dressing table. She scrabbled around at the back and found her small purse. Shaking out the ten shillings she'd been saving, but keeping a penny back, Bobbie tied the coins in one of her handkerchiefs, stuffed it in the middle of the bundle and then hid it under the bed.

She sat back on her heels to regain her breath, then went over to her writing desk to quickly scribble out a letter, address it and slip it in her pocket. The tall clock in the hall chimed nine o'clock. In a short while, they would have to leave to walk to church, so Bobbie retrieved the bundle and opened the door to the landing again. At the end of the hall, through her grandmother's open door, she could see her arranging herself for church.

Flattening herself against the wall, Bobbie slid along to the top of the stairs and then dashed down the three flights to the kitchen.

She burst through the door just as Mrs Woodall was hooking a joint of meat on the jack.

She blinked in surprised. 'Miss Robina, shouldn't you be getting ready for Church?'

Bobbie held out the bundle and Mrs Woodall's gaze rested on Josie's distinctive paisley shawl.

'Mrs Woodall, I have heard of a deserving family in Walburgh Street – I don't know what number. I would be grateful if you could ask Sam to take this to them,' she said, wondering how long she would be locked in her room if she'd misjudged the cook's loyalties.

Mrs Woodall studied her for a long moment, then wiped her hands on her apron and took the bundle.

Bobbie pulled out the letter. 'Would you also be kind enough to post this for me tomorrow? I have a penny for the stamp.'

Mrs Woodall took the letter and glanced at the address.

'I don't want to bother my grandmother with such a small errand,' Bobbie said with the hint of a squeak in her voice.

Mrs Woodall slipped Bobbie's letter in her pocket. 'I quite understand, Miss Robina, I'll take it to the post office myself in the morning. I'll pay the stamp, so you just put your coin in the church collection and pray that the letter reaches its destination without mishap.'

Chapter Twenty-One

Josie kicked open the back door to the kitchen and set the pails of water down next to the fire. She straightened up and put her hands into the small of her back to ease the ache. With Sarah living with Mattie for the foreseeable future and Kate working from dawn to dusk at the bakery, the running of the house fell squarely on Josie's shoulders.

She caught sight of the washing draped over the cast-iron clothes horse hanging from the ceiling

302

and her lips twisted in a rueful smile. How many times had she seen such a sight when she was a child? Of course, then it was her mother and her gran who'd spent the morning up to their elbows in suds, not she. Although her knuckles were raw, Josie had a warm sense of satisfaction seeing Patrick's shirts hung over the wooden rails all mended and clean.

She had risen that morning, as she had every morning since Brian's funeral, to see Patrick off to work, then she'd queued at the pump with the other women in the street for water. She'd fetched her two pails back and boiled two kettles full, ready for the children's morning wash, after which she'd strip the sheets from the beds and set them to boil in the copper as she waved Annie and Mickey goodbye. She'd clean and tidy the house before making her second trip to the pump for more water. Once she'd finished the washing, she would walk the half mile to Watney Street to buy the family supper. It was all a very far cry from her life at Stepney Green and, if she were to be totally truthful, she hadn't yet adjusted fully to this new life.

Although she had cooked in America, and had helped Mrs Woodall each day, she hadn't had to stand in line at the butcher's counting the pennies or carry her own quart jug of milk back from Johansson's Dairy on Fairclough Street. Tradesmen didn't call to take your orders in Knockfergus; you had to go and fetch what you needed yourself.

Rolling her shoulders in their sockets to ease the stiffness, Josie picked up one of the pails of

303

water she'd just carried back and carefully poured it in the huge kettle. She momentarily thought of the kitchen in Stepney with its own pump, and the cooking range with a built-in water heater, but she pushed the thought aside.

Thinking of the home she'd been forced to leave only amplified the nagging anxiety about her brothers and sisters. Bobbie had sent her clothes and a note saying they all loved her but it wasn't the same as seeing them. She knew she could rely on her eldest sister to look after the other children, but Bobbie was only twelve after all and could hardly stand up to Mrs Munroe as Josie had done.

Also, she couldn't rid herself of the fear that, with nobody to restrain her, Mrs Munroe's regime would become even more dour and austere if that were at all possible.

The rattling lid of the kettle cut through Josie's troubled thoughts. She used a cloth to grasp the handle and poured the hot water into the washing tub. As she set the kettle back, the yard door opened and Patrick's mother walked in. Josie's heart thumped but she gave her a friendly smile.

'Morning, Sarah,' Josie said.

Mrs Nolan gave Josie a guarded smile. 'Morning yourself, Josie. I thought I'd drop by to pick up a few bits for Mattie.'

Josie and Patrick had thought it best to arrive separately at Brian's funeral so as not to cause a furore on such a mournful day. Patrick had taken his mother aside later in the day and told her what had happened the night before. Sarah had come over and hugged her, but they had not had a chance to speak alone. When Josie visited Mattie two days ago Sarah had been friendly enough, asking about the children and such, but Josie knew that there was something on her mind.

Sarah went through the house and returned with a bundle of clothes.

Josie set the kettle back in the centre of the fire and spooned tea into the pot. 'If you're not in a hurry to get back why don't you take the weight off your feet and I'll make you a cup of tea.'

'I don't mind if I do,' Sarah replied and sat in her usual chair.

Her eyes flickered over the newly washed windows and scrubbed table, then moved on to the rag rug that Josie had thrown over the washing line and beaten only the day before. Josie poured the tea and handed it to Sarah.

'How's Mattie?' Josie asked, picking up the block of soap and setting the scrubbing board in the tub.

'Not sleeping, and weeping fair to break your heart, but the baby's kicking and her waist's spreading, thank the Virgin,' Sarah replied. 'How's my Pat? He tells me he's all right but as you well know, him and Brian were as close as brothers. He looked like a ghost himself standing at the graveside.'

Patrick had held himself together manfully through Brian's funeral, with only a trace of moisture in his eye betraying his grief as the coffin was lowered, but he'd sobbed in her arms when they were alone that night.

305

'You know what men are like, they keep it all in, but he's been to the Virginia Street chapel after work each day to light a candle for Brian. I know he mourns him deeply, as we all do,' Josie replied. 'Thankfully, with the fair weather there's been plenty of work to keep his mind busy.'

'I can see he's not the only one who's been busy,' Sarah said, casting her eyes around the room.

'Well, while you're taken up caring for Mattie I'm trying to make sure everything stays just as you like it,' Josie told her.

Sarah expression softened. 'Well, truth where it's due, I couldn't have done better myself, and the children are forever telling me how Miss Josie has done this and that for them. Annie even said you were giving them a bath twice a week. That's a lot of water to fetch in. Wouldn't it be easier for you and the children to make do with a strip wash like Patrick does?'

'We do most nights but Patrick goes to the bathhouse in Smithfield each Saturday, and the children and I can't. So despite the fetching and carrying I've decided to set a bath in front of the fire like Ma, Gran and me used to.'

Sarah laughed and Josie's shoulders relaxed. 'Pat said he'd come home and found you soaking yourself in the tub the other night.'

Josie felt her cheeks glow as she remembered what he had done after he walked in on her – and without giving her time to dry herself either.

Sarah set her empty cup on the table. 'Well, I can't say that you haven't brightened Patrick's and the children's lives. There's no doubting they couldn't be in better hands, but I'd bet a crown to a penny that you've discovered muscles you didn't know you had in the last week.'

This time Josie laughed. 'Aye, and that there's such a time as five in the morning.'

Sarah's smile widened. 'I heard you've been sending Pat off with a clean shirt and full belly each day. I used to do the same for my Pat, God rest his soul.' She crossed herself.

'I may not be able to be Patrick's wife in law, but I am his wife in every other way,' Josie said firmly. 'After Rosa, he and the children deserve a proper home, and while I'm caring for them they'll always have clean clothes, mended socks and a hot meal each day.' She gave Sarah a quirky smile. 'But I had forgotten just how much work that actually took. No matter. I'll get used to it.' She picked up her chemise and plunged it into the soapy water.

The reserved expression returned to Sarah's face. 'I'm sure you will but, Josie, *whatever* will your mother say?'

A lump settled on Josie chest and her shoulders slumped. 'That's just what I've been asking myself for the past week,' she replied. 'I just pray that when she hears the whole story she'll understand why I left.'

'I hope you're right and Ellen does see it that way, but you're not little Josie running the streets in second-hand clothes any more. You're Miss O'Casey, the stepdaughter of the Chief Medical Officer at the London Hospital. You have grand prospects; at least you did have before all this trouble.'

'I know, but now I have Patrick instead, and perhaps that's how it should have been all along,' Josie replied. 'Anyhow, I have written Mam another letter explaining everything but I'm not sure if it will reach her. She was in Edinburgh but I'm sure she's gone north by now. If I remember rightly, Robert's sister was leaving to visit a friend for a few weeks after they'd left. I just hope that she got my first one so at least then she'll know what's going on at home while she and Robert are away, even if I have to wait until she returns to tell her the whole story.'

'But what about the children? From what you've said about Mrs Munroe aren't you bothered about them?'

At Sarah's words all the nagging fears that kept her awake at night while Patrick slept peacefully beside her came screaming back into her mind.

Josie stared at the dirty water. 'No, Sarah, I'm not bothered.' She looked up at Sarah. 'I'm nearly out of my mind with worry,' she replied, as the images of Bobbie, Lottie, George, Joe and Jack sprang into her mind and a lump rose in her throat.

'There's not a day goes by without me imagining what that foolish old woman might be doing to the children, but I can do nothing about it. Patrick said he'd send Gus around but I said not to as Mrs Munroe would probably have him arrested.' She looked at Sarah through shimmering tears. 'The only consolation I have is that despite all her old-fashioned ways and pious attitudes Mrs Munroe *is* their grandmother. She does care for them in her own way and would not do anything purposely to harm them. All I can do is pray they remain safe until Mam and Robert return.'

'May the saints hear you,' Sarah replied.

Josie pressed her lips together and, as much as she could, she put aside her concerns for her brothers and sisters.

Perhaps she could wait for Mrs Woodall when she went to market and see if she could get news of the children from her.

Sarah stood up. 'Ah, well, I can't be sitting here all day,' she said. 'Mattie's trying to run a coal yard and grow a baby so I'd better get what I came for and head on back.' She went over and rested her hands on Josie shoulders. 'You know I've always thought of you as a daughter.' One corner of her mouth raised slightly. 'But it won't be an easy task for your mother to see you living with Patrick without the benefit of the church as an advantage for you, or the rest of your family.'

She kissed Josie on the cheek, picked up her bundle and left.

Josie watched the door close and then turned back to her task, her mind full of thoughts of her mother. She rinsed the washing in the cool water tub and then hung clothes next to Patrick's laundry. The cuff from one of his shirts fluttered against her cheek and she smiled as she thought of the man it belonged to. Images of herself and Patrick entwined in each other's arms came back so vividly that a thrill of excitement shot through her. Then she recalled his whispered words of love as he caressed her body. Her troubled heart quietened.

As long as she had Patrick's love she would never regret her actions the night of Harry's attack because it brought them together and gave her more joy than she ever thought possible. She was Patrick's completely, and she would never regret giving herself to him as she had. Even so and despite everything Josie fervently hoped that when her mother *did* find out about her and Patrick, her estrangement from her family would not prove to be permanent.

Patrick's head nodded forward and he woke with a start. He blinked a couple of times and then glanced around the scullery. The light from the window was almost gone and he judged it was almost nine o'clock at night. He must have closed his eyes for a moment and fallen asleep. It was hardly surprising – he had been up since before dawn and, after a belly full of pork and potato stew, he must have drifted off.

His eyes rested on Josie, Annie and Mickey sitting at the table. Illuminated by the soft lamp-light Josie, with Mickey on her lap, traced her finger over the words of a book he was reading softly and slowly, while Annie sat on the other side stitching the turned collar of her brother's shirt.

It had been three weeks since the night of the Tugmans' violence, followed by Brian's funeral, and Patrick still hadn't got used to the joy of returning home each day to find Josie waiting for him. He knew he never would. When he told the children that she was staying they were overjoyed and, thankfully, didn't ask any questions as to how or why. Having Josie with him made his life complete and, in truth, he didn't know how he could have gotten through the past few weeks without her. He'd nearly unmanned himself when Brian's coffin was lowered and it was only Josie's love that made the aching loss of Brian bearable. But, despite his need of her, Patrick's conscience continued to trouble him for bringing her into such a situation.

It had started on the morning of Brian's funeral, when they'd arrived back and found that one of the Munroes' servants had delivered a bundle of Josie's clothes sent by her younger sister.

Josie had sobbed when she read the note inside and remorse took a hold of him as he thought again about what she'd given up. It flared yet again when he'd come home a few days later to find she'd sold her three good dresses to buy two workaday ones for herself and new coats and boots for Mickey and Annie. He reproached himself when he saw her cooking with her sleeves rolled up, whereas less than a month ago she had had her meals not only prepared by the Munroes' cook, but also served to her in style.

It wasn't right, and he was determined to provide her with a better home. He'd put a little by from his overseas voyages and with the *Mermaid* constantly in work, he'd already decided that he would quit Walburgh Street and rent one of the houses at the back of St Dunstan's church. They were no bigger than the house they had but they did have gardens. Kate was going to live with poor Mattie and help her run the business when the baby arrived, so it would just be him, Josie, Annie, Mickey and his mother Sarah in the house. There was also a school nearby for the children. Of course, it didn't compare with the luxury he'd taken her from, but it was a start.

His head jerked again. He stretched his legs and put his hands behind his head. 'I just dropped off for a moment there.'

Mickey put his hand over his mouth and chuckled.

'Have I missed a joke?' Patrick asked, forcing himself to forget about their present circumstances and enjoy his family.

'Oh, Pa. You were snoring,' the children said almost in unison.

Patrick shot up and gave them an incensed looked. 'Snore? I don't snore!'

The children laughed and Josie joined in but she frowned slightly.

'Now, Mickey, Annie, your pa's been up before dawn and working like a farmer's mule all day. You get yourselves to bed and let him have a bit of peace,' she said, tousling his son's hair.

The two children hopped down from the table and each gave him a swift kiss before going upstairs.

Josie kissed both children as they left the room and a lump settled across Patrick's Adam's apple.

'Mickey's reading is coming on a treat,' Josie said, as she folded away Annie's thread into the sewing box.

'Thanks to you.'

Josie put the lid on the box and went over to stand in front of him. Even in her faded green

312

gown she looked like a queen. He remembered the feel of her against him and rested his eyes on her slim waist.

After the first few days, when he couldn't have held himself back if he'd wanted to, he'd tried to withdraw just at the crucial moment; however, on more than one occasion his passion had overtaken him. The thought of Josie's middle swelling with his child filled him with joy because he wanted nothing more, but also with dread – because he felt it would remove her even further from her family.

He forced a smile. 'That was a meal fit for a prince.'

Josie ran her fingers though his hair and looked down at him. 'What's troubling you, Patrick?'

He caught her around the waist, pulled her onto his lap and kissed her. 'What could be troubling me?'

She settled in his arms and gave him a considered look. 'That's what *I* asked.'

'This colour suits you,' he said, running his hands over her thigh, and reached up to kiss her but she pushed him away. 'Patrick Michael Nolan, are you going to tell me what's on your mind or am I going to have to nag you for another hour?'

Patrick managed to maintain his guileless smile for a few seconds longer but then let out a sigh. 'There were three more boats damaged today – two with their rudders smashed, and the *Pegasus*' engine was filled with syrup.'

'The Tugmans?'

He nodded. 'Of course. Also two of the men

who stood against Ma had their houses go up in flames last night.'

Josie gasped. 'Was anyone injured?'

He shook his head then let it fall back to stare up at the ceiling. She caressed his face and he caught her hand and kissed it.

'I knew there would be comeback after I'd practically brained Charlie. Ma won't let that go and now everyone is suffering because of what I've done. What's happened to Brian doesn't seem to matter.' He blew out hard. 'I know some of the men in the association have already started shipping her contraband again. I don't blame them, but to my mind they are putting their family in the shadow of the workhouse by running her stolen goods right under the coppers' noses.'

Josie shifted on his lap. 'Why don't you go to the police?'

'A man sorts out his own problems and doesn't go bleating to the nabbers,' he said, running his finger over her cheek lightly. 'Don't you worry, sweetheart, I'll see it right.'

He reached up and managed this time to capture her lips. He kissed her deeply, hoping that would be the end of the matter. With Josie sitting on his lap he could think of a number of things he'd rather do than talk about the Tugmans. She melted into him for a few moments but then pushed him away again.

'I know you think you can sort it out, Patrick, but now we have a chance at happiness I can't bear to think of it ruined by you ending up at the end of someone's knife – or worse.' She looked him squarely in the eye. 'Think, my love. You send them packing and they sink someone's boat. Ma's thrown out of Mattie's wedding and more boats are damaged. You all join together and they smash up the Town, kill Brian – God bless his soul – and then try to sabotage the *Mermaid*. Charlie attacks me and you all but kill him.' She grasped his face in her hands. 'I know it's hard to admit, but the police are the *only ones* who can put a stop to Ma's gang for good, otherwise there'll be more widows and orphans queuing up for parish relief. And don't try to tell me that Ma isn't biding her time until she can pay you back for Charlie,' she said, with just the hint of a tremor in her voice.

Patrick enfolded her in his arms. 'There, nothing's going to happen to me,' he told her. 'And I won't let anyone harm you again, I promise.'

She struggled against his embrace and sat up. 'For goodness' sake, I'm not afraid for myself. It's *you!* I don't want to lose *you.*' A twisted smile played over her lips. 'Don't you understand, you great lummox? I love you and want to spend my life with you. My whole life – for years and years – not just until the next fight when Harry catches you out one night.'

A tear swelled up over her lashes and Patrick hugged her to him. This time she snuggled down with her head on his shoulder.

She was right of course. From the moment the pipe had connected with Charlie's head there was no going back. He didn't fear for himself. If anything happened to him his family would look after the children, but Josie would be alone and then what would become of her? She wouldn't be able to go back to her family and society would shun her without him. Josie would be destitute.

He looked over to her bonnet hanging on the back of the chair. He had fished it out from the bottom of the *Mermaid's* hold where it had tumbled on that fateful night. The shape of the brim was intact but the ribbons were ripped off. Coal dust had sifted itself in between the woven straw. Josie had dampened it and dried it several times in an effort to remove the black specks but its brightness had gone. Even the fresh ribbons couldn't restore it to its former pristine condition and, unfortunately, the world Josie had turned her back on would regard her in much the same way as her bonnet – beyond rescue.

But would he wish her anywhere else? he asked himself silently, enjoying her head resting on his collarbone and her hand slipped around his body. In truth, with the joy of loving her each night he couldn't – and he thought she had the right of it: if the docks were ever to be free of the Tugmans it would need more than street law to remove them.

Chapter Twenty-Two

Josie pushed open Mattie's door and called out a hello before making her way down to the kitchen at the back of the house. As she'd expected, Mattie was there with her mother Sarah preparing the midday meal. Queenie Maguire sat in a rocking chair in the corner of the room.

'You're looking well,' Josie said as she gave Mattie a kiss on the cheek.

Mattie smoothed her hand over her swollen stomach. 'I feel fine. I still can't...' she bit her bottom lip and gave Josie a bright smile. 'I'll be glad when the young 'un's out in a few months and not doing a jig in my belly all night.' She glanced at Brian's mother rocking back and forth. 'He'll soon be here, won't he, Mother?'

Mrs Maguire gave a vague smile but didn't answer. Josie nodded at her and then turned back to her friend. 'Is she any better?'

'Well, she's talking now – sometimes,' Mattie replied, putting the pot back on the stove. 'But she's still wandering about at night.'

Mattie put her hand onto the small of her back and her mother waved her to a chair. 'Sit down and fold those clothes while I peg the sheets on the line,' she said, picking up the basket full of damp linen, and smiled across at Josie. 'It's good to see you,' she said, as she went out the back, leaving Josie and Mattie to talk.

317

'You'll be needing these in a week or two,' Josie said, and handed Mattie the baby clothes she'd been sewing.

'Oh, they're beautiful,' Mattie said, holding them up and inspecting them. She gave Josie a crafty look. 'You might need some of these yourself soon.'

Josie cheeks grew warmer. She should have had her monthly visit by now, but with all the upset of the past few weeks she was out of rhythm – or that was what she kept telling herself. 'Not this month,' she said.

'I suppose you're relieved,' Mattie said. 'I mean with your mam and pa being away and all.'

Josie sighed. 'Patrick has this strange idea that they would look more kindly on us if I wasn't with child.'

Mattie tutted. 'Men do have some odd thoughts, so they do.'

Josie bit her lower lip. 'I tell you, Mattie, I'm a bit worried that I haven't heard back from Mam. What if she's taken a turn for the worse?'

'I'm sure she's fine and dandy. You told me that she and Dr Munroe had been out and about and even went to see the military band,' Mattie said, reassuringly.

'I know, but that was a month back. What if the fever's returned?'

'Josie, I think you're just getting yourself all het up over nothing. You father wouldn't have taken her if he didn't think she was fit enough to make the journey safely.'

Josie's heart sank. It was just what she'd been telling herself for the past three weeks, and it left only one explanation for her mother's silence.

'I know Mam would have been as mad as a captured elf when she read that Patrick was still married but I hoped she might have been a bit more understanding. Especially as Bobbie's birth certificate is a year older than her and my step-father's marriage lines.' Josie shrugged. 'But as she hasn't written back I'm starting to think I was wrong. Perhaps, after all the scandal she and Pa went through before, and what with her recent illness, she just can't bear any more heartache. If that is the case, I can't see it matters if I'm in the family way or not.'

'Maybe Mrs Munroe has your mam's reply.'

'It's possible, but Bobbie sent Sam around with a letter from Aunt Mary. If Mam had written a letter back, I'm sure she would have sent that too.'

'Well, I must say, I have to hand it to your sister. She's got some pluck, smuggling out your clothes like that.'

'That she has,' Josie replied.

'I hear Patrick wasn't very pleased though,' Mattie said.

'It wasn't the clothes that riled him; it was the fact that I sold them. Oh, he didn't say anything but he got his what-have-I-done-to-you look in his eyes again,' Josie said. The image of her family sitting in the parlour loomed up in Josie's mind and sadness washed over her. 'I won't lie to you Mattie, it has been so very hard to think that my parents have turned their backs on me and I'll never see my lovely sisters and brothers ever again... But I would still rather be with Patrick, even as we are now, than not at all.'

'Pat feels responsible, and you know he's as stubborn as a mule.'

A satisfied glow spread across Josie's face. 'I know, and I love him for it. But I do wish he wasn't quite so obstinate about the Tugmans.'

Mattie was shocked. 'You don't mean he *should* ferry their gear upstream?'

'No,' she laughed. 'I mean about going to the police and helping *them* put the Tugmans where they belong – on the gallows. My stepfather worked with the police to put an end to Danny Donovan so why can't Patrick do the same with the Tugmans?'

Mattie looked doubtful. 'I don't know about the police, Josie. Our men like to right their own wrongs, you know that.'

'But at what price?'

Mattie shrugged, then looked down at the baby clothes again. 'You're so good with the needle. My wedding dress wouldn't have...' She stopped, and let her hands fall on her lap. One large tear dropped onto the tiny white-work garment.

'Oh, Josie, I miss him so much! It's as if he's taken my heart to the grave with him,' she said, her bottom lip trembling as she spoke.

Josie pulled her chair next to Mattie's and gathered her friend into her arms. Mattie buried her face in her shoulder and sobbed.

'I lie there each night with his empty place beside me and I wonder how I'm going to get through another day without his cheery whistle as he harnesses the horses or puts on his boots sitting by the fire.' She lifted her head from Josie's shoulder. 'How can something that hurts so much not kill you?'

Josie kissed Mattie's tear-stained cheek. 'I don't know and I don't want to find out, which is why I urged Patrick to forget about how scores are usually settled and go to the police.'

Mattie wiped her eyes with the back of her hand.

'Maybe you're right,' she said. 'I couldn't bear to see Pat end up like Brian. Oh, Josie, everyone tells me I'm young and I'll find someone else one day. I know they mean well but there can be no one else for me now. Not after Brian.'

'I know,' whispered Josie. And she did. Many a night she'd start awake with a vivid image of Patrick rather than Brian lying in a coffin. She would calm her frantic heart by putting her hand on his chest and feeling his steady breathing and, as the daylight filtered in, she would study every feature of his sleeping face.

As the first few lights appeared in the windows, Patrick flipped his collar up to his ears and pulled his cap down over his face. Keeping to the shadows he quickly opened the yard gate and slipped into the narrow alley at the back of the houses. A dog barked a couple of streets away but then fell silent. Without looking either side of him and with his shoulder scraping the brick wall he headed towards the new police station in Arbour Square.

He had spent three days chewing over Josie's words and, although it went strongly against the grain, he knew she was right. Still he had to be careful. Ma didn't just have eyes and ears in the streets, she had them amongst the local police, too.

It was for that reason that he now skulked around in the shadows praying to God that he could get into the station to see Superintendent Jackson before anyone knew what he was doing.

The gaslighter was already setting the lamps ablaze when he passed a couple of drunks stumbling about in Commercial Road. Skirting around them, he continued on towards Turner Street. The old Wapping Police office was nearer but Arbour Square was now H-division headquarters and also where Superintendent Jackson worked.

Dangerous was not even half the word to describe the risk of crossing Ma Tugman in normal circumstances, but with her precious Charlie still paralysed from the blow he'd inflicted, reckless might be a more accurate description of his present plan.

Picking up his pace, he soon reached the front of the new, stone-clad police station then, with a quick look left and right, he slipped through the double doors. The front office had a wooden screen from floor to ceiling with a couple of notices pasted on poster boards. Overall, it resembled a small shop – even down to the polished counter behind which sat a sleepy-looking constable writing up the evening ledger.

With a swift glance around to make sure no one was lurking around who might recognise him and high-tail it back to the Tugmans, Patrick whipped off his cap and went to the desk.

'I'd like to speak to Superintendent Jackson,' he said, turning his face as far to the wall as he could.

The sandy-haired officer, who was probably around Patrick's age, stared at him from under a straight, fair brow.

'What about?'

'I have information,' Patrick replied, in a firm voice.

The officer pursed his lips. 'This is irregular, sir. I don't–'

'Tell him I was there when Danny Donovan was taken,' Patrick said, holding the officer's gaze.

At that, the policemen barked an order at a younger constable, who clicked his heels and disappeared into the body of the station.

He pointed to the wooden bench fixed to the wall. 'You'll have to wait.'

Although every moment he sat in the front office was a moment closer to Ma getting wind of what he was about, Patrick calmly took a seat.

The clock beat heavy, rhythmic time for several moments before the door to the side of the desk opened and Superintendent Jackson stepped out.

He was much as Patrick remembered him: tall, ferocious and, please God, still straight as an arrow.

Patrick stood up.

'I know you, don't I?' Jackson said, tilting his head to one side. 'Weren't you the lad who cracked Danny Donovan across the skull when he tried to murder Mrs O'Casey?' Jackson clicked his finger. 'Patrick Nolan, isn't it?'

Patrick extended his hand. 'It is.'

The superintendent grinned. 'I never forget a face. Good to see you, Nolan, after all these years. Went to sea, didn't you?'

Patrick nodded. 'I did but I work on the river now to look after my family. We live in Walburgh Street.'

The door to the front office swung open, bringing in an officer holding a swaying drunk.

'Come,' Jackson said to Patrick, 'we'll find somewhere quieter to talk.'

After walking down several echoey corridors they finally reached the superintendent's office.

'Sit, sit,' Jackson said indicating the chair in front of the desk, and sat himself down opposite. 'Now, Nolan, what have you got for me?'

It took Patrick half an hour to spell out his plans for dealing with Ma Tugman and, when he'd finished, Jackson let out a long whistle through his teeth.

'That old sow's a sharp one, I know that, and what you've thought through to catch her is quite impressive, I must say, but' – the superintendent's face grew grim – 'not without considerable risk.'

'I know,' Patrick replied firmly, 'but someone has to step forward. I don't want my children, or any others for that matter, sucked into her web because no one has the courage to stop her.'

Jackson eyed him for a moment then stood up. He tore open the door. 'Fetch Sergeant Plant,' he bellowed down the corridor.

Within a few moments, a puffing Sergeant Plant appeared in the doorway. 'This is one of the sergeants on the Wapping Beat,' Jackson told him as Plant regained his breath.

'We've met,' Patrick said.

Plant acknowledged him with a nod.

'You've been around Wapping for years, haven't you, Plant?' Jackson said.

Plant doubled-stepped on the spot. 'I have kept order in the streets by the river for nigh on fifteen years. First as parish constable, like my father before me, and now as a police officer.' He gave a good-natured chuckle. 'I've always got my ear to the ground and the villains say I have eyes in the back of me head.' He pulled his shoulders back, putting considerable strain on the buttons on his uniform jacket.

Jackson slapped the sergeant on the back. 'Good man. Now, Nolan here has a plan that could put an end to Ma Tugman and her scum.'

Plant smoothed his moustache with his finger. 'You don't say.'

'It *must* put an end to Ma Tugman, because if she gets wind of it I won't live long enough to get another crack,' Patrick replied.

'What plan would that be then?' Plant asked.

Jackson waved his hand. 'Never mind the details.'

'Of course,' Plant replied.

'As soon as I've set it in place I'll give you the nod,' Patrick said to the superintendent.

'Good.' He offered Patrick his hand.

Patrick took it and gripped it firmly. Jackson regarded him for a moment. 'You were sweet on Mrs O'Casey's daughter, what was her name?'

'Josephine,' Patrick replied, careful to keep his voice an even tone.

'Whatever happened to her?' Jackson asked.

'She went to her family in America with her mother,' he replied, suddenly conscious of Plant's eyes on him.

Patrick frantically re-ran the conversation he'd had with Plant in the tunnel. Had he given Josie's full name to Plant? He was sure he hadn't.

Why did it matter? He couldn't think it did but somewhere, deep inside him, Patrick's instinct told him to keep her name and whereabouts to himself.

'I had better go,' Patrick said, noting that the gas lights in the corridor were being lit.

Jackson shook his hand again. 'I'll get my constable to see you out,' he said.

'No need, sir,' Plant said standing to attention. 'I'll let him slip out the back door, discreet like.' His jolly face turned up in a smile. 'After all, it wouldn't do for Ma to rumble what he's up to until everything is in place.'

Ma Tugman sat in her usual chair beside Charlie and watched the customers in the Boatman supping their ale. The apple of her eye was propped up on his left side by a folded bolster to stop him slipping onto the floor, and clutched a large brandy in his right hand.

In the last four weeks he had made some improvement. Although his left arm still had no feeling and became stiffer each day, he could stand now if someone helped him up and also just about shuffle across the floor without taking a tumble. His speech had slowly come back, although it wasn't easy to understand him as the left side of his mouth and jaw still dangled loose and drool constantly needed to be wiped from his lips.

Although each day someone pointed out a little something Charlie was doing that he hadn't done the day before and reassured her that he would soon be back to his old self, Ma wasn't so sure and, if the truth were told, she didn't want him to be.

She could play with his hair now and he couldn't move his head away. She would make a show of cleaning the dinner from his mouth as she used to when he was a child. Even his slack bladder meant he was reliant on her for a change of clothing.

Of course, that didn't mean she'd forgotten who'd put her son in such a state. Oh no. She was going to make sure Patrick Nolan *and* his fecking precious family paid for what he'd done to her sweet boy. And that included that whore, Josie O'Casey, who now played wife to him.

She chuckled quietly. That bit of news was carried to her swift enough by those women who'd hoped Nolan would do them the favour he was now doing the O'Casey woman each night.

Harry's boys were now rampaging through the docks and streets and it was paying off handsomely. Although the police had managed to seize a couple of shiploads last week, she had still shifted more goods than she'd been able to for a few months, thanks to those boatmen who, knowing what was in their best interests, had sneaked back and almost pleaded with her to help them out. It was just as well. With the nobs up west away in the country for the summer, leaving their houses crammed with movables behind, there were a great deal more stolen clocks and jewellery to be shifted out of London.

With the streets coming back in line she could now concentrate on Nolan and make him regret what he'd done to Charlie for the rest of his bog-trotting life.

A smile formed itself on Ma's lips. She glanced at her son. 'Quiet tonight, ain't it, Charlie?'

He grunted and threw the brandy down the back of his throat. He slammed the glass down a couple of times and glared at the girl behind the bar. Ma whipped the rag from her sleeve and patted it on his chin where a small rivulet of the spirit trickled down. He jerked his head away.

'Now, now,' she said, continuing with her fussing. 'We don't want it all over your nice shirt, do we?'

Charlie banged the glass again but she snatched it from his hand.

'Better wait awhile, you know,' she whispered, casting her eyes down to his crotch.

Charlie ground out a series of Fs and Cs as the door swung open and Harry strolled in. He clicked his fingers and the girl at the bar shot over quick as could be with a drink in her hand.

'There you go, Harry,' she said, simpering at him.

Ma regarded her through narrowed eyes. She hadn't given Harry the time of day until Charlie was carried back half dead and now she was all over him, ungrateful slut.

Harry gave the girl a slap on the rump as she

turned to go. She giggled and cast an inviting glance at him over her shoulder.

'Don't you go too far in case Charlie needs you,' Ma told her. The girl gave her a resentful look and scurried away.

'How's Charlie tonight?' Harry asked, nodding towards his brother.

Ma folded her arms and tutted. 'Like you care.' She waited a few moments before giving a sharp nod. He shuffled to his feet, caught hold of a chair and sat in front of her.

'We got two boat loads from the *Kittymore* and the *Pride of Aberdeen* and swifted a wagon load of silk from the Gilmore and Sons warehouse. The boys are already storing it,' he said, giving her a beseeching look.

It was a good haul and no mistake, but it would give them the problem of moving it. The *Kittymore* carried spirit and, although profitable, the barrels were bulky. She'd already got two crates of silver waiting to be transported to her buyer in Old Pye Street, but she couldn't complain. She let her smile return.

'Not bad,' she said. 'We'll set about parcelling it up–'

The murmuring in the bar stopped and instead of listening to her, everyone was staring openmouthed at the door.

Ma turned and her mouth, too, dropped open as her eyes fell upon Patrick Nolan standing alone in the middle of her bar.

Chapter Twenty-Three

Patrick ran his gaze slowly around the dingy interior of the Boatman and wondered why anyone, after breaking his back all day for a few pennies, would want to drown his sorrows in a place like this. Even the whores selling themselves for six pennyworth in the alley alongside were a repellent collection of crones. Ma's pub must be the last stop before the grave, or the pox ward at the London Hospital. With his hands in his pockets, Patrick mentally counted Ma's men draped over the bar.

Twelve. With a rueful smile to himself, he thought he might just get out alive.

The door swung closed behind him and Patrick looked at Ma. In her shapeless gown and with her swollen ankles she looked more like a vagrant than the head of the most successful criminal outfit on the river, and he wondered in passing where all the money she made went to. Clearly not on her person, judging by the rat-tail hair crammed into a loose knot or the food stains down her front. A brief flash of admiration crossed her face as she looked him up and down. Although his heart pounded in his chest, Patrick gave her his friendliest smile.

'I heard you wanted a word,' he said, striding towards her.

Snapper did what was expected of him and

growled in Patrick's direction but didn't bother to get to his feet. Harry stepped forward and took up the task.

'Let me slice him, Ma,' he called over his shoulder, spraying Patrick's face with spit.

Patrick regarded him coolly. Others now peeled themselves off the bar and gathered behind Harry, jeering and spitting on the floor at Patrick's feet.

'Let him pass,' Ma called out.

Harry balled his hands into fists and jerked towards Patrick a couple of times before he stood aside.

Patrick stepped forward and Ma gave a hard laugh. 'You've got some balls strolling in here after what you've done,' she said. Her fingers clawed around Charlie's arm. 'Look at my poor boy.'

Patrick did. Charlie glared at him out of his good eye but the left side of his face slid downwards like a wax candle left in the window on a hot day. His left leg seemed well enough although the foot was turned out at an odd angle, and his left arm had already contracted up. One of the crew on the *Seahorse* had fallen from the mast and lost the use of one side of his body as Charlie had. By the time they'd reached port his arm was fixed to his side as if it had been nailed there. By the way Charlie's left fist was clenched, it was clear his arm was heading in the same direction.

'I see him well enough. But what you can't see is what your Harry did to my sister's husband because now he's in his grave.'

The drinkers in the bar began sliding towards the door to avoid being caught in the blood bath that was beginning to seem inevitable.

Patrick shrugged. 'I came to talk business, but if you just want to go over who's done what to who, then I might as well go.' And with that, his hands still in his pockets, Patrick turned to leave. But, for all his studied nonchalance, he could almost feel the sting of a blade on his windpipe, and the hair on the nape of his neck pricked up.

Like all predators, the Tugmans could smell fear. He had to hold his nerve and with slow deliberation he sauntered to the door.

'Business is it?' Ma's voice called after him.

Patrick turned slowly, the relief swelling in his chest almost painful.

'What sort of business?' she asked, leaving off pawing Charlie's arm.

'The sort that will profit us both.'

Harry began to speak but Ma shot him a look so sharp it could have cut a diamond.

Patrick put on his artless grin again. 'See, me and the boys have something you want – boats – but up till now some of us have been working with you and not been getting our fair share, so to speak.'

'They get paid enough, why should I pay them more?'

'Because the police are on your tail and they've been capturing more boats each day. If they go on at this rate you won't be able to move the stuff you've got stashed around the area and you know it.'

Ma's watery blue eyes fixed on him. 'Why

should I cut you in?'

'Because without me you'll be finished in a month. I have the boats you need, but not for the few pennies you pay.'

'And what's brought about this change in the wind?'

'I have responsibilities.'

Ma let out a long cackle and rocked backwards. 'You mean the O'Casey woman you're fecking,' she said. The men beside her snorted and Ma ran her eyes slowly over him. 'You must be a bit of a he-goat, Nolan, to tempt a bit of quality skirt like that to warm your bed, and without a wedding band.' Her tongue traced along her thin lips. Patrick's skin scrawled.

'Does your wife know?' Harry called out, and the men around him sniggered. Even Charlie's lopsided mouth lifted on the mobile side, and, though Ma laughed too, her rheumy eyes never left Patrick's face.

He held back his fury. He'd known Josie's name would come up but it didn't make it easier to hear it on Ma's filthy lips. She studied him for a moment then clicked her fingers. Harry sprang forward, as did the man behind Charlie. Before he could move they grabbed him, shoved both arms up his back and pushed him onto his knees in front of her.

'Feck you, Nolan,' Harry snarled in his ear.

The blood pounded in Patrick's brain as an image of Josie shot into his mind. It looked as if the nightmare that woke her up sobbing was about to come true and her next sight of him would be lying on a cold slab at the coroner's.

Ma fished around in the folds of her ragged skirt and pulled out a short-barrelled pistol. With slow deliberation she turned it in her hands and pointed it at him.

'My Charlie loves his old ma, don't you, son,' she asked.

Charlie grunted something and a simpering expression lit her face. 'Nice bit of workmanship on this one, see?' She fingered the fine tracing on the lock mechanism. 'And not just any old pistol but, as you can see, I get two goes at hitting my target.'

Patrick stared briefly down the double barrels of the gun as Ma pressed them to his forehead.

Images of Josie, Annie and Mickey flashed through his mind as the cold metal dug into his skin.

'I've been practising in the yard on some old bottles and I'm missing more than not but,' she clicked both firing locks back, 'I guess my aim would be true enough this close.'

Sweat sprang out along the length of Patrick's spine and for one awful moment he felt his nerve waver. Clenching his jaws together until his teeth grated, he gave Ma as cool a look as he could muster under the circumstances.

'Now that's no way to treat someone trying to do you a bit of good,' he said, praying that his voice didn't betray the terror thundering through him.

The barrels moved between his eyebrows. If he reacted he was dead, so he conjured up an image of Josie sewing by the fire, forcing his mind to focus on that and not on Ma's swollen old finger resting on the trigger.

'Is there some reason why I shouldn't just pull the trigger and splatter your brains across the far wall, Nolan?' she asked, in a conversational tone.

'Because if I'm not sinking a pint in the Town by half-nine every Irishman on this river front will be down here. There'll not be a man alive when they leave.'

There was an agonising pause when, for one alarming moment his panic nearly overwhelmed him, then Ma uncocked the gun and slipped it back in her pocket. She nodded. Patrick was released instantly. He stood, hardly believing he was still alive and, suppressing the urge to run from the pub, he gave her a hard look.

'I'll send you word,' she said. 'We'll talk money then.'

'No, we won't. We'll talk now. I'll take the first run for ten percent. After that I'll consider sending my men.'

What could have been a smile curled its way over Ma's lips. She nodded. 'Next week.'

'I'll need two days' notice,' Patrick said, as the sweat rolled down the centre of his back and soaked though the shirt under his jacket. He was still having trouble believing she'd taken the bait.

'You fecking well *have* got some balls on you, Nolan, and that's a fact,' she said, with grudging admiration.

Patrick pulled the lapels of his jacket down hard and nodded. As slowly as he could he strolled back to the door and left as casually, and purposefully, as he could.

He sauntered along the alley, turned into Narrow Street and continued west. After a few more paces he ducked into the shadows of a doorway and waited as people passed along the street. He remained hidden in the doorway until he was certain that none of Ma's knife men had followed him, then he leant back, shut his eyes and did something he hadn't done for a very long time: recited Hail Mary Mother of God in its entirety then crossed his forehead, lips and heart.

Josie started awake with her hand outstretched to the empty space beside her. Rolling over and looking around, she saw Patrick standing motionless at the window, one arm resting on top of the window frame as he stared out towards the river.

Although the threat of the Tugmans still hung over their heads, up until a week ago Patrick had been more or less his usual contented self, but Josie had noticed that he'd become preoccupied over the last few days. She had also caught him several times watching her and the children with a troubled expression on his face.

At first she thought Patrick's change of mood might have been because he'd noticed that she'd been queasy for the last couple of mornings, but when she mentioned making Mattie some more baby clothes as a way of broaching the subject, he'd just smiled mildly. Most telling had been the passionate, almost frantic way he'd made love to her recently. There was clearly something wrong, and she wasn't going to be put off getting to the root of the matter by allowing him to tell her that she was just being fanciful.

She sat up, gathering the sheet around her.

Patrick looked around and his eyes rested on her bare shoulders. The hard lines of his mouth softened.

'I don't think I'll ever get used to how beautiful you are,' he said, his dark eyes renewing the excitement in the pit of her stomach.

'What's wrong, Patrick?'

He looked back at the river. 'I've been to the police.'

Thank God for that, Josie thought, but said, 'It's the only way,' and smiled at him. 'All they need is the evidence.'

'I agree,' he said, giving her an odd look then striding across the floorboards to sit on the edge of the bed. Taking her delicate hand in his large, work-calloused one he smoothed over the palm and the tips of her fingers. A shiver ran up Josie's arm as he kissed it lightly.

'Last Tuesday I went to the Boatman to see Ma Tugman,' he said, capturing her gaze with his own.

'Alone?'

He nodded.

No wonder he'd been pensive, Josie thought. He'd probably been trying to make sense of how he'd been allowed to walk out of that drinking hole alive.

'I told them that, because of Brian's death and the number of damaged boats, the boatmen in the association have had second thoughts about carrying her stolen goods,' Patrick continued in a calm voice.

'Have they?' she asked, running her hand up his forearm and disturbing the smooth hair just to assure herself that he was still whole.

The corners of Patrick mouth lifted and he kissed her hand again. 'Not a bit of it. If anything they are even more determined to stand against her.'

'Then–'

'I told Ma we would help her out but we wanted more money.' He slid his arm around her. 'And that I would take the first shipment as a show of good faith. I plan to find out everything I can, then give the information to the police so that they can catch Ma and her thugs. Handling stolen goods carries the sentence of transportation, but only if there's enough evidence to link the Tugmans to the crime, and not some poor bargeman.'

'You don't actually trust her, do you?' she asked incredulously.

'Of course not. She's only biding her time until she can pay me back for Charlie,' he said, kissing her hair. 'But I'm going to set her up before that can happen.'

Josie braced her hand on his chest. 'No, Patrick! No!'

'Shhh, sweet, you'll wake the children.' He tried to gather her back to him but Josie held him off.

'Maybe when you see them you'll realise what a stupid idea this is.'

A determined expression set on his face. 'It's the only way, Josie. You said so yourself.'

She grasped his upper arms. 'I said to tell the police, not to act as bait.'

Patrick was resolute. 'Trust me, Josie. I know what I'm about.'

It was only just early morning, probably no more than five o'clock, but already her stomach felt unsettled. She wasn't yet certain that she was carrying his child but thought perhaps she should tell him as a way of dissuading him from his course. She studied his face, noting every small detail, including his unwavering gaze. She raised her hand and traced her finger along his cheekbone. 'Of course I trust you.'

He slid his arms around her, drew her to him and then rolled her on her back, covering her mouth with his to end further discussion.

She knew that if she told him her suspicions about her condition it wouldn't change his mind – indeed it would only add to his burdens. So she gave herself up to the pleasure of Patrick's hands and lips and tried to blot out the sense of foreboding that had suddenly coiled itself deep within her chest.

Having seen Annie and Mickey to bed, Patrick waited an hour or so for the surrounding streets to fall silent before he slipped out of the house.

Once Josie had said her piece on the morning he'd told her of his plans, she hadn't tried to dissuade him again. For that he was truly thankful.

He had qualms enough without having to argue and talk the whole thing over with her every time they were alone. He smiled to himself – Talk? The last thing they did when they were alone was talk!

From the first time they had lain together, Josie had responded to his lovemaking in a way he could never even have dreamed of, but since the morning he'd explained how he was going to rid

339

the area of the Tugmans they had made love as if judgement day was coming. Hopefully it was – for Ma.

His big gamble was that Ma's need to get her goods shifted would override her desire to pay him back in kind for Charlie. So far her greed seemed to have the upper hand, but he had to set the trap swiftly before she changed her mind and the police found his gutted corpse floating face down in the Thames.

Although the new police force, with its headquarters in Scotland Yard, was concerned with more than just theft from the docks, the tradition of telling them absolutely nothing was deep-rooted in people's minds. But Patrick knew it couldn't continue and was now prepared to defy the custom.

The constable stopped scratching the quill across the open book and looked up.

'We haven't had any women brought in yet,' he informed Patrick from beneath his fair moustache.

'Women?'

The constable gave Patrick a pitiable look. 'You're looking for your old lady and I'm telling you there's none in the cells.' He waved the pen towards the front door. 'Come back later, when the pubs are chucking out.' He went back to his task.

'I've come to speak to Superintendent Jackson,' Patrick said in a firm voice.

The officer looked up and raised his eyebrows. 'What about?'

'Is he here?' persisted Patrick, in as calm a voice

340

as he could manage. 'It's important that I see him.'

Important wasn't the word; vital was. He hadn't heard from Ma all week and was beginning to doubt if she was actually going to take the bait until late this afternoon when she'd sent word that the cargo would be ready tomorrow. This left him precious little time, but if he tried to stall Ma, she would smell a rat and his swim in the Thames would surely follow.

Chewing his lips, the constable behind the desk regarded Patrick thoughtfully for a moment. 'Superintendent Jackson isn't on duty until tomorrow morning.'

This was a fine fecking kettle of fish. Patrick mentally ran through his options.

It was common knowledge that Ma had a couple of rotten peelers in her pocket but Patrick couldn't be sure who they might be. The constable keeping the front door could be honest, but equally it could be that if Patrick told him about Ma's shipment he would send word straight to her.

He studied the constable, still scratching his quill across the open ledger. No, he couldn't chance it. This venture was risky enough without telling any one else, even a decent looking station officer.

'I'll come back at eight tomorrow then,' Patrick said as he headed to the door. The officer shrugged and returned to his paperwork.

Patrick slipped back around the corner of the station and bit the pad of his thumb while he tried to get things straight in his mind.

By eight o'clock, Ma's stash would already be aboard the *Mermaid* and her contact would be waiting for him below the horse ferry jetty just past Westminster. He had to get to the superintendent before he set off, to allow him time to apprehend the shipment. There was nothing for it – he would have to go home, return at dawn, and pray that the commanding officer of H-division arrived early.

Furious and frustrated but with no other course of action open to him, Patrick flipped his collar up around his ears again.

St Dunstan's church sounded out eleven o'clock in the distance. The back gate opened and the night patrol marched out with the sergeant in charge of the watch at their head. Patrick remained in the shadows as their boots crunched over the cobbles and then the lamp light illuminated the man at the head of the column. He almost laughed out loud and could have wept with relief. Plant!

Patrick waited while the column of men disappeared. Plant would march his constables to their beats and then start his own supervisory patrol. Following the rhythmic stamp of their feet Patrick set his cap down over his face and emerged from the shadows.

Chapter Twenty-Four

Ellen rested her hands on Robert's shoulder as his hand encircled her waist. With a light step she jumped down from the dog cart and stood in the gravel drive in front of the hotel. She drew in a deep breath, noting that the temperature had already dropped.

They had hired a local trap and spent a lovely day in the hills, walking and drinking in the spectacular scenery of Great Cumbrea Island. Mrs MacKay, the hotelier's wife, had packed them a hearty lunch which they'd eaten at one of the island's high spots, where they enjoyed the fine late summer day.

'Ready for tea, Mrs Munroe?' he asked and offered his arm as the groom led the pony back to the stable.

Ellen smiled up to his much loved face. 'I certainly am,' she replied. 'All that walking has given me an appetite.'

A crease furrowed his brow. 'It wasn't too much for you?' he asked, his experienced eyes looking over her face for any signs of fever.

'Not at all.' She squeezed his arm as they started towards the front door. 'It's been a beautiful day – one of the last I'm sure, as I feel autumn in the breeze.'

'You like Scotland then?' he asked, as they went up the steps together.

'I don't *like* Scotland, I love it. Next year we shall bring all the family with us,' Ellen replied with a twinkle in her eye. 'Just as the Queen and Prince Albert do.'

Mr MacKay, the hotel manager appeared. 'Good afternoon to you, Dr Munroe, Mrs Munroe. Would you like tea in the sitting room?'

Robert looked at her.

'May we have it in the conservatory so we can watch the fishing boats return to Largs?' she replied, taking off her hat and gloves.

Mr MacKay hurried towards the kitchen.

Ellen and Robert sat beside the large windows looking out over the bay to where the small fleet of fishermen sailed in on the evening tide after a day of dragging their nets in the Firth of Clyde.

Ellen settled back to enjoy the view until the tea arrived. Robert picked up yesterday's copy of the *Scotsman,* which had arrived that morning on the early ferry, and pulled his glasses out of his top pocket. She felt her eyelids start to droop but it was from the healthy tiredness of fresh air and exercise, not the bone-weariness of illness she'd suffered when they'd first arrived at Robert's sister's in Sterling.

After the dreamlike childbed delirium that had engulfed her, it had taken her weeks of rest before she'd begun to feel like her old self again. But thanks to Robert's constant love and attention she had returned to full health.

'You would think, with the House in recess, that the two sides would stop calling each other names over the Factory Act debacle,' Robert said, shaking out the paper. 'Don't they realise that children are dying while they act like over-grown school boys?'

'You'll be back soon to put them straight,' Ellen replied.

At the end of the week they planned to continue their tour of the Western Isles, across to Arran and Bute for a month before travelling back to Edinburgh and taking the steamer home to London.

Robert looked over his half-rimmed glasses at her. 'Only if you are well, my love.'

Mrs Mackay arrived with the tea tray. 'There's some of my own plum jam you're so fond of, Mrs Munroe, to go with the scones,' she said, in her soft lilting voice as she set the over-laden tray beside Ellen. 'And today's post. It arrived after you'd left this morning.'

Ellen thanked her and handed the two letters to Robert to open while she poured the tea.

A twinge of disappointment tugged at her. She had hoped to hear from Josie a week ago but there was still nothing. Since they'd left London, the children's letters had arrived regularly each week. The younger children wrote of what they had been doing and how much they enjoyed being with dear Grandmama, but Lottie's and Bobbie's had phrases like, 'we are following your progress on a map and see that you will be back with us in eight weeks' and 'Grandmama was pleased that, because of the rain, we were able to spend an extra hour at our prayer today', which frankly unsettled Ellen. She had seen the disquiet in Robert's eyes, too, but he hadn't commented.

The one consolation Ellen had was knowing that Josie was with the children. However, whereas the children's letters were usually full of what Josie said and did with them, the batch that arrived last week hadn't mentioned their older sister at all, which is why Ellen was even more concerned. She hadn't had a letter from Josie for almost three weeks.

'Hermione sends her love and says she hopes we enjoy the rest of our holiday and looks forward to visiting us in London in the Spring,' Robert said, refolding his sister's letter and picking up the next one. 'Hello,' he said slipping his finger under the seal. 'This looks like Bobbie's handwriting. I wonder why she didn't send it with the rest.'

Robert scanned the page and his mouth dropped open. 'I cannot believe what I am reading!' He handed her the letter.

The words seemed to rush at her from the page and dance in front of her eyes. 'Robert!' she said, as the paper fluttered to her lap.

He jumped to his feet and pulled on the rope by the fireplace. He snatched his glasses from his nose and clasped his hands behind his back. With his mouth pulled into a tight line he stared out of the window. Although he stood stock still with his broad shoulders pulled back and an impassive expression on his face, Robert's knuckles showed white.

Ellen read Bobbie's letter again and tears sprang into her eyes as fury swept over her. 'How could she? After all–'

Mr MacKay stepped into the conservatory and Robert turned. 'Mr MacKay, I am afraid that we are required at home immediately. My wife and I will be leaving tomorrow. I would be grateful if you would make arrangements for our luggage to be collected for the morning ferry. Please convey our regrets to you wife for us having to leave your establishment so abruptly.'

The hotelier bowed and left the room. Robert glanced down at his mangled spectacles then threw them in the fire grate. 'I don't know why she did this, Ellen, but I'm going to damn well find out.'

Annie held tight onto her brother's hand as they made their way along The Highway to their school. She smiled when she felt her long plaits bounce against her back, knowing that each one was tied with a bright blue ribbon that Miss Josie had said suited her dark hair perfectly. Annie had always been conscious that she was darker than most of the other children in the Highway School but Miss Josie, when she was combing out her tangles after their bath, pointed out that freckled faces and fair hair were two a penny in the playground, whereas Annie's raven hair and creamy skin was distinctive.

Since Miss Josie had come to live with them, everything in Annie's life had changed for the better. She had two new dresses and Mickey had two new shirts and a pair of trousers; they both had new boots, and a new coat each for the winter. They were much too big for them but, as Miss Josie said, they would have to last a few years before they could be replaced.

Pa wanted her and Mickey to call Miss Josie Mam, but Annie couldn't quite manage it yet. And it wasn't that she didn't want to or had some loyalty to the mother she couldn't remember, it was just that, even dressed in the same poor clothes as all the other women, Miss Josie was still different.

And she wasn't the only one to think so. When the news got around that Miss Josie had come to live with them it was on everyone's lips. Whenever she went into the corner shop or passed a group of women they had nudged each other. She even heard a couple of the younger women call Miss Josie dirty names, but when she asked Gran about it she'd told them they were just jealous because Patrick loved Miss Josie and not them. And Annie knew it was the truth of the matter because Pa did love Miss Josie and Miss Josie loved him.

They laughed for no reason in that special way that Aunt Mattie and poor Uncle Brian used to do. Pa was always hugging Miss Josie and, although she pushed him away and told him to stop, Annie could see she didn't really mean it.

But Miss Josie had been quiet this morning when she filled their new satchels and waved them off. She looked tired too, with dark rings under her eyes and hugged them for a long time before she'd let them go.

Annie thought it was because Miss Josie's tummy had been upset for the past few weeks. She was worried at first to think that she might have to go home, but when she told Gran and Aunt Mattie about it they gave each other one of those looks that told Annie it was the sort of thing women knew about but didn't mention out loud, so she was reassured.

As they reached The Highway, Annie took hold of Mickey's hand more firmly. With the wagons rolling by in both directions they had to keep their eyes peeled so they didn't end up under the hooves of the huge horses that pulled them.

'Come on, Mickey,' she said, as she spotted a gap that they could dash across.

They started off but halfway there Mickey let go of her hand.

'I've dropped my satchel,' he called, as a heavy horse with his muzzle in a sack cut him off from view.

Annie turned to follow him but was blocked by a brewery cart so she continued onto the other pavement then turned to look for her brother. Crouching down so she could see under the traffic, she tried to spot his legs amongst the people making their way to work on the other side of the road, but she couldn't.

Straightening up again, she retraced her steps but he was nowhere to be seen. Normally she would have thought he had slipped away from her to bunk off, but since Miss Josie had been helping him with his letters Mickey had been eager to go to school and had even talked about getting the form reading prize. She couldn't understand why he wasn't waiting for her with his retrieved satchel.

She looked around and spotted a fat, squat man who seemed to be in danger of bursting out of a brightly checked jacket.

'You lost your brother?' he asked in a cheery voice, the cigarette dangling from his lips wagging up and down as he spoke.

Annie nodded.

'He went down there.' He jerked his head backwards to the narrow alley behind him, nearly dislodging his short-crowned hat as he moved.

Annie peered around him but couldn't see Mickey. She bit her lower lip.

Pa, Gran and Miss Josie had told her to stay on the main road and not to stray into the narrow passageway that ran through the neighbourhood, but the school bell would be rung soon and she didn't want to have to explain to Miss Porrit why they were late.

With her heart thumping in her chest she stepped past the man lolling against the wall and into the alleyway. There were stacks of boxes on one side and a couple of doors leading in to the shops but she couldn't see Mickey.

'Mickey must be hiding,' the man said.

Annie spun around to find the man right behind her. 'How do you know—?'

One of the doors opened and another man stepped into the alley. He grinned at her and the breath left Annie's lungs as her gaze fixed on Harry Tugman.

'Hello, Annie,' he said with a grin. 'My ma wants a word with you.'

Chapter Twenty-Five

Ma couldn't remember when she'd felt so jolly. Sitting on her chair in the corner, she swung her legs backwards and forwards as she watched the door.

'Give us a brandy,' she barked at the girl cleaning the bar.

Nine o'clock was a little early, even for her, but she was celebrating and thought an exception just this once wouldn't hurt.

The door to the back parlour opened and two of her men struggled through with Charlie hanging between them. His head still lolled a bit but his good leg managed to find its footing with the forwards step although the other scraped along behind.

'Put him here,' Ma said indicating the chair beside her. 'And you–' she slapped the girl who'd just brought the brandy, '–go and fetch him his breakfast.'

The girl scarpered away.

They heaved Charlie into the chair and Ma stuffed the cushions in place to steady his balance, then went back to watching the door.

She patted her son's arm. 'You'll enjoy this.'

Charlie grunted and his focusing eye followed her gaze to the door. Almost immediately, it swung open and Patrick pushed through with Harry and Ollie close on his heels.

Ma forced the smile off of her face as she studied him striding towards her. She ran her eyes over him, understanding why the O'Casey woman had turned her back on her comfortable life. Even the two sluts at the bar were giving him more than just a passing glance. He stopped just before her with a furious expression on his angular face.

'I thought we'd agreed that you would stash the gear overnight and I'd turn up and sail off as I always do. Instead of which I have these two,' he thumbed at the men behind him, 'stop me in the middle of the docks, in front of everyone, and haul me back here. I thought this trip was a show of goodwill on both our parts.'

Goodwill! She'd give him goodwill, all right. Lying, cheating bog-trotting bastard that he was.

Ma smiled artlessly. 'There's a bit of a change of plan,' she said, hardly able to keep her merriment from bursting out. 'When Harry went down at dawn there seemed to be a nabs fair on by the docks. Know anything about it?' She fixed him with the stare that had made grown men blubber like infants.

'No,' he replied, without moving a muscle.

'The place was swarming with Peelers so I told Harry to wait,' Ma said. 'And while I waited I got to thinking. Say someone had slipped along to the police station and told a few tales they shouldn't...'

'Then we'd be in trouble wouldn't we,' Patrick said, his expression unchanged. 'If you've just called me to tell me that then I'll be on me way.'

He was fecking good and no mistake, Ma

thought. There weren't many who could stand there with a face like the archangel Gabriel, knowing they'd double crossed you. She reached under her chair and grabbed the articles hidden beneath her skirts and slammed them on the table.

Patrick eyes focused on them and his nonchalant expression vanished.

'Where did you get those?' he shouted, moving to snatch Mickey's satchel and Annie's blue ribbons off the sticky beer-stained surface.

He lunged at Ma but Harry caught him and he pitched forward, taking Harry with him. Another one of the men in the bar stepped in to hold him.

'Where are my children?' Patrick bellowed.

Ma savoured both the agonised look now spreading over his face and his impotence against the forces holding him pinioned.

'Somewhere safe,' she said, and let her smile grow wider. 'For now.'

He tried to surge forward again and almost broke free. 'You hurt one hair on their heads and Holy Mary Mother of God, I'll kill you with my own hands, so I will.' The studs on the sole of his boots scraped the floorboards as he fought to be free.

Ma continued to smile. 'They'll not get hurt as long as you keep up your end of the bargain. But if, say, the police were to get wind of our arrangement, or you decide to negotiate your own price for the cargo...' She shrugged and went on, 'Well, there's many a ship in port would pay fifty pounds for a boy.' She winked. 'Especially those Arab ones off on a long voyage. And as for that sweet

Annie of yours. I could name you a dozen fine gentlemen who would snatch her off my arm for the chance to purchase her innocence.' Horror took hold of Patrick and he tore his arm away from the henchman's grip and punched him square in the face.

He stepped forward. For one moment she thought he would grab her and choke out her last breath but he stopped just short of her and clenched his fist. The bones cracked but he kept them tight by his side.

'We had an agreement,' he forced out.

Still smiling, she crossed her arms under her bosom. 'Now, now. Nothing's going to happen to those little sweet darlings as long as you make it back here with my money and without a regiment of nabbers on your tail. Your boat's loaded so you'd better be off.'

He stared at her and if looks could kill she'd be facing her maker at that very moment. She watched as Patrick battled to keep his temper in check and then he jabbed his finger at her.

'One hair.'

One of the men behind him sneered. Patrick drew back his fist and smacked it into his nose. The thug fell like a rag doll and lay motionless, blood pouring from his nose. Ma's eyes rested on Patrick's powerful frame as he thrust his way past Harry and his men.

Bastard lying Mick though he was, Patrick Nolan had a brain as sharp as a razor, the nerve of the devil and could handle himself better than most of her own men. If she were honest, all things taken into account he was a rare one, and worth three of her men any day of the week.

Some of her gang started after him but Ma held up her hand. She didn't want Patrick dead in a pub fight. He had to live to rue the day he'd tried get one over on Ma Tugman.

Patrick couldn't remember getting to the *Mermaid,* nor how he'd managed to manoeuvre it out of its berth. He supposed he did it automatically because when the furies cleared from his mind he was already midstream and heading west. He did remember growling at the Chinese shovelling coal on the jetty, but his uncharacteristic temper got his barge loaded in double quick time so, despite losing an hour, he would still be able to dodge though the tall ships just before noon.

Although the brisk, late summer wind blowing the salty smell of the sea up river cleared his head, the image of Mickey's satchel and Annie's bright ribbons under Ma Tugman's dirty hand remained.

And, although he was almost insane with worry, there were two things he was thankful for: one, that he'd managed not to show that he knew anything about the police at the docks; and two, that he had managed to hold his temper against every inch of him wanting to grab hold of the dirty old trollop and squeeze the life out of her. But he knew he had to stay calm and focused – everything depended on it. As his temper cooled, he cursed Plant roundly for blundering about on the docks.

For the love of Mary, hadn't he explained his plan clearly enough? What more could he have done to make the sergeant understand? When Ma's men brought the goods to the *Mermaid* the superintendent was supposed to order his men to follow them back to their secret warehouses and catch them red-handed with their stolen goods. The idea was that the police act with stealth, not march up and down with pipe and drum, as seemed to have happen. Patrick had even made Plant write the details of the plan in his pocketbook to make sure he had it straight, but still he got it all arse about face.

He would deal with Plant later – the what or why didn't concern Patrick now. All he was intent on was getting the tobacco off his boat and getting Ma her money. If by the end of the day he had Annie and Mickey back and Josie waiting for him at home, nothing else mattered.

Well, that wasn't strictly true. Just getting them home in one piece today wouldn't keep them safe tomorrow unless Ma was removed permanently. He had started on this course and had to see it though to the end.

By the time he had the green tranquillity of Temple Garden on his starboard side, Patrick's brain had begun working again and he began to formulate more plans. Although Sergeant Plant had been eager to act as a go-between, Patrick decided that tomorrow he would talk to Superintendent Jackson himself. St Margaret's church at Westminster was just chiming three when he guided the *Mermaid* between the busy passenger steamers crammed with shoppers heading for Fulham. Leaving Westminster Palace behind him, Patrick trimmed the *Mermaid* for the last half

356

mile of their journey to the horse ferry by Market Street, where Ma's accomplice would be waiting. It wouldn't take more than a half an hour or so to offload the bales stowed under the front of the hold. With a swift passage to Vauxhall, he would be back to the Boatman before the sun met the horizon.

Pulling out to the centre of the river for an instant before swinging back, Patrick steered the *Mermaid* towards the jetty and nudged it between two ferries loading coaches and passengers bound for the south side of the river and the coast roads.

Tying up, Patrick climbed up to the quayside and looked around. Iggy pulled out his pipe and laid himself down, his head resting on a coil of rope until Patrick gave the orders to cast off again. It wasn't unusual for them to stop off on the way to the final destination. River men always earned an extra few shillings by taking small items for individuals as they passed along.

The road to the ferry was packed with people, animals and carts waiting to make it across to the other bank of the Thames. The driver of the Portsmouth Mail Coach argued loudly with a waggoner trying to jump the queue, while a small herd of cattle heading for a slaughterhouse lowed as they nosed nervously around.

Over the heads of the throng, Patrick spotted three policemen making their way down the quayside towards him. As with Wapping, the police officers at Queen Anne's Gate kept an eye on the riverside that ran though their division.

They seemed unhurried but as Patrick watched

their steady progress towards him a coil of unease lodged in his gut.

As the cattle were poked and prodded onto the ferry Patrick leant back and studied the men heading his way. They had the same look as the Wapping officers: tall, bewhiskered and plodding along at the regulation two miles an hour.

The one leading the way studied the names of the craft moored up as they passed along. Sweat broke out between Patrick's shoulder blades. What if the old harpy had double-crossed him and betrayed him to the police?

His heart was thundering now. If they discovered Ma's stash on board it would take too long to explain about his links to Superintendent Jackson, and if he didn't get back with Ma's money God only knew what she would do to the children. He couldn't take that chance.

Don't be stupid, he told himself. She might hate him for Charlie but she needed the watermen to move her stuff too much to set him up for a couple of pounds of tobacco. He'd get a month inside, the streets would be in uproar and she'd be worse off than she was now.

Patrick glanced around again. *Where was Ma's contact?* he wondered, trying to ignore his jumpy guts.

He sat on a stack of crates waiting to be loaded and rested, trying to look as casual as possible. The officer a few steps in front of his colleagues stopped alongside Patrick and looked him over.

'Your boat?' he asked, nodding at the *Mermaid* bobbing in its mooring.

'Aye,' Patrick replied.

The constable gave him a dubious look. 'You don't mind if I take a little look around, do you?' he said.

'Not at all,' Patrick replied, as the blood pounding in his ears nearly deafened him.

The two policemen on the dockside came and stood at his shoulder while the stout officer jumped down onto deck surprisingly lightly for someone his size.

The policeman marched to the fore and peered around. Ma's stash was almost directly under the crates Patrick was sitting on and he had to force himself to keep calm. The tobacco was well hidden under the coal and there was a good chance that if they weren't looking for it they wouldn't find it.

Whilst maintaining his outwardly relaxed appearance, Patrick prayed the officer would have enough of scuffing his polished boots and go on his way. His prayer seemed to be answered when the policemen on the ship marched back to the stern. Patrick tried not to look too relieved. They were obviously just having a look-see, nothing more.

But at the stern the officer stopped and studied the rope cabinet, then flipped back the lid. Turning slowly, he looked back at Patrick and the corners of his mouth rose under his moustache.

He reached in and the clink of metal on metal sounded as he pulled out a massive silver platter with a crest stamped in the centre. 'Beats hauling coal, eh?'

Patrick froze with icy horror, which swamped him and robbed him of speech, as the officer raised up a tankard and punch bowl out of the rope store. Strong hands grabbed him and he saw the pipe fall from Iggy's mouth.

Holding the plate high, the policeman twisted it in the afternoon sun. A blinding beam of narrow light bounced off over the ship.

'Is it the Pettit silver?' asked one of the officers.

'It is – and just where we were told it would be,' the policemen on the ship replied.

Told!

Fury and fear collided together in Patrick's head as images of Annie, Mickey and Josie flashed into his mind.

No, it wouldn't be worth her while to set him up for a pound of tobacco, but it would for a load of stolen silver that would send him to Botany Bay for seven years. He'd walked right into it. What now threatened Patrick's sanity wasn't the prospect of a trip to the other side of the world but the knowledge that Ma had his children and that Josie, without his protection, was totally at her mercy.

Josie stared at the back of the fire and stirred the stew in the pot. She'd taken out a few extra pennies from the money Bobbie had sent in her clothes, walked up to Watney Street market and bought some scrag end of lamb to make a special supper.

She been awake half the night trying to reassure herself that Patrick's plan was secure and that, by this evening, Ma Tugman and her gang would be in custody. Somehow though she couldn't quite manage it. With a heavy heart she had watched

Patrick dress silently at dawn to go down to the *Mermaid*.

They had made love last night, but afterwards, as Patrick slept, she lay staring at him and chewed over the fact that he had alerted Sergeant Plant to Ma's consignment rather than Superintendent Jackson.

It was stupid of course. Plant had been vocal enough about the criminal nature of the Tugmans when he'd sent Harry about his business, but something about the way that Harry had smiled at him gave her a nagging doubt that wouldn't go away. There was something else that wouldn't go away either.

She was certain now that she was with child. The joy of carrying Patrick's baby would have been complete were it not tinged with the sadness of being estranged from her family. She had posted the letter to Scotland seven weeks ago and had been expecting a letter back from her mother if only to upbraid her – but now it was clear to Josie that her mother was so shocked and angry that she couldn't bear even to reply.

Bobbie had managed to send a scribbled note which brought a lump to her throat with the news that Mrs Munroe had threatened to dismiss Miss Byrd for encouraging the children to laugh too much when they should be concentrating on their studies; that on Sundays the children couldn't play outside, sing or read anything but their Bibles, and that Jack had started to wake in the night, screaming. Josie ached to see them, but if her parents had turned their backs on her who knew how long it would be before she could.

George was leaving for school soon and the younger children might not even recognise her in a few months.

The potatoes in the pot boiled over and hissed on the grate. Sighing, Josie moved the pot off the heat.

The front door slammed. The children were back from school. But instead of Annie and Mickey, Billy and Georgie Conner stood in the door way.

'Er ... er ... we've come to see if Mickey is sick like, Mrs Nolan,' Billy the taller of the two boys asked as he screwed his school cap into a ball.

'Sick?'

'Yes, Missis, on account that he wasn't at school,' Georgie added, sniffing a line of clear snot back up his left nostril.

'Was Annie at school today?' Josie asked, fear welling up in her.

Billy and Georgie shook their heads.

All the nagging doubts about Sergeant Plant and Ma's duplicity came screaming back to her. There had been no mention of a police raid when she'd stood in the butcher's that morning. Surely, if Patrick's plan had gone as it should, Ma's downfall would have been on everyone's lips, but she'd heard not a word.

Maybe, it was so quietly done that no one knew and Patrick was still at the police station helping, she told herself, but it didn't ring true. Someone would have seen something.

Josie took in a deep breath. She had to stay calm and in control of her wits. She wouldn't do any one any good if she allowed panic and fear to take over.

'Thank you boys,' she said, picking up her bonnet and setting it on her head.

The boys shuffled out, followed by Josie. They ambled off, kicking a stone as they went, and Josie looked around.

Perhaps the children had bunked off and had been playing in the streets all day, she thought, but she knew it wasn't so – and she knew she had to get help to find them.

Her first thought was to dash to Mattie's where Sarah and Kate were, but four women – one of them heavily pregnant at that – couldn't search the wharves and docks alone. It was too dangerous. To find Annie and Mickey, and quick, she needed more help.

Without a second thought she turned and headed down to The Highway. She crossed over Old Gravel Lane to Wapping High Street.

Since the fight at the Town of Ramsgate, the wooden frame and the small panes of the front windows had been replaced and the paintwork redone. Through the bulls-eye glass she could see the drinkers in the packed bar.

Only trollops wandered into a public house alone, but without breaking her step Josie put her hand to the brass plate and pushed open the door. Every inch of the bar was crammed with men in their work clothes. Some wore drab jackets with patched elbows and worn, misshapen trousers, others dark canvas reefer jackets over lighter, baggy bell-bottoms. Most had stud boots but all had a drink in their hands. A thick veil of tobacco smoke stung Josie's eyes and irritated her nose as she glanced around, looking for Gus.

Thank goodness, she thought, spotting him at the far end of the bar chatting to the young woman serving. Ignoring the astonished looks on the drinkers' faces, she shoved her way through.

'Gus!' she called as she got near to him.

He looked around. 'Josie?' he said in a disbelieving tone.

'Annie and Mickey didn't go to school today.'

A smile, very like Patrick's, spread across Gus's face. 'Well there, they probably thought to have a day with their mates instead of being cooped up in a classroom.' He winked at the barmaid, who giggled. He looked back at Josie. 'Don't worry. They'll be home when they're hungry.'

She shook her head and drew him away from the bar. 'It's not like that.'

She briefly told him Patrick's plan and Gus's jaunty smile vanished. 'I need your help,' she shouted above the hubbub.

The noise continued as if she hadn't spoken. Gus picked up a tankard and banged it on the counter. The hubbub ceased.

Josie took a deep breath then spoke. 'I'm Patrick Nolan's—'

'Little dearie,' someone shouted. There were a couple of sniggers, but others shushed them quiet.

'Watch your mouth, Eddy,' Gus bellowed across her head, 'or my brother'll watch it for you.'

There was silence again.

Josie cheeks burnt but she continued. 'You know about Patrick's stand against Ma Tugman and what he did to Charlie.'

'Good man himself,' shouted someone at the back.

'Today he set up a trap to put an end to her for good but I think she's got wind of it and snatched his children,' she said.

One of the older men with a dirty cloth cap low over his brow left his drink and sidled over to her.

'Now there, Missus. Don't you fret yourself none,' he said. 'Pat's kids are better than most, but they can still find trouble if they look for it. I wouldn't wonder that while you're here getting yourself riled up they're sitting at home wondering where you are.'

Another man, this one with a coal-blackened face, grinned at her. 'There, luv. My nippers are always going missing.'

There were murmurs of agreement and the hum of conversation resumed.

'But the *Mermaid's* not back yet,' Josie shouted above the noise.

'He's probably got caught upstream at London Bridge,' another drinker told her. 'It happened to me last week. Sat there for hours, I did, waiting for a space to squeeze through.'

The men in the bar turned back to their drinks. Panic rose up in Josie. 'I have to find the children before Ma Tugman harms them,' she shouted, but no one answered.

The landlord leant across the bar. 'This ain't the place for you, Miss.' He looked over her head at Gus. 'Why don't you take her home and if Pat drops by I'll tell him you were looking for him.'

A rapid fluttering rose up in Josie's chest and

threatened to swamp her. 'No you don't understa–'

The bar door burst open. The men in the bar turned.

Iggy Bonny staggered in, clutching his chest. 'Pat's been arrested.'

Chapter Twenty-Six

With the damp from the wall at his back seeping through his jacket, Patrick watched as the morning light filtered through the high window of the police cell. He shifted his position and rubbed his wrists under the iron shackles he'd been bolted into the day before. All around him, men in dirty clothes slumped against walls or curled up on the stone floor oblivious of the stream of stale water and urine that trickled down to the drainage channel. Patrick guessed that the cell was below the level of the nearby Thames as the musky, chilly air mingled with the pungent smell of unwashed bodies.

He'd been too stunned to argue as the three officers dragged him from the *Mermaid* and marched him through the streets of Westminster. His mind had focused on only one thing – his children. Thankfully, he'd regained his wits by the time he stood in front of the duty officer, who had read the charges to him. It was then that he'd managed to convince them that Iggy had nothing to do with it and tell them of his involvement with Superintendent Jackson. They had looked dubious but dispatched an officer to Arbour Square nonetheless.

Although bone weary he hadn't slept a wink. Annie and Mickey had been in Ma's clutches for a day now and anything could have happened to them. Fury surged up in him but he shoved it aside again. He'd spent the last ten hours calling himself all kinds of a fool for not realising that Ma wouldn't just want him dead because of Charlie, she'd wanted him to suffer and she'd succeeded.

Then there was Josie. She'd be frantic by now too, and God only knows how she'd be when she heard he was taken.

The bundles of rags snoring all around him began to rouse themselves.

The barred door opened and a warden wearing a dishevelled jacket and an indifferent expression entered, with a pot in one hand and half a dozen dingy plates in the other. The old hands alongside Patrick shuffled over, but he remained where he was. He might be starving but he still didn't think he could keep down the grey gruel being slopped on the plates.

The groans of the night gave way to the slurp of men eating. The day staff eventually entered and threw the drunks who weren't worth dragging into court back onto the streets. Then the warden returned, accompanied this time by three police officers one of whom unlocked the barred door.

Patrick and the other men formed themselves into a single line and marched up the stairs to the daylight. Across the road a small crowd watched with mild interest as they stepped into the back of a closed wagon for the two miles to Anne's Gate Magistrate's court.

He was shoved into a tall waiting room with cream-tiled walls. There were a dozen or so men from other police stations already there, so he was thankful that the court started almost immediately. The pickpockets and beggars were taken up first, presumably because they could be dealt with quickly and dispatched on to the various correction houses. Finally, he heard his name called, so he picked up the chains joining his wrist and feet shackles and made his way between two prison officers into the court.

The steps took him straight up into the dock opposite the magistrate. He glanced around and his gaze shot to the public gallery. Josie stood gripping the metal railings, her knuckles white. Behind her stood his mother, two sisters, Gus, Iggy and two of the boatmen from the Town of Ramsgate. All of them stared across at him, but Josie alone held his attention.

All the guilt and self loathing he'd managed to keep at bay during the long night in the cell surged back. She was wearing her best dress covered with her paisley shawl, and her bonnet was secured with its usual side bow. Compared to the other women in the gallery she looked like a duchess.

Judging by the dark shadows under her eyes, she'd probably had as little sleep as he had. She gave him a small encouraging smile which tore Patrick's heart wide open.

The clerk of the court stood up and the noise

in the courtroom ceased. All eyes turned to the high bench where the magistrate sat.

The magistrate shook out his black gown and peered around. Satisfied that he had everyone's attention, he examined the charge sheet over his half-rimmed spectacles then looked back at Patrick.

'You are Patrick Michael Nolan of number twenty Walburgh Street, Wapping?' he asked, with just a trace of a London twang.

'I am,' Patrick replied.

'You are charged that on the twenty-fifth of August you were in possession of stolen goods to the value of two hundred pounds – the property of Sir William Pettit of Bedford's Park, Havering. How do you plead?'

'Not guilty,' replied Patrick.

The magistrate looked up at him from under an oversized wig. 'It will not do you any good to waste the court's time.'

'Not guilty,' Patrick repeated.

'Have it your own way,' the magistrate answered. 'The evidence if you please, officer.'

The police officer who had discovered the silver plate took the witness stand. 'I am Constable Grant and, acting on information received, I and Constables...'

Information received. He knew it!

He glanced over at Josie. Even with the iron rings dragging on his wrists and ankles he felt her love surround him like a warm blanket.

Constable Grant came to the end of his evidence and the magistrate shuffled the documents, sniffed over the paper for a moment and then looked back again to Patrick.

'The evidence in this case seems very clear to me, but I suppose I must ask you if you have some explanation for being found in possession of Sir William's family silver. What have you to say?' He jabbed his finger at Patrick. 'I've seen your type in court before so I don't want to hear any of your cock and bull stories. I don't look kindly on people wasting my time.'

Patrick drew himself up and looked him in the eye. 'Mrs Tugman organises and oversees all of the criminal activity in the London Docks and has tried to force the honest rivermen who earn their living ferrying goods along the Thames to take her stolen goods on their ships. I refuse to do this and, two weeks ago, I went to speak to Superintendent Jackson of H-division with a plan to trap her. He agreed, and the arrangement was that I inform him of when the trap was ready to spring. Which I did last night.'

The magistrate leaned forward. 'Are you telling me that you are a police informer?' he asked.

A low muttering started in the court. Patrick took a deep breath. 'I am an honest man who tried to help the police put a criminal gang behind bars. I sent word to Superintendent Jackson,' Patrick said in as even a voice as he could manage. 'Unfortunately, he was not on duty that night but I told Sergeant Plant all the details so that he could put his men into action.'

The magistrate sniffed and turned to the prosecuting officer in the witness box.

'We sent a constable to speak to Superintendent Jackson but he has gone to Northampton to assist the chief constable there with a murder inquiry. The constable, however, spoke to Sergeant Plant, who said he has no knowledge of last night's events,' Constable Grant said.

No knowledge!

Patrick looked across to Josie. Her face was ashen. He gripped the railing around the top of the dock and his chains jingled. 'Plant's lying! I told him everything.'

The magistrate pounded the gavel. 'Don't compound your offence by besmirching one of Her Majesty's constables. I will not have it, do you hear?'

'Plant's a liar and in Ma's pocket, I shouldn't wonder. I told him. It was as we planned. He even wrote it in his pocketbook.'

The magistrate stacked the papers together and handed them to the clerk. He banged the gavel again. 'Patrick Michael Nolan, you are remanded in custody to appear at the Central Criminal Court for trial,' he said, without even glancing up at Patrick.

Anger exploded in Patrick's head, blotting out all coherent thought. The gavel banged again somewhere but was almost drowned out by the blood rushing in his ears.

Annie and Mickey! Sweet Mary, he *had* to find them!

Ma's words about what she planned for his children flooded back into his mind and cut off his breath. Mickey sold and brutalised and Annie's innocence torn from her.

Patrick threw off the two men holding him. They stumbled as Patrick tried to scale the dock

371

but his chains held his hands together and stopped him raising his legs. He kicked the board and something cracked. The two wardens caught him again and one hit him across the shoulders with his stick. Patrick barely felt it as the pain in his heart overruled everything.

'Patrick!'

The voice calling his name wrapped around his heart and steadied it. Patrick looked across.

Josie had pushed her way to the end of the gallery nearest to him and was stretching her hand out to him over the railing.

His mind calmed and his breath began to steady. Heaving his chains up and almost welcoming the pain as they cut into his skin he too reached out but was pushed back.

'I'll find them, Patrick,' she shouted above the clamour of the court room. 'I promise I'll find them.'

'Josie.' He stretched for her again and the warden smashed the stick across his shoulders. Patrick sunk to the floor.

'I love you, Patrick,' she called, as a grey fog clouded his mind. 'And I *will* find them,' were the last words he heard as blackness closed around him.

Ma sat in her usual chair in the bar surveying her domain with a benevolent eye and a rare, unrestrained smile.

Although Harry had said he'd stashed the silver out of sight on the *Mermaid*, she couldn't rely on him pointing his prick downwards when he pissed so there was always the chance that Patrick might have found it and rumbled her game. She also fretted that, despite Plant's evidence, Patrick might still be able to convince the judge of his story, especially if Jackson started poking his nose in. But fortune had smiled on her when the bastard superintendent was called away up north. Without Jackson to back his story Patrick would go down like a cannon ball in water when he came up at the Bailey.

She swallowed the remains of her drink and turned to Charlie, propped up in his cushions in the chair beside her.

'Are you all right my love?' she asked in a sing-songy voice as she moved a lank strand of hair out of his eyes.

Charlie grunted something that she couldn't understand. 'Good,' she said, and patted his arm.

A laugh boomed across the room and Ma turned her attention to Harry, dressed in his flamboyant best at the other end of the bar. He was leaning on the counter with his arm around Lucy. She giggled as she pressed her body into his, her faded dress showing the curves of her slender body. Her cheeks glowed red in the lamplight and her eyes already had a glazed appearance as she smiled up at the man beside her. She had clearly taken advantage of the free booze.

The men in the bar were throwing drinks down their throats as if Judgment Day was about to dawn. Ollie Mac dragged himself up from his seat and swayed dangerously across the floor. He took hold of the squat barrel on the counter and thrust his glass under the spout. He tipped the keg forward but nothing came out so he threw it sideways. The empty barrel bounced onto the floor with a hollow sound.

He swung his arm out and nearly lost his balance. 'You load of bastards,' he bellowed at no one in particular. 'You've drunk the lot.'

A couple of other men lurched across to investigate and one tripped on an uneven floorboard, colliding with Ollie. He shoved him back, sending him reeling onto a spindle-legged table and spilling the drinks set there.

Chairs scraped on the wooden floor as others stood to join in the fray, but Ma banged her glass on the table in front of her and the noise stopped instantly.

'I suppose if I don't want you breaking up the place you'd better tap the other barrel,' she chuckled.

A cheer went up and those squaring up to each other forgot their differences and turned back to their drinks. Ma regarded the brutes attacking the second barrel with a maternal eye, reflecting that they were good boys really, they just needed keeping in line. Now, with Nolan gone, she thought, life would settle back to its natural order and the bog-trotting Micks could crawl back under their stones again.

A happy glow settled over her. She couldn't remember when she'd felt so cheerful– Probably when she'd watched her husband Harry's coffin being lowered, if the truth were told. A smirk spread across her lined face as she thought how Patrick Nolan tried to pit himself against her. Bloody nerve of it. She, Ma Tugman, who took over when Harry had croaked, and who saw off the Poplar crew when they thought to muscle in.

She chuckled to herself again as the tap was hammered into the next barrel. She might be getting on a bit but she could still outwit better than Nolan in her sleep. If he'd had half the sense she was born with he'd have realised she would have him the moment he thumped Charlie over the head.

Harry raised his glass and swung it around his head sprinkling brandy on those nearest to him. 'Here's to you, Ma,' he shouted, sliding along the bar towards her and bringing Lucy with him. 'No Paddy bastard could get the better of my ma.'

There was a roar of agreement.

Ma beckoned to Ollie. 'Come and tell me again what happened in court.'

Harry's right hand man stood up and swept his gaze around the room. 'I sat at the back of the flea pit, keeping meself to meself, but wiv me eyes sharp. First I saw Nolan's women come into the court with his brother and that darkie who works with him.'

'What did she look like?' Ma asked, relishing the thought of Josie O'Casey pressed into the public gallery alongside Whitechapel's pimps and trollops.

A grin spread across Ollie's face. 'Bad. Eyes like coal holes and a face like a sheet.'

Ma would liked to have seen that but, instead, she pictured Patrick, not proud and defiant as he was at his sister's wedding, but filthy and lice-ridden held between two prison officers.

Charlie gave a choking laugh. Ma turned to

him. 'See? I told you I would take care of him for you.'

He snorted and a stream of snot slid out of his left nostril. He wiped it on the cuff of his good arm.

Ollie continued. ''E was a flash one and no mistake. He stood there as bold as brass and told the world his plan to double deal you.'

'Fecking cheek of it!' someone shouted.

A crafty smile spread across Harry's face. 'But it didn't do him no good, did it?'

'No it didn't.' Ma slapped her thigh, the joy of her victory bursting out of her. 'Tell me again what happened when the magistrate sent Nolan down. I want every last bit, mind.'

'You should have seen 'is face! Like a mad animal it was. He would have jumped right over the rail too, if the chains hadn't held him back. Still, he kicked the box so hard he dislodged the wood. It took the wardens beating him – with blows that would break another man's back – to stop him.'

Ma leant forward. 'And what about 'er? Tell me what she did.'

Ollie's grinned widened. 'It was just like one of them plays at the hippodrome. He's being dragged away, like, and she's calling out, "I'll find them, Patrick, I promise. I'll find them,"' Ollie warbled in a falsetto voice, his arms outstretched and a simpering expression spread across his craggy features.

Tears of laughter gathered in Ma's eyes. She would have given half the stash in Burr Street to have seen that.

'Well, she won't have to find 'em now, will she?' a small voice slurred. 'Not now Nolan's ba ... ba ... banged up and away.'

The men in the bar, who only a few moments before had been rolling around in high spirits, were suddenly quiet.

Ma's eyes fastened on Lucy. 'What?'

Lucy blinked and screwed her thin face into a puzzled expression. 'I ssssaid ... the O'Casey woman won't 'ave to find Nolan's kids 'cause you'll let 'em go now.'

Ma heaved herself up from the chair and waddled over to the girl. The drink had made Lucy forget herself but, even so, she'd noticed that since Harry had taken up with her the slut had become less biddable.

Typical, she thought studying the girl coolly. Harry never could keep his women in order.

She smiled and several of the men around flinched. 'Will I?' she asked in a pleasant tone.

Lucy forced her eyes to stop roaming and looked at her. 'Well, it ain't right to keep 'em. I mean, you got what you wanted and they are only young 'uns after all.' Lucy eyed her nervously. 'It's sort of understood, aint it? Nippers are left be.'

'Is that right?' Ma asked in an icy voice.

Harry stepped forwards and put his hand out. 'Now, Ma, Lucy's not–'

Ma's hand shot up and Lucy jolted back.

'See the teeth marks?' she said holding the back of her right hand close to the girl's face.

Lucy's eyes focused on the curved row of teeth marks on the back of Ma's hand. 'Nolan's snotty little bugger did that only yesterday. Drew blood, too, he did. And the other one, that girl, with her slanty dago eyes kept staring as if she's trying to hex me.'

Harry stepped forward and Lucy's head lolled back as she grinned up at him.

Lucy's fair eyebrows drew together. 'But you said yourself, 'Arry, it wasn't right to keep them locked up in Burr Street.'

Harry gave her a hard look and she put her finger to her lips and giggled.

'Lucy's a bit tipsy,' he said, giving his mother a conciliatory smile. 'You didn't mean anything, did you, sweet?'

Sweet! Ma's eyes narrowed.

She studied her eldest son. 'So you think I should go down to the nasty dark cellar and untie dear Mickey and darling Annie, do you, Harry?'

There were a couple of titters and he shuffled on the spot.

'I ... er ... I'm just saying that now Nolan's taken care of, if we don't release his brats there'll be grumbling in the streets.'

Fury shot through her and she pulled her face into an ugly expression. 'Grumbling! What the feck do I care about grumbling? And how you can stand there and say that after what that bastard did to your brother I just don't know. Or have you forgotten?'

'No I haven't forgotten but–'

Ma jabbed her finger towards Charlie. 'Look at him,' she screamed. 'You, too.' She grabbed Lucy and pulled her around. 'Look what Nolan did to my darling boy.' She let her eyes rest on Charlie's contorted features for a moment then turned back to Harry. 'And you say I should let his brats go so Miss Josie fecking O'Casey can trip off to the jail and tell him his kids is safe?' She let go of Lucy and the girl fell against Harry. 'I'll tell you this. A man like Nolan could do a stretch and walk out smiling if his kids were safe, but I want him to suffer up here.' She tapped her forehead with her finger. 'Suffer every day of his life, just like my Charlie does.'

'But even Pa and Popeye Wells didn't touch each other's families,' Harry said with a hollow laugh. 'I mean, if they had, half of us wouldn't be here now.'

Ma cast her eyes around and unbelievably, she saw agreement in the men's expressions. Alarm started in her chest. They looked loyal enough, but who knew for how long? There was plenty of life in her yet, but with Charlie injured there was only Harry to enforce her will, and what if he turned against her? Her eyes returned to Lucy.

She'd always used the fact that men thought with their balls to her advantage – it was how she'd caught her Harry after all – but until now the women her sons had used to scratch their itch had come and gone. What if Lucy, with her willing smile and body, turned Harry to her ways? If he stood against his ma, the men he led would follow and then where would she be? She chewed the inside of her mouth with her few remaining teeth.

With a lightning move her hand shot out and caught hold of a clump of Lucy's blonde hair. The girl screamed but Ma dragged her closer until their faces were only a hair's breadth apart.

'Who asked your sodding opinion?' she asked, shaking the girl's head.

Lucy's face crumpled. 'I only said–'

'Who?' Ma bellowed, shaking the girl's head again.

Lucy screamed and a thin line of red appeared along her hair line. 'No one,' she sobbed.

Ma let go of the lank strands but grasped the back of her head and, digging her nails into the girl's scalp, forced Lucy to look at her. 'Then keep your fecking mouth shut,' she shouted, then she smashed the girl's face into the edge of the bar. There was a sickening crunch as she connected to the wood.

Ma let go and Lucy collapsed among the empty bottles and sawdust on the floor, blood pouring from her nose. Harry made as if to bend down but Ma fixed him with a look and he stayed where he was.

She gazed down at the unconscious girl as the splattered blood soaked into her gown and congealed on her cheek. Then she looked up, flexed her hand, and smiled. 'Anyone else got an opinion about the Nolan kids?'

Meg handed over her shilling and gathered up her bundle. She haggled with the rag seller and got down from sixpence to fourpence for a new dress for Polly, two shifts, a bonnet for the baby and a serviceable dark dress and petticoat for herself. Of course, she would have to soak the filth off the garments before they could wear them, but they would be sound enough when she had.

Meg had been pleased when she'd heard that Miss Josie had moved in with Patrick Nolan. The news had shot around the streets like lightning and while some pretended to be shocked Meg had been glad for her. Of course, at the moment Miss Josie could do with some help from the Almighty with her man locked away and his children missing.

Patrick Nolan was a good man. None better, as far as she was concerned. Everyone admired him for standing up to Ma Tugman, although much good it had done him and his own, and Meg couldn't help but worry what would become of them now that Ma was back in control.

And where were those poor children? It was the talk of the streets. Miss Josie had put up posters all over but there was still no news of them. It weren't right taking children, no matter who their father was. Until they could do proper damage kids were left to roam. Someone knew where they were of course, but they weren't saying, and Meg understood why. You might as well slit your own throat if you crossed Ma.

Meg turned the corner into East Smithfield and knocked straight into a woman with a shawl pulled tightly around her face. She murmured her apologies and was about to walk by but then stopped.

'Lucy Moss? Is it you?'

The woman nodded.

Meg and Lucy had grown up in the same street and although she had been fond of Lucy, she kept well out of her way since she'd taken up with Charlie Tugman.

'Hello,' Lucy whispered, moving the shawl away slightly.

Meg gasped. Lucy had always had fine-boned features with sharp cheeks and a pointed chin framed by pale blonde hair, but now her once straight nose looked like a squashed and bloodied piece of offal on a butcher's slab, and her pale blue eyes stared out of mauve, green and yellow bruising around their sockets.

'For the love of God, who did that to you?' she asked, as she stared in horror at the young woman's battered face.

'That evil old bitch, Ma Tugman,' Lucy replied, sucking in the spittle that had escaped from her lips.

An icy hand of fear clutched at Meg and she quickly looked around. Thankfully, the street was practically empty and those nearby couldn't have heard what Lucy said over the noise of the wagons passing by. Meg drew her into the wall and out of sight.

'I was out cold for a day after she smacked my head on the bar. And the pain! I can't tell you,' Lucy added.

Meg could imagine. Even in the shadows it was clear to see that there wasn't one part of Lucy's face that wasn't either swollen or discoloured. She must be in agony just breathing, never mind eating or speaking.

Meg chewed her lower lip. She ought to go. The children would be waiting and, besides, anyone who'd fallen foul of Ma wasn't someone you wanted others to see you hobnobbing with. There were plenty of people who would slip a titbit of information to Ma to stay in her good books.

Meg adjusted the basket on her arm. 'Well it's good to see you again, and mind how you go.'

Lucy gave her a forlorn look, and Meg realised what a stupid thing she'd just said. Mind how you go?!

The memory of how Josie O'Casey had defied Ma came back to Meg. Josie hadn't turned tail and run; no, she'd stood up to her and sent her packing.

Meg studied the downturned face of Lucy again. Thinking of Josie's daring overcame Meg's fear and allowed her motherly instincts to rise. As much as Ma Tugman's face woke her from sleep in a cold sweat of terror, she couldn't just leave Lucy as she was.

'Right,' she said putting her free arm around her old friend. 'You're coming home with me, my girl, and no argument.'

Lucy didn't argue, in fact, she slumped against Meg all the way home. Meg should have collected her children along the way but, in view of the state Lucy was in, she didn't think Mrs Olly would mind if she were a bit late. After shutting the door to her room she guided Lucy to the easy chair, lit the fire and put the kettle on.

She turned back to find the young woman had closed her eyes and appeared to have drifted off to sleep. Her shawl had slipped off her head showing that, in addition to her other injuries, her friend had a line of torn skin on her forehead. Within a few moments the kettle was hissing and Meg made a cup of tea. She judged that Lucy needed something to build her up so spooned in the last few lumps of sugar in her tea.

'There you go,' she said, handing Lucy the mug.

Lucy opened her eyes and took the cup. She cradled it in her hands and gave as near to a smile as she could manage with her twisted lips.

'I thought you'd be gone from the Boatman long before this,' Meg said, as she watched Lucy sip up her tea. 'I mean, with Charlie not too well and all.'

Although Charlie's condition was common knowledge, most thought it no more then he deserved and a great deal more besides, but you didn't speak about it if you knew what was good for you.

'When Harry brought him back I thought he would be fine and dandy in a day or two, but now he can't even hold his water and she's got me tending to him like I was a nursemaid or something, cleaning him up, feeding him and the like. It ain't right. I tried to leave but that old bitch wouldn't let me.'

'You're not going back now though, are you?' Meg said. 'Not after this. I mean, you could be waiting for a space in the poor end of the church-yard instead of sitting here sipping tea.'

Lucy shrugged. 'I haven't got anywhere else *to* go. It's there or the workhouse.' She looked around at Meg's snug little room. 'Could I come and live with you?'

An image of Ma Tugman's wrinkled face floated into Meg's mind and she shook her head.

'Don't think me hard, Lucy, but I have my children to think of and I don't want her or

Harry coming around here looking for you.'

Lucy shoulders sagged. 'I understand.'

Guilt shot through Meg. As much as she didn't relish the thought of any woman having to live with the Tugmans she really couldn't take the chance of Ma turning her beady eyes on her and the children again. Then an idea came to her.

'I know!' she said sitting up straight and beaming at Lucy. 'You can go around to the Mission hall in Settle Street and get saved.'

'What?'

'Get saved. The doxies in Whitechapel do it regularly. You go in and they ask you if you repent your sins. You say yes and then they give you a bath, a set of clothes and a bed with no questions asked.'

Lucy's eyes popped open as far as they could. 'Is that it?'

'More or less. And then if you go to their Bible study each week they feed you again,' Meg explained.

'Sounds fair to me,' Lucy said, looking quite perky at the thought.

'I also heard that they are looking for suitable young women to go to Australia.'

'Whatever for?' Lucy asked as she finished her tea.

''Cos there are too many men there and they're looking for wives,' Meg replied. 'Girl like you could do well there, I shouldn't wonder.'

She left Lucy thinking about her words and went back to the table. She unpacked her basket and set aside the basin of chicken stew. She was going to save it but it would be a kindness to share it with Lucy. They were having mutton stew tomorrow in the doctor's mess and there was bound to be some left over.

'Why don't you stay and have a bit of supper with me and the kids and go off to the Mission later? They don't shut their door until midnight.'

'You're a kind soul,' Lucy said, standing and joining Meg at the table. 'Why don't I do that while you go and get your little 'uns?'

Meg let her take over setting the plates out and grabbed her shawl from the back of the chair.

'I won't be a moment,' she said as she reached the door. She turned back as Lucy started to slice through the bread. 'By the by, you didn't say why Ma hit you?'

Lucy's pale blue eyes looked across at her. 'Because I told her that it wasn't right to keep Patrick Nolan's kids tied up in her cellar in Burr Street.'

The guard swung the chain at his waist, caught the dozen or so keys in his hand and unlocked the door to the room. He pushed Patrick in. From the other doors leading to the visitors' room various prisoners shuffled forward for the once-a-month visiting hour.

The prison officers in their buttoned-up navy uniforms and peaked caps stood with their backs to the wall, batons in their hands. The long hall was devoid of all fittings except a bench. One side of the room was punctuated at regular intervals with arched, barred windows. It was through this grille, like the monkeys at a fair, that the inmates received their loved ones at the governor's pleasure.

Pentonville, the New Model Prison, had been open for less than two years but was already filled to capacity. The silent regime kept men in their own cells for hours on end. When allowed to exercise, it was done under the watchful eye of the officers, who forbade all communication.

Even the officers were silent as they moved around the place. At first, this lack of noise suited Patrick, but over the last few days he had begun to wonder how he would manage if he was sentenced to years of this regime.

He was allowed his own clothes, although these were becoming dirty and he already had flea bites. With one bucket of water a day for personal use, it was almost impossible to keep himself and his clothes clean but he'd done his best. Years on board ships had taught him a few things, including soaking his smalls in urine before rinsing them through to help keep the lice at bay.

Patrick took his place on the stool opposite the grille. His mother sat on the other side of the bars with Gus, in his best suit, perched on a stool alongside her. She gave him a brave smile.

'It's good to see you, son. You don't look as thin as I thought you might,' she said. Her tone was too jolly.

'It's grand to see you, Mam,' he said, thinking how old and tired she looked. He turned to his brother. 'I'm even pleased to see your ugly moosh, Gus. How's Mattie?'

'As well as can be expected. Kate's with her,' Sarah told him.

'Don't you worry, Pat; I'm looking after everything just as you would. You'll soon be out of here,' Gus said.

Patrick managed a faint smile in response, thankful at least that the Nolan women had Gus to look out for them. 'Have Annie and Mickey been found yet?' Patrick dared to ask.

His mother shook her head.

He thought he was prepared for the answer, but hearing the words out loud crushed him all over again. He tried not to dwell on what might have happened to them but at night, in a bare cell, he could think of nothing else. 'How's Josie?'

'Well enough, although out of her mind with worry, like the rest of us,' Sarah told him. 'She sent this.'

She unfolded a letter and held it up for him to read.

Patrick scanned the bold hand telling him of her love and renewing her promise to find the children. He read it three times to memorise every word before he allowed Sarah to refold it and slip it back in her pocket.

The sounds of voices echoed around him. He glanced at an old man beside him in the dark blue uniform of a compliant prisoner, then through the bars to the woman in rags sobbing quietly in the grille beside his mother's chair.

'God, I feel so useless!' he shouted, and the warden tapped his stick on the side of his leg. Patrick forced himself to calm down. He was still bruised from the blow in the court.

'Come on, Pat,' Gus said, his eyes darting to their mother on the chair beside him.

Patrick nodded and pulled himself up. He gave his mother as much of a smile as he could muster.

'What's being done? Is Jackson back yet?'

'No. And no one knows when he will be,' Sarah said.

'It was in the paper that he was helping the Northern police with a double murder,' Gus told him. 'The report said the victims were found in their own beds with their throats cut.'

Sarah gave her youngest son a sharp look.

'I reported it to the desk officer,' she continued. 'But he said they had hundreds of missing children and didn't have time to look for all of them.'

Despite his resolve to put on his best show for his mother, Patrick hung his head in his hands.

'Don't you mind none,' Sarah said, moving her chair nearer to the grill. 'Josie has the whole neighbourhood searching for them. She found some packing-case paper and made posters with Annie and Mickey's description and has been from The Highway to Whitechapel High Street and everywhere in between, sticking them up in any shop that'll take them.'

'She's done the same around the riverside eating houses, too,' Gus added.

The chill in Patrick's heart thawed slightly.

'You should have seen her march into the Town to get the dockers and boatmen to help. Thanks to her they are keeping a sharp eye out to stop anyone trying to force Mickey on a ship.'

'She's even been down Betts Street and Rose-mary Lane to have a quiet word with some of the trollops about Annie,' Sarah added.

Images of Josie wandering down the dark alleys where every shabby house was either a brothel or gin shop filled him with horror.

'Now, now, Patrick she came to no harm,' Sarah said, seeing his shocked expression. 'The women might pay Ma for their pitches but, as Josie said, most of them have a child or two to care for, and might just come forward with a bit of gossip as to Annie's whereabouts.'

Patrick tasted bile at the back of his throat.

'Josie, God and all his blessed saints preserve her, is a fighter and one of the best.' Sarah went on. 'I've known from the first moment I saw you and her together that you were made for each other. A rare pair you are and no argument in it. I'm glad you and she have made it together at last.'

'I don't think she's glad,' he said. 'She gave up everything and what have I given her?'

'Aroon, lad,' Sarah said, in a tone he hadn't heard for many years. 'She'd rip your ears off if she heard you talking gloomy like that, and you know it.'

He knew his mother was right, and he wished he had Josie in front of him now as well, if only to give him one of her royal pastings for voicing such dark thoughts.

Of course, she couldn't come as only legal wives were allowed to visit. As much as he didn't want Josie to see him chained and dirty, being apart from her was sapping the life out of him. What with his fears about Annie and Mickey and his separation from Josie, Patrick was beginning to wonder if he'd survive with his sanity intact.

Sarah reached out and gripped the bar. The prison officer to one side of them placed his stick on the table. Sarah withdrew her hand and folded it on her lap.

'Don't fret, me lad,' she said in a soft voice. 'Josie's raised the neighbourhood and it's only a matter of time before we find the children and bring them home.'

Patrick prayed that her words would reach the saints in heaven – and soon.

'Although the boatmen were a bit unsettled about you getting involved with the police and all, once your Josie explained why, they've pledged a sixpence a week to pay for a solicitor for when you go to court,' Gus added.

A lump formed itself in Patrick's throat.

'That's really good of them,' he said, touched by the gesture but wondering what difference it would make against Plant's testimony.

'Also, this arrived.' Sarah put her hand into her pocket and drew out a large crumpled envelope.

Patrick stared at it. It had a colourful stamp on the corner and several ink marks over its surface. But what caught his attention was the large VR Fort William, Alexandria, stamped above his name.

'Open it, Mam.'

His mother ripped the seal off and held it up.

I am sorry to inform you that your wife, Rosa Nolan, along with twenty-seven other members of the garrison succumbed to typhus fever on the 17th January 1844 and it is recorded as such in the garrison records. I offer

you my sympathy and can assure you that she was laid to rest in the garrison cemetery.
Rev Adolphus Watson

Patrick let his head fall back.

God, how the Devil liked to twist his fork in a poor man and no mistake, he thought, as all the possibilities that had been snatched away from him rose up in his mind. He had the urge to laugh out loud but knew that the sound he made would instead be a howl of pain.

Patrick gave a humourless laugh. 'Rosa is dead. I have been a free man since January.'

Sarah and Gus crossed themselves rapidly.

'Praise the Virgin. Wait until Josie hears,' Sarah said.

'I don't want you to tell her,' Patrick said.

Sarah looked puzzled. 'But why not?'

'Because, even though she hasn't heard from her parents, I am sure they will try to help her when they return and see the danger she is in. And they won't be able to do that unless she gives me up. If she finds out about Rosa I know, and you know, she won't.

'But Patrick, now you can marry Josie before—'

'No, Mam!' Patrick clutched the iron bars between him and his mother. 'I might be free to marry her, but without a blessed miracle, I won't be able to for seven years.'

Chapter Twenty-Seven

Josie rested her hand on the brick wall outside the yard door and let the wave of nausea subside. Since she'd watched Patrick being dragged half conscious from the court she'd started each day outside the house losing her breakfast in the gutter. Although she hadn't yet fainted, she had to be careful when she stood up suddenly or moved too fast. There wasn't a day that passed without her having to stop and steady herself against a nearby wall. The misery of her morning sickness was compounded by lack of sleep and constant worry.

Each night she crawled under the covers, her mind and body aching with fatigue, and rested her hand on Patrick's side of the bed, but sleep refused to come. She prayed for a few hours' peace but images of Patrick's anguished face played over and over in her mind.

Quite apart from the constant fear for Annie and Mickey, there were other troubles, not so urgent but just as real, like the rent, and money for food. Without Patrick's income there was precious little coming into the house. Sarah still did her bit of home sewing but that only brought in a few pennies and, although Kate had given her mother five shillings, together the two women's income didn't cover half of what the landlord demanded. The last few shillings from the money

Bobbie had sent had paid last week's rent and there was enough food for six or seven days, but after that they would be on the streets.

Mattie would take them in but she couldn't support them for long with a new baby due any moment.

Josie could not allow herself to stand idly by. She decided that she must take action to find a way of supporting Patrick's children and the baby she was carrying. Neither she nor Patrick's children would ever be forced into the workhouse so, despite her stomach's morning rebellion and her head begging for rest, she straightened up. She wiped her mouth with her handkerchief and made her way back inside the house.

Kate had already left for work so Josie splashed boiling water on the damp tea leaves in the pot and waited for them to brew.

Her nausea had subsided a little and she smoothed her hand over her stomach. She had only just missed her second monthly visit so the small life inside her hadn't yet changed her shape but already she loved the child. Although the Nolan women had guessed her secret almost as soon as she had, Patrick didn't know. He had enough to torment him and she was glad not to add to it.

It wasn't yet eight so Josie poured her weak tea into a mug and settled down in the chair by the fire. Putting the mug beside her to cool she closed her eyes and let her head fall back. She must have nodded off because she jumped awake with her heart beating wildly at the click of the back door being quietly opened.

Her eyes darted around the room, then her shoulders relaxed as she spotted Meg Purdy's face peeking around the edge of the back door. Although it was already warm outside, Meg had a large shawl around her head almost covering her face.

Meg's gaze darted around the scullery for a moment before she ventured further into the room. 'Mrs Olly next door is minding the kids so I thought I'd pop by. Are you alone?' she asked, looking warily towards the front door.

Josie summoned up a brave smile. 'I am,' she said, and gave Meg a questioning look. 'You didn't need to come down the alley, the front door's open.'

'You know I ... I...' a bright smile lit up the young woman's face. 'How are you faring, duck?'

'Not so bad,' Josie lied, as the contents of her stomach rolled again. 'Pour yourself a cup.'

Meg slid into the room and, keeping the shawl over her head, got herself a cup of tea. She perched on the chair in the corner.

'Any news?' she asked, the cup in her hand trembling ever so slightly.

Josie shook her head and wished she hadn't as the floor under her feet went off kilter for a couple of seconds.

A man's voice bellowed suddenly along the alleyway at the back of the house and another answered. Meg jumped, splashing tea over her skirt. She stared at the door to the yard in wide-eyed terror.

'What on earth's the matter?' Josie asked.

The shouting stopped as the men continued

down the alley. 'They gave me a start, that's all,' she said, with a hint of a warble. 'What about the police?'

'The police aren't interested,' Josie said. 'My only hope is Superintendent Jackson but he's still away. I am so afraid that when he does come back it will be too late and Patrick will have already been found guilty.' Suddenly, from nowhere, a sob burst from her. 'I haven't slept for two hours together for days on end and my head is fair split asunder; and half of what I eat I bring back as soon at it hits the bottom.'

Meg's gaze slid down to Josie's still slender waist and her mouth dropped open.

'But just at the moment, I tell you, Meg, as the Virgin is my witness, I don't care about Ma, or the police, or the rivermen or even myself. All I want is just to have my family home and safe.'

Meg's face crumpled. 'Oh, Miss Josie.' She buried her face in her hands for a moment then raised her head. 'I should have come last night but I was too scared.' She ran the back of her hand across her nose. 'And you have been so good to me, you have, Miss Josie, and how have I repaid your kindness? I have dallied, that's what I have done, dallied, when I should have come straight around as soon as I heard.'

'Heard what?' Josie held her breath.

'Where the children might be.'

Annie woke and heard her brother whimpering quietly in the dark. So, gathering up the slack from the rope that held them to the wall, she shuffled closer to him.

'Don't worry, Mickey,' she whispered. 'Pa'll soon be here.'

'You said that yesterday,' Mickey replied, 'and the day before.'

'But today he'll come and find us and he'll give Ma Tugman and her Harry a bashing they'll never forget.' She looped her tied hands over him to hug him.

'Promise?'

Annie kissed his forehead. 'Promise,' she said as firmly as she could, stifling a sob.

If she'd had her hands free she would have crossed herself as her gran had taught her, so she just prayed silently to the Blessed Virgin and guessed the Queen of Heaven would understand that with her hands tied she couldn't manage the proper reverent attitude.

When they were first left in constant darkness, with only scurrying rats for company, Annie thought they would starve, but each morning Ma came down and threw a bowl of slop at them. They had screamed themselves hoarse the first day until they realised that no one could hear them, then they had saved their strength.

Ma Tugman would call them her little chicks and sweeties and cluck over them but Annie knew the old woman hated them and would as soon slit their throats as feed them. Annie guessed that the reason she stayed her hand was because she had some nasty fate in store. From the whispers of conversation she'd heard, Ma was negotiating some payment for something but she wasn't sure what.

The door at the top of the stairs rattled and

Annie felt Mickey start to shake. 'She's c ... c ... coming,' he said.

'Now, remember what I said, and eat everything she gives you without saying or doing anything,' Annie whispered. Mickey nodded his head against her. 'We have to keep our strength up, don't we? Pa will come and then we'll be going home to Miss Josie and we'll all be happy.'

The door opened and a light shone in and Mickey shuddered against her.

'Now, Mickey, be brave,' Annie whispered, with a great deal more bravado than she felt.

Mickey tucked himself behind her and jammed his head between her shoulder blades. Slowly, the crack in the door widened and the light from the lamp illuminated the barrels, crates and boxes piled high in every corner of the chamber. Annie squinted to allow her eyes to become accustomed to the light and blinked up to the landing at the top of the stairs.

She blinked again as she could scarcely believe her eyes. 'It's all right, Mickey,' she called over her shoulder. 'It's Miss Josie!'

Josie cast the light around, creating blocks of shadows and eerie shapes as the beam illuminated crates and boxes. As her eyes adjusted to the darkness she saw bales of silk and lace, tins of tobacco with wax seals splodged on the side, and draped sheets of sail canvas obviously hiding other items underneath.

'Miss Josie!' a small voice called across.

Josie swung around and saw Annie's dirty face

and then Mickey's peeking over his sister's shoulders.

Thank God!

If he knew that Annie and Mickey were safe, Patrick could endure imprisonment and separation but if they had come to harm...

Josie started down the stairway. 'Don't worry, sweethearts,' she said, as the wooden treads bowed and creaked under her weight. 'I'll soon have you out of here.'

Careful, she told herself. If she missed her footing and fell they'd all be done for. She clung onto the flimsy banister and made her way down in to the mouldy cellar.

'Hurry, Miss Josie,' Annie urged as Mickey started to cry.

Josie hurried down the steps but a loud crack stopped her in her tracks. She felt the tread under her foot sag and dirt pitter-pattered to the floor.

Annie screamed. Josie gripped the banister. Something fluttered over her hand but she forced it to remain, grasping hold of the rough handrail.

'It's all right,' she said, in as calm a voice as she could manage.

Keeping her head high and not daring to glance down into the stairwell that curled down beside her, she said, 'We'll soon be out of here and home.'

Slowly Josie lifted her foot off the faulty step and lowered it on to the one below until she reached the cellar floor. Dodging around the boxes and barrels she made her way to the children. She knelt down beside them and looked them over.

They were dressed in the same clothes as they'd been wearing when they'd left the house for school but now Annie's blue dress with its cover-over apron was filthy and her hair tangled. Mickey, too, was covered in dirt, and even in the dim light she could see that he had cuts and grazes over his face.

Fury rose up in Josie. What sort of evil being would treat children like animals?

She ran her hand quickly over their faces almost to reassure herself that she really had found them, then she set to work and tore at the bindings around Annie's fragile wrists.

Annie wriggled over towards her. 'Where's Pa?' she asked as Josie's nails caught in the thin rope.

'You'll see him soon,' Josie told them.

She loosened Annie's hands and the young girl rubbed her wrists before starting to pick away at the strapping around her ankles.

Josie turned her attention to Mickey.

'I'm scared,' he said as she crawled behind him. The damp from the floor spread through her skirt.

His childish voice echoed around the chamber and Josie glanced up at the cellar door at the top of the stairs. She hugged him and kissed him on his cheek.

'Shush, my honey,' she crooned in his ear, 'we'll be out of here soon and back with Gran. She's got two big sugar buns for you and Annie when you get home. Now be a good boy and stay as quiet as a mouse while I get you free. Will you do that?'

Mickey nodded.

Annie threw away the rope from her ankles and huddled closer to Josie and her brother.

'What time is it?' she whispered.

'It's just after nine by now,' Josie replied.

'The old woman will be here soon with our daily mush,' Annie said, a quiver in her voice.

Trying to keep the screaming threat of danger in her mind at bay, Josie ripped off the last of Mickey's lashings and stood up, lifting the boy to his feet and then hugging both children briefly.

'Oh, my poor loves,' she said, as she pressed her lips to each forehead in turn.

She took hold of Mickey's cold hand. 'Now, you hold my hand, and Annie, you take his other hand and follow my lead.' She lifted the lamp from the peg.

Mickey gripped her hand and all three of them picked their way towards the stairs. Above them, through the collapsed old shutters at the front of the house, the morning light was starting to filter in. Josie could now see more of what was in the cellar. In the far corner, she could make out some long boxes with VR stamped on the side and fitted with stout rope handles. A dozen or so coffee sacks, all sewn up tightly across the top, sat strangely at odds with the other items in the cellar. Gilt-framed canvasses, taller than she was and half concealed by tarpaulins, leant against the back wall.

They squeezed though some of this and through the packing cases full of spices and tea towards the bottom of the stairs.

'Just a few moments and we'll be up the stairs, out into the back gardens and free,' she said in as jolly a voice as possible. 'Right now you go ahead, Annie, and mind that–'

The door above them creaked open and a light shone down. Mickey slid behind her and held onto her skirt. Annie, too, clung to her as Josie stared up to see Ma Tugman standing on the landing above them with her old dog at her heels.

The old woman's mouth dropped open in surprise giving her grimy face an almost girlish look, then a calculating smile crept across her face. Leaving the basket in her hand on the floor, she waddled over to the top stair, her dirty skirt dragging along the floor. Gripping the banister, she leant over and a few particles of dust floated down through the cracks in the boards.

'Well, ain't that touching,' she said. 'A proper little family reunion. Almost brings a tear to your eye.'

Josie's mouth drew into a mirthless line. No old woman and mangy dog was going to stop her from taking Annie and Mickey out of this cellar and back home.

She put the children behind her and stepped forward. 'Get out of my way.'

Ma's face formed itself into a mockery of surprise. 'You're very big with your orders aren't you, miss high and mighty. You're forgetting that you're nothing but the whore of a Paddy who's looking at seven to ten at Her Majesty's pleasure.' She gave a hard laugh. 'And what will you be then, eh? Just another skirt trying to keep yourself from the workhouse, that's what.' She tilted her head. 'But don't despair, a pretty girl like you could earn yourself a good living if you keep yourself clean.' She lumbered down another step, the board creaking beneath her feet. 'If you ask me nicely I'll put in a good word for you in one of those fancy houses in Piccadilly. That's where she's going.' She nodded her head at Annie. 'Of course, the boy won't be with you, he'll be on the other side of the world or up some chimney.'

Mickey whimpered and Josie shushed him softly, but didn't take her eyes off the old woman.

'Get out of my way,' Josie repeated, gathering the children to her and stepping over a coil of rope.

Ma slapped the railing and chuckled but then her jovial expression grew venomous. She drew a pistol out of her pocket, pointed it at Josie and cocked both barrels. 'That poxy man of yours is a fool to think I wouldn't make him pay for what he's done to my poor Charlie...'

Josie huddled the children to her. As far as she could tell, the gun in the old woman's hand was a flintlock, like the one her cousins kept in the house in New York. She heard two clicks and realised it was doubled barrelled, which gave her two shots. Although it was risky, if she could get her to waste one shot into the wall then at least the children had a chance of dashing up the stairs to safety.

'...his arm's all curled up like a crab's claw, thanks to that bastard father of yours,' Ma shrieked above them.

Josie lowered her head. 'When I push you, dive behind the tea chest,' she whispered, rocking them to the left.

Annie turned her face up. 'But–'

'No buts,' Josie cut in firmly, holding the frightened child's gaze.

Annie nodded.

Ma was still yelling. 'Well, now he'll know what

it's like to see your children suffer,' she continued, moving down another step. 'But now it's even better because I've got you, too. See if he's still as mouthy and...'

'Now!'

Josie pushed the children, who dashed behind the chest while she dived between the nearby barrels.

Ma gave a laugh. 'That's right, run and hide. Harry'll be here soon, he'll flush you out,' she said.

Josie bit her lip. She had to keep the old woman from calling for help or they'd be doomed along with Patrick. She jammed her back into the barrel behind her and pushed the one in front of her with her foot. It was only chest high but full of spirits. It swayed a little, then tipped forward and upturned. It rolled across the floor, smashing a crate of bottles.

'Quit that,' Ma yelled.

'Kick the tea chest,' Josie shouted to the children.

They did as they were told, pounding the side of the flimsy crate with their feet.

'Stop that you, buggers,' Ma shouted, lumbering further down the stairs.

The children continued to attack the side of the tea chest and Josie picked up a bottle that had escaped from the broken crate. Gripping the smooth neck she smashed the bottom away and raced over to the sacks of coffee. With a wide arc she slashed through the hessian cloth and beans burst out and rattled around her feet.

She grinned up at Ma. 'Go and get your thugs,

404

but you won't have much left by the time you get back!' She turned to the next sack, tearing a gash across it.

'Fecking stop that,' Ma bellowed, pointing the barrel of the gun at Josie.

'Make me!'

She jabbed the broken bottle into another sack and the pungent aroma of cinnamon rose up as the russet coloured powder spilled onto the earthen floor.

Ma levelled the barrel of the gun at Josie and a flash of light obscured her for a second before pain burst in Josie's shoulder.

Annie and Mickey screamed and the bottle fell from Josie's hand as she staggered back, blood on her sleeve. Shaking her head to clear the fog crowding around her vision she glanced at the children.

'Stay there!' she shouted, but it was too late, they were already rushing towards her.

Annie reached her first and placed her hand over the wound. Pain shot thought Josie's arm but she flexed her fingers and they moved. She struggled upright and shielded the children with her body.

'She's only got one shot left and if she fires it I want you to dash up those stairs fast,' she whispered as they huddled into her. 'Do you understand?'

'I'm not leaving you, Mam,' Annie sobbed.

'Me neither,' Mickey added.

Josie thought of the baby growing inside her. The first bullet had only grazed, but the second could be fatal. She wasn't dead yet, though, and until she was, she would fulfil her promise to Patrick by getting his children safely away from Ma Tugman.

'If you don't get me help then who will?' she asked, giving a bright smile despite the throbbing in her arm. 'Now do as I say.'

They nodded and Josie turned back to face Ma. 'I thought you wanted us to suffer like that half-dead son of yours,' she said, pleased to see the unhealthy tint under the old woman's skin darken.

'The children will suffer, don't you worry,' Ma told her. Lifting the pistol she aimed it square at Josie, who protected the children in the jumble of spilled tea, brandy, coffee beans and spices.

Ma squeezed the trigger, but suddenly the ground beneath her feet shifted. She screamed and grabbed the banister. For a brief second, nothing moved, then there was a loud crack and a space opened under her feet. Sharp edges of broken stair treads scraped her arms and face as she began to fall.

Snapper barked, and Ma flailed her arms about desperately snatching for something to stop her fall but her hand grasped only air. The roof of the cellar moved further from her as she plummeted to the floor. Splinters and dirt obscured her vision, then something hit her under her shoulder blades and she felt, rather than heard, a sickening snap.

Above her, through the haze of dust, she saw Snapper teetering on the broken stair and heard his sorry whine. He barked again, jumped across the space and dashed down to her. She couldn't move her neck but she felt his damp nose on her cheek as he nuzzled her. Ma watched as Josie and the children ran up what remained of the steps.

Harry had warned her not to touch the children but he was too soft in the head. If he'd been here as he should have been, instead of snoring in bed, then Nolan's brats and his bit of slap wouldn't have got the better of her. With Nolan coming up for trial next week, she would have finally been able to sell the children on, but now her profits – and her revenge – were escaping and it was all that bone-headed Harry's fault. She had near on ripped her innards out birthing the bastard – the least he could have done was do show a little gratitude...

She saw Josie help the children clamber over the broken stairs and heard them stomp up to the corridor above.

Josie looked back and then turned her head to one side. With a puzzled look on her face she came back down the stairs.

Ma smiled to herself. She hadn't fired the second shot in the gun.

Stupid doxy, she thought, as Josie picked her way across the dirt and splinters towards her, I'll give her another couple of feet and then blow her fecking head off.

Snapper barked a couple of times then shuffled off as Josie stopped beside Ma, wincing and holding on to her injured arm. It was clear she was in a great deal of pain.

Good, thought Ma as she closed her hand around the gun. But something was wrong – very wrong. Although her mind told her fingers to move, they wouldn't. She tried again, using every last effort of will to get her hand to do as she bid, but still nothing.

Ma's breath caught in her throat and threatened to choke her. Beads of sweat sprang out on her forehead. She tried to shout, but while her mind formed the words and her mouth opened, nothing came out.

Josie reached down and Ma's head rolled as the girl slid something out from beneath her. As she held it up, the small dish twinkled in a narrow shaft of sun that had crept in through a crack. Josie turned the plate back and forth for a moment and then glanced down at the old woman. 'I think the police will be interested to hear where they can find the rest of the Bedford silver,' she said, stuffing it down the front of the gown.

Josie retraced her steps to the stairs. As she put her foot on the first rung, she turned and crossed herself. 'May God have mercy on your soul,' she said.

Ma stared soundlessly after her as she disappeared.

When I get my hands on her... Ma stopped and, swivelling her eyes in their sockets as far as they would go, she caught a glimpse of her flaccid right hand. She tried to move it but it didn't even twitch.

As she studied her motionless hand her mind began to drift, conjuring up memories she didn't know she still carried. A dim image of the dirty cellar she'd lived in as a child flared up for second, then the face of her dead sister floated by and

408

merged into Harry her husband's winning smile, then Harry her son's thick features loomed up, and finally the image of Charlie.

He was such a pretty boy. And sharp? Why, my Charlie was so sharp he could cut himself. And such a dandy. Dapper, that's what he was, with real style...

The old images faded to be replaced by a picture of Charlie as he'd looked that morning with his withered arm and dribbling mouth. She felt something crawling on her cheek and realised, with some surprise, that it was a tear.

'He was a beautiful boy, my Charlie,' she whispered.

Her mind reached for him, but instead of his dear face, other images crowded him out. Men whose names she'd forgotten swirled around with their eyes full of hatred and lips snarling, reminding her that it was she who had sent them to their early graves. A black fog started to creep in from the side of her vision but she pushed it away.

From a long way off, Harry's voice called. She opened her eyes and the fog in her mind retreated. Although she was suddenly very weary she forced herself to focus and then found herself looking up at a different angle. Harry was there, and she realised he'd lifted her from the floor.

'Ha... Ha... Ha,' she choked out.

'It's me, Ma,' he said, his piggy eyes swimming with tears, his shoulders shaking. Harry hugged her and the sweet pomade he slicked through his hair filled her nostrils. 'I'm here, Ma. Don't worry I'm here.'

Something gurgled in her throat and Harry put

his ear near to her mouth. 'What did you say, Ma?'

'I said, where the feck have you been?' she asked with her last breath.

Chapter Twenty-Eight

Sergeant Plant's boots rang out as he climbed the stone stairs to the superintendent's office. Superintendent Jackson had only returned to H-division the day before and Plant had managed to keep himself well away all day. Unfortunately, he had been summoned by his superior officer, so couldn't very well avoid him any longer. Besides, it was tipping down and now at least he could spend the last hour of his patrol in the dry.

Since Patrick Nolan had been arrested, things in H-division had settled back into their old ways. The villains had gone back to filching anything that wasn't nailed down and killing and maiming each other, whilst any bobby with his head screwed on turned a blind eye, only arresting the odd drunk or two to show willing and draw his pay in good conscience without putting life and limb at risk to earn it.

Stopping halfway up the stairs to catch his breath, Plant reflected that, all in all, he was content with his lot. With the money Ma had promised him for turning in Nolan and his cut of the reward for the recovered Pettit silver, he was considering quitting the force and taking the

410

lease on a pleasantly situated public house in Forest Gate, right by the new railway line. After all, he'd done his duty to Queen and country and was now entitled to take it a bit easy.

Grasping the brass handrail he mounted the last dozen or so steps and marched along the landing to the door at the end. Pulling down the front of his jacket and straightening the shiny belt around it, he rapped on the door.

On hearing the superintendent bark, 'Enter', he stepped into the room.

'Sit,' Superintendent Jackson said, without looking up from the collection of papers in his hand.

Plant took the chair in front of the desk and a faint sneer rolled his lip under his moustache.

Why couldn't Jackson be more like the old super, he thought as his eyes ran over the papers and warrants scattered across the desk. Old Chalky White didn't upset the apple cart. Live and let live was old Chalky's way and the lads under him were the better for it.

Plant glanced at the window where the rain lashed against the glass. Yes, on a night like this a glass of ale in your hand in front of a warm fire was better than checking the constables on their beat. Maybe it *was* time to call it a day.

Jackson set the papers down and Plant gave him his full attention. Even though the superintendent could only have been a few years younger than he was, by the look of his massive frame, he could still take a fellow to the floor and handcuff him if the need arose. Jackson sat back and the chair creaked under his weight. There was a hint of amusement in his grey eyes as they settled on Plant.

'It's very good to see you back sir,' Plant said.

Jackson smiled. 'Thank you, Plant, and I must say my first day back has already turned into a very interesting one.'

'Has it sir?' Plant replied.

'Indeed. Do you remember Patrick Nolan, who came to us some while back about the Tugman gang?'

'Vaguely.'

'Well, I had his – his wife in here this afternoon and she gave me this.' Jackson drew a small silver dish from his side drawer and placed it gently on the desk.

Plant put a puzzled expression on his face. 'Did she hand it in?'

'No, she found it.' Jackson leant across the desk. 'She also told me a very interesting tale of kidnapping, theft and corruption. Involving you, Sergeant Plant.'

Plant blinked. 'Really, sir?' he answered as a rivulet of sweat trickled down his spine.

'Yes, really. She found the plate, and the Nolan children, in a boarded-up cellar – along with a whole haul of interesting bits and pieces.' Jackson fixed Plant with an icy stare. 'Like canvasses from Mount Finching House and Orsett Manor, rare medieval church fittings, jewellery, and all other manner of stolen objects which have yet to be identified, but which I am certain will be found to have come from burglaries from all over Essex and probably beyond.'

Alarm shot though Plant but he cut it short.

There was no evidence to link him with Finching or Orsett, or with Nolan and his brats, and if Ma was in trouble she wouldn't turn him in. She'd need all the friends she could get to keep herself out of gaol.

Jackson set the plate down in the centre of the leather inlay on his desk. 'Mrs Nolan tells me that on the night before he was arrested, Patrick Nolan came to see me to alert me that he was springing the trap the next day.'

The moisture evaporated from Plant's mouth.

I told Ma, he thought, forcing his ingenuous expression to stay where it was. *I said that she was asking for trouble snatching Nolan's kids. But would she listen...!*

Superintendent Jackson continued, 'The desk sergeant on duty that night, PC Woolmer, remembers a man fitting Patrick Nolan's description asking for me, but leaving after finding out I was not on duty. In court, Patrick Nolan's defence was that he had informed *you* that night, when he met you on patrol.'

'That was a bare-faced lie,' Plant answered, hotly. 'He ought to have the key to his cell thrown away for trying to implicate me, an officer with a spotless record.'

'So the magistrate at Queen Anne's Gate court believed, after your statement to that effect was read out at Nolan's hearing,' Jackson agreed.

'They're cunning fellows those boatmen, as you know yourself, sir.'

'So you say.'

Under the stiff, tailored navy jacket of his uniform, Plant's shoulders relaxed. He'd been in tight

413

squeezes before but believed that things would right themselves if he held his nerve. He'd had a few sleepless nights after Nolan's trial and no mistake, but who would be believed – a jumped up bog-trotter, or that old fleabag Ma, against one of London's finest? It would go against reason and nature.

'I do say so,' Plant replied. 'And with Ma Tugman in the cells–'

'Oh, Mrs Tugman's not in the cells,' Jackson said calmly. 'She's on a slab in the morgue at the London Hospital with her neck snapped.'

Even better! Plant suppressed a grin and asked, 'And Harry?'

'Missing. I sent the morning patrol to storm the Boatman but they only found Charlie, who's now been taken to the incurable ward at the workhouse.' Jackson's tone was matter of fact.

Deliverance! With Ma dead and Harry on the run, he was definitely in the clear. Harry didn't have half his mother's brains, and without her he was no more a threat than any of the other drunken thugs in the area. With a bit of luck, someone would slit Harry's throat before the constabulary cornered him.

Yes, it was definitely time to hang up his truncheon and start pulling pints.

'Good show,' Plant said. 'I'm sure that the commissioner will be pleased that you've uncovered Ma's stash in Burr Street.' He ventured a comradely smile. 'I shouldn't wonder if there isn't a promotion for you in this, sir. And well deserved I'd say, and so would the men, every one of them.'

A wry smile curled the superintendent's lips.

'Why, thank you, Sergeant,' he replied. 'But you haven't heard the best bit of the story yet.' A jovial expression crept over Jackson's face, which was strangely more alarming that his tough one. 'Mrs Nolan informed me that not only did Patrick Nolan *tell* you everything about the operation the night before he ferried Mrs Tugman's stolen goods upstream but also that he made you *write it down*.'

The pocket book! The small, manila-covered book with its notated pages and serial number that the officer had to sign for and keep safe or incur a fine of three days' pay.

Fear and panic now engulfed Plant as his pocket book seemed to burn through the lining of his jacket.

'Ha!' he forced out, as he held himself back from bolting for the door. 'Bunch of liars the lot of them,' he said. 'Of course you can't blame her, poor woman, but surely you don't believe the ranting of some ignorant Paddy skirt? And I tell you something, if it's the woman I think it is – curly auburn hair and mature figure, if you know what I mean – well, she's not his wife just his bit of tickle. She'd say anything to get him out of clink for her own sake.'

Jackson's expression remained implacable and he leant back in the chair again. 'Do you remember Danny Donovan's trial?' he asked conversationally.

Plant relaxed again. 'I do. You were the one who sent him to the gallows,' he said, thankful to have the conversation move from Patrick Nolan on to Jackson's past triumphs.

'Well, not me alone,' Jackson replied. 'Dr Robert Munroe gathered most of the actual evidence, along with his wife.'

Plant smiled, encouragingly. 'I remember some such, sir.'

'Of course she wasn't his wife then, she was Mrs O'Casey, the mother to one Miss Josephine O'Casey, who, because of an assault by Harry and Charlie Tugman, is now under Patrick Nolan's protection. It was Miss Josephine O'Casey, educated stepdaughter of Dr Robert Munroe, Medical Officer of the London Hospital and adviser to Her Majesty's government, whom you have just described as "an ignorant Paddy skirt" and "a bit of tickle", who brought me this silver salver as proof of Patrick Nolan's innocence. It was *she* who told me about the cellars under *Burr Street*, that *you* seem to know all about, too.'

The sweat on Plant's spine turned cold as the Superintendent stood and loomed over him.

'*And* the notes in your pocket book.' Jackson's long fingers stretched out. 'Hand it over.'

As her grandmother went to the window for the fourth time in a quarter of an hour, Bobbie glanced at her sister sitting next to her and grinned. Lottie grinned back. Bobbie looked across at George and Joe opposite in one of their best outfits and smiled at them. George smiled back, showing his missing front tooth, and Joe put his fingers in his mouth and pulled a face at his grandmother's back.

Since Papa's letter had arrived last week telling them that their parents were cutting short their

416

holiday and coming home a month early, the happiness in the house was fair bubbling over. Bobbie had wished she could somehow get word to Josie that Pa was on his way back and that all would be well but she could not.

Daisy had told Grandmama when Bobbie had sent Aunt Mary's letter to Josie around to Walburgh Street. She had been marched in front of Grandmama and given an almighty dressing down for giving succour to her degenerate sister.

After that, Grandmama had kept such a tight eye on Bobbie and Lottie that neither of them could even speak Josie's name without fear of it being reported. So, although every inch of her wanted to defy the old woman and sneak a note to Josie, she didn't dare. But all this would be over soon because Mama and Papa were coming home. Bobbie knew it was because they had received her letter.

'I don't know what can be keeping them,' Grandmama said, as she let the lace panel fall back.

Joe let go of the side of his mouth and changed his features from devilish to angelic as she turned to face the room. Mrs Munroe glanced at Jack sitting on Nurse's lap in the chair by the fire and her brows drew into the all too familiar frown but said nothing. Before the arrival of her parents' letter a week ago, Bobbie thought, Grandmama would have reproved Jack for sucking his thumb; now she seemed suddenly more indulgent towards such a childish shortcoming.

'I expect they are caught in traffic,' Bobbie said.

Her grandmother nodded. 'I am sure you're

417

right, Robina.'

Mrs Munroe sat down and folded her hands on her lap. Her face took on a jolly expression which was at odds with her frowning, thick eyebrows and pursed upper lip.

'I expect you are all eager to tell your Papa and Mama what a lovely time we have had while they were away,' she encouraged.

All the children looked at her blankly, without uttering a word. Mrs Munroe's hands went to her throat and she fiddled with the edge of her lace collar. 'George, you can tell them how we visited the Horse Guards to see the Queen's cavalry, and that you decided you wanted to become an officer like my brother, your great-uncle Rob.'

'I'd rather be like Nelson,' George replied.

The corner of Mrs Munroe's eye twitched and Bobbie suppressed a smile. George's resistance to Grandmama's rule took the form of mentioning the senior service whenever he had the chance.

'Perhaps as Joe likes to make things with his bricks he will be an engineer like Mama's brother, Uncle Joe, in America,' Lottie said, with a look of pure innocence on her face.

A quiver touched Mrs Munroe's cheeks. Mention of Mama's Irish family had the same effect as the Navy on Grandmama's composure.

'I don't think so, Charlotte,' Grandmama replied. 'I think that by the way he pores over the scriptures Joseph is being called by God to higher things,' she said, with her God-has-told-me-so expression.

Joe devoured books, and as Grandmama considered *The Swiss Family Robinson* and *German Popular Stories* totally unsuitable for impressionable young minds, her brother had to sate his appetite for adventure stories with the only book she approved of.

'I have noticed,' Bobbie said. 'He was showing me a section only yesterday in the Old Testament. Judges, chapter four verse twenty one.'

Grandmama's considerable brows drew together. 'I'm not very familiar with–'

'It's the one where someone's wife nailed a man's head to the floor,' Lottie chipped in.

A coach rattled to a stop outside and Grandmama rose and hobbled to the window.

'They are here,' she said, and waved them off the chairs and into a row with Nurse behind them. The children complied and lined up by seniority.

Bobbie held her breath as she heard the front door open and the deep voice of her father in the hallway. Papa! He would make everything all right.

The door opened and Ellen and Robert stepped in to the room. Mama looked very well now, with a blush on her cheeks and her eyes bright, while Papa's face had a light tan.

Grandmama stepped forward. 'Robert, dear Ellen, you had a good journey, I hope,' she said with a rare expression of goodwill on her face.

Papa's eyes narrowed.

'Tolerable,' he replied, shortly.

Ellen stared at her coolly. 'Where is my daughter Josie?'

419

Grandmama's neck flushed bright red and her eye began to twitch again. 'She's not here at the moment and–'

'So Bobbie wrote,' Ellen cut in.

Grandmama gasped and then her eyes narrowed as she looked across at Bobbie.

'We will discuss the matter in private later, Mother,' Robert told her.

Grandmama gave a hesitant laugh. 'Yes, that would be better. Now children, tell your dear Mama and Papa what fun we have had.'

Bobbie, Lottie, George and Joe rushed at their parents. Ellen caught the boys in a close embrace, telling them how they had grown, while Bobbie and Lottie hugged Papa, burying their heads in his chest and clinging to his jacket as if never to let him go.

As her father's strong arms closed around her and Bobbie smelt the familiar bay rum cologne a weight fell from her shoulders. His lips pressed on her head and she hugged him even closer. She and Lottie then hugged their mother as Papa hunkered down to talk to the boys and, finally, somehow they all managed to hug each other at the same time.

After everyone had kissed everyone else, Papa straightened. 'Well, you all look none the worse,' he said, glancing at Grandmama.

She bustled forward, twisting her lace handkerchief in her hands. 'As I was saying, Robert, the children have all–'

'Papa,' Joe said, tugging on his father's jacket bottom.

Robert scooped his son up. 'Yes, son?'

'I want Josie to come home.'

All eyes fixed on Mrs Munroe.

She flipped the lace square in her hand up and down. 'They don't–'

'You're looking tired, Mother,' Robert said in his stern voice. 'Perhaps you should lie down for a while.'

Two splashes of crimson burst onto Mrs Munroe's cheeks. 'I am perfectly well, I assure you, Robert.'

Robert's mouth curled but it wasn't a smile. 'You must allow me to be concerned about your health, and I insist that you go and have an hour or two's rest in your room while the children tell us what has been happening since we left.'

Mrs Munroe knocked on her son's study door and waited. After a few moments he called 'enter' and she went in. Robert was standing with his back to her, staring up at the family portrait. Since Robert and Ellen had arrived back the day before she hadn't had a chance to speak to him alone. Dinner last night had been a haphazard affair, with the children all talking at once as if they'd forgotten every word she'd ever said to them.

But she hadn't reprimanded them. After all, poor Robert had already had his homecoming marred by having to explain to the children about their wayward half-sister. Well, at least most of them were young enough to forget all about her in time...

She should have written, she knew that now, but hadn't for fear that telling her of Josie's

421

descent into depravity would hinder poor Ellen's recovery. Of course, if she'd known that Bobbie would be so deceitful as to write to her parents in secret, she *would* have put pen to paper. She only hoped that Robert would deal with his eldest daughter's lack of honesty appropriately. Deviousness was a trait to be nipped in the bud.

She studied his rigid back. She didn't relish a conversation about Josie O'Casey but she knew her duty.

Mrs Munroe ran her eyes over him and a swell of motherly pride rose up in her. He was a fine son and one any mother would be proud of. Perhaps now, when all was said and done, it was a blessing that he hadn't gone into the military all those years ago. The army wasn't what it was when her dear brother had worn his red coat for balls and assemblies and the occasional battle against the French. Now, English soldiers were sent to the four corners of the globe to fight naked savages. No – better that Robert was at the top of his profession here, at home, not in some far-flung garrison of the empire.

He turned and regarded her coldly but indicated that she should sit. He remained standing, with his hands behind his back.

The pain in her neck started to throb.

'Mother, Ellen and I are very distressed about Josie,' he began.

Mrs Munroe summoned up a sympathetic smile. 'I am sure it is a great shock to you both. It was not easy for you especially to hear that the young woman whom you have loved like a daughter has turned her back on all respectability and attached herself to a married man.'

Robert winced. Mrs Munroe shrugged her shoulders. 'I'm sorry Robert, I truly am,' she said, hoping she sounded so. 'But I did warn you about Miss O'Casey's wayward and impetuous nature. Had I known sooner about her involvement with this Nolan man then maybe I could have saved her from total disgrace. By the time I found out about the liaison, it was too late.'

Robert turned away from her and stared up at the picture again.

Poor boy, she thought, gliding across the room to him. His eyes remained on the canvas.

Giving him time to let the enormity of Josie's infamy sink in she, too, gazed up at the portrait and her eyes rested on Josie, on what she considered the girl's brash smile.

She laid her hand gently on his arm. 'You mustn't blame yourself, Robert, for her present situation. It's in the wild blood she inherited from her drunken father.'

Robert stared down at her with a look of astonishment on his face.

'I don't blame myself–'

'Good. You have no rea–'

'I blame *you.*'

'Me!' Mrs Munroe's hand flew to her chest. 'How am I to blame for–'

'I blame you for bolting *my* daughter out of *her* home in her hour of need.'

The pain in her neck started to throb again. 'She left of her own free will and I don't think you understand the depths to which Miss O'Casey has fallen.' She drew in a dramatic breath. 'Patrick

423

Nolan is *married!*'

Robert's brow furrowed as he took in her words.

'How do you know that?' he asked, after a long moment.

'Because...' She stopped.

'Because you took her letter to her mother and read it, didn't you?'

'But she was–'

'Did you read Josie's letter to her mother?'

Mrs Munroe drew a long breath through her nose and pulled her shoulders back. 'I did, and it was full of her monstrous lust for Nolan and lies about me. You should have read it.'

'I would have liked to. Perhaps we could have helped poor Josie sooner.'

'Poor Josie!' she shrieked. 'Poor Josie! Poor Josie has thrown aside all propriety and decency.'

'As I understand the matter, on the evening Josie left this house, she had been attacked by ruffians. Patrick Nolan saved her and brought her home,' Robert said.

'She said she'd been set upon but I thought she was trying to explain away her ripped dress.' Mrs Munroe went to lay her hand on his sleeve again but stopped when she saw the frosty look in his eye. 'Robert, I saw them. They were in each other's arms swearing their eternal love when I found them at the back door. I shudder to think how long they had been deceiving us to carry on their sordid affair. As far as I am concerned, she turned her back on those who cared for her and chose a life of sin with Nolan.'

'After you threatened to have her locked in an

asylum,' he replied, though gritted teeth.

Mrs Woodall!

'I never thought my own son would take the word of a servant against mine.'

'Did you threaten to send Josie to an asylum?'

Mrs Munroe held his stare as the tenth commandment danced in her mind. 'In my mind, her unbridled actions indicated mental instability.'

Robert let out a colourful oath, crossed the room and stood staring out of the window, his hands gripping onto the frame.

'Blaspheming will do you no good,' she said severely. 'After all, Saint Paul in his epistle to the Galatians tells us the adulterers and fornicators shall not inherit the Kingdom of God.'

Robert turned and glared at her. 'You quote scripture to *me* after forcing Josie out on the streets with nothing more than the clothes on her back?'

'But, Robert, I did it for *you*. For you and your dear children, my grandchildren. I couldn't bear to see you ostracised again because of Miss O'Casey's disgraceful behaviour. It gave me no pleasure to expose her lewd nature but, as you well know, I have never flinched from my duty. My only thought when I saw them in each other's arms was to safeguard your reputation and save those precious children upstairs from being tainted by Josephine O'Casey.'

'By throwing her onto the streets,' Robert replied in a leaden stare.

Mrs Munroe fixed him with the look she used to pull his father into line on many occasions. 'I must say, in view of all I have been through and sacrificed I am deeply hurt by your tone, Robert. So much so that I am of a mind to cut short my visit and return home.'

Robert reached for the bell pull. 'I will organise your travel arrangements immediately.'

Chapter Twenty-Nine

Josie turned into Walburgh Street just as the light had begun to fade. In several windows the glow of lamps began to flicker. The wind gusted and she put her hand to her head to catch her bonnet and then wished she hadn't. The gunshot wound was only superficial and after Sarah and Mattie had cleaned it and packed salt on it for three days, it was healing nicely, but it hurt like billy-o if she moved her arm suddenly. It ached even more because she, along with Sarah, had struggled since early morning to birth Mattie's baby boy.

She smiled as she pictured herself in the same situation next spring. Please God, let Patrick be with her when their own baby was born.

Sarah's and Mattie's eyes had fixed on her belly when they saw the blood on her arm but the baby remained tucked away unharmed.

Although outwardly Annie and Mickey were unharmed from their ordeal, it was only in the last couple of nights that they had both managed a full night's sleep without one of them waking up screaming. So, as much as she would have loved to stay and fuss over Mattie's new son, Josie had gulped down her tea to dash home. Kate was there with the children, but she would, no doubt, be in a rush to go over and see Mattie's baby for herself. Josie wanted to make sure she was back in time to get them ready for bed.

Colly Bonny waved at her as she gathered her own children, who were kicking a half-inflated ball up and down the street.

'What did she have?' she called across.

'A boy, as big as his father. They have called him Brian,' Josie called back. 'They're both well.'

Colly laughed. 'God bless her. I've just pulled a tray of toffee out of the oven; send your two over for a couple of chunks, if you like.'

Josie grinned. 'I'm surprised they haven't smelt it and been over already.'

Colly went in and Josie pushed open her front door.

'I'm home,' she called down the passage as she took off her bonnet.

Nothing! Josie's brows drew together. Annie and Mickey usually raced up the hall right away.

A cold hand of dread closed around Josie's heart. Ma was dead, but Harry Tugman was still at large, and although Superintendent Jackson had assured her that he had every officer available out looking for him, it wasn't impossible for Harry to come back to harm the children.

Josie covered the distance to the scullery door in seconds and flung the door open. For one moment her brain didn't quite believe what her eyes were seeing: her mother and father sitting in the two chairs by the fire, with a child on each of their laps.

She saw them, as if looking at them for the first time. Ma, who had looked so pale when Josie had waved her goodbye, now sat in her dark green day dress, with a healthy glow in her cheeks, while Annie explained something about her embroidery hoop to her. Robert, in his charcoal jacket and pin-striped trousers, traced his finger over a page while Mickey read his storybook.

She tried to speak then four pairs of eyes turned on her.

Annie and Mickey jumped down and ran towards her. Josie tore her eyes from her parents and caught the children to her.

Ellen stood up and crossed the room. 'Josie! Oh, sweet Mother, Josie, are you all right?' she asked holding her at arms' length and running her eyes over her rapidly. 'I haven't slept a wink since we got Bobbie's letter. Tell me you're all right, my darling girl.'

'I'm fine,' Josie assured her mother, still not quite believing that her parents were actually standing in Sarah's scullery.

Robert gently tilted Josie's head to the light. 'Are you sure? Young Mickey here tells me you were *shot.*' He was already taking her injured arm and gently articulating it. 'Has anyone looked at it? Has it been dressed properly? You can't be too careful with a dirty wound like that. Fragments can be left and set off a fever.' He let her arm fall and studied her closely in the available light. 'I'd better look at it myself in a while, just to be sure.'

Josie threw herself into her mother's arms, buried her face in her shoulder and burst into tears, unable to hold back her relief and joy. Robert came over and put his arms around them both. When he pressed his lips to Josie's forehead she started to sob uncontrollably.

How she could ever have thought her parents would turn their backs on her, she didn't know, but in the wild and dangerous weeks since they'd left, her love for Patrick had turned her whole world on its head. It was little wonder she'd forgotten how unshakable her parents' love really was.

'Mam,' she sobbed, her tears making dark spots on the fabric of Ellen's jacket. 'Oh, Mam, I'm so sorry, when you didn't reply to my letter I thought–' She stopped and buried her face in her mother's shoulder again.

Ellen hugged her tighter. 'There, there,' she said as she ran her hand lightly over Josie's damp face.

'Your mother didn't answer your letter because she never received it,' Robert said in a controlled voice as he dragged a chair over so that Ellen could sit next to her daughter.

'If we'd known the trouble you were in, we would have come straight back,' Ellen said.

Trouble! thought Josie, remembering that she'd had to let out the laces in her stays that morning.

She gestured to Annie and Mickey and put her arms around them. 'Colly has some toffee cooling, why don't you pop over and have some while I talk to my mam and pa?'

Annie went to take Mickey's hand but he screwed up his face. 'But I want to tell Dr Munroe how Ma Tugman fell though the stairs and we got away.'

Robert leant over and ruffled the boy's hair. 'You've already told me twice, *and* how Josie found the stolen silver plate and took it to the police. Now you do as she says and when you come back we'll read the rest of the story.'

Annie took her brother's hand and this time Mickey trotted off after her.

After she heard the front door close, Josie took a deep breath. 'Mam, Pa. I know I should have told you before and I'm truly sorry. It has hurt me to be dishonest with you both but I must tell you the truth now,' Josie said, as her heart thundered in her chest. 'I love Patrick and since I left, we have been living together as man and wife.'

'So I understand,' Ellen replied. 'Now why don't you tell me it all from the beginning.'

Josie explained all about how Patrick had met and married Rosa and what happened to her. 'And, although Annie and Mickey think their mother is dead, she is not. So Patrick is still married.'

Although frowned upon, premarital relationships could be remedied in a chapel. An adulterous one could not.

There was a long pause and then Robert spoke. 'I won't deny that this doesn't create huge problems, Josie.' He took hold of Ellen's hand and pressed it to his lips. 'Your mother and I know how unforgiving society can be to those who love outside the accepted boundaries.' Ellen gazed up at Robert and then they both looked at Josie. 'But you are our daughter and we love you, so let us deal with one thing at a time. What can we do to

430

get the case against Patrick dismissed?'

Harry swilled the gin around in his glass and threw it down his throat. The gut-rotting liquid burnt but he welcomed the pain. Slamming the glass on the table before him he glared at his surroundings.

The Blue Coat Boy was two miles from the Boatman with a ceiling so low that even an averaged sized man had to stoop. It was also so deep within the Wentworth Street rookery that, even with the nabbers out in force looking for him, he could sit in the bar without fear. The bar was crammed with men and women escaping their damp and dreary hovels in order to drink themselves into oblivion in the warm companionship of the public house.

Porters from the market rubbed shoulders with butchers, cheesemongers and barrowmen, while raddled trollops tried to persuade them to part with their cash for a quick knee trembler in the side alley.

Ollie Mac lumbered to his feet. 'I'll get you another, 'Arry. That'll see you right.'

Harry knew another gin wouldn't set him right; no more than all the others he'd poured down his neck since Ma had died, cursing him with her last breath. The image of her motionless face and staring blue eyes came back to him again. With all the craftiness gone from her face she looked like the mother Harry had remembered as a lad. Bitter remorse and misery gripped his chest and made him choke and cough.

If only he'd gone with her that morning he

could have caught the O'Casey woman, and Ma would still be alive – not mouldering in her grave.

Lifting his eyes from the bottom of the empty glass he watched Ollie chatting to a pert-looking girl with an eyeful of cleavage and painted lips. Ollie had stood by him, and Harry didn't wonder at it – the wiry Scotsman was always his most loyal man, but others of the gang had scarpered as the police closed in.

Ollie gave the strumpet pressing herself into him a lavish kiss and then fought his way back. He plonked a bottle on the table.

'It'll save me another trip,' he said, slopping gin into both their glasses.

Harry threw another mouthful down. 'I shouldn't have left her like that,' he slurred.

'Now, now, man,' Ollie said, shaking his arm. 'What could you have done? The peelers were on their way and your old Ma wouldn't have wanted you taken, now, would she?'

Harry wasn't so sure. He had the feeling that his ma would have shopped him to the nabbers herself if she'd known where her 'sweet' Charlie had been carted off to.

He wiped his nose on his sleeve. 'But you didn't see her, lying there all broken.' Ollie gave him a sympathetic look but said nothing. 'What sort of son am I, to let his own mother be buried in a pauper's grave?' Harry swallowed the rest of the gin and Ollie poured another. Harry drank that too.

Somewhere a woman started to sing and others joined in. Harry peered through a haze of tobacco smoke at the happy drinkers. He heaved

432

himself up, swaying for a second or two before he found his balance.

'Shuurrup,' he bellowed. 'Me ma's dead. Show a bit of respect.'

A couple of men at the bar turned and shoved two fingers up at him. Harry ripped the front of his jacket open and started to peel it off but got tangled in the sleeves. There were snorts of laughter and Ollie pulled him back into his seat.

'Look, Harry. What say you and me find ourselves a nice bit of skirt each and have some fun?' he said encouragingly.

Harry shook his head and drew the small, double-barrelled pistol out of his pocket and turned it over in his hand, remembering Ma's rare smile when Charlie had given it to her. He sniffed loudly.

'I took this from her cold hand, I did,' he said, running his thumb over the handle and held it up. It was a nice piece, perfectly balanced.

Ollie grabbed his hand and shoved it under the table. 'You trying to get arrested or something, waving that thing about?'

'Don't you understand? It's my fault Ma's dead,' Harry snivelled.

Ollie shook his head. 'Look, you're not to blame. I tell you, Harry, no muvver had a better son, than you.'

Harry forced a smile. 'Do you think so?'

'I do. Honest, mate. If anyone's to blame for your ma it's that bastard Nolan, devil take him. If he'd been straight and honest and taken her booty upstream as he'd agreed, instead of ratting to the coppers, none of this would have hap-

433

pened. Things would have worked out fine if he hadn't crossed her. If you want to blame anyone, he's your man, and now that Plant's in custody, Nolan's going to get off clean as a whistle when he comes up in front of the judge next week.'

Harry blinked his eyes a couple of times as Ollie's words sank in. 'You're right. It's all that bastard's fault.' An image of Patrick and Josie laughing and dancing at a wedding rose up in Harry's mind. 'Him and that swanky woman of his. It was her who broke in to Burr Street. If she hadn't poked her nose in where she had no business, me ma would never have fallen down the stairs.'

'That's right, Harry.' Ollie slapped him on the back heartily. 'See, they did it, both of them. So don't go on there blaming yourself because there weren't nuffink you could have done.'

A weight lifted from Harry's back. Ollie was right. He shoved the table away and staggered to his feet. He raised the gun and shook it above his head. A woman screamed and men backed away.

'It was Nolan and that fecking doxy of his.' He stumbled back and crashed into the table behind and those sitting around it darted away. A bottle smashed under his feet as people screamed and dived for cover.

He ran his hands over the smooth barrels of the pistol. 'He thinks he's got the better of us, Ma,' he said cocking and uncocking the hammers. 'But don't you worry none. I'll make sure Nolan *and* his woman pays!'

Chapter Thirty

There wasn't a bone in Patrick's body that didn't ache after the mile or so's journey from Pentonville to the Old Bailey. As he was on remand and still presumed innocent, Patrick had tried to get permission for his mother to visit again. This had been denied, leaving him without any hope of relief from his dread of what had happened to Annie and Mickey and of course, Josie.

Therefore, unlike his travelling companions, Patrick was eager to get to London's central criminal court because he would get the last glimpse of the woman he had loved for such a very long time and, please God and all his saints above, she would tell him that Annie and Mickey were safe.

The carriage juddered to a stop and Patrick looked towards the back door as it swung open and one of the two wardens flanking the door waved them out with his truncheon. All six of them stood in line to avoid the drag on the chains that bound them, and then marched into the back door of England's foremost court.

Patrick was unchained from his fellow prisoners, squeezed between two court officers, and marched along the short corridor up to the dock.

His gaze shot to the public gallery and his eyes raced along the crowd of men and women crammed into the small space at the back of the court.

She wasn't there!

He looked again and bitter disappointment rose up in him, soon replaced by a feeling of powerlessness.

Oh, my God, what had happened to her?

Was she ill? Had Ma Tugman taken her too? Had she been attacked by Harry again and injured or was she...?

He had to stay calm. Any moment now he would be called to give his testimony. He had to keep a clear mind if he had any hope of convincing the court of his story about Sergeant Plant. He had, at the very least, to throw enough doubt on the whole incident to sway the jury.

He glanced across at the twelve good men squashed together in the benches to the side of the judge and his heart sank. They stared across the well of the court at him with tight-lipped disapproval. The judge pounded his gavel on the bench and the room fell silent. Patrick took a deep breath and turned his attentions to the man behind the bench.

Then he rose to his feet and faced the judge. The clerk of the court read aloud the same charges that the magistrate's official had read two weeks before.

The judge chewed on his gums for a moment then looked down his nose at Patrick. 'How do you plead?' he asked, crisply.

Mr Vaneweather, the thin lawyer with the worn cuffs the boatmen had engaged on Patrick's behalf, jumped to his feet. 'Mr Nolan pleads not guilty,' he said, in a strident tone at odds with his insubstantial frame.

The judge's lower jaw ruminated again. 'Very well,' he said at length. 'Mr Gilchrist, let us hear the evidence in the case.'

Mr Gilchrist, a sallow, paunchy individual, stood and flourished the papers in his hand.

'My lord, members of the jury,' he said, inclining his head towards the bewigged judge and then the jury. 'This is a most distressing case. I am afraid the heinous crimes of this man,' he jabbed his finger towards Patrick, 'will shock you as I lead you through the dishonesty, the duplicity, nay, the very immorality of his actions. I will—'

The door at the back of the public gallery burst open and the men and women in front of it muttered loudly as they shuffled to one side to allow the latecomers in. A door at the back of the main court also banged open and several police officers marched to the front of the court but Patrick's eyes were fixed on only one thing: Josie.

Joy flooded over him and he suppressed the urge to laugh aloud at the sight of her pushing her way to the front.

She was wearing her best dress, with her bright Indian shawl over her shoulders and her bonnet on the back of her head. Worryingly, she had her left arm in a sling and, judging by the small grimace that flickered over her face when she moved it, it caused her some degree of pain.

His eyes ran over her as if he'd never seen her before, noting the sparkling brightness of her green eyes and the pleasing sweep of her cheek-

437

bones. An escaped curl had tucked itself around her ear and Patrick remembered how he had woven his fingers through those lovely locks as they streamed over his pillow.

The hubbub of the court faded, as his eyes locked with hers. She smiled across at him and nodded.

Oh, praise the Lord, Annie and Mickey were safe.

Then Patrick noticed who stood behind her: could it really be Dr Munroe? He could hardly believe it, but it *was* her father who stood there behind her, his hands resting lightly on her shoulders.

The two men stared at each other across the courtroom and Josie's father inclined his head slightly. Patrick acknowledged it with a cautious nod.

The gavel silenced the court and Patrick forced his attention back to the court proceedings.

The officer, who had just arrived, was arguing with Mr Gilchrist. Patrick stared, and hope flared inside him as he recognised Superintendent Jackson.

The prosecuting lawyer shot Jackson a furious look and then approached the judge's bench. Superintendent Jackson sat back and crossed one leg over the other while Gilchrist and the judge spoke.

'Well, this is all very irregular,' the judge said after a moment. 'You had better explain.'

Jackson unfolded his legs and rose. 'It is a grave miscarriage of justice for Mr Nolan to be charged with the crimes laid against him. Motivated by his desire to rid the riverside area of criminal

438

elements, Patrick Nolan came forward and offered information and his help to assist my officers to put an end to a ruthless criminal gang led by a Mrs Tugman, aided and abetted by her two degenerate sons. After a plan to trap Mrs Tugman's gang was formulated between Mr Nolan and myself, Mr Nolan, at great personal risk to himself and his family I might say, began to set the plan in place. On the twenty-third of September last, when he visited Arbour Square police office to inform me of the time and place so that my officers could apprehend the villains in full possession of their ill-gotten gains.' Jackson's face grew dark. 'Unfortunately, I was not on duty that night so Mr Nolan spoke to another officer. I am ashamed to tell the court, but that officer, a Sergeant Plant, was in Mrs Tugman's pay and told her of the plan. She then set about secreting stolen items, notably some of the Pettit silver, from the Bedford Park robbery on Mr Nolan's boat and kidnapped his children to force him to take his boat up river to the Horse Ferry Landing at Westminster that same day. Plant informed the constabulary at St Anne's Gate police office, who duly arrested Mr Nolan.' Jackson turned and looked at Patrick. 'It is only now by the courageous actions of Miss Josephine O'Casey that all the real evidence in this case has come to light.'

Patrick's gaze rested on Josie. *God, how he loved her!*

Mr Vaneweather sprang to his feet. 'I move that all charges against Mr Nolan be dropped and that he be released at once!' he demanded.

From the lofty height of his bench the judge looked down. 'Mr Gilchrist?'

The stout barrister at the other end of the polished oak table ground his teeth for a second, then grabbed the side of his black gown and puffed out his chest.

'I have no further evidence to offer the court,' he said, with as much good grace as he could muster.

Josie's heart fluttered and her stomach turned over and over as she stood in the entrance hall of the Old Bailey, her eyes glued to the oak door that led to court number one. Beside her Annie and Mickey could hardly stop from jumping on the spot and Sarah hadn't stopped crying since Josie and her father had come out of the public gallery and told her that the case against Patrick had been dismissed. Even Gus, who'd accompanied his mother to court, turned and quickly wiped his eyes when he heard the news. Ellen sat with her old friend on the bench while she dabbed her eyes, while Robert and Superintendent Jackson shared a joke over by the staircase.

'Mam, how much longer?' Mickey asked for the tenth time in as many minutes.

'I'm afraid, Master Nolan, there are procedures to be followed,' Superintendent Jackson said, as he and Robert came over to join them. 'They can't just take your father's chains off and let him stroll out. English Law works slowly, and with attention to detail, so your father has to be recorded, logged and signed for.' Superintendent Jackson leant down closer to the boy until they were almost nose to nose, and added, 'In triplicate.'

Mickey pulled a face. 'Well, I think it's daft,' he announced.

Superintendent Jackson and Josie's father laughed.

'You want to be *very* glad that it does, young Mickey,' Robert said, 'because it was Sergeant Plant's recorded, logged and signed for pocket book that proved your father's innocence.'

'That, and Miss O'Casey's bravery in rescuing you two and discovering the Bedford silver,' added Superintendent Jackson. He glanced at Robert. 'You should have heard the ruckus she made in the police station to make them fetch me.'

Robert's face creased into a smile. 'I don't have to; I've lived with her for twelve years.'

'Mam was very brave,' Annie said, as she squeezed Josie's hand.

'Aye,' Robert replied in a softer tone. He put his arm around Josie's shoulders, avoiding the still tender wound, and kissed her lightly on the forehead.

Josie swallowed. Despite the difficulties of her choice that living out of wedlock with Patrick posed for Robert, he had worked tirelessly, pulling all the strings he had over the last week to try and have the charges against Patrick withdrawn and get him released, but due process of the law had to be observed. She only hoped that any gossip about her living in sin with a married man wouldn't revive the old scandal about Robert's marriage to her mother.

But that was for the future, and she couldn't dwell on that now because every part of her longed for the moment she would be in Patrick's arms again.

The door opened and Patrick stepped out into the open space. Josie's eyes ran over him. He was dressed in the same clothes she had waved him goodbye in three weeks ago. Although he was clean shaven and his hair had seen a comb sometime that morning, it was over-long and in need of a wash. But, even so, Josie had never seen him look finer.

Annie and Mickey let go of her hands and, dodging through the black-gowned barristers and the less well-heeled plaintiffs and witnesses, they dashed across the floor and threw themselves at their father. Sarah rose from the bench and joined her grandchildren.

Patrick scooped them up in one movement and held them to him with his eyes shut. They clung to their father and sobbed and he kissed each one in turn as if to assure himself that he was actually holding them. With Mickey and Annie still in his arms, Patrick turned to Sarah and put the children down. He hugged his mother and she sobbed in his chest then she pulled something out of her pocket and handed it to him. He looked at it briefly before hugging Gus for a moment.

He turned to Josie and crossed the space between them in seconds. She smiled up at him and he took her in his arms.

Josie clung to Patrick with her uninjured arm and sobbed incoherently into his chest for a full two minutes and then held him at arm's length. 'You've lost weight. Are you well?'

'There, there, my sweet,' he said, enjoying the way her eyes ran over him. 'I'm fine and dandy. But what have you done to your arm?'

Mickey spoke. 'Pa, Miss Josie was–'

'I'll tell you later,' Josie said, as Annie nudged her brother.

Before he could ask any more questions, Josie hugged him to her again. 'I can't believe it's over.'

And neither could he. He kissed her again and then became acutely aware of her parents behind her. Keeping a proprietary arm around her, Patrick stood her beside him in order that they might look slightly more respectable as they faced Dr and Mrs Munroe.

'Mr Nolan,' Dr Munroe said offering his hand. Patrick took it. 'It's good to see you.'

'Thank you, sir,' Patrick replied, and turned to Ellen. 'I'm very pleased to see you fully recovered, Mrs Munroe.'

'Thank you, Patrick,' she said. 'We had a lovely time in Scotland, but we've been fair beside ourselves to hear of all the happenings since we've been away.' Her expression was severe but there was a twinkle in her eye.

Some of the tension left Patrick's body. Ellen Munroe might not reach up to her husband's shoulder but you'd be better fighting with a tiger than tangling with her if you'd wronged one of hers.

Superintendent Jackson came forward. 'Fine show, Nolan,' he said, pumping Patrick's hand enthusiastically. 'I'm glad I returned to find out the truth before you had to suffer a spell in the Surrey House of Correction.'

'Thank you, Superintendent. So am I.'

'I must get back to the station,' Jackson said. 'I still have to catch Harry Tugman. Also, when you've recovered from your brush with the wrong side of the law, make an appointment to see me, Mr Nolan.' The superintendent touched the side of his well-formed nose twice. 'It will be to your advantage.'

He shook Robert's hand again and left.

Patrick and Josie turned back to face Ellen and Robert. The fact that they were here was an encouraging sign but Patrick had still taken their daughter from her home to his bed. Any father would, rightly, take exception to that.

He pulled the letter from inside his shirt and handed it to Robert.

'This is from Mr Watson, chaplain to the garrison in Alexandria.' He glanced at his children. 'It confirms that my wife Rosa is dead.'

Ellen, Josie, and his mother crossed themselves swiftly. Josie turned to him and threaded her fingers through his. He took her hand to his lips and pressed it before turning to her father.

'I know it's not the usual way of doing things, Dr Munroe, but I would like to ask your permission to marry your daughter.'

Holding on to Patrick's arm, Josie stepped through the double doors and out into the sunshine. Mickey trotted next to her while Annie skipped along beside her father. Behind them strolled Ellen, Robert and Sarah. Josie could already hear her mother and Patrick's making wedding plans, just as they had done years before when she and Patrick were little more than children.

The thoroughfare outside the Old Bailey was packed with a mass of people from bewigged lawyers to city clerks. Sellers of hot potatoes and coffee hawked their wares in raucous voices, while piemen balancing full trays on their heads rang bells to attract buyers. But Josie barely saw or heard the hustle and bustle – every part of her was focused on Patrick.

There had been times in the past weeks, in the dead of night when her need for Patrick had robbed her of sleep, when she had almost despaired of this moment. But now he was here, close beside her, and she was holding his strong arm. Yet she couldn't quite believe that all the fears and dangers of the past months were over and soon they would be married.

Josie almost gave in to the overwhelming urge to throw her arms around Patrick and kiss every inch of his face, but of course she couldn't. Her parents might have accepted what had gone on in their absence, but that didn't mean they would sanction its continuation. She would have to live the life of a respectable young woman until her father gave her away at the altar. As her eyes ran over the firm line of Patrick's jaw and the shape of his mouth, Josie hoped that they could have the banns read soon.

As if sensing her gaze on him, Patrick turned. He placed his hand over hers and she smiled up at him. In fact she'd done nothing but smile since the judge smacked down the gavel and dismissed the charges. And if that weren't reason enough to smile, when Patrick produced the letter proving he was free to marry, Josie thought her heart would burst with happiness. It also meant she didn't have to tell Ellen and Robert just yet that they were to be grandparents.

Patrick stopped the party at the top of the steps and drew in a deep breath. 'I didn't think I'd feel the sun on my face for a very long time,' he said, tilting his head back to feel the autumn warmth.

'Well, if it hadn't been for Josie, you probably wouldn't,' Sarah said, taking hold of Mickey before he ran down the steps into the road.

Patrick's right eyebrow rose and he gave Josie a questioning look. 'And just what *did* you do, may I ask?'

Josie laughed. 'It's a long story.'

'And one you'd be better off hearing after a good meal and a brandy, I can tell you,' her father cut in. 'If you all stay here, I'll fetch us a cab or two,' Robert said, walking off towards Ludgate Hill.

Suddenly, there was an uproar at the bottom of the stairs as the milling crowd objected to someone pushing between them. Men shouted, a woman screamed, and a young man was sent sprawling to the floor. Josie turned.

There was something familiar about the stocky figure shouldering his way through the throng. At first, seeing the ragged jacket and dirty face and hair, Josie thought he was one of the vagrants she'd seen begging for a few coppers from passers-by as she went into the court. But then he raised his head, and Josie found herself gasping for breath as Harry Tugman climbed the stairs towards them.

He acknowledged her recognition with a crooked, crazed smile.

Two women selling lavender on the steps screamed and dropped their baskets. The lilac-coloured stems scattered and Harry crushed them underfoot. For a brief moment their heady fragrance filled the air. Then he reached into his jacket pocket and drew out a gun.

'Patrick!' Josie screamed.

Patrick turned and, pushing Josie aside, sprung at Harry. He collided with him just as Harry squeezed the trigger and the hammer ignited the charge. There was a flash and an ear-splitting crack as Josie shielded the children. A lawyer on the step above them shrieked and fell to the floor.

Patrick grasped Harry's arm and bent it upwards, twisting his wrist as he did so to force him to drop the weapon. But Harry, with the strength of the deranged, held on, his face flushed purple and hatred contorting his heavy features.

He shoved Patrick away but Patrick caught him again and people around them fled as the two men grappled on the steps. Harry disentangled himself from Patrick and aimed the gun at him, but before he could discharge the second barrel, Patrick lunged and caught his arm again. Holding the gun away, Patrick snapped his head forward and smashed the bridge of Harry's nose, splitting it instantly – but still Harry held on.

Paralysing terror took hold of Josie as she watched the two men battle for their lives. Patrick could match Harry for strength and speed any day of the week, but he'd been in prison for over a month and her heart pounded with fear that at any moment Harry would get the advantage and blow Patrick's brains out.

'Police!' screamed Ellen and Sarah, while Mickey and Annie clung to them, sobbing, and others took up the cry. Gus stood with his mouth open for a moment then started down the steps.

The lawyer who'd been injured by Harry's first bullet was being tended to by those around him; court officers streamed out in response to the furore. Harry would be captured for sure, but would it be too late?

Patrick lost his footing and, although he stayed upright, he stumbled down two steps. Harry saw his opportunity and cocked the gun but Patrick landed a bone-crunching kick to Harry's knee cap and he grunted and lurched sideways. Patrick crouched for a second to judge the distance and then pounced again.

Police officers from the court were beside Josie now, but Patrick and Harry, locked together in combat, rolled over each other down the steps. As they crashed on to the pavement there was a muffled shot.

The crowd around them drew back as Harry staggered to his feet.

'Patrick!' Josie screamed, and tore down the steps. She threw herself onto her knees beside him, her skirts spreading over the muddy pavement. She covered her mouth as she caught sight of the blood splattered over his shirt and face. Heedless of her parents, the crowd and her own aching shoulder, Josie threw herself on him and sobbed helplessly on his chest. She tucked her head under his chin and clung to his shoulders.

How could it be, that after all the danger and heartbreak they had been through, their happiness was now to be snatched away from them again – this time forever...

'Patrick, Patrick,' she sobbed, feeling the steady beat of his heart under her hand and fearing that at any moment it would stop.

His finger hooked under her chin. 'It's all right, Josie,' he said, raising her head and smiling at her. 'It's not my blood, sweetheart.'

Lifting herself off him and pushing her bonnet back, she saw Harry Tugman standing a few yards away, holding his stomach as blood oozed through his fingers. He stared at Josie and Patrick with an astonished look on his face, his mouth open and his lower lip trembling. He pulled his hand away and looked at the sticky redness covering it for a moment, then staggered back.

'Ma,' he croaked, as his eyes rolled up and he crashed to the ground.

The police swarmed around Harry's inert body as Mickey and Annie ran down the steps to their father. Gus reached them just an instant before Ellen and Sarah. Robert, who had just returned, crouched down beside Harry. Patrick got to his feet and helped Josie up as Ellen, Sarah and the children gathered around them.

'Is he dead? Patrick asked.

'Not yet,' Robert replied, 'but he will be in a day or two. The bullet's gone straight through his bowels and even my old friend Chafford, chief surgeon at Bart's, would not be able to extract that slug without corruption taking hold.' He pointed to the injured lawyer, who wore a makeshift bandage around his shoulder. 'Thankfully, Tugman only winged that young man. I've told them to take him to Mr Chafford and say that I sent him.'

Suddenly, the ground under Josie's feet swayed and she caught hold of Patrick. His arm slipped around her. Feeling his strength, Josie's dizziness passed.

'Josie, are you unwell?' Robert asked.

She shook her head and the floor shifted again. 'It's the shock, I think, that's all,' Josie said, giving him what she hoped was a reassuring smile.

'Well, I'm not surprised,' Robert said, raising his cane to signal the hansom cab to come forward.

Ellen tilted her head and studied her daughter and Josie's cheeks grew hot under her mother's gaze.

Mickey and Annie demanded Patrick's attention so, leaving Josie with her mother, he made a fuss of them, hugging and tickling them until they squealed.

Ellen put her hand on Josie's forehead. 'You look very pale, sweetheart,' she said.

'It's the shock,' Josie repeated, not quite able to meet her mother's eye.

Ellen's lips twisted into a wry smile. 'Is it now? And is it the shock that made you turn your nose up at breakfast since you've come home? And shock that's straining at your waistline?'

Josie cheeks flamed. 'I ... that is to say...' she started, then her father returned.

'This way,' he said, ushering them all forward.

Patrick strolled over, holding his children's

450

hands with Sarah walking alongside them.

Robert opened the cab door. 'You, Josie and Sarah ride in this one, my dear,' he said to Ellen. 'Patrick, Gus and I will follow on with the children.'

'Ah, well, Patrick, why don't you and Josie take the first one and we'll all squeeze in the next one,' Ellen said, giving Robert a telling look as she ushered Patrick forward.

Sarah took the children from Patrick, who then held out his hand to Josie. She took it and his fingers closed around hers.

Their eyes met and Patrick's intense gaze sent a shiver through her. He squeezed her hand and she squeezed his back before climbing in to the cab. He got in beside her and closed the door then, under the cover of her billowing skirts, took her hand again.

Outside, Mickey and Annie held Sarah's hand while they jumped up and down on the spot, happy to see their father free and unharmed, Robert's brows knitted together.

'I don't know, Mrs Munroe,' he said to his wife. 'Is it right to let our daughter go home alone in a cab with a man?'

Ellen slipped her hand around his arm. 'Go away with you, Dr Munroe. It's no more than three miles and we'll be right behind them.'

Robert nodded. 'Very well. After all, they are to be married soon.'

Ellen smiled happily. 'That they will, and the sooner the better.'

451

Chapter Thirty-One

Patrick strolled past the shops in Stepney High Street and turned right in front of St Dunstan's, where he and Josie, surrounded by their family, had been married five months before. The front door of number four sat opposite the alms house at the back of the churchyard in the grand sounding Belgrade Road. He had called on Superintendent Jackson as instructed and the something to his advantage had proved to be a two-hundred pound reward for the recovery of the Pettit silver, so in one stride the new Mr and Mrs Nolan had stepped up in the world.

The reward, and the dowry Dr Munroe had settled on Josie, meant they could afford one of the smart new houses surrounding the church-yard. Their new home had a parlour and a sitting room as well as the kitchen and scullery on the ground floor. It also had its own privy at the bottom of the garden, four good-sized upstairs rooms and all in all a far cry from number twenty Walburgh Street.

He could also afford to purchase his own barge, and now the newly launched *Smiling Girl* had Nolan and Son proudly painted on its side.

Pushing open his freshly painted front door, Patrick was greeted by his mother-in-law at the bottom of the stairs.

'The baby's coming,' she said, walking past him

and heading for the kitchen at the back.

'Now?'

'In about an hour, I'd say. Josie started just after you left this morning. She sent Annie to fetch me.'

He followed her down the hallway. 'Is she all right?' he asked anxiously, as they entered the kitchen.

Mattie stood at the kitchen table peeling potatoes. She looked up and for an instant Patrick glimpsed her ever-present sadness.

'Well, she's not too fond of you at the moment,' she told him.

He went over and hugged his sister. Mattie leant into him and he kissed her forehead. She looked up and gave him a too-bright smile.

'And how's my best nephew today?' he asked, as he hunkered down beside the basket at her feet.

Young Brian hiccupped then went back to chewing his knuckles as he stared up at Patrick from out of his father's blue eyes. Patrick felt a lump in his throat as he ran his hands gently over the infant's light brown hair.

'He's had me up half the night teething,' Mattie replied, as Patrick stood up.

Ellen draped clean linen over her one arm and took hold of the pail of hot water in the other.

'But don't you worry none,' she said, as Patrick opened the door to the hall for her. 'Dr Pym visited earlier and is satisfied with how things are going on. He said to call him at the hospital if he's needed but I think your Mam and I will manage fine.'

Patrick took the bucket and walked beside her to the end of the passage. She went to take it back but Patrick started up the stairs.

'And where do you think you're going?' she asked.

'To see my wife.'

Ever since Josie had told him on their wedding night that she was carrying his child, so many conflicting emotions went through his mind that he thought his brain would turn to mush. He was furious when he realised that Josie was already with child when Ma had shot her. But fury gave way to gratitude for his freedom to marry Josie now, meaning also that their child could be born in wedlock. His mind then went into a state of anxiety for six months as he worried about the perils of childbirth while he watched her stomach swell.

Patrick mounted the stairs two at a time and stepped through the open door of his and Josie's bedroom. His wife stood in her nightdress, gripping the iron frame at the bottom of their bed. Sarah was beside her with one arm around her shoulders and her other hand resting lightly on Josie's stomach.

He had expected to see Josie lying down, but was reassured that, apart from her flushed face and tightly pressed lips, she looked much as she had when he'd kissed her goodbye that morning. She let out a deep breath and relaxed her shoulders.

'That's another good one,' Sarah said as Josie gave her an unreadable look, then turned to her son. 'This is no place for you, Pat.'

Patrick, ignoring his mother, crossed the room and put his arm around Josie. 'Is it very painful, sweetheart?'

'Oh, no more than slamming the same finger in the door every five minutes,' she replied in a sharp tone.

'Oh!'

Josie's hands relaxed. 'It just hurts like billy-o when the pains start, but it's not so bad in between.'

He kissed her hot, damp forehead and she looked up at him. 'Mam said it won't be long now.'

Ellen entered the room and poured the hot water into the wash basin.

'I told Pat this was no place for him,' Sarah said to her.

'Oh, Sarah, he's grand,' Ellen replied, smiling at him and Josie.

Patrick gave his mother-in-law a grateful look then, suddenly, Josie dug her nails painfully into his hand as beads of perspiration sprang out on her forehead. Sarah placed her hand on Josie's stomach again.

'Another strong one, Ellen,' she said as Josie gritted her teeth and twisted Patrick's hand until his knuckles cracked.

He held her firmly as the contraction gripped her, then she pivoted forward and grunted.

Panic and fear shot through him. 'Josie!'

She lifted her head. 'It's all right.'

'Don't you worry, Josie'll be fine,' Sarah shooed him toward the door. 'Now we have work to do, so away with you.'

Patrick relinquished Josie to Ellen, who walked her daughter carefully to the bed. 'We'll call you when it's all over.'

As he reached the door he turned and Josie looked across at him. 'I love you,' he said.

She opened her mouth as if to reply then another pain caught hold of her. Patrick closed the door and went back downstairs.

Her mother slipped the fresh nightdress over Josie's head and she enjoyed the crisp starchiness of it against her clean skin. Ellen and Sarah had already washed the sweat and blood of her labour off her body and legs and changed the sheet underneath her. Feeling fresh and clean, Josie lay back on the pile of plumped pillows while her mother gently brushed her hair and tied it back in a ribbon, as she used to do when Josie was a child.

Ellen straightened the sheet and kissed Josie gently on the forehead. 'Well done, my love.'

She went over to the basket and picked up her first grandchild, awake and niggling for his mother. She handed the baby to Josie, who smiled up at her mother through a haze of tiredness; then her half-closed eyes drifted down to the not-so-small bundle in her arms and joy swept over her.

Ellen tilted her head to look at her grandson. 'He's just like his father.'

Josie traced her fingers over her son's damp hair. 'You mean with his grand curly hair?' She studied the small fingers curled around hers, the damp eyelashes, and budded mouth.

Her mother laughed. 'He's looking for his

dinner. Now support him at the back of the head and hold him on. After a moment, he'll do the rest.'

Everything below waist level seemed to groan as Josie wriggled up and unbuttoned her night-dress. She offered the baby her breast and after a couple of rubs over he clamped his mouth on the nipple, his little chin working hard for his food. Her breast tingled and a lethargic haze settled over her.

'You won't have proper milk for a couple of days, sweetheart, what he's having now is only the cream,' Ellen told. 'But put him on each time he niggles and it will encourage the flow.'

Josie did as her mother said and gazed down at Patrick's son, hardly believing that he was actually here at last. All the hard work of the last few hours evaporated and, in truth, even though it was less than an hour ago that she was pushing him into the world, she couldn't recall the pain. The door opened and Patrick entered the room. Josie's gaze left her son and rested on his father, standing anxiously in the doorway still in his work clothes.

She smiled at him and he was at her side in an instant. Ellen collected the last soiled linen sheet and left the new family alone.

He edged up the bed next to her and slid his arm around her. She rested her head on his shoulder and he pressed his lips to her forehead. 'He's a handsome lad.' He ran his finger gently over the baby's head. 'And such a mass of hair.'

'Just like his father, then,' Josie replied, changing the baby onto her other breast. This time young

457

Nolan knew what was required and latched on straight away. The warm languid feeling stole over Josie again.

Patrick grinned. 'Mam said he's a big baby for a first one, but he looks tiny to me.'

'He certainly felt large enough squeezing himself out,' Josie said, fighting off the weariness that suddenly swept over her. 'What shall we name him?'

Patrick held his finger out and his new son curled his tiny hand around it. 'If you have no objections, I'd like to call him Robert.'

'Pa will be pleased,' Josie replied, feeling her eyelids starting to droop.

Patrick bent forward and kissed his new son on the head. 'Thank you,' he said with a crack in his voice.

Young Robert's head rolled back and a small trickle of milk rolled down his cheek. Josie wiped it with her finger then handed him to his father. Patrick scooped him up in his large hands and held him in the crook of his arm as Josie re-buttoned her nightdress.

'Why don't you call Annie and Mickey up?' she said, suppressing a yawn.

Patrick pulled open the door and called down. The children clattered up the stairs, burst into the room, then skidded to a stop.

'Give your mother a kiss, then come and see your new brother, Robert,' Patrick said as he sat down on the chair next to the bed.

Annie and Mickey gave Josie a quick peck on the cheek then dashed around to their father. Mickey scrambled up and sat on his leg while

Annie stood next to him.

Josie's eyelids felt weighted down but she forced them open to look at Patrick, the man she'd fallen in love with as a young girl and whom she lost for a while, before the blessed angels brought them together again, never to be parted now. So, as sleep stole over her, Josie let it have its way. Who knew what tomorrow would bring, but that was the way of things. All she knew was that with Patrick by her side she could meet whatever life threw at them.

The publishers hope that this book has given you enjoyable reading. Large Print Books are especially designed to be as easy to see and hold as possible. If you wish a complete list of our books please ask at your local library or write directly to:

Magna Large Print Books
Magna House, Long Preston,
Skipton, North Yorkshire.
BD23 4ND

This Large Print Book for the partially sighted, who cannot read normal print, is published under the auspices of

THE ULVERSCROFT FOUNDATION